The Works of
Jeffery Farnol

THE BROAD HIGHWAY
THE MONEY MOON
THE AMATEUR GENTLEMAN
CHRONICLES OF THE IMP
THE HONOURABLE MR. TAWNISH
BELTANE THE SMITH
THE DEFINITE OBJECT
THE GESTE OF DUKE JOCELYN
OUR ADMIRABLE BETTY
BLACK BARTLEMY'S TREASURE
MARTIN CONISBY'S VENGEANCE
PEREGRINE'S PROGRESS
SIR JOHN DERING
THE LORING MYSTERY
THE HIGH ADVENTURE
THE QUEST OF YOUTH
GYFFORD OF WEARE
THE SHADOW
EPICS OF THE FANCY
ANOTHER DAY
OVER THE HILLS
THE JADE OF DESTINY
CHARMIAN, LADY VIBART
THE WAY BEYOND
WINDS OF FORTUNE
JOHN O' THE GREEN
A PAGEANT OF VICTORY
THE CROOKED FURROW
A BOOK FOR JANE
THE LONELY ROAD
THE HAPPY HARVEST
A NEW BOOK FOR JANE
A MATTER OF BUSINESS
ADAM PENFEATHER, BUCCANEER
MURDER BY NAIL
THE KING LIVETH
THE "PIPING TIMES"
HERITAGE PERILOUS
MY LORD OF WRYBOURNE
THE FOOL BELOVED
THE NINTH EARL
THE GLAD SUMMER

ADAM PENFEATHER BUCCANEER

HIS EARLY EXPLOITS

Being a curious and intimate relation of his tribulations, joys and triumphs taken from notes of his Journal and pages from his Ship's Log, and here put into complete narrative

By

JEFFERY FARNOL

SAMPSON LOW
25 Gilbert Street London W1

New Impression 1952

MADE AND PRINTED IN GREAT BRITAIN BY PURNELL AND SONS, LTD.
PAULTON (SOMERSET) AND LONDON

CONTENTS

BOOK ONE

BOOK TWO

BOOK ONE

CHAPTER I

TELLS SOMEWHAT OF A FATHER—AND A SON

THE executioner adjusted his noose and spoke hoarsely in the doomed man's ear; but the eyes of this man, staring widely, gazed very wistfully at one small, pallid face low down amid the jostling, murmurous throng, an eager, yearning look wherein his every faculty was centred so that he seemed blind and deaf to all else,—therefore the executioner (a busy soul) pushed him suddenly. . . . The man fell, the deadly rope jerked violently, tightened, quivered. . . .

Then from the awed and silenced crowd rose a voice in shrill, agonized scream:

"Father!"

A frantic, small figure pushed and strove desperately to win nearer that awful, quivering rope, but, finding all efforts vain, screamed once more, cast hands wildly heavenward, sank and was like to have been trampled by the gaping concourse but that a strong hand clutched and dragged him up, a powerful shoulder drove through the press, out into a corner of the market-place, along a narrow street, across a pleasant green and so to a rustic bench set about the massive bole of a shady tree. Here they paused and upon this bench the so dreadfully bereaved son cast himself face down while his rescuer, a tall, bronzed fellow with gold rings in his ears, tilted his be-feathered though somewhat shabby hat to scratch curly head, rasped fingers across jut of blue-shaven chin and finally spoke in voice unexpectedly rich and musical:

"Your father, eh, my lad,—your very own dad!"

The slim shape on the bench writhed as in agonized convulsion yet made no sound.

3

"Well, now, my poor orphan, I says you can scupper, sink and burn me if this an't a precious sorry business for any dutiful son, and mighty heart-breaking! So, my lad, your present need is rum forthwith—rum and plenty on't. So bowse up, lad, stand away wi' me and rum it shall be." Reaching forth powerful arm, the speaker lifted this quivering shape of horror to its feet and thus saw how this youth was something older than he had deemed, for, though small-made and slender, the face of him showed strangely arresting,—a smooth oval, pale as death, lit by wide-spaced eyes very keenly bright, with pallid lips, close-set to stay their quivering, and long, pointed chin.

"Rum's the word, messmate, with an R a U and an M writ large,—rum!"

"No, 'twould choke me."

"Ay, but 'twill hearten thee . . . or stoup of ale, for, next to rum, there's nought for trouble o' mind or body, like nappy ale, 'tis a true Englishman's panacea. Ay, and there's a right classical word for ye, my lad, for though a tarry mariner something inclined for the nonce to be out at elbow, I was and am and shall be very much beside. Rouse up, messmate, and bear away along o' me."

So this tall, strange sailorman sought to comfort his small companion whose frail body was shaken violently ever and anon by violent shudderings and once, faltering in his stride, a groaning outcry broke from him:

"They've killed . . . my father . . . the world's an emptiness! Oh God . . . the rope . . . that murderous, cruel rope!"

"Courage, lad! What's done is done, and grief shall not better it. Whereof I'll now make a rhyme and pipe it to thy comfort,—hearkee!" And forthwith, setting long arm about his companion's slim, trembling form, this mariner began to sing these words in voice richly mellow:

> " For thee, m'lad, I pipe this lay,
> So mark and stint thy sorrow,
> For since they've hanged thy dad to-day,
> He can't be hanged to-morrow.

And, messmate, there's comfort, too, in this, to wit,—when a man's dead and gone aloft, he's risen 'bove all cares o' mind or plagues o' body—we hope! And now, what might your name be? "

" Adam."

" Why I've heard worse name,—though Father Adam proved snivelling tell-tale on Mother Eve anent that apple business,—howbeit Adam is goodish name, being Biblical, like mine own—mine's Absalom by reason, as I've heard tell, that I was born with uncommon long hair. Absalom Troy am I. And what name hast beside, messmate? "

Instead of answering, Adam lifted clenched hands towards heaven and said between shut teeth:

" It was . . . murder! My father wrought 'gainst Papistry and cried down this Spanish marriage . . . and for this . . . for this they murdered him ! And he was so gently kind . . . so good a man . . . ah God, would I had been a better son. To-day he hangs dead yonder . . . his innocent blood is on me, crying for vengeance. Oh God, make me strong, a man's strength. Oh Lord!" Breathless and shaken by the wild passion of his grief, Adam would have fallen but for his companion's clutching hand.

" Avast, messmate!" quoth Absalom, with friendly shake. " Such grief's a shoal for shipwreck. So haul your wind and bear away afore it, large and free, until I can physic ye wi' rum, for hearkee:

> " When sorrow and black troubles come,
> Then souse 'em—drown 'em—deep in rum;
> And if so be as rum do fail,
> Then drown 'em deeper yet in ale.

So here's yet another song as I've contrived to thy comfort, boy! I've made the words to many a chorus and chanty, as you shall hear sung lustily all along the Spanish Main from Tortuga to Santa Catarina. Ah, many's the song I've made and sung and wrote down likewise, especially two as be now chanted right hearty aboard ships o' the Coast Brotherhood, true songs, my lad, and of real men—Black Bartlemy for one and Roger Tressady for t'other and hell-fire roarers both or strike me dumb! And there lieth our haven—in the lee o' yon trees. 'The Mariner's Joy,' kept by an old shipmate, and a snug berth for any poor sailorman.''

So came they to a sequestered tavern bowered amid the green and into a small, pleasant chamber, its wide lattice open upon a sunny garden fragrant with herb and flower.

"Ho, Ben,—Ben Purdy ahoy!" cried Absalom, sitting down upon roomy settle and beckoning Adam beside him. "Ahoy, Ben, show a leg—and rum, Ben, rum and ale—and lively ho!"

"Ay, ay, sir!" came an answering hail. "Rum it is, wi' ale as ever, sir." And presently to them came a squat, trim, merry-eyed fellow who rolled in his gait yet bore well laden tray very deftly none the less.

"Where be the lads, Ben—Abnegation and lubberly Abner?"

"Abroad, sir."

"Ha. And Captain Smy?"

"He be aloft, sir, wi' his Book. Shall I pass him the word?"

"Nay leave him to his meditations, and see to it we are nowise interrupted, Ben, off with ye! And now," said Absalom, so soon as they were alone, "here's to thy consolation, my poor boy. Sluice the ivories, drink deep and drink oft—come!"

Adam drank and choked, but at earnest solicitation of his new friend, drank again; he sipped rum, he gulped ale, he quaffed both together until at last he nodded drowsily, sank back upon the settle and forgot awhile his sick horror, his grief and heartbreak in the blessedness of sleep.

He awoke to a hoarse rumble of voices at no great distance, and, sitting up, found himself very heavy and languid, his faculties dulled by the pain of his aching head; so for some while he crouched miserably, staring blindly at the opposite wall, for before the eyes of his mind was ghastly vision of a rope that jerked horridly . . . quivered . . . swung . . . and was still. He groaned and bowed pain-racked head between clutching hands . . . and now the murmur of these hoarse voices was like the vague, harsh muttering of a pushing, jostling crowd that watched a man die. But in to him through the open lattice came a soft, fragrant air that touched his hot brow like the hand of a loving friend and soothed his rising horror like the blessing of God.

At last, rising uncertainly, he came to this open window and saw that it was evening and three men rolling dice in a rosy sunset. Then he heard the door open behind him and therewith the pleasant, cheery voice of the man Absalom:

"How is 't with ye, lad, how d'ye do now, I wonder?"

"My . . . head . . . aches!"

"Good, and 'tis no wonder, considering how I dosed thee, boy, for better head that acheth than heart that breaketh."

"It is . . . broke."

"Good again, for sink and burn me but ye look all the better for 't, more manly, my lad, I lay my oath ye do! There's some must needs break their hearts or ever they are men enough to mend 'em. Look at me! I broke my heart five year agone and ha' been better man ever since, ay and got me more out o' life, or damme! I changed me from dreaming young fool, sighing and puling for the impossible, into sober man and right cheery soul content to take whatsoever comes and make the best o't, a fellow bold in adversity and jibing at woe, ay so, or may I rot! So, never grieve, m' lad——"

"How should I—not?" groaned Adam.

"By other thinking. Lookee, Adam boy, I was once a mother's darling, then an Oxford scholar, next a fool-lover sick for love, but she proved false, and with my friend, so her I trounced, him I killed in fair fight, bundled me off to sea and to-day here am I a shipmaster without a ship, low in pocket yet high in heart, bold to dare Fortune and spit in the very eye of baleful Circumstance,—and what o' thee, boy, what?"

"That . . . rope!" said Adam, staring on vacancy with eyes wide in horror. "You'll mind that murderous rope . . . how it . . . jerked . . . quivered? 'Twas death. Oh, 'twas agony manifest."

"Ay, lad, but by death, agony may be transmuted into abiding joy—if the God of my good mother sits aloft indeed, so comfort thee, Adam."

"Ah but—the rope! I see it yet! I shall see it so long as I live . . . so would God I die soon!"

Bowing head, Adam twisted both hands in his long hair and cast himself face down upon the floor to lie there writhing; and when Absalom stooped to lift him, cried out as in bodily agony and bade him go away, which at last the tall mariner did, shaking his curly head and muttering as he went, and so left Adam prone in his misery.

Now as he lay thus, heedless of time and all else save horror and grief, a heavy foot spurned him painfully and a harsh, jeering voice spoke above him:

"Eh, what cursed younker be you, and what doing, eh, kid, eh?" Adam neither spoke nor moved, wherefore this foot stirred him more savagely and the voice jeered him again:

"How then, are ye sick, or drunk, or only dead, eh, boy? Curse ye,—if y'ain't dead, pipe up and answer me." Still Adam made no response and was kicked till he gasped. Then was sound of other feet and a familiar voice:

"Ha, Abner, is't you, and must ye boot my messmate?

Why then feel my toe and be damned t' ye, and now my fist, ye lubberly scum!" Here ensued sounds of violent movement with howl of savage pain cut short by slamming door.

More than once, through the long hours, this door opened softly, and though Adam sensed eyes watching him, yet he lay mute and still, face hidden and clutching fingers buried in his long hair.

And so at last came slumber, lulling him to forgetfulness.

His next awaking was to a dazzle of sun and the feel of a hand upon his shoulder, and though he did not look up, he knew this for the hand of a friend.

"Adam," said a voice. "Adam, my poor lad, how are ye now? Speak to me, boy, speak!"

Now in this familiar voice instead of usual jovial ring was something so much the reverse that Adam, moving cramped limbs, turned, then sat up with an effort to blink at the down-bent face of Absalom Troy.

"What now, sir?" he demanded huskily. "Why do you look on me so strangely?"

"Why, Adam, lad, 'tis because yourself is so . . . ay, so mighty strange . . . very marvellous strange! Something hath befallen you in the night . . . and I'm wondering how . . . and what. Come, lad, and see for yourself!"

So saying, he lifted Adam to his feet and pointed to a little mirror that hung on panelled wall nearby. Thither, stiff-legged, walked Adam and, looking at his reflection, started, peered close, then fell back a pace, to gaze wide-eyed, for the long, tousled hair framing lined brow and haggard face, hair that should have been glossy black—was white as snow.

"Well, Adam, well? How of it? What d'ye say?"

"Mighty well!" he answered, turning from the looking-glass with strange, mirthless smile. "My loved father was white-haired . . so this white hair honours me and shall be his memorial to bear with honour whiles I live."

CHAPTER II

TELLS HOW ADAM SMOTE SAVAGERY

"AND now, sir," sighed Adam, "if you'll show where I may wash me and comb my old man's hair, I'll thank you and go about my business."

"Ay, ay, lad. I'll bring thee with clean towel to pump i' the yard and thereafter shalt feed, my poor boy." Adam shook white head wearily.

"Mr. Troy, you are crassly blind to so mistake me. I alas, am no boy! A man am I these two years, and to-day am aged beyond my years, as you may see."

Tall Absalom looked down at this small, slim figure, this shape of youth crowned by hair silvery white; he looked away, rubbed his chin, shook his head and finally spoke:

"Why then, friend Adam, go along o' me and I'll pump new life and hunger into thee with sweet, fresh water."

So forth went they into a morning bright with sun and glad with song of birds, for the day was young. And presently, stripped to the waist, Adam bowed white head and slender body and was pumped upon and deluged with sparkling water until he gasped, then towelled and rubbed down by Absalom until he glowed and thrilled with new life. Now as Adam, thus half naked, turned for his garments, he chanced to catch his companion's eye, and flushed:

"Ah," said he, frowning, "Master Troy, I perceive you are considering what small, puny wretch I am, eh, sir?"

"Why now, Adam, let me die but there a'n't a vasty deal o' thee,—now is there?"

"Howbeit, sir," retorted Adam in the act of donning

shirt and therefore speaking in tone a little muffled, "I have wrought and studied in divers ways and with a painful diligence to make the utmost of what there is of me. I must not be measured by my inches, sir,—or lack of them. Moreover, I——" He broke off with a gasp and ducked suddenly behind his tall companion, for a buxom woman was nodding and smiling at him from an open window nearby.

"Breakfast, Capten!" she cried in laughing tone. "And the little gen'leman needn't show so fearsome modest and coy, I've seen growed men aplenty and I be old enough to mother him, ay and you too, Cap'n Troy!"

"Why so ye do, Martha, Lord bless your handsome face, and never was younger mother or more dutiful, loving son! Messmate, you behold our hostess, commander and general mother—dame Martha Purdy."

"Not as I won't say," chuckled Mrs. Purdy, as Adam struggled desperately with his shirt, "but what your little gen'leman 'ave got the prettiest smooth skin and white as any maid's. Hows'ever, my Ben's this moment a-drawing your ale, there's gammons a-frizzling, likewise eggs, so come your ways this moment, both o' ye, and eat 'em."

And presently eat indeed they did, Adam with such appetite as was his own astonishment.

"Mr. Troy," said he, when at last his hunger was satisfied, "sir, I have very much to thank you for . . . your sympathy, for this I am grateful beyond words."

"Dost reckon me thy friend, Adam?"

"Indeed, needs must I."

"Then never 'master' or 'mister' me that is thy friend, call me Absalom or, since 'tis such plaguey mouthful, make it 'Lom' as do certain others, a few . . . and tell me this, have ye many friends, Adam, or relations?"

"No."

"Good! For one staunch friend is better than many, and relations, dammem, are generally a curse and plague.

So then you've no ties or grapples to hold ye fast aground here in England ? "

"Not one!"

"Good again! For, damme, Adam, but I'm mighty set on carrying ye off along o' me, shipmates, you and I. . . . The broad ocean, the clean winds, and the Main, Adam, the Spanish Main! The golden Indies, Hispaniola, Tortuga, Santa Catarina, the Isle o' Pearls. Ay, and 'twill be noble venture besides,—to save from the hell o' slavery divers goodly gentlemen, poor souls and woeful prisoners, bound for the plantations. Well, how say you, friend, will ye sail with me?"

"With you," Adam murmured thoughtfully, "yet who beside?"

"Certain lusty fellows, well chosen and prime sailor-men all, here with me lie four o' the chiefest, namely— Captain Smy Peters, Nicholas Cobb, Abnegation Mings and Matt Appleby."

"There is also," said Adam, pinching his long chin between nervous, sinewy fingers, "the man Abner."

"Ay, ay, though he's no more than mere lubberley rogue. But for the rest, they be all tried and sober men, well beknown to me and to each other. . . . Hast ever heard tell o' the Brotherhood o' the Coast, Adam?"

"Never."

"Ah well, 'tis a staunch company, and powerful in the Indies and along the Main, and made up of English, French, Scots, Hollanders and others, good, bad and indifferent,—like Life itself, Adam. So now, will ye 'list with us, wilt hazard thy life—first to the rescue of these doomed prisoners and thereafter dare Fortune on thine own account?"

"How so, Absalom?"

"Join the Brotherhood, as my sworn comrade."

"And what then, Absalom?"

"To live a man's life, Adam, hearty and free, or die

as a man should—on his feet and in fullness o' strength, hailing Death as friend and cheerily."

"To die—suddenly," nodded Adam, "on my feet to welcome Death as kindly friend,—ay, this were better than to perish by inches—cowering in a bed! So, Absalom, I'll with thee,—to win fortune and power or six foot of earth, or say—five foot and an inch. So, when do we sail?"

"Three days hence, from Shoreham."

"Then shall be time a-plenty for that I have to do, and the sooner the better. Pray lend me weapon of some sort,—pistol, hanger or rapier, any shall serve."

"Ay, but to what end, Adam?"

"The performance of a sacred duty."

"Ay, and might a friend ask—what?"

"I go to kill my uncle."

"*Madre de Dios!*" murmured Absalom, opening his blue eyes wider than usual, while Adam, leaning head on hand, sighed deeply and explained:

"It was he betrayed my father, his own brother, to shameful death . . . that ghastly, twitching rope . . .!"

"Art sure o' this, Adam?"

"Beyond all doubt."

"Then 'tis case of homicide justifiable, eh, Adam?"

"So I believe, for he is murderer beyond reach of the law, therefore I must be his death—or he mine."

"How then, you'll fight him, messmate?"

"Indeed!" nodded Adam.

"Nay, lad, I protest 'tis fools' way to deal with a murderer."

"Agreed!" answered Adam. "Yet, for my father's sake, I had rather die such fool than live and feel myself a murderer. So this guilty man shall fight for his life, and howsoever it end, I shall be content, myself now having no least fear of death."

"Why then, Adam, an thou't be Nemesis and slaughter thy nunks. I, like trusty friend, will——" He paused and turned sharply as the door opened to disclose a shock-headed country fellow in smock-frock who beckoned with back jerk of thumb, saying:

"Oh, Cap'n, youm wanted main bad in kitchen or bloody murder will be for sure. There be Must' Abner in kitchen, wi' loaded dag, all full o' rum and Old Nick 'e be—in kitchen along wi' Cap'n Mings an' landlord Ben and dame in kitchen, sir, and all on 'em backed rearwise into corner —in kitchen 'e be and swearin' very 'orrorsome."

Up leapt Absalom with swirl of wide coatskirts and a pistol which seemed to have leapt to his fist from the air.

"Burn him! Is he drunk again, Tom?"

"Ay, sir—leastways, fightin'-sober, I'd say—in the kitchen, Cap'n, and——"

"Devil take the sot! I'll go wing him——"

"Pray—no!" said Adam, rising very nimbly. "This Abner kicked me, yester evening, so this morning, by your leave, I'll deal with him."

"Eh—you, little master?" quoth Tom, shaking shock head. "Nay, he'd eat ye, 'e would,—bolt and swaller ye at jest one mouthful 'e would."

"Yet should I choke him—mayhap. Howbeit, friend Absalom, put up thy pistol and suffer me to try."

"Why now, messmate," said Absalom dubiously, "'tis murderous rogue very powerful and should ye fail——"

"'Twill be an end o' my grief, Absalom—come!"

A stone-flagged passage brought them to a wide, pleasant kitchen where, crouched in a corner stood two men and the buxom hostess fronting a great, brawny fellow, stripped to the waist, who pounded on broad, hairy chest with one fist and flourished a pistol in the other.

"Lookee now," cried he fiercely, "when I goes for to kiss a woman, she ain't agoin' for to deny me, no nor nobody else ain't neither, and anybody as says me different——"

"Swinish beast!" hissed Adam, in such a voice that the fellow started and turned to stare in open-jawed amazement. "Fool!" cried Adam, pointing suddenly. "Look! Look behind ye, there, fool—there!" Instinctively this man Abner glanced back across his wide shoulder and, in that moment, Adam leapt, grasped the pistol by lock and barrel, wrenched, twisted, and sprang back and with the weapon levelled at the scowling face of Abner who, blinded by rage, groped for the cutlass a-swing at his hip.

"Good!" exclaimed Adam, and gave the pistol into Absalom's ready hand saying, "Lend me a hanger, somebody." A cutlass was thrust into his grasp; he balanced the weapon, shook his head and sighed at it, then with the broad blade advanced, fronted his mighty adversary and instantly their steel rang together in vicious cut and dexterous parry; then, with these sharp, curved blades grinding together they circled one another.

"Now, fool," said Adam, gazing up at his brawny antagonist narrow-eyed, "do your utmost best or I'll blood ye—fight, numps—fight!"

Wrought thus to a very frenzy, the man Abner uttered a beast-like, inarticulate howl and smote full-armed, terrible blows that were somehow deftly turned or narrowly eluded by this small, puny creature who seemed always only just out of reach, who moved so nimbly on dancing feet and who, bobbing white head, laughed and mocked.

"One!" cried Adam, out-flashed his levelled steel—and there on Abner's brawny arm was thin trickle of blood. Abner gasped a curse and smote the wilder; but his furious, cutting strokes were avoided or turned aside and each parry was followed by instant, lightning thrust, for whereas Abner used only the edge, Adam plied the quicker point, rapier-fashion.

"Two! Three!" he cried; and presently, "Four! Five! Six! . . ." And now Abner's great, bare arms and chest were flecked by small spots and scarlet runnels.

"I'm blooding ye, fool, I'm—blooding ye!" Adam panted. "Drop your . . . useless steel or . . . I'll cut ye into . . . foul gobbets." Abner gasped hoarse curses, his attack grew feeble, he gave back and back until at last, stung beyond endurance by these ceaseless pin-pricks and cowed by the sight of his own blood, he staggered aside to the window, dashed his cutlass to the floor and clambering out through the wide casement, reeled away like a drunken man.

Then Adam laid by the weapon he had used to such purpose and turned to be gone; but to him came a sprightly man, a ruddy, smiling fellow who slapped him on the back, grasped and shook his hand, with joyful oath and question to every shake:

"I'm Mings, I am, mate! Abnegation Mings, that's me. And you can choke and let me rot if I ever see the like! 'Twas woundy miracle or let me drownd! And here's me to ax how 'twas done—and Abner twice the size o' ye, how, friend how?"

"It was because," answered Adam, putting his too eager questioner aside, "the man Abner is an ignorant clod and afraid to die, and I am neither." So saying he went from the kitchen, leaving clamorous amazement behind him.

Going forth into the garden, and the sun now very warm and glad all about him, he wandered here some while until he came upon a small arbour bowered in honeysuckle, and entering this pleasant shade, sat down and presently fell to troublous meditation. Bees hummed drowsily, birds chirped and piped above and around him and then, borne to him on the sunny air came a man's voice upraised in song and these the words:

"There are two at the fore,
    At the main be three more,
    Dead men that hang all of a row;
    Here's fine, dainty meat
    For the fishes to eat,
    Black Bartlemy—Bartlemy ho!"

And presently forth into the sunshine came Absalom Troy to breathe deep of the fragrant air, while Adam

watched him with a wistful envy,—such handsome fellow,
blithe in his strength and vigorous manhood, all careless
grace from curly head to spurred boot (thought Adam),—
such tall, commanding figure despite shabby garments
which had once been things of splendour. Now glancing
from this shape of stalwart manhood to his own puny
form with look of bitter dispraisal, Adam sighed very
despondently. Then was a cheery hail and Absalom came
striding to halt without the arbour, to fold his arms and
gaze down at woeful Adam with a new interest.

"Messmate," quoth he, shaking comely head, "I protest
you become my astonishment, I vow you do, or damme!
For I perceive in thee a sucking Achilles, Ajax and Hector,
one and indivisible. There's curst Abner bleeding like
stuck pig and yourself untouched,—there's Mother Martha,
Ben and Abnegation swearing 'twas spells and magic,
here's myself astounded, as I say, and very fain to know
the how of it."

"Here is nought for wonder," answered Adam, "the
art of weapon-craft was born in me, and hath been well
nurtured from my boyhood up, and by a very perfect
swordmaster . . . my patient tutor at each and every
weapon, broadsword, backsword and rapier . . . a tutor
very able, very wise and kind."

"Ah," said Absalom, sitting down to set long arm
about Adam's drooping form, "this was——?"

"Yes, my . . . father," Adam answered, choking on
the word. "By his will I had divers other famous instructors beside,—and this the reason. Upon a day, and I a
schoolboy, my father found me in tears and bloody of face
for I had been at fisticuffs, and I told him I wept not for
my hurts but because God had made me so small and
weak. Then he kissed me, saying: 'Comfort thee, my little
son, for, though Nature hath cast thee in mould so small,
the Lord hath blessed thee perchance in other ways,
and there is a strength of soul nobler than power of body.
But now because 'tis a harsh world for the weak and more

especially if weakness be valiant and bold-hearted to dare
the strong, I will show thee a craft, a mystery of weapons
that, God aiding, shall make thee terrible as a giant, yet
first promise me, little son, thou wilt be terrible only
against the aggressor.' So I promised, and so was I
instructed, and so . . . may God rest and cherish the
sweet soul of him!"

"Amen!" said a deep voice, and, glancing up, Adam
beheld a lean, dark man, grim and somewhat sinister of
aspect though very neat as to person and clad in garments
of sober black.

"Messmate," said Absalom, gesturing towards this
man, "you behold my good friend and shipmate Captain
Smy Peters. Smy, here sitteth my young Achilles, Hector
and Ajax called Adam. He hath mayhap another name,
but no matter. Come you in, Smy, and sit likewise. So,—
now here are we and presently, with somewhat to wet
our whistles, we'll confer on what is to be, and the how
and what o' things." Here, lifting his pleasant voice in
mellifluous bellow, he hailed the house:

"'Mariner's Joy'—ahoy! Ho, Ben—ale, ahoy. Three
tankards! And lively ho!"

"Young master," said Captain Smy, his harsh look
softening, "sometimes,—let's say—occasionally—a good
sire begetteth a good son, and thy so late sire, as I hear,
was good and noble man, for Absalom telleth me he was
of The Elect, a zealous servant o' the Lord. Now, by
accounts, thou'rt a right lusty smiter, maugre thy size,
and this should be a bond betwixt us, for I am myself a
pre-destined smiter of Iniquity, and come of such Godly,
hard-smiting stock that my good father, Lord love him,—
had me christened Smite-Sin-With-Both-Hands, which,
though original name, is yet one calling for such excess o'
wind or breath that 'tis of necessity reduced and shortened
to Smite, and this again to Smy. Being so named, I was
so bred that smite sin I did and do when and wheresoever
found, ashore or afloat. Ay verily, I've smote and been

smitten right heartily ere now to the chastening o' poor,
erring humanity,—in especial cursed Spanishers, Portu-
gales, Papists and Pirates, rot 'em! Well now, I am still
very zealous to 'smite the wicked in his sin and uproot
the unrighteous in pride of evil', for, as saith Holy Writ,—
'the soul of the transgressor shall eat violence'. Thus,
friend, for thy right worthy father's sake, I humbly proffer
my service to the proper and needful avenging of his
innocent blood, even though I do but keep the door
whiles Justice achieves."

"Sir," answered Adam, "I thank you gratefully, yet
think I may better despatch alone."

"Nenny, messmate, no, no!" quoth Absalom. "For
such business as this slaughter o' guilty nunks, two is
better than one and three than two, and three are we.
Moreover we languish in idleness very damnably, so—
when shall the matter achieve, Adam?"

"To-night."

"Good! And whereaway, near or far?"

"But twelve miles or so."

"Good again! There be nags in stable, we ride to-night
then, after supper. Now for thyself, Adam, what o' thy
gear, clothes and so forth?"

"They lie at the 'King's Head', in Horsham, all I shall
need."

"Very well. To-day, Ben or his man shall bear a writing
from thee and fetch 'em away. Meanwhile since we shall
be aboard ship pretty soon, 'tis but right we should tell
thee—somewhat, eh, Smy?"

"With discretion, brother."

"Well then, Adam, you'll have heard tell of the Buccaneers and Pirates of the Main?"

"Yes."

"Good! Then, first and foremost—a buccaneer is no
pirate."

"The Lord forbid!" quoth Smy, fervently.

"A pirate, Adam, lives for murder by murder. He is a

lousy, pestilent fellow, a plague o' the seas, who will plunder and destroy any vessel weaker than his own—and of any nation. His sport is rape and slaughter of the defenceless, he is, in fine, a very bloody, vile rogue and damned rascal,—eh, Smy?"

"Ah, 'tis even so, friend Adam," nodded Smy, grimly. "He is an abomination, a rank offence whose iniquities reek to heaven."

"On the other hand, messmate, your true buccaneer hath but two enemies, to wit—himself by reason of drink and the devil, and the accursed Spaniard with his hellish slave-galleys, cruel *autos da fé* the which are public burnings—crowds of poor men, ay and women too,—and the most horrid torments of his Inquisition. Three good friends o' mine were tortured to death at Lima for no more than sailing those seas that the prideful Dons esteem their very own. The buccaneer, afore he rose against the Spanish tyranny, was a peaceful hunter,—beef and pigs, their flesh he dried and flavoured above a fire of spic y twigs called a 'boucan', and so cometh this name 'buccaneer'. And of all the Buccaneer captains o' the Main, Adam, none better esteemed or more fortunate, up to a point, than Captain Smy Peters, of the *Hope of Glory*, thirty guns, and Absalom Troy, of the *Golden Venture*, twenty. And—of all pirates that foul the seas, no greater rogue or bloodier villain than Black Bartlemy, of the *Ladies' Delight*."

"Black Bartlemy," repeated Adam, "you were singing of him awhile ago, I think."

"'Tis like enough, messmate. I sing often without knowing. This was song I made after a voyage with him and his mate Tressady, and what I wrote, I saw. Belike I shall write other verses of him some day."

"This was of dead men, Absalom, five of them, and all a-swing."

"And they were hove aloft together, Adam, and—Englishmen all, not a cursed Spaniard among 'em."

"And you—watched this done?"

"I did, Adam, and dumb as any oyster lest I should make a sixth. And 'tis to sink, burn and destroy Bartlemy's accursed ship and make an end of him that Smy and I are pledged and sworn."

"Verily and indeed!" sighed Captain Smy. "It is my constant prayer that I may be so blest to let out his evil soul by incision of steel beneath his fifth rib, or—watch him hang, for 'tis very son of Belial."

"And yet," said Adam, "you sailed with him, Absalom!"

"Perforce, messmate. I'd been cast away on a lonely island where his ship chanced to put in for water."

"What like is this Black Bartlemy?"

"A smiling, fiendly gentleman, Adam, all niminy-piminy affectations, and, save for lace ruffles, all sable black from trucks to keelson. Yet none the less an apt rapier man and vastly proud of his skill,—a notable swordsman, eh, Smy?"

"Verily, brother. I watched him kill the famous Italian Vincenzio at St Kitts, in masterly fashion,—a feint, a parry, two beats and—through Vincenzio's eye,—extreme neat and dexterous."

"Some day, Adam, you may see Bartlemy for yourself and find chance to take his measure, eh?"

"I should embrace the opportunity," said Adam, rising. "And now I'll go see about my few worldly possessions."

"Ay, ay, messmate, and tell Ben we shall want horses for to-night, after supper."

CHAPTER III

TELLS HOW ADAM RODE TO HIS VENGEANCE
AND THE MANNER OF IT

THE moon was well up and very bright when they reached the top of a hill; and here Adam reins in his horse to point where, plain to see in this pale light, rose the chimneys and gables of a comfortable farm-house.

"So ho!" exclaimed Absalom. "A sizeable place. There'll be servants aplenty, womenfolk to scream and make alarm, dammem!"

"Yet this shall not let or stay the hand o' Justice," quoth Captain Smy.

"No whit, old lad, or burn me! So, Adam, to avoid such female clamours, your best course should be to lure nunky forth and do his business out o' doors—if ye be still o' the same mind, ha?"

Answered Adam, between shut teeth:

"When so I close my eyes I needs must see . . . that murderous rope . . . jerking . . . swaying. . . . Follow me!"

Down the hill he led them, and by a winding lane that brought them to a place of trees and in this shadow they dismounted and tethered their horses.

"You ha' the swords, Adam?"

"Yes."

"Dogs, now?" enquired Absalom, taking out his pistols to glance at their flints and primings. "Any dogs, messmate?"

"In the rickyard at the back; however, they know me. Come!"

So through a night very close and still, they began to approach this house, all three, and very silent.

"Aha!" whispered Absalom, as they drew near. "Yon window, lad, its lattice wide open to thy purpose! Easy all now."

Being come to this open window, Adam looked into a small, arras-hung chamber where, at littered writing-table, a man sat poring over one of the many papers before him, a rosy, full-bodied personage who, starting to soft, unexpected sound, glanced up to behold a small, grim figure with pale, set face beneath close-fitting seaman's bonnet and two naked swords beneath one arm.

"Uncle," said Adam, approaching this staring man on slow, soundless feet, "they hanged my father . . . yesterday morning!"

"Adam? Eh—it is nephew Adam, I think? Adam, be welcome . . . eh . . . but . . . what is it? What would ye, boy? How are you here . . . so . . . so suddenly . . . so unexpected. Ha! what is 't, Adam . . . what——?"

"Death, sir! They killed your brother and my father .. . yesterday . . . in the morning . . . and the sun so glad and bright."

"Why this . . . this I know, my poor Adam. Alas, 'tis so I've heard and——"

"Alas, uncle, 'tis so you contrived."

"I, boy? My own brother? No, no! Who says so lies! Ay, 'tis lie, 'tis most foul and wicked lie!"

"'Tis known and grievous fact, sir. Indeed 'tis truth so sure that I am here to do justice on you. Choose now one of these swords,—and make no least outcry or alarm lest I strike you dead,—choose, I say!"

"No! No! Oh God forgive thee, nephew, such basely cruel, such wicked accusation . . . I am innocent! I vow . . . I swear it before——" He gasped and cowered as through the casement one after another, came Absalom and Captain Smy.

"Oh, sirs . . . sirs," he quavered, "what . . . oh what would ye?"

"Justice!" answered Absalom.

"The Great Tribunal!" nodded Smy.

"So, Uncle," said Adam, "take now one of these swords to kill me if you can, or—die like a gentleman."

"No, no! Have mercy on me, Adam. Show pity——"

"Sir, I watched a . . . twitching rope that had neither. So, Uncle—fight."

"Nay, spare me. . . . Oh, for God's sake, spare me. . . . I did but my duty to the King. . . . Oh, pity me!"

The wretched creature was down upon his knees, a pallid, sweating, grovelling shape of terror with arms outflung in frantic entreaty—arms that were seized by powerful hands quick to strangle all outcry, and thus to gag and pinion him in tall elbow chair.

"Bell-rope!" snarled Captain Smy; the which and instantly Absalom cut asunder, wherewith the half-swooning wretch was speedily trussed and bound to the heavy chair.

"Better so!" quoth Smy, as he tested the cunning, seaman's knots he had tied. "Better we leave him to the Lord his mercy. The Lord shall decide if such rogue murderer live or die!" So saying, he took a candle from its sconce and set fire to the many papers on the table and then to the arras on the walls that went up in instant flame; which done, he grasped Adam by the arm and led him towards the window.

"Nay, but," gasped Adam, holding back, "to die—such death?"

"Even so!" nodded Smy. "The purging, fiery torment here and the flames of Hell hereafter—except the Lord will otherwise. Come now!"

Reaching the open air, Adam paused to snatch off his seaman's bonnet and breathe deep, glancing back wide-eyed upon that place of fiery torment.

"Come," said Absalom, clapping him on shoulder, "cover that white head o' thine and let's sheer off and——"

"My . . . white head . . ." repeated Adam, and gasped, and began to run. . . .

Back through that open casement, back into a hell of smoke and crackling flame; choking and half blind, he cut asunder the bonds of this swooning man, to drag him towards the window through eddying smoke and the fierce leap of red fires. Blinded and failing, he struggled on . . . reached the window at last and sank there groaning. . . . Then strong arms were lifting him.

"No!" he gasped, struggling. "Him . . . first!"

So, in his turn, Adam was hauled forth of that terror of smoke and mounting flame and lay awhile on cool, dewy grass to breathe deep of the sweet night air; then a powerful arm raised him and a voice spoke above him.

"How are ye, messmate?"

"Very well . . . thanks to the both of you," he answered, struggling to his feet.

"And what o'—this?"

Now glancing round, Adam saw his uncle crouched nearby upon his knees.

"Oh, Adam!" he sobbed. "Oh, Adam. . . . 'Twas you brought me out of hell . . . am I to live? Ah, God of mercy . . . is this life?" But, with no word, Adam turned and limped away between his two silent companions, through a darkness shot now by a red and awful glow.

CHAPTER IV

CONCERNING ANTONIA THE WOMAN, AND AN
OATH OF BROTHERHOOD

IT was as they breathed their horses after the ascent of a steep hill that the girl came tumbling down upon them, —a wild, breathless creature who, bursting through hedge that crowned the steep grassy bank, rolled and slid into the narrow road so suddenly that their startled horses danced and Absalom slipped from saddle.

"Don't . . ." panted the girl, clinging to him with desperate hands, "don't . . . for dear God's sake . . . let them . . . take me."

"Not I, or damme!" he answered, clasping ready arm about her. "But what the——" His question was forbidden by a loud, hoarse shout above:

"Hey there . . . hey, you down there," cried this voice breathlessly, "hold me fast the . . . bloodsome, curst . . . Jezebel . . . hold her!"

"I am," answered Absalom, stealing hand into deep side-pocket. "Then what?"

"Keep her so . . . till us gets our claws on 'er. Hey, Jacob . . . Oh, Jake, 'ere she be! Come ye now . . . down this yere bank . . . foller me!" Down the slope scrambled a burly fellow armed with a stout bludgeon.

"Thankee, gemmen," quoth he, "thankee for saving my legs and breath. She run like a stag, ah, like a perishin' deer, she did. So now I'll take the curst jade and——"

"Good fellow, tut-tut!" said Absalom, putting the girl behind his broad back. "Easy, my pretty cut-throat lurcher, and very gently now."

"Eh—what?" demanded the man, handling his bludgeon.

"You gimme that there gallers-vixen now or 'twill be the worse for ye. I got the Law, I 'ave."

"But not the lass—yet!" said Absalom, speaking with an extreme of mildness. "First I must beg to know the wherefore and the why——"

"Oh, Jacob!" cried the man. "Come on down! Yere she be——" At this, there descended another man even burlier than his fellow.

"What's to do yere?" he growled. "Come on now, us don't want no 'by-your-leaves' nor 'ow d'ye do's, us wants the gell and we're a-goin' for to tek 'er, one way or t'other, so which is it for to be? Does you give 'er up or do we set about the lot o' ye?"

"Fie!" exclaimed Absalom, spreading his feet slightly. "Such a fearsome, violent fellow! Pray don't terrify me, speak me kind and say why you want this trembling child,—what hath she done?"

"Ho, child, d'ye say? A f'rocious vixen! And, wot's she done? Robbery, ah and—murder, that's wot she's done! So 'tis prison, 'tis rope and gallers for 'er! Now give 'er up,—we're the Law."

"Why then," quoth Absalom in his rough seaman's voice and diction, "sheer off, afore I rip out your livers, —both 'o ye! Aha, is that it?" With these words, he leapt, very suddenly, in beneath up-swung bludgeon and instantly felled his would-be assailant with down-smiting pistol-barrel, while Captain Smy seemed to fall bodily from saddle upon the second man, bearing him to earth. So, for brief space, was dust and sounds or strife.

"All fast . . . messmate?" panted Absalom, at last.

"Ay, ay, brother, my rogue is peaceful awhile. Don't forget to belay and make fast their jaw tackle."

"Not I, shipmate, my fellow's fast, and dumb as a damned oyster."

"Then, brother, it's loose moorings and stand away."

Hereupon, they mounted their horses that Adam had been holding; but, being in the saddle, Absalom turned to look at the girl who stood leaning in shadow of the bank between the silenced but writhing forms of her late pursuers who lay expertly gagged and bound with their own belts and neckcloths.

"Sink me!" he exclaimed, "what o' the lass?"

"Yes," she answered, in tremulous voice yet without moving. "What shall become of me? I can run no farther. I'm . . . faint with hunger and have no money——"

"Then," said Captain Smy, leaning down to her, "take these few coins, child, and may the Lord bless and be thy protection."

"And, lass, take my purse," cried Absalom. "I would 'twere heavier."

"Get you up on to my horse!" said Adam. "Come,—here before me. Give me your hand,—now your foot on my toe—up!"

Swiftly, lightly she obeyed, and with this quick-breathing, soft-trembling fugitive within his bridle-arm, Adam rode forward, his two companions following after, wide-eyed.

Now as they rode thus, said Absalom to his old shipmate:

"Well, Smy, what say ye to this?"

"Yonder I see trouble!"

"Ay, a petticoat,—and in it a young murderess!"

"Brother, since Eve ate the apple, man's chief trouble hath been woman!"

"True enough, Smy, and the sooner we are rid o' this one, the better for all concerned. . . ."

Meanwhile, the subject of their talk was stealing sidelong glances at Adam and, the moon being so very bright, caught him glancing askance at her.

"Well?" she enquired timidly and almost whispering.

"Yes, I . . . I hope so!" he answered, almost as shyly.

"But," said she, emboldened by this, "you ask me no questions . . . my name . . . who I am . . . what —I have done."

"I . . . I wait to be told . . . if you will."

"I struck down my master with his own sword."

"And—killed him?"

"I don't know . . . the sword was sheathed. I . . . oh, I for the moment . . . meant to kill him. I struck him very hard because he would have whipped me . . and . . . worse."

"Then," said Adam, looking on the distance, "I grieve the sword was sheathed."

"I struck so hard that he fell and hit his head—I saw blood on his face! Then I was afraid and ran away."

"And . . . the things you stole?"

"These clothes that cover me. I was to pay for them out of my wages and have not. His servants came after me, but I hid in a wood."

"Were those two men his servants?"

"No, they were law officers from Horsham. They caught me once and told me I must hang on a gallows. I broke from them and ran and ran till I thought I should fall dead, and then . . . I found you. But I know. . . . Oh I know if I'm taken they'll prison and hang me . . . as they did a girl that stole five yards of lace . . . only last month. . . . My master and mistress took me to see. . . . Oh it was horrible. . . . She screamed and cried . . . just as I should! So I'm afraid for my life."

"Then you must not be taken."

"No—no! I pray merciful God! Yet is there any place in England I shall ever be safe?"

"Ay, to be sure! Never doubt it," he answered, and so confidently that she took comfort from his mere look and tone.

"Pray what is your name?" she asked him.

"Call me Adam."

"And I am Antonia Chievely—because I was found by a rich lady named Chievely in the porch of Saint Anthony's church. She adopted me, educated me but—ah, most of all she taught and learned me how to love her. Six months ago nearly, her horse ran away and killed her, and because there was no will, her nephew took everything, all her property, and they turned me away. So, to live, I became a serving maid . . . and to-day I am penniless . . . afraid, and very lonely."

"I am lonely too!" said Adam.

"Where are you taking me?"

"To safety, I hope."

"But where—where?"

"A tavern called 'The Mariner's Joy.'"

"A tavern!" she repeated, whispering, and glanced fearfully from the speaker's pale, strange face to the grim horsemen behind.

"What now?" Adam questioned, for he felt her shudder violently.

"I'm wondering . . . wondering what is to become of me? It was to 'scape one man that I struck and fled, and now . . . three!"

"However," answered Adam, "these three are men indeed, moreover, of these three, I am one."

"You!" she repeated, hopelessly. "But they are so big and you so . . . young."

"And—small!" said he, bitterly. "But as for young— look at this!" And snatching off his seaman's bonnet, showed his long white hair all glistening to the moon. "How say you now—child?" he demanded, somewhat grimly.

"Sir," she answered, viewing him with very wistful, humbly-questioning eyes, "I know not how or what to say. Your face—so young and your head—so very old! Sir, indeed I cannot tell what to say."

"Well," quoth Adam, covering his hair again, "if my head be old it should be wise, and if it be wise, it should scheme how to save and keep a poor lonely child safe from all harms and dangers."

"Sir," said she, after they had gone some little way and no word, "there is something you may tell me, if you will, a thing that puzzles me . . . why do you smell of fire?"

"Because," he answered, looking up at the serene night sky, "I have come through the fire of . . . Great Tribulation."

It was about now that Absalom said to his solemn companion:

"Love my eyes! Smy, wilt look now at my young Adam. He's said more to his slip of a murderess in this short while than to me since I hauled him to his spindle-shanks. Ay, he has so—or I'm a forked radish!"

"Absalom, I ponder how best and soonest we may dispose of the poor creature to her own safety and good. For, as the Lord knoweth, she shall find neither along of us!"

"True enough, messmate, we are no company for any young lass, so—how and when is the question. Ha, damme, she's a woman's concern and care,—we be men and bent on plaguey desperate course. And besides there's Mings and t'other wild lads. The 'Mariner's Joy' shall be no harbourage for any maid, murderess or no."

"How so be, Lom, we shall supply her with what o' money we may and thereafter leave her in care o' the Lord that hath been our protection hitherto, bringing us, thou and I, all unscathed through such stress o' tempest, shipwreck, battle and bloody strife as is my abiding wonder and cause for gratitude."

"True enough, Smy, we should ha' been bleached bones long since, otherwise. . . . And yonder, where the ways divide shall indeed be a parting o' the ways. Forrard, messmate!"

Thus being come to these cross-roads, Adam suddenly found his two companions beside him.

"What now?" he questioned, reining up.

"Why here," answered Absalom, "when we have bestowed what monies we may, we bid farewell and good fortune to young mistress here——"

"Leaving her," Captain Smy added, "unto the Lord, his care."

"Why very well," said Adam, looking from one to other, "ride on and leave us to go our way alone."

"Ay, but whither, Adam?"

"The 'Mariner's Joy' and Mother Martha."

"Nenny, Adam, 'tis no place for any young maid, or damme!"

"Yet, Absalom, thither she goes, or curse me!"

"Eh, lad, eh? Lord love us, wilt snap at thy messmate? I tell thee, Adam, this is impossible."

"And I tell you, Absalom, I esteem few things to be impossible."

"Oh, I'll go!" said Antonia miserably. "Loose me and I'll go——"

"Ay, let her away, messmate, 'twill be best for her and us."

"Best?" demanded Adam, in a still fury. "Best d'ye say? Man, d'ye know what you are doing? Will ye dare to leave her—the defenceless prey for any loose night-prowler,—horror o' mind and shame o' body . . . will ye leave her to hazard o' this? 'Yes!' says you. 'Then damn your friendship and let's be enemies,' says I. In such case I'll fight you or any man, kill or be killed and joy in it."

"'S death!" exclaimed Absalom, peering at this small yet resolute speaker. "Sink and burn me but I believe you would."

"Sir, be very sure of it! And of this also,—to-night this child of ours shall lie secure at the 'Mariner's Joy'."

"Ours, d'ye say? Our child, Adam?"

"Indeed. Since she lieth in our care, ours she must be. So here's the reason she goeth with us. Now if this reason suffice, let us ride on, if not, we will debate the matter with steel. Perchance you shall find reason on my rapier-point."

"How,—a challenge? D'ye dare me, Adam?"

"Ay, with all my heart."

For a long moment they fronted and stared on each other, eye to eye; then Absalom's shapely lips curved, he smiled, he chuckled, he threw back his head and laughed joyously.

"Adam!" said he. "Oh Adam! I'm going to love thee some day—except thou force me to shoot or hang thee for insubordination and mutiny! Smy, how think ye of my hell-fire roaring boy?"

"That verily he is his father's son, for here is no boastful bragster, Absalom, the youth hath bowels! Mayhap the Lord hath raised him up to some purpose, and 'tis for us to abide the issue. Ride on."

So came they at last, and silent all, to the tavern; but having stabled the horses:

"Belay now!" muttered Absalom. "Easy all and softly by reason of our Martha for, though good soul, she's a woman and therefore overly apt with her tongue."

"And," sighed Captain Smy, "the tongue of woman is very disquieting member, being tipped with a viperish gall."

"Therefore," continued Absalom, glancing up at the silent house, "our best course shall be to steal us softly within doors and——"

"House!" shouted Adam, loudly as he might, "Mistress Purdy! Oh, Mother Martha!" And deaf to Absalom's commands and Smy's exhortations he continued his shouting until a lattice swung wide to let forth Mrs. Purdy's indignant face framed in a large nightcap.

"Ha!" cried she, "stint this drunken clamour . . what, is it you and—oh my soul, with—a woman! A drabbish trollop, as I'm a vartuous creetur! Pack off . . . pack off . . . away wi' her. Nay but I'll see into this!" The head vanished swiftly, lattice closed angrily, Absalom cursed pettishly, Captain Smy groaned, and Antonia trembled.

"Adam, fool, what i' the Fiend's name——? Damme, but you've done it now!" quoth Absalom.

"I hope so!" said Adam, and taking Antonia's trembling hand he led her forward as the door opened and Martha Purdy fronted them, a fierce-eyed, night-capped figure of Judgment.

"Lord bless and save us all!" she cried angrily. "What's this wickedness. Fie shame on ye, here's no place for your naughty baggage, 'tis a good house, mine, so pack now —pack!" And she waved them off with imperious hand. But, stepping lightly forward, Adam had taken and kissed this so forbidding hand, all in a moment.

"Mrs. Purdy," said he, uncovering his white head, "dear Mother Martha, if I tell you this is my sister and she and I orphans and, for the time being, homeless, will you turn us away? Life hath not been kind to us and she is sore distressed. So, if I ask of your compassion to take her to your gentle care, to shelter her for this night at least, will you deny? Also I can pay well. See—she droops with hunger and weariness! Wilt now open thy generous heart and mother her—this little while?"

Mrs. Purdy glanced at Adam, looked at the woeful girl and instinctively reached forth her arms.

"Why now," said she. "Lord love her sweet, sad eyes, this will I! Come thy ways, my poor, pretty lamb, there —there! As for thee, young master, if I thought wrong, forgive me for 'tis naughty world and most men so wicked, 'specially"—here she rolled bright eye at Absalom, "'specially sailormen! Come now, my sweeting, shalt eat and to bed, and—within hearing and call o' me! Now go along o' Mother Martha."

"Well!" exclaimed Absalom, so soon as they were alone. "Smy, old shipmate, my young Adam hath found his tongue and to some purpose, or I'm a shotten herring! Now let's stay for a noggin afore we turn in."

"Thank 'ee," answered Adam, "but for myself I'll to bed."

"Ay, but where, messmate?"

"Any hole or corner shall serve."

"Aloft, sir!" said landlord Ben, appearing with lighted candle. "'Tis but attic 'neath the eaves, young master, but the best us can offer. We ha' stowed your gear there, a portmantle and two saddle-bags, sir."

"Nay, there should be a sword also, a rapier with its girdle and carriages."

"All's there aloft, ay ay, sir. But there was two swords. Us took care to have away all o' your belongings from Horsham 's arternoon, young sir."

"Why then, here's for your trouble, Ben,—nay take it, man! And now pray show me up to bed."

"Though first," said Absalom, "I've somewhat to tell thee, Adam. Give me the glim, Ben, and bring that you know to Mr. Adam's attic."

So up they went to a chamber beneath the thatch which, though small, being neat and clean, Adam thought well enough, And here to them came Ben with a flask of wine and large goblet which he set forth on little table beside the bed and with salute smart and sailorly, departed.

"Messmate, sit down," said Absalom, seating himself at the table, "for I've a thing to propose. But first, Adam, How d'ye like me?"

"Why," answered Adam, viewing the comely face opposite with his shrewd yet wistful gaze, "very well and sometimes—better than I suppose."

"Hum!" quoth Absalom, rubbing square chin. "Art a non-committal soul! Is your liking deep enough to trust me with all you own in this world?"

"Yes, for this is very little."

"Then wouldst trust me with thy very life, Adam?"

"Yes, for I hold it very cheap."

"Experience perchance shall make it dearer to thee anon, Adam. However, dost esteem and trust me sufficiently well to take me henceforth as thy comrade sworn?"

"Gratefully, Absalom, for you showed me kindliness and sympathy in . . . my black hour."

"Well then," said Absalom, drawing a broad-bladed knife from his belt and testing its point on his thumb, "let us together now swear the Brotherhood Oath,—do you as I shall do." So saying, he filled the goblet with wine, then taking knife snicked his wrist with the keen point and from this small wound squeezed a few drops of blood into the wine; this done, he passed the knife to Adam who followed his example.

"Now, Adam, give me thy hand, swearing this oath after me. I, Absalom Troy, do take thee, Adam, to be my blood brother. I swear on the blood to keep thy counsel faithfully, to aid thee in all things 'gainst all men soever, to cherish and comfort thee in every adversity and to be faithful to thee until death,—or may I perish everlastingly."

So, with hands locked Adam swore this oath also, whereafter they pledged each other in the wine.

"Well now," quoth Absalom, setting down the empty goblet, "henceforth thy foes and woes are mine and mine are thine. . . . Yet dost ask no question as to what hast pledged thyself, brother, and wherefore not?"

"Because, having only my life to lose, I care not. Sufficient unto the day,—and so Good night, brother Absalom."

CHAPTER V

TELLS OF TWO IN THE DAWN

AROUSED by sounds of furtive, stealthy movement Adam sat up in bed, blinking in the dawn; heard a stair creak and, quick to guess what this meant, leapt from the sheets to dress speedily as he might and beside the open window. Thus, after a little while he saw Antonia come stealing out into the misty garden where no leaf stirred and no bird sang, for the sun was not yet up.

Very soon Adam was dressed and, shoes in hand, went creeping down the stair in his turn and so, very silently out of the house; then, having slipped on his shoes, he began to run and thus presently espied her going on before, a drooping, disconsolate figure in the dawn. He ran upon his toes and so silently that he was close before she heard and started about in sudden terror, but seeing him, clasped hands to resurgent bosom and closed her eyes so that he thought her about to swoon, and set his arm about her.

"Oh!" she gasped, shuddering violently. "I . . . I thought 'twas . . . them . . . to drag me to . . . the gallows! And 'tis . . . only you!"

"Yes, only me," he repeated. And now she clung to him, sobbing so violently that he questioned her very anxiously:

"Why d' you weep so, poor child?"

"For . . . joy that . . . 'tis indeed . . . only you! I was so very terrified, and now . . . so marvellous glad."

"Then don't cry. Suffer me to wipe your tears,—sit down." So together down they sat and all heedless of the dew, leaning near each other in this windless, misty

37

dawn, while Adam, doing his best with his handkerchief, proved so inept that she laughed, then gazed on him in wide-eyed amazement.

"Oh—I laughed!" she whispered. "And I do never laugh—now! But, oh Adam, why did you fright a poor body so?"

"Nay, why did you run away, Antonia?"

"Because I cannot . . . dare not bide still in any place for fear they creep and . . . take me ere I know . . . drag me away to prison and . . . Ah! My master and mistress carried me to see them hang a poor serving maid not so old as I——"

"Hush! Never think on it, child!"

"I cannot help but think on it . . . her dreadful weeping . . . and screams . . . and for five yards of lace——"

"But you are no thief."

"Yes, yes, I am! They cried me for thief . . . I thought it was for my clothes, but now I know 'tis more. . . . Oh much, much more! Last night when I undressed I found—this!" And into his hand she thrust a man's large signet ring. "You see . . . it is terribly valuable, much more than . . . five yards of lace,—gold, Adam, and a great ruby stone."

"No, a garnet," said Adam, scowling at it. "And you found this?"

"Yes, in my bosom. My master must have thrust it there whiles we struggled."

"Ah?" said Adam, with show of white teeth.

"So now . . . if I'm taken, they'll swear this against me, and surely hang me for thief. Oh, if I'm caught, this ring shall be . . . my death!"

"No!" said Adam softly, but clenching his hand upon this ring. "Oh no, 'stead o' your death this vile thing shall perchance be his."

"How? Oh—how?"

"The liar shall swallow it. Where lives he?"

"I . . . no, I shall not tell."

"Ha, why not, child, why not indeed?"

"Lest you kill him,—if I have not,—and they hang you with me."

"Yet, Antonia, I do beg you'll tell me."

"No, Adam, I never will . . . never!"

"Then—here's for your lying master's false evidence!" And dropping the ring into the dewy grass, he spurned and stamped it deep from sight beneath scornful heel.

"So!" he said, hissing between clenched teeth. "I would 'twere your rogue-master's villainous face!"

"Nay now, Adam, prithee don't look so—murderous."

"Why then tell me, Antonia, where you were going?"

"Oh—anywhere! London, I think . . . it doth not matter."

"Afoot, child, and without money?"

"Nay, your friends gave me money."

"And when this is gone, how then, Antonia?"

"I shall work my way . . . or beg."

Adam looked at her ripe, young shapeliness, her pale though lovely face, saw the terror and despair in her wide, grey eyes, and began to tremble, even as she was trembling.

"No, by God!" said he, between grim lips, "there you shall meet death—and worse, so this you shall not do!" Then he was up and seizing her nerveless hands in masterful grasp, drew her to her feet with unexpected strength and compelled her to go beside him.

"What . . . ?" she gasped. "Where do you take me?"

"Back to present safety. Come, I want to talk and you to listen. For if you'll trust to me, Antonia, as you must, I have a scheme shall keep you safe."

"No," said she, breathlessly. "No! I shall never be safe in England; no matter where I go there will always be a shadow behind me,—cold,—cold and dreadful, the shadow of . . . a gallows."

"But see, Antonia, see—yonder cometh the kind sun to fright away shadows. Old Sol shall be an omen of happiness to come. Let us sit here and warm us in his glory. So,—now hearken to me."

Thus seated in the growing warmth and splendour of this rising sun, Adam told his scheme in few words, whereat she sprang afoot, gasping in breathless whisper:

"No,—ah no, I—dare not."

"You must, Antonia."

"'Twould be impossible."

"Not with me beside you."

"They . . . I should be found out, and then——"

"Not if you are quick-witted and able as I do believe you, Antonia. Besides, I shall instruct you very fully. Do this and 'stead of fear o' death shall presently be joy of life,—and, whiles I live, no one shall anyways harm you. And this I swear on . . . the white head of my dead father! So now, wilt do this, Antonia, and trust all to me and thine own mother-wit?"

"Yes! Yes!" she whispered, reaching him both hands in pretty, instinctive gesture. "Yes, I will trust you. . . . I do, and shall so long as you be Adam."

"Then go with me indoors before the house is astir and I'll tell you more."

"Yes, Adam. And when . . . when must I . . . ."

"Not until I give the word, nor stir abroad even then until—you hear me whistle."

"Ay, but what shall you whistle?"

"Do you know this merry song called 'Sellinger's Round'?"

"To be sure, Adam."

And presently back went they side by side through a world all bright now and glad with the piping chorus of birds; and in Antonia's grey eyes, instead of terror and despair, was the dawn-light of Hope.

CHAPTER VI

HOW ADAM BECAME PENFEATHER, AND ANTONIA, ANTHONY

THE three had finished breakfast and now, leaning back in his chair, Absalom glanced from one to other of his companions and propounded this question, solemn of tone yet with a twinkle in his blue eyes.

"Brothers and messmates both, resolve we now this troublesome question of curst, troublous subject, to wit, —what of—our child?"

"Eh—child?" repeated Captain Smy. "D'ye mean——"

"The female child, shipmate, foisted upon our fatherly care by young Adam here. I mean this nymph o' bloodshed, this dryad o' slaughter, this soft-spoke goddess o' death! What must we do with her?"

"Leave her snug here with Mistress Martha," answered Smy.

"Ay, ay," nodded Absalom, "'tis so I think. And what say you, Adam?"

"Take her with us."

Now at this, Captain Smy opened grim lips yet spake not; Absalom, starting erect, swung round to stare at the speaker, while Adam finding his pewter yet held some ale, finished it and wiped his lips daintily on snowy handkerchief.

"Smy, you heard him," said Absalom, still staring on Adam 'neath cocked eyebrows, "he's neither mad nor a fool and yet talks like both—or I'm a stockfish, damme!"

"Moreover and finally," quoth Captain Smy, at his very grimmest, "a rule o' The Brotherhood is—no women aboard-ship. And 'tis good rule and nowise to be broke."

"However," said Adam, "out of England she must go,
—this England where the Law never rests, for if she remain
I am persuaded she will be retaken—and then——"

"Nay, bethink you," said Smy, grimly pious, "we leave
her in the good Lord's care."

"Ay," nodded Adam, "but how if the Lord hath set
her in ours?" Now at this, Absalom looked from the
speaker's pale, strange face with its firm mouth and bright,
steady eyes, to Smy's lean visage; but, before he might
speak, Adam rose and took the long rapier that dangled
from his chair-back.

"Look at this!" said he, unsheathing the narrow, glittering blade. "This is my father's sword, he showed me
how to use it to mine own defence and the protection of
suchlike weaklings as myself. See my white hair that grief
hath bestowed upon me for a memorial of this father that
feared no thing under heaven save only dishonour, and
who dying so shamefully, left me—only this sword and this
white hair to mind me how I must be faithful and still
keep his honour clean and bright. Well, sirs, how may
I so do and yet leave this maid, this child, this innocent,
to be hunted down . . . strangled in a rope even as he
was,—or perchance dragged down to shame of mind and
body? I cannot and will not, for my so honoured father
his noble sake. Therefore she sails with us or I bide with
her in England!"

"Then," quoth Captain Smy, harshly, "bide ye must,
for woman aboard-ship is death and worse."

"And what," demanded Absalom bitterly, "what o'
the sacred oath ye swore, the Oath o' Brotherhood, what
o' this?"

"Master Troy, to save this innocent from gallows or
viler thing, I will break a thousand such oaths and abide
the consequences with good heart."

"Talking o' hearts, lad," Absalom retorted, "you aren't
fallen souse in love wi' this wench, eh?"

"Now this," retorted Adam, scowling, "this is very base

thought in you, Mr. Troy! No, sir, I have not. All I do
for her I would do for any defenceless creature, 'tis duty,
sir, laid on me by memory of . . . my father."

"And damme," exclaimed Absalom, "but I believe thee
and so crave thy pardon,—'twas indeed unworthy thought."

"Nathless," growled Smy, "this girl must and shall not
with us!"

"Ay, ay, 'tis so I say!" nodded Absalom. "For lookee,
Adam, a ship is vile place for any woman, ay and most
especially this ship, the *London Merchant*, where there is
like to be some unlovely business,—except matters go
better than I can hope. Of the which I had best, it seems,
give thee some notice that you may——"

But at this moment in through the open casement came
the rosy, smiling face of the young man Abnegation Mings.

"Ho, Cap'n Lom," quoth he, "Sir Benjamin Trigg be
in the offing, standing in and bearing down on we, aboard
of a black 'oss."

"Ha, d'ye say so, Abny lad? Why very well. Smy, do
you go meet him, what time I warn young Adam. Ay,
there he is,—hark to the bellowing jackass!" And indeed
from the stable yard now rose clatter of horsehoofs and
voice of a booming arrogance very loud and commanding:

"House-ho! Where's everybody? Stand by to take my
horse somebody. Hell's fury, am I to be served?"

Smy scowled and went striding away while Absalom,
leaning across the table, jerked head towards the sunny
garden, saying:

"Yonder cometh Master Hector Peevish, in velvet and
lace, a very gentlemanly hellfire roarer, Adam, a swashing
blusterer, a yelping dog whose bark is worse than his bite.
But, mark this, Adam,—he is our—means to an end,
though little he knows it! Now mark me again,—afore
any man of us may claim his share of any treasure that
may bless our enterprise, his name must be writ down in
Articles, so down your name must go. But, Adam, should
he blast your eyes or curse your hide, you shall take it

smiling cheerily, and in good part,—if not, then do your
best to out-curse and down-roar him,—do anything save
to stand mumchance and meek. Is 't understood?"

"Yes," answered Adam, pulling on the close-fitting
seaman's bonnet Absalom had bestowed to hide his silvery
hair. "Yes, I understand." So, when he had belted his
father's sword about his so meagre form, he followed whither
he was led. To a neighbouring room where at table beside
the open lattice sat a personage bedecked in magnificence,
as it were, from the crown of wide-brimmed hat with its
gemmed brooch and noble sweep of feather, to spurred
heels; a very modish though somewhat rotund personage,
for his face, eyes, nose and form were all of a certain
roundness. But, though plump, this personage was also
petulant, for, at mere sight of small, pallid Adam, he
recoiled violently, stamped loudly and bounced in his
chair.

"'Od's m' life—what's this?" he bellowed, stabbing at
Adam with the long feather of the quill pen he had been
using. "'Swounds and blood, Absalom, never tell me you'd
'list this little misery, this poor atomy? 'Tis but shadow
of a shade,—remove it—take it away, out o' my sight!"

"Sir Benjamin, belay now!" quoth Absalom, frowning.
"You've guessed right, here stands my latest recruit and,
if no giant, better than he seems and older than he looks.'*

"Eh—looks, d'ye say? 'S blood—he looks like small
vision o' creeping death! Tush and curse it, Captain, 'tis
no more than petty boy, a sickling, a lousy lad, a puling
manikin not worth shiproom! I want hearty fellows,
seadogs and tarry mariners, not spindle-shanked whifflers!
Besides, my company's complete——"

"Not so," said Absalom, shaking his head, "your
damned company will lack Captain Smy Peters, John
Fenn, Nicholas Cobb, Abnegation Mings with myself and
others, except my comrade Adam be signed on."

"But 's death and blood, Captain Troy, don't I tell
ye——"

"No, Sir Benjamin, 'tis I tell you,—except my brother Adam sail, neither sail we, and may you and your rogues all perish and rot——"

"Eh? Stap me vitals, your brother, Captain, your brother?"

"Sworn on the blood!" nodded Absalom.

"Then why i' the fiend's name not say so?" cried Sir Benjamin scowling and bouncing in his chair again. "If so be—be sure he sails. Hey, boy, hey, boy, with a curse, —what's your name?"

"Adam."

"Ay, ay, and what beside—what?" bellowed Sir Benjamin stabbing at Adam again with the feather of his pen, "your t'other name—pronounce!"

Now with his gaze on the feather of this quill pen Adam answered:

"Penfeather."

"So,—then down I write ye! Now come and make your mark."

"Nay, first, sir," sighed Adam, "I have to tell you that I am neither lousy nor a lad,—look at this!" And snatching off bonnet he showed thus his white hair. "Furthermore, sir, you have jibed me, jeered and belittled my littleness, and this I can by no means let pass. So——"

With one movement, as it seemed, he stepped back, whipped blade from scabbard and Sir Benjamin's magnificent hat, transfixed on darting steel, was whisked out through the window.

"Now, sir," said Adam, bowing, "let us walk after your hat and see if such mannerless man as yourself may outman manikin such as I,—come, sir!"

Clapping hands to his round, cropped head, Sir Benjamin uttered a choking roar, he bounced to his feet and, emitting rageful clamour, stamped and strode out into the sunny garden and here, not staying to remove coat or even shoes, drew his own weapon, whirled it dexterously, brandished it fiercely and fell to his guard. Scarcely had the blades crossed than he thrust, was met by a strong parry, leapt back from lightning counter-thrust and, being out of distance, lowered his point to survey his small, so agile assailant; and his eye was bright, his peevish scowl clean gone, he skipped, he bounced, he flourished.

"'Od's body, a pretty manage!" he exclaimed. "This lad is none so lousy as methought. Come again!"

Once more the swords rang together and, joined thus, whirled in flashing arcs, parted to clash in slithering flurry, their flickering points darting, now in the high line, now in the low, until Adam's blade seemed to waver from this line, flashing wide but, in that same instant, he stepped nimbly aside and as Sir Benjamin passed in the expected lunge, Adam smote him lightly across broad back with the flat of his blade.

"There, sir," said he, turning to front his now hard-breathing antagonist, "there was time-thrust had transfixed you had I so willed. Thus, sir, I suffer you to live. Now if this prove me worthy your company let us cry enough and you shall sign me on, if not let us endeavour each other's despatch featly as possible. I await your word. Meanwhile, sir,—your hat!" And reaching this noble adornment whence it lay, Adam tendered it to its puffing owner with humble obeisance.

Sir Benjamin accepted his hat dumbly, he put it on, took it off again, bowed, flourished and made answer briefly with never an oath:

"Master Penfeather, sir, my first word is,—enough! My second,—regret! And my third,—sack!" Then seizing Adam's hand he shook it violently, drew it within his arm and strode back indoors bellowing:

"Oho, landlord,—sack! Sack and plenty on't! Sack-ho!"

And presently, seated all four with brimming glasses, they solemnly pledged one another; they drank to good-fellowship; to the stout ship *London Merchant*; to a prosperous voyage, success on their venture and general good fortune. They (Adam excepted) drank indeed oft and deep until the wine getting low and their voices high, Adam contrived to steal away unnoticed and so to the kitchen,—a place of quiet orderliness with its gleaming copper and pewter, its wide hearth, roomy ingle and great ceiling beams hung with smoked hams and fragrant bunches of dried herbs. Here he found Mrs. Martha, this buxom yet so capable person, who, at sight of him, laid finger on lip, then laughed, clapping her hands, and still laughing, drew him within the deep inglenook and whispered:

"Oh, Master Adam, 'tis wonderful sure-ly! She do fit your clothes to a hair, she do! And, Lord bless her pretty limbs, a more lovesome young gen'leman she do make as no eyes never see afore,—never!"

"Is she dressed correctly, good Mother Martha?"

"That she be, ay marry is she, sir! Every single stitch, innards and outards, I did on her my own self—wi' these two hands, I did. And a lovely creeter your sister be, Master Adam, white-skinned as yourself though plumper."

"And is she girt with my spare sword?"

"She be, sir. I belts it about her pretty middle wi' these same two 'ands, I did. Likewise I've been a-learning her to stride large and strut,—manlike."

"God love thee, Mother Martha,—hast been such kind friend to us,—'tis beyond my poor words to show."

"Nay, sir, nay, how should I not be—and ye two orphan waifs so young and helpless like . . . and yet none so helpless neether, not yourself, Master Adam, not when it do come to murderous steel! First that toad Abner and now yon bellering fury Sir Benjamin! You be the quickest thing as I ever see on legs,—and you so small too and thin! As I says to Mistress Antonia while us watched ee fight Sir Benjamin—'tis like David and Goliath, I says."

"Pray where is she . . . my sister?"

"'Bove stairs busy wi' needle and thread for me, in-sisted, she did,—my Sunday gownd, and so quick and

clever as ever I see! Ye should do well in life, the both o'
ye, I'm sure."

"Indeed I hope we may!" said Adam fervently.

"Now what o' t'other gen'lemen, sir? Be they still
a-guzzlin' their sherris wine? 'Tis not like Cap'n Absalom
for to fuddle like so many fool men do, specially sailormen!
Ay, but 'tis proper gen'leman, Cap'n Absalom, and one o'
the quality to boot, wonderful rich they was, his family,—
but now all dead and gone save himself,—and the gert
house little better than empty ruin! Though he weren't
called Absalom in them days, nor yet Troy."

"You knew him well?"

"Ay, born were I on his father's manor. And my Ben
sailed 'boardship wi' him to the Spanish Main, two voy-
ages and come back wi' money enough for to marry—
which marry him I did. And now 'tis yourself."

"Me?" exclaimed Adam, blinking.

"Ay, you, sir, and sweet sister are to sail along o' him,
and may the good Lord prosper and bless ye. Which do
mind me o' that wrigglesome snake Abner, hast seen aught
of him since you trounced him so proper?"

"Not a glimpse."

"Ah well, take care lest he crawl and sting afore ye're
aware. . . . And yonder be Sir Benjamin a-bellering for
ee, Master Adam."

"I heard him. Pray now go summon my—sister."

"This will I, Master Adam, and I vow you shall scarce
know her. . . ."

Meanwhile in stable-yard Sir Benjamin, after one or
two earnest though vain efforts, had at last contrived to
get astride his somewhat mettlesome horse when to him
came Adam accompanied by one—at sight of whom
Captain Smy goggled while Absalom stared mumchance;
for this other was a tall, slim, dark-avised young gentleman whose hair, cut long in the new mode, was tied below
each shoulder in curling love-locks that framed a handsome
though swarthy visage; a gentleman this who swaggered

in his walk, left hand posed gracefully upon rapier-hilt, right hand waving be-feathered hat,—perceiving which Sir Benjamin instantly flourished his own, whereat his horse jibbed and was cursed, thickly though with fervid eloquence,—and when this animal had stopped capering and Sir Benjamin ceased bouncing responsive, Adam addressed him:

"Sir, I take leave to make known yet another adventurer, namely—my half-brother Anthony."

"Honoured, sir, honoured!" cried Sir Benjamin, a little indistinctly. "Brother o' thine . . . brother o' mine! Brothers all 'n' hearty good f'lows! We meet in Shoreham t'morrow . . . and there we'll crack a bottle to——" But here his impatient steed reared and set off at such pace as very soon bounced Sir Benjamin out of sight.

"So ho!" quoth Absalom, his shapely lips upcurving in quirkish smile. "Here then is your brother, eh, messmate?"

"Half-brother!" Adam corrected.

"Lord," exclaimed Captain Smy, piously. "May the Lord aid and bless us!"

"Gentlemen, your . . . your servant!" said Mr. Anthony, bowing, and if his voice was a little uncertain his air and carriage were sufficiently masculine.

"But," said Absalom, returning this salutation, "Mr. Anthony, sir,—your present complexion astounds me, your dainty skin once so delicate, so purely white, now so fiercely tanned and sunburnt! Pray how cometh such sudden metamorphosis?"

"Walnut juice, sir!" answered Anthony with look and tone virile as possible. "Our clever Mother Martha's doing . . . and suits me, I think." So saying, this manly-showing Mr. Anthony glanced at Adam, at goggle-eyed Captain Smy, looked at handsome, smiling Absalom and then, flushing swift and painfully beneath his quizzical gaze, turned and fled into the house with grace of movement extremely feminine.

This same evening after supper, said Absalom, yawning:

"Brother Adam, I've that to tell ye touching our venture overseas the which is but right ye should hear afore we sleep. So presently, over a noggin, I'll talk and you shall hearken."

"So be it," answered Adam, gazing pensively out through the open lattice where a full moon was filling this summer night with a pale splendour. "Meantime I'll go walk in the garden."

"Ay, ay. I'll with ye there anon."

So forth went Adam slow pacing to breathe deep of this sweet air, to gaze away at great, rising moon to see there, as his childish eyes had so often seen,—the dog, the man with his bundle of faggots—or face of that serene and gracious lady the Moon Goddess. But to-night, and for the first time in all his life, he visioned there a face he thought far lovelier, a face quick and vivid with life and framed in hair of a tawny brightness; and as he visioned thus Antonia's features, so in his ears was the sweet echo of her soft, deep voice. At rustle of leaves behind him, he checked to turn, but in that moment, moon and face and dreamful fantasies were smitten into nothingness . . . he staggered, pitched headlong and lay as motionless and heedless of all things as the dewy turf that pillowed his pallid, bloodstained brow.

CHAPTER VII

HOW ADAM CAME ABOARD THE STOUT SHIP "LONDON MERCHANT"

HE opened his eyes to sense of pain in a creaking gloom dim lit by a lanthorn that swayed dizzily to and fro, and himself half-dressed upon narrow bed that heaved beneath him with rhythmic yet uneasy motion. Against the panelling hard by hung his coat, girdle and father's sword, and these also swung and swayed, while, with their every to and fro movement came that strange, never-ending creak and groan. And in this moment of slow awakening to pain of body and distress of mind the mere sight of this, his father's sword, its cut-steel pommel and gracefully curved quillons and counter-guards, brought him strange comfort and solace. Little by little above the persistent groan and creak that seemed to fill the very air about him, he distinguished other sounds remote and indefinable,—a vague stir and bustle above and around him, a piping wail that rose and fell, distant voices, faint and dream-like . . . and then, close at hand, a real and unmistakable sniff . . . a sob . . . a stifled moan.

Now lifting hand to aching head he found it bandaged, but, the moan being repeated, he contrived to sit up.

"Antonia?" he murmured.

A dim curtain was pulled aside and the swaying lamp showed him the bright sheen of tawny hair. Then she was beside him on her knees.

"Yes, 'tis me, Adam!" she whispered. "Only me! And oh, thank God you are come alive again, 'or I am nigh dead with fear."

"Why then," he answered, venturing to touch her bright hair, "now is the time to show your boldest."

"Nay but . . . this great ship . . . so very many rough men . . . and now a dreadful storm o' wind and monstrous waves to drown us!"

"So then . . . we are at sea, Antonia?"

"And a fearsome tempest raging, Adam! Do but see . . . see how everything tumbles and sways and shivers . . . and the ship squeaking . . . crying out in every timber as ready to break and let in the awful waves. And all this dreads me, for I ha' never been to sea."

"Neither have I," he answered, "and a very uneasy business I prove it."

"Then you will not be angry with me that I am so fearful?"

"Not I, Antonia, for there are few creatures that have not known fear at some time. And yet my . . . my wise father showed me how terror should make us but the more valiant,—the which, though a paradox, is yet very truth as well I do know, for I am ofttimes very fearful. . . . So now," said he, glancing up at the swaying sword, "if we are to drown indeed . . . there are worse deaths."

"Oh, I know . . . I know!" she gasped, pressing closer against him. "I know this—but if I am to live on this great ship . . . so many fearsome men . . . and I . . . alone!"

"Nay, Antonia, I am here also. And no man shall harm thee while I live. But do thy best to show manly as possible . . . and I must take all heed to name thee always Anthony. Now be thy boldest, Anthony, call on thy valiant soul and be of good heart. . . . Tell me, how came I on this ship?"

"Oh, Adam, now what selfish wretch am I! You were sore hurt and I do but think on and grieve for myself."

"I was struck down in the garden and, as I guess, by the man Abner."

"Indeed, he would ha' murdered thee, Adam, but looking from my window, I chanced to see, and screamed murder on him till came the Captain and Master Troy and shot him, but vainly, for he got him away."

"So have I a sore head, Antonia, and serves me right, Anthony, for being dreamy fool and unwary dolt."

"At the first we thought thee dead, Adam, and they were for leaving us behind, next day, but Master Troy would not. 'Twas he bore you before him on his horse all the way and carried you in his arms like a baby, Adam. Oh, he is very tall and strong."

"And I so small and weak, Anthony! Howbeit, I am no baby."

"No indeed, indeed no, Adam, thou'rt strong too yet in manner so . . . so different."

"So it was Absalom brought me into this ship?"

"Yes, Adam. And when Captain Smy would have left poor me, Master Troy would nowise suffer I should be so deserted. He is a very kind man, Adam."

"He is indeed, Anthony."

"And yet I . . . hate him!" said she, and so fiercely that Adam stared in wonder.

"Why so?" he questioned.

"For that when he looks on me and . . . smiles, then and despite this manly guise, I know myself a . . . a woman."

"Hum!" quoth Adam, pinching his chin and gazing up at the lanthorn very wistfully.

"Adam, why should this be, think you?"

"Mayhap because he is . . . so very much a man!" Adam answered, and sighed very deeply.

"Well, I hate men! They are no more than mere beasts on two legs 'stead o' four."

"My poor child!" sighed Adam, venturing to touch her shining hair again. "Some man shall teach thee different, one day . . . mayhap. Now tell me when did we sail?"

"Last night."

"And what o'clock is 't now, Anthony?"

"Late afternoon . . . and oh, my poor Adam, you must be famishing! I'll go find Mr. Troy——"

"No, no!" said Adam, getting afoot, with an effort, "where is he?"

"Somewhere above-stairs, let me show you."

"No, Anthony, your poor eyes all red with tears might betray you. Pray bide here till I return."

"But . . . 'tis so fearsome dark . . . so close and airless."

"Ay, true enough, Anthony. This shall be amended, you shall be better lodged, and this right soon. Meanwhile wait me here . . . you have my spare rapier?"

"Yes, and your pistol, I took it on the sly, Adam."

"Good! Dost know how to use it?"

"Ah no,—no indeed!"

"Good again, you can then do no great harm to yourself. I shall teach you the manage of pistol and rapier, if you will, Anthony."

"Then I will this shall be soon," cried she with a quick eagerness. "I shall feel myself so much more man-like."

"Good yet again!" he nodded. "As you know, I have taken you for my brother——"

"Half-brother!" she amended, with ghost of a smile.

"Howbeit," he continued, earnestly, "as brothers we must live on this ship . . . so . . . brother Anthony, let us like brothers trust one another, have faith in thyself and . . . trust ever thy faithful brother Adam."

"Yes. . . . Oh I will, I will!" cried she, giving him both her slim hands with look and a grace so prettily feminine that he came near kissing them, but flushed at himself and shook head at her instead; whereat she drew herself up, squared her shoulders, straddled shapely legs with swaggering air and said with look and tone as much like Absalom as possible: "I'll be resolute, brother Adam, and play my part to please thee—or damme!"

"Why then," smiled Adam, "be patient awhile and bide here till I come very soon and bring you to better lodgment. Is it agreed?"

"Yes, dear brother. Yes, I'll wait unfearing. Go you now, eat and drink at leisure nor hurry for me. Come, let me aid you into your coat. So! You'll find the stairs on your right, beyond this little, narrow door. Lord ha' mercy—how dreadfully this ship sways! Be careful how you go, Adam!"

So he opened this door though with some ado, by reason of the vessel's violent lurches, and stepped into a dim spaciousness where, to right and left, loomed the grim shapes of cannon one beyond another with neat coils and hanks of rope with blocks and tackle. And presently, stumbling with his landsman's legs, he came on a steep flight of stairs up which he clambered to another deck bright with the ruddy beams of sunset and where a sweet, fresh wind buffeted him joyously.

He was blinking dazzled eyes in this welcome radiance and drinking deep of this clean, salt air when a hand clapped his shoulder, a long arm embraced him and a cheery voice greeted him.

"Adam lad! Ha, messmate, now I joy heartily to see thee or I'm a soused gurnet! Come aft to my quarters and eat whiles I talk."

"This," gasped Adam, reeling to another lurch of the deck, "this is a vastly . . . unsteady ship and . . . marvellous uncertain!"

"Lord love thy lubberly pins!" chuckled Absalom. "She's something lively on a bowline, I'll grant ye, and we're in mid-channel. Moreover you ha'n't your sealegs yet. Shalt soon find the trick on't."

"Not soon!" Adam sighed, staggering again. "And never in such wild storm as this."

"Storm?" laughed Absalom, folding him in long arm. "Here's no more than sweet breeze—as yet! A jolly capful. Come, make fast to my girdle,—now—ease thy legs

to it. Though we shall ha' more weather to-night, I reckon,
and plenty on't, ay there's wind i' the offing. Now, come
thy ways, brother."

Across the wide, heaving deck, through an arched doorway brave with gilding and carved work, along a dimming
passage and so at last into a small cabin, very neat and
orderly.

"Now lie ye down on this locker, Adam,—what, art
faint, messmate? Is't thy head?"

"Somewhat!" he answered, and sinking down weakly
full length, closed his eyes, half blind with the pain of his
throbbing head.

"Rum!" quoth Absalom. "A noggin or say, a brace,—
rum it is!" And away he strode and very soon came
striding back followed by a negro bearing a large, well laden
tray, an immensely tall creature with the blackest face
Adam had ever seen, which face seemed suddenly split
asunder by a white-toothed smile.

"This is Jimbo o' the larboard mess," said Absalom,
tweaking this grinning black man by the ear; "should'st
lack for aught at any time, give him a hail and he'll to
thee with a run, eh, Jim?"

"Yassah, come pretty damcurse queeck, yassah!"
answered the black giant, then at Absalom's nod, grinned
and vanished.

"First, drink this, messmate, toss it off now!"

Submissive in his weakness Adam gulped and choked,
but, revived by this potent spirit, sat up and, urged thereto
by Absalom, began to eat, though with no great appetite.

"How's thy cracked sconce, shipmate, thy sore-battered
nob, now? 'Twas that Abner rogue, curse his murderous
soul——"

"No matter for him, Absalom, I have but my just
deserts for being so fool-like unwary. Instead I would thank
thee heartily for bringing us safe aboard—both of us!"

"Aha! Meaning our confounded and most confounding
young female cut-throat——"

"Hush, man! You speak of my half-brother, Anthony, so pray not so loud."

"Why there's none shall hear us aft here, the crew's forrard and the rest aloft on deck."

"Then, Absalom, first and foremost, Anthony must be better lodged."

"Messmate, she shall be. I did but have her—him out o' the way below there whiles we were getting under way, d'ye see, so much foul cursing and swearing as no maid— I mean young gentleman—should hear, a right delicate thought o' mine as you must admit! And then she would by no means be parted from you, Adam, not she—or I'm a radish! For she—I mean he—must have ye in her care,— ay care's the word, Adam,—for when I brought Perks, our chirrurgeon, to bleed and comfort ye, damme if she didn't withstand the two of us,—claps a pistol 'neath our noses and cries 'hands off!' Vowed you'd lost blood a-plenty, which was but truth, for you bled nobly for your size at the 'Mariner's Joy'—and there was she and Mother Martha sponging and cosseting and bandaging and yourself sense-less as any poor, small corpse."

"Then God bless them!" said Adam, rising. "Now pray show me where brother Anthony may be lodged secure and in more comfort."

"Come then, Adam, 'tis aft and just forrard of the stern-chase, and, though none so large or fine as the new banquet chamber at Whitehall, it should serve! I've had all pre-pared, swept and garnished, a hammock slung,—ay and a looking-glass likewise,—the which is yet another delicate thought o' mine."

"A hammock?" questioned Adam.

"Ay so! If you've never slept in hammock you'll find there's no bed ashore to match it for comfort, 'specially when 'tis blowing hard and yourself bone-weary. Come and see! Easy now,—clap on to my girdle again." Thus supported, Adam stumbled a yard or so, to another narrow door whereat Absalom paused, saying:

C

"Here's for thy Master Anthony, confound her! And, lookee, this being the last berth to larboard no one shall need to pass this way,—except of course to fight our stern-chase pieces yonder, if needful." Then he opened this door, showing a small, trim apartment where swung the first hammock Adam had ever seen.

"Bowl . . . and ewer?" he enquired, clutching at the door to steady himself against the ship's dizzy roll.

"All here, Adam, in this locker, all right and tight and shipshape. And other lockers yonder for clothes and so forth. Ay—and stout bolts to secure the door, I'll ha' ye to observe. Your pestilent brother shall be safe enough, ha?"

"Therefore," nodded Adam, "the sooner he is here, the better. Now where must I be housed?"

"Yonder, 'twixt this cabin and my own. Well, shall I go fetch your plaguey brother?"

"Half-brother, Absalom. And I'll go myself, as promised."

"Why then, Adam, take heed ye don't pitch down the companion and break neck along o' head."

So, very carefully though with many slides and stumbles, Adam made his way below and after some desperate groping, found and opened the door he sought—to have his own pistol thrust into his face and hear a voice of extraordinary harshness bid him 'Stand Back!' Then the weapon was tossed upon cushioned locker and he was clasped in eager arms while a voice now trembling between laughter and sobbing, cried:

"Oh, Adam . . . you've been so long away . . . and I frighted out o' my poor wits by sounds like dreadful, creeping footsteps beyond the door . . . and then a great, horrid rat very monstrous and so bold he sat up and looked at me so fierce I should have screamed but for my promise to you,—so instead I pulled out sword and poked at him, very manlike though a little wild, but he fled."

Adam chuckled (to his own surprise), then gently loosing

those too-feminine arms, grasped Antonia's hand and shook it, saying:

"Well done, brother Anthony! God love thee! Now shalt be lodged as valiant gentleman should be, ay—and sleep right sailorly in a hammock!"

"Nay but, Adam, what manner of thing is that?"

"Follow and see for thyself, my bold Anthony."

Together they stumbled and clutched their way out and up the companion ladder and thus at last to that passageway where Absalom met them.

"Aha, Master Anthony," quoth he, raising hand in smiling salute, "hast come armed to the teeth, I perceive —sword and pistol now, is it?"

"Indeed, Master Troy," she answered, head aloft and shoulders squared, "also, brother Adam hath promised to show me their proper manage."

Then she turned to survey her little cabin, to exclaim in wondering surprise at the hammock, and with pleasure because of the many lockers,—but espying the mirror, she clasped her hands and uttered a sigh of such truly feminine joy that Absalom chuckled, whereat she instantly scowled on him and clapping to the door, bolted it violently.

"Faith now," he laughed, "'tis fine-spirited wen— youth!"

"And," sighed Adam, hand to aching head, "I would have you regard him, whiles on this ship, as my brother Anthony."

"Why so I must—and will, be sure, for I've seen many a boy more maid-like, or damme! Now come and sit ye, for I've divers matters to discuss."

"Nay, not—ah, not now," sighed Adam, "for I feel a marvellous discomfort within me, Absalom."

"'Tis Nature, messmate, 'tis curst frail Nature,—and none so wonderful neither, since these narrow seas, breaking short, are apt to prove troublesome at first, making the mere thought of ripe, rich, fat pork extreme disquieting, ha? Come aloft into the good wind."

So up they went into a blusterous evening shot by fiery sunset that crested every rolling billow with glory.

And thus for the first time Adam Penfeather beheld the wonder of a stout ship cleaving her trackless course through a riotous sea, rising graciously to the surge and onrush of mounting waves, to plunge forward and down in smother of hissing foam; and he felt such profound awe of these wide, ever-moving waters and this noble ship with her towering masts, mazy rigging and great spread of sail that, for the moment, he clean forgot aching head and bodily discomfort.

"A right joyous prospect, eh, messmate?" cried Absalom, glancing aloft at taut canvas and away to windward with sailorly eye.

"Glorious!" Adam answered breathlessly. "Surely 'tis a very great ship, this?"

"Middling, Adam. She's pierced for forty pieces and carries poor twenty. But she's stout and trim and sweet on her helm. Hast ever been aboardship afore?"

"Never."

"Why then, this is the quarter-deck,—below there is the waist, forrard o' that the forecastle. Aft there is the round-house or coach and above it the poop. Ha, and there ye may see Sir Benjamin, with Dodd the Master and William Sharp, our sharp-nosed, sharper-tongued, curse and damn ye fool of a captain."

"I perceive you love him not, Absalom, and wherefore?"

"For that he's no sailor,—a portentous ass too fond of himself, his own cursed importance and the bottle. He'll run foul o' trouble anon, or I'm a flounder! The only true sailormen aft here are Smy and myself. And we're due for a blusterous night by the look o' things, there's weather i' the offing. How's thy stomach, Adam?"

"So queasy I would to heaven I had not eaten."

"Better so, 'twill be the easier for thee by and by, 'tis Nature, Adam, yet once over 'tis soon forgot. And now the better to forget, come and watch me bait our Captain

Numbskull Arrogance. Shalt see him very presently foam with prideful rage."

"Nay, why quarrel with the man?"

"First, for pure joy of it, and second—to very good purpose anon and hereafter. Go with me."

"No, Absalom. The unhappiness within me waxeth. . . . I'll to my cabin."

"Wouldst be better i' the clean air, Adam. Howbeit go thy ways and luck with thee, brother."

Adam merely groaned and went staggering and clutching his way below to shut himself into his berth and be alone with his misery.

And now ensued for him long hours he was not soon to forget; for as his trouble grew, so, as it seemed to him, the movements of the ship became ever the more violent until came one dizzy heave and sickening plunge that rolled and tumbled him to the sloping floor where he lay, a mere huddle of wretchedness, faint with nausea and racked by pain of his wounded head, outsprawled in a coma deepening at last to a merciful unconsciousness.

CHAPTER VIII

"PENFEATHER, ahoy! Ho, Adam Penfeather!" A loud, harsh voice, with powerful fist that smote and thundered on the door, troubling him greatly.

"Adam Penfeather, ho there! Rouse out and open! Penfeather ahoy!"

Distressed by this insistent clamour, he stirred, groaned, and sat up.

"Who calls me?"

"Myself—thy friend Captain Smy. Open the door!"

"No . . . no. . . . Begone. . . . Go away!"

But now, being thus drowsily awake and finding the ship much steadier, Adam clambered back upon the cushioned locker and there outstretched, presently fell into a refreshing slumber—until once again came a knocking with a voice crying his name. And knowing this voice, he rose up, though feebly, and answered:

"Yes, Anthony. What is it?"

"Come you out to me, Adam. Come out."

So when he had bathed hands and face and ordered rumpled garments, he opened the door and was seized by two hands that drew him forth of foetid gloom into a life-giving air made glorious by a fugitive sunbeam that showed him Antonia's face, a pale though radiant vision.

"Oh, Adam," she cried, leading him towards the sunshine, "I feared you had died in this dreadful night!"

"And indeed," he answered, "I thought so, too."

"Such terrible storm, Adam, it broke some of the riggings and washed men overboard to die in the horror of black waters. And they've taken him away to prison and in fetters . . . and he did but smile!"

"But," sighed Adam, "the tempest hath abated, thank God! And now, Anthony, pray tell me who is prisoned and in fetters?"

"Why—him,—Master Troy."

"Absalom . . . in fetters! Art sure?"

"Adam, I saw him led away . . . and he smiled at me."

"But . . . Absalom prisoned? Why so?"

"Nay, Adam, see yonder . . . a great, fierce sailor-man beckons us!"

"Ay. I see him!" nodded Adam, and coming to the quarter-railing looked down on this man, a tall, young, though very hairy fellow who, standing on the deck below, knuckled an eyebrow, saying in lowered tones:

"My sarvice to ee sirs, and which of ee be Master Adam Penfeather, if ye please?"

"I am."

"Why then, sir, I be Bym. Joel Bym, gunner's mate, and I be ordered to ax ee to bear away down along o' me."

"By whose order?"

"Cap'n Absalom, sir."

"Why then, Anthony, do you wait me here. Lead on, Joel Bym." Forthwith they descended to a lower deck in which place of gloom they came upon Captain Smy sitting upon a gun with a small lanthorn in his fist, who rose and beckoning silently led them forward and down another companion ladder into the very bowels of the ship as it seemed to Adam, who now, halting suddenly in this unsavoury darkness, demanded:

"Captain Smy, pray where d'ye take me?"

"For to visit Absalom, our messmate Lom."

"But what does he down here in this foul-smelling darkness?"

"Sits in fetters and makes a song on't, eh, Joel?"

"Ay, by cock, sir,—carols 'e do, blithe as any chirping cricket."

"And the foul reek you complain of, Adam, is sweet to sailorly nose for it proves a tight ship."

"But why is Absalom so prisoned?"

"For saving the ship and kicking lubberly Captain into the scuppers, Adam. There was the *Merchant*—which is lubberly name for any vessel,—nigh on her beam-ends, being taken aback, and the Lizard in our lee. So Absalom takes charge, turns up all hands and, with Abel Challen and myself at the helm, cons the ship to make an offing and it's touch and go if we shall weather the point. Yet we did, by Lom his seamanship, and beat out to sea though it took us all night. Then, first thing this morning, Absalom is clapped by the heels for mutiny, and the crew mighty downcast and sullen therefore—the which last is just as well. So, yonder in the black hole lieth our messmate, yet a-singing right cheerily and as only Absalom may,—heark to him!"

And now, above the ceaseless creak and groan of the ship's labour, they heard a rich, clear, baritone voice singing very melodiously with rhythmic clash of jangling fetters, and these the words:

> "Here in bilboes fast be I,
>   As we sail, as we sail (*clash of fetters*).
> Here in bilboes clamped am I,
>   As we sail (*clash and clang of fetters*).
> But—'stead o' me, by and bye,
> Cursed Sharp himself shall lie,
> So now damn his eyes! say I,
>   As we sail" (*clash of fetters*).

They had reached the forward bulkhead wherein was a small, stout, grim-looking door, and now while Smy held the light, Joel Bym fitted ponderous key to lock and opening this door, showed a narrow cell where, seated cross-legged amid heap of tumbled straw, Absalom Troy blinked and smiled up at them.

"Aha, messmates," quoth he, shading his eyes against

the light, "be welcome to this place o' tribulation; a martyr gives ye right hearty greeting. Sit ye down here on my throne o' straw. So! How is thy poor head and stomach now, brother Adam?"

"Better, I thank you, Absalom. But I grieve to find you thus."

"What, Smy, hast not told him then?"

"Nary word, Lom."

"Why then, Adam, Lord love thee,—never waste thy pity, for I can be out o' these irons whenso I will. For, d'ye see, ere I suffered myself to be locked into 'em, I took care to have a duplicate key in my pocket. Moreover, my present abasement is but a means to my soon exaltation. There's not a man or lad aboard but knows I saved their lives, wherefore I sit here very martyr-like for their sakes, and therefore they are all ripe to up and follow me for my sake whenso I give the word."

"Meaning—mutiny, Absalom?"

"Ay, some would so name it. Now hearkee, 'tis for talk o' this I sent for ye, having meant to speak on 't afore, yet found no chance. Well, Adam, this ship called *London Merchant* is bound for Hispaniola with cargo for traffic with the planters and Indians thereabout,—ha, but— among the various oddments for sale are five poor gentlemen now languishing in bonds, shut up like cattle on the orlop, and of these—one is kinsman to Sir Benjamin, one an old shipmate o' Smy, and one well beknown to me. Five are they, Adam, all political prisoners, gentlemen o' condition and haters o' Papistry who, being something too froward o' speech or act, were doomed to axe or rope by King Jamie our Scottish, Royal Sycophant o' Spain. Later, his Majesty changes his royal mind and, 'stead o' death now dooms 'em to banishment, and 'stead o' giving them to the Headsman, bestows 'em on divers of his court favourites, which languishing, pampered pets have sold 'em to our Captain Sharp who will sell 'em again at much profit overseas, and so to death as sure yet less merciful than block or gallows. So, Adam, we are here aboard this ship with intent most determined to rescue these same prisoners."

"Well and good, Absalom, but—how?"

"By taking this ship—and not to Hispaniola but to St. Kitts or Tortuga, this to be decided later."

"And this," said Adam, pinching his chin nervously, "this shall be rank piracy."

"Ay, ay, shipmate."

"And the penalty—death!"

"True enough, Adam,—execution dock, tar and irons and gibbets alongshore for warning to like rogues."

"And," said Adam, blenching, "to take such great ship you must do—murder!"

"Some small effusion o' blood, messmate, mayhap, 'tis but natural and to be expected. And because o' this, Adam, and by our brotherhood oath, I bid thee to stand neutral in this business, so that, should things go foul and our schemes a-wrack, thou at least shall be within the law and clear of its sure vengeance. Well, how say'st thou?"

"Nothing. I ponder how best this may achieve—without bloodshed."

"'Twill yet be piracy, Adam, blood or no."

"Though not murder of honest men. How stand your chances with the crew?"

"There be twenty-five stout lads all listed for this purpose by Sir Benjamin, Smy and myself, men we can trust—blow foul or fair, the rest have been sounded by Joel and Abnegation and are mostly heartily disposed towards us since Smy and I saved the ship."

"Even so," sighed Adam, "there shall be many honest among them will balk at piracy."

"Ay, like as not. Yet if we must fight, to shed blood to such good purpose is——"

"Wrong," said Adam, "and crass stupidity, since it should be needless."

"Eh? How needless? How?"

"When shall you attempt this?"

"Two nights hence i' the middle watch, two days and nights further from Old England."

"Then, Absalom, 'stead of force I would suggest method strategic."

"Oho!" exclaimed Smy, grimly sardonic. "I perceive a sucking Solomon, a youthful, prattling sage, a young Daniel to inform us! A fico, Adam lad, what know ye o' strategy —and aboard ship moreover?"

"Sir," answered Adam, pinching chin again, "no more than caution and my mother wit do teach me."

"Aha!" cried Absalom, clashing his fetters. "And what then? Speak out, Adam."

"Then Absalom, I'll answer your question with another, to wit—what is it all mariners do most fear at sea?"

"Mist and fog!" growled Smy.

"What say you, Joel Bym?"

"Why, sir, I du reckon as it be fire,—ay, by cock, I du!"

"And fire say I!" nodded Absalom. "And how then, shipmate?"

"Then," continued Adam, "since fire is the terror most dreadful, let this terror work for ye instead of murderous steel. At time appointed let some trusty man, hid below here, contrive a fire shall nowise peril the ship yet make great plenty of smoke. Then let other chosen men set up mighty baloo and cry o' 'fire'! Whereat, as I nothing doubt, all on board shall haste below to save the ship and themselves from such calamity. Then you above may shut these all below by pointing cannons as to discharge down each stairway. Thus ye shall have them at your mercy to parley with them at leisure, with offer and choice of serving under you or sailing to land in such of the boats as they will— and all without shedding of blood."

Absalom glanced from Adam's small, earnest face to Smy's pensive visage, then at Joel Bym's goggling eyes— and chuckled, then laughed, clashing his fetters as in an ecstasy.

"Smy," said he, at last. "Oh, Smy, hast said it, man, hast said it, or I'm a salted codfish!"

"Eh, Lom—I? Now what a plague said I?"

"A sucking Solomon, a prattling sage, a young Daniel, for so he is, or damme! Though one of internal disquiet by his looks,—how now, Adam, is 't thy head or stomach ails thee?"

"Both!" answered Adam, faintly. "Pray get me to my cabin."

So thither he stumbled, supported by Joel's brawny arm; and there, somewhat revived by the cleanly, buffeting wind, he suffered Antonia to bathe and re-bandage his aching head, and thereafter sank to heavy slumber.

CHAPTER IX

HE awoke early next morning to new vigour, with such unwonted hunger that, making all haste to wash and get into his only other shift of garments, forth he went to seek breakfast.

But reaching the open deck he paused to shade dazzled eyes against the level beams of a sun that, new risen in fiery splendour, made a sparkling glory of the sea through which this stately vessel rode with a smooth and gracious pride.

Coming to the lee bulwark he leaned there, all else forgotten, to gaze down at radiant ocean and up at spreading sails and the multitude of ropes and cordage, marvelling now at God's vast and awful handiwork, and now at the ingenuity of Man whose brain could thus conceive and hands construct this floating miracle of wood and canvas. And in this moment Adam knew he was henceforth to love the sea, the dreadful beauty of it, and the brave ships that dared its might.

Now as he stood thus rapt in a sort of ecstasy, he was startled by a shrill, agonized scream, with a heavy fall and crash of breaking crockery, and speeding instantly towards these sounds, beheld a small urchin who lay sobbing bitterly amid a litter of splintered plates and dishes.

"Why how now?" said Adam, stooping above this small person. "Art hurt, my child?"

The boy raised a blood-smeared face, blinked away blinding tears and stared up at his questioner, then, gulping his sobs, answered manfully as possible:

"Sir, I bean't a child, ho no, sir! I be Capn's cabin boy ay, sir, and I be powder boy to number four gun starbard battery. And I only cried a bit 'cause when he kicked me I falls and cuts me,—though I don't mind blood—much! So I ain't a child, sir, if you please."

"No no," smiled Adam, raising the little fellow to his legs, "I crave pardon, my man, pray what's your name?"

"Charles, sir, but they calls me Smidge aboard ship, and I likes Smidge better nor Charles, so call me Smidge, sir, if y' please. But have you been in a war, sir,—your figure-head all lapped in a clout, so?"

"Somethin' o' the like, Smidge. Now tell me who kicked you so hard."

"Only the Cap'n, sir, him being a bit angry-like this morning."

"You show something young for the sea, Master Smidge, and don't speak like a ship's boy, I think."

"But I tries to, sir, only my . . . my mother learned me to speak soft and read and write . . . but when she died I . . . I run away to sea, being so very lonesome —like."

At this moment a bell tinkled nearby and a harsh voice shouted, whereupon little Smidge caught up his fallen tray in shaking hands.

"Boy!" shouted the voice again.

"There be the Cap'n, sir, I must go."

"To be kicked again, Smidge?"

"I hopes not, sir, yet go I must."

"No!" said Adam, taking the tray. "I will. Bide you here." Then guided by the Captain's shouts he came to a certain door, opened it and stepped into a very spacious, handsomely furnished cabin where, at well laden table, sat Captain Elihu Sharp with James Dodd the Master and another officer. Clapping the tray beneath his arm, Adam saluted them with a bow, saying:

"Gentlemen, a very good morning to ye."

The two officers stared, Captain Sharp scowled.

"Now who the devil may you be?" he demanded.

"Adam Penfeather, sir, entirely at your service."

"So? Then serve me by sheering off. Begone, d'ye hear? Ay, and send me that cursed, snivelling little brat, and lively."

"Not I, sir!" answered Adam, approaching the table and laying the tray there. "You have kicked him so hard that I came in his stead."

"Hey—you? Now what the devil d'ye mean?"

"That you shall not vent your splenetic, foul humours on such poor, small child, sir. So now, if you must kick someone, pray kick me and you shall bleed for it."

Captain Sharp seemed to stiffen in his chair and opened his eyes as if shocked and amazed beyond speech; he gazed at Adam's puny form from spindle shanks to bandaged head, he blinked, gulped and finally spoke.

"Bleed?" he repeated disbelievingly, his ferocity tempered by breathless astonishment. "Bleed was it? Did dare . . . blast your eyes . . . ha, bleed me, will ye?"

"Sir, 'tis you shall decide," answered Adam, whereat the two officers looked from his lean, pale face to their passion-shaken captain, glanced at each other and averted their faces.

"Why, you . . . you . . ." gasped Captain Sharp, "you little, cursed, pitiful whelp, will ye dare to threaten me . . . and on my own ship?"

"Nay," sighed Adam, "I venture warning. Kick me and bleed, invite me to breakfast and I shall be glad to join ye."

Uttering foul invective, Captain Sharp made to rise; taking knife from the table Adam tried its edge on his thumb, staring into his would-be assailant's glaring, bloodshot eyes the while. Suddenly, his quick ear caught a stealthy sound behind him, he swayed nimbly aside and a tall, barefooted mulatto, missing him by inches, crashed sprawling across the table, scattering plates and dishes, and all was confusion. Adam was backing towards the door when he was checked and staggered by an unseen fist, then smitten to his face; but as he lay thus helpless to be kicked and cuffed, glimpsed a pair of stout legs that skipped in familiar bouncing manner, heard an arrogant, full-throated bellow:

"Sblood and death—what's here? Ods wounds, what's doing? Hold off or I'll mischief ye! You trample friend o' mine! What a plague——?"

"Here's murder, Sir Benjamin!" cried the Captain. "'Tis mutinous rogue drew knife on me."

"Tush and ten thousand curses!" roared Sir Benjamin, his bouncing legs becoming passionate. "I tell ye this gentleman you outrage is friend o' mine."

"And, sir, I tell you 'tis murderous villain would ha' knifed me!"

"Od's my life, Captain, will ye dare me? Ha, Penfeather, you hear him?" cried Sir Benjamin. "What says't thou, Adam?"

"Sir," answered Adam, getting to unsteady legs, "you behold here the knife, but——."

"How?" cried Sir Benjamin, recoiling in dismay. "You took knife to the Captain?"

"Ay, I did,—but to mine own defence."

"Nay," cried the Captain, "'twas with most fell and bloody intent o' murder . . . we be all witnesses thereto! And how then?"

Sir Benjamin sighed dismally, shook head dejectedly, his very legs (these so eloquent members) appeared to languish.

"Ha!" cried Captain Sharp. "Sir Benjamin, I perceive you are acquaint with the old rule and law o' the sea— to wit: Whoso draweth knife aboardship with murderous intent, shall lose his right hand! 'Tis good and ancient custom and shall be duly observed. Master Dodd, at the next bell, let sound trumpet with beat o' drum to muster all hands aft to see justice done and infliction o' punishment. Meantime the young, murdering villain shall be seized to the main, and the knife slung about his neck

and set two armed men for guard. See to it, Mr. Sprot,—
away with him!"

So Adam was haled and dragged away into the waist
of the ship and here, with back to the great main-mast
and arms drawn painfully about it, was tied securely and
with two brawny mariners to guard him.

And now by the pain of his head and blood that was
half blinding him, it seemed his wound had been re-opened
in the struggle; and this blood, creeping into his eye-
sockets, began to tickle and teaze him so intolerably that
to be rid of it he shook his aching head, but finding this
vain, groaned, and was about to ask one of his guards to
wipe it away, when a hand did this mercy for him, then
glancing round, he beheld the boy Smidge.

"Now," sighed Adam, quick to read the pity in this
small face, "now God love thee, my Smidge man!"

"Do it hurt ee bad, sir?" whispered the boy: but at this
instant one of the guards glanced round, and this a young,
plumply-pallid, smiling fellow who, grasping Smidge by
the hair, smote the writhing boy cruelly with the flat of
his sword. Then ere he could repeat the blow, Adam
spoke as he deemed Absalom might have done and using
his remembered words:

"Avast, ye scum! Strike again and soon or late I tear
out your vile liver, or damme!"

Loosing Smidge, who vanished instantly, the man
touched his bonnet instinctively, as to familiar authority
of words and tone, then recoiled slowly before the narrow-
eyed, venomous look of their speaker.

"Lord, sir," he whined. "Lord love and bless your dear
'eart, never threat pore Sam so fierce. I be Smiling Sam,
sir, and the Smiler be everybody's freend and only does
'is dooty as dooty so com-pels and all along o' bleed'n
boy as——"

"Belay your cursed jaw-tackle!" snarled Adam, whereat
the Smiler, in the act of smiling, groaned instead and
turned away.

And now in his pain and shame Adam looked about for little Smidge, yearning for some friendly face or mere look of kindliness and seeing none, bowed his head again and began to think on what might soon befall; this horror imagination made so real that he felt a nervous twitching in his right hand, this good hand which must be shorn from his quivering flesh unless. . . . He closed his eyes and began to pray. . . . Presently, as if in answer, a voice cried his name, and he beheld Antonia, who would have run to him but was prevented by his guards, whereat he called on her to begone, until she turned unwillingly and sped away.

Slowly the time dragged by . . . up rose the sun, high and higher . . . a trumpet blared shrilly with slow solemn beat of drum, and, twisting in his bonds, Adam saw four men bearing a great block painted an ominous red, and behind this the grinning mulatto bare-armed and fondling a short-hafted, broad-bladed axe.

And now was tramp and scurry of many feet where the crew was mustering, every man and boy, to behold and take warning by his dreadful punishment. Suddenly trumpet and drum sounded again as with his officers behind him, came Elihu Sharp, the Captain, brave clad for the occasion; halting within a few paces of the block he lifted his hand, whereat trumpet and drum instantly hushed. But before he might speak,—forth before the company strode Sir Benjamin who, being for once somewhat unsure of himself, bounced and strutted, flourished and bellowed even more arrogantly than usual.

"Hold!" cried he, with flash and glitter of brandished rapier. "Hold, I say! Od's body, this shall not achieve! Death and damnation—no!"

"Silence, sir!" roared the Captain, harshly. "As commander o' this ship I bid ye stand away and suffer the law be done upon this——"

"Hell's fury!" roared Sir Benjamin. "Am I denied then?" And from somewhere about his rotundity he drew a long-barrelled pistol. "Now hearkee, Sir Captain,—I, as part owner o' this same ship and cargo, demand instant release o' your prisoner, for, knowing him gentleman and therefore honourable, I do here and now pronounce and will maintain him innocent! Am I explicit, sir?" Here, and very ostentatiously, Sir Benjamin cocked his pistol, whereat Captain Sharp recoiled, crying:

"Ho, musketeers, stand by! Handle your pieces——"

"Halt!" bellowed Sir Benjamin. "Let one so much as level at me, Captain, and I send a ball through your brisket, forthwith. Do I persuade?"

Now for a space was a hush wherein it seemed none stirred . . . then, suddenly, from the deeps below, rose a wild and fearful cry:

"Fire! Fire! Oho—help! The ship's afire!"

With this awful cry and making it the more terrible, came smoke upcurling from the nearby hatchway, a thick column growing ever denser—whereat other voices took up the cry and all was clamour and wild uproar.

Now presently Adam saw the deck about him all deserted except for a few men who were busied with one of the smaller guns, heaving at and aiming it to sweep and command the companion stairs, with Captain Smy to direct them while Joel Bym stood blowing lustily on lighted match. Thus watching these warlike preparations, Adam felt a hand upon his shoulder and glancing round beheld a grimy though very cheerful Absalom who chuckled.

"Like a charm, Adam!" he nodded. "Thy smoke strategic worketh like spell o' witchcraft or I'm a pickled mackerel! The ship's good as ours."

Then Adam felt his galling bonds fall away and turning, saw Antonia beside him, grasping a knife.

"Thou'rt bleeding again!" she cried, breathlessly. "Oh, did they hurt thee? I made all haste possible."

"And now," said Absalom, glancing at the priming of a pistol that had appeared suddenly in his smoke-grimed fist, "make haste again,—off with thee, Adam, take this loving brother o' thine to tend thy hurt—away from chance o' stray shot."

"'Tis good thought, Absalom,—and here's another,—spill no life, I pray you."

"Never a one, messmate—except o' necessity. Aft there," he shouted. "Ahoy, Abnegation! Is the hatch battened down?"

"Ay, ay, sir, all 's fast!"

"Then stand by to watch lest they break through. Cock your pieces,—they'll ha' discovered our trick by now . . . ay, they have! Hark to 'em!"

From the crew below rose an angry hum, hoarse murmur swelling to fierce clamour of angry voices with patter of many feet, hushed and stilled all at once by sight of that down-pointing gun-muzzle that menaced them. Now coming beside this gun, Absalom hailed them cheerily:

"Below there, my lads! Pass the word for Captain Sharp."

"I'm here, Troy, I'm here!" answered the Captain. "And demand your reason for this outrage——"

"Hearkee then, sir,—hearken to me one and all o' ye! Here stand I with twenty-five stout lads, to tell our several reasons why you behold me in command o' this ship, to wit: First, Captain Sharp, your drunkenness. Second, your lubberliness. Thirdly, and for mine own part, because I love not the sight, sound, manners or nose o' thee, in fine, sir, thou art my aversion. Wherefore and therefore it is decreed that you and such fools as will follow you, shall have one o' the boats with store of arms and victuals, and be cast loose——"

"Ha—mutiny," cried Captain Sharp. "I call on all men to witness here is rank, black mutiny!"

"Ay, ay, mutiny it is," nodded Absalom, patting the gun beside him, "whereto this is yet another witness shall bear loud and eloquent testimony whenso I will. This ship that was the *London Merchant* is now the *Bold Adventuress* to dare Fortune on the golden quest. So now, my lads, who of ye will be bold adventurers? Who'll sail with me for the Main and chance o' Spanish gold, doubloons and pieces of eight? Whoso will 'list let him step forrard."

At this was a muttering among the men, then a cheer; and cheering up they came, first by two and threes, then in a jostling, eager crowd, to be counted by Captain Smy and marshalled in orderly ranks by Abnegation Mings.

"Smy, how many do ye muster?"

"Ninety and two, sir."

"Well and good! See a boat be prepared, Smy, and then we'll heave-to and be quit o' this lubberly Sharp and his fellows forthright."

And presently, with creak of yards, rattle of blocks and flapping of canvas, the ship was brought to; Captain Elihu Sharp with four of his officers and the nine men who remained faithful to him, went over the side into the small boat prepared for them, and there, standing in the stern-sheets, he cursed Absalom Troy living and dead, with dire threats of rope and gallows, tar, irons and gibbet. The law's dreadful and inevitable vengeance. To all of which Absalom, lounging above on lofty poop, hearkened with a polite interest and acknowledged with cheery smile and gracious flourish of hat. Then, at his command, the braces were manned, sails trimmed, and the course set for the golden west.

And so, in this most fateful hour, the *London Merchant* now the *Bold Adventuress*, bore away, with fair wind and smooth sea, for those far latitudes where all were to find peril, many death, some few great fortune and success, two a wondrous happiness, and one—triumph, greatness, heartbreak and failure.

CHAPTER X

CHIEFLY CONCERNING A KISS

FOR a week, owing to bodily hurt and affliction of mind, Adam kept his bed, with the surgeon, Tobias Perks, to doctor him, Jimbo, the black giant, to wait on him, the boy Smidge to creep on small, bare feet to steal furtive peeps at him, and Antonia to preside and rule all of them in her own serene though determined manner.

This morning, finding himself sufficiently recovered, and moreover being for the moment alone, Adam determined to get up, and looked about for his garments, and seeing them nowhere, scowled pettishly; then noting his father's sword had vanished also, fretful annoyance changed to swift anger, and he cried out in dismay—whereupon, round the jamb of narrow doorway came a shock of curly hair and the boy Smidge inched himself into view with a rag of grimy canvas in one small fist, Adam's rapier in the other.

"Oh, sir," he whispered, "I be main glad as youm well again—do ee lack for aught, sir?"

"Ay, my clothes, boy. And what do ye with that sword?"

"Nuffink, Mis' Adam, only shine it up a bit like. I've cleaned your shoes, bofe pair, sir. I've polished your belt and buckle, sir, and all your buttons."

"Thankee, my man. Now where are my clothes?"

"He's took 'em, sir—Mist' Anthony, your bruvver, Mist' Adam, sir."

"Then go fetch 'em, Smidge,—stay, where is he—my brother?"

"On deck, sir, along o' the fat gen'leman, and another on 'em named Mr. Melord——" But at this moment was jingle of crockery and in came Antonia, followed by Jimbo carrying a large, heavy-laden tray.

"I shall get up to-day," said Adam, with the utmost resolution and glancing at Antonia, "so bring me my clothes, Jimbo."

"Yessah!" answered the great negro with flash of white teeth, "I bringum dis instantannyious moment, sah!" But, instead of so doing, he too glanced enquiringly at Antonia who shook her head, saying:

"After breakfast, Adam—mayhap. Set the tray here, Jimbo, my hearty. Ahoy, Smidge, hang up that sword and bring me the stool yonder. Now—this cake for thee and run off like a good child."

"Ooh, thankee sir, I'm sure . . . only, Mist' Anthony, I ain't no child—eh, Mist' Adam, sir?"

"Nay, thourt my trusty old shipmate."

"So there's for ee, Mist' Anthony!" cried the boy, making a face at Antonia's back; then with salute, smart and sailorly, to Adam, he sped away.

"This boy worships you, Adam. He's forever hovering around,—he hath cleaned your shoes so often that I've hid them lest he rub and polish them into holes!"

"He told me you were walking with 'the fat gentleman' the which I guess will be Sir Benjamin."

"It was," said Antonia, and giggled.

"And some other gentleman he said is named Mr. Melord."

"This," said she, laughing merrily, "was my lord Perrow, one of the rescued prisoners, Adam, and though such great gentleman very gracious and kindly but very sad too, and small wonder considering his many sufferings, poor gentleman . . . and with his every tone and gesture puts me in mind of someone, though who 'tis I cannot think. Hath your fine Captain Absalom been to see you this morning?"

"No,—unless this be he," answered Adam, as came the sound of approaching footsteps.

"It is not!" quoth Antonia. "Your grand Captain goes with leisured stride scornful of haste. No, hither speeds our surgeon that hath mixed you potions that looked noisome as they smelt."

"Yet I have taken none, surely?"

"Surely not, Adam! And so be humbly thankful to thy brother Anthony."

"Good morrow t'ye, gentlemen!" cried a cheery voice, and in bustled Master Perks, the surgeon. "A day o' promise, sirs. Aurora blusheth, sly jade, i' the lap o' Neptune on our starboard beam, the hoary wag! A sweet morn, a gladsome dayspring!" Master Tobias Perks, though small of person, was great of speech and if skilful surgeon in treatment of wounds, by reason of long and much experience, knew little or nothing of medical arts, which ignorance he was wont to veil in pomposity of words and sounding phrases. All of which Antonia's womanly sense had been quick to perceive, of course.

"Well, well?" exclaimed the little surgeon, clapping plump hands softly, and beaming down at pale-faced Adam, "here is very obvious betterment, Mr. Anthony. Though our young patient, like Peter's wife's mother, hath lain sick of a fever, this is now happily reduced. Tongue, sir—ha! Pulse now—hum! You gave him the draught, Mr. Anthony?"

"No, sir!" answered Antonia, serenely.

"Eh? Not? Then—what did you?"

"Threw it out through the scuttle, sir."

"Eh, sir? Oh! The devil, sir! Most irregular! Yet no matter. He showeth none the worse."

"He is better, Master Perks."

"Much better!" quoth Adam, with vehemence.

"Ha! Good! This will be effect o' the pill, 'tis potent, sirs, 'tis remedy radical and prescription o' my own! 'Tis most rare stimulant o' the aortic nerve whereto the heart responsive induceth a more liveliness in the vital spirits, a flux, sirs, a flow o' the secretions animal. Pray, when took he the pill?"

"Sir, he did not."

"Not, sir—not? Gad's my life! Why not?"

"Sir, he showed so much better without it that, minding how wisely you said: 'Nature is nature's best physic', I

withheld your pill lest Nature approve not of my so
meddling therewithal.''

"Hem! Ha! And yet—he is better and shall anon be
well, thanks to Great Nature, to Tobias Perks—and—thine
own littleness, Mr. Penfeather, thy paucity o' person and
lack o' length, sir.''

"And what,'' Adam demanded, scowling, "what hath
my lack o' size to do with it?''

"Everything, sir, everything! Look at yourself, Master
Adam,—regard me! Little men both, ha? But little men
be usually of an amazing vitality,—and for this most
especial and very cogent reason, to wit: As the blood is
the life, the chiefest life member is the heart, this sponge,
this pump, this most lovely organ! Now perceive me,—
if the body be small o' size and trimly compact, this same
pump needeth the lesser force to pump or drive blood to
the extremest limits thereof. But if the body be o' dimen-
sions grossly large, plethorically bulky,—oh, conceive then
how poor heart must laborious surge, must heave and con-
vulsive strive, and so—be weary! And when heart lan-
guisheth, body fainteth,—so cometh disease, till weary
heart swooneth, stoppeth and—body dieth! So be grateful,
sir, for your vital smallness o' body, your poverty of
inches, as I am, good faith! In health or sickness, peace
or war, better be small and sweetly compact o' person
than giant, like Jimbo or great, brawny fellow like Troy.''

"Speaking of him, Mr. Tobias, how go things aboardship these days, since he took command?''

"Better and better, sir! 'Tis sweet ship now, ay and
nobly handled and cared for. Such scouring and scrubbing,
such prodigious business alow and aloft, such drilling with
small arms and great, this crew o' scowling slovens are
being worked and kicked and transformed into fighting
men now they've a man to rule 'em. Troy knoweth men
and hath with 'em a method unfailing.''

"As how, pray?''

"Why, t'other morning he has all hands piped aft and

tells 'em roundly that he means to drub and drill 'em into
lusty fighters and seadogs all. Then offers a guinea to the
first man shall reach and straddle the main-guard—and
himself wins the prize. Ay, 'tis prime seaman Tory, and
hearty fellow 'til crossed, and then—beware! He kicked
one, Tucker, adown the poop-ladder yesterday forenoon for
back-answering, and levelled Smiling Sam with his fist for
kicking one o' the little rascal boys—and half-throttled Tom
Tranter for fouling the new scoured deck with spittle. And so
'tis the men begin to love him and jump at his word as
seamen should. Ay, a notable captain and mariner is Troy."

"Yet sounds one extreme harsh and violent!" said
Antonia. "A word and a blow,—and sweareth most vilely!"

"Ay, true sir! True indeed, Master Anthony, and 'tis
by such violence, instant and just, by such speech, elo-
quently to the point, that a man winneth the high respect
and instant obedience of his fellows, more especially such
fellows as these that are, or were, for the most part regular
gallows-meat. Yet is Troy shaping 'em anew, trouncing
and learning 'em to be sailormen and mostly by act o'
fist or boot. Verily, I never saw more captainly captain
since I was such fool accursed as to follow the sea, the
which I've done this twenty odd years."

"And how," enquired Adam as the loquacious surgeon
rose to depart, "how do the erstwhile prisoners, Mr. Perks?"

"Excellent well, sir. My potions have recovered 'em of
their much suffering and late incarceration. Such cure by
any other had been miraculous,—by myself 'tis but the
reaction expected to my purge, bolus, vomit, and pill.
Truly they bloom, sir, saving one only and he, alas, being
a very long and therewith expansive gentleman and something stricken in years is beyond even my skill by reason
of an over-weary heart. So, once again, Mr. Adam, be
thankful for your vital shortness o' stature—as I am!" So
saying, the little surgeon beamed, nodded, and bustled away.

"Some day," said Adam, speaking his thought, "I will
to be such mariner as Absalom! For I love God's sea, its

might and fearsome majesty, and must needs wonder
and admire at the ships that brave the fury of ocean for
there, methinks, God walks. . . . To die at sea in storm
and tempest, this were surely to sink forthright into the
arms of God, the Almighty Father of us all. . . . How say
you, Antonia?"

"Why," she answered, thoughtfully, "I think this is
wise thought, Adam, and brave with comfort."

"'Tis so I would pass when cometh my time . . . on
the deck of my own ship, dying as she dies . . . in the
good, clean deeps of ocean. . . . Someday I shall sail my
own ship. . . . Someday I shall rule and lead men . . .
winning to fortune, to power and honour."

Now here, seeing how she looked on him, he sat up to
glance from her intent face down at his own puny form outlined beneath the bedclothes, and frowning, said bitterly:

"You think how such dreams be all too vast for achieve-
ment by body so paltry and weak. Art thinking so?
Tell me!"

"I am thinking," she answered, in the same musing
tone, "how you are of mind so resolute and body so vital
you shall win all this—and more! Riches, power, glory
. . . and what beside?"

"I'd fain have all these for mine own sake, Antonia,
but for my father his sake I choose honour, for this is the
one glory that fadeth not, and he—was an honourable
man and now surely an angel in glory."

"You loved him greatly, Adam, your father?"

"Ay I do, I do indeed!"

"And your mother?"

"She died or ever I might know her."

"So you will make yourself a mariner?"

"Ay, with all my heart."

"And make Captain Absalom Troy your pattern?"

"I could find none better, surely."

"Howbeit, Adam, I like him less and less!"

"Yet he befriended thee, ay and me too in the past as——"

"Ay but how of the future?"

"This should bring but increase o' friendship, for——"

"True, Adam. Yet friendship may change, as changed is he since he made himself great."

"Absalom is not the man to veer with change o' fortune."

"Are you so sure?"

"I am marvellously deceived else."

"You begin to love him, Adam?"

"Ay, I believe I do. I have been lonely soul o' late and yearned for such friendship. Besides he is my blood brother, the which should——"

"And so, Adam, I ponder why your fine captain and blood brother hath scarce troubled to come anigh you this two days!"

"He hath many concerns, Anthony, the business of this great ship. And now, if you'll be so good to bring my clothes, I'll——"

"What were you in England, Adam, I mean your trade, profession?"

"A student of divinity."

"Oh! A—parson? You?"

"It was my father's wish, his hope that I might speak forth the love of God for His children and show how man should love his fellow therefore. And because 'twas so his hope, I might have become an eloquent preacher, with time to overcome my natural timidity."

"Timid? You, Adam?"

"Indeed! I was weak and timid as a child, I am so yet."

"This I can nowise believe."

"Alas, 'tis veriest truth!" he sighed. "I am of nature so extreme fearful, Antonia, that dreading lest fear prove my master, I do all I may to shame fear by a forced and furious boldness. Dost see what I mean, Anthony?"

"No!" she answered vehemently. "No, I do—not! You show so bold and fearless I must needs think you braver than others . . . and most terrible with your sword, and the more so because you are so . . . not big."

At this he smiled, though wistfully, and shook his head.

"I must be rarely good play-actor," he sighed, "for 'stead of murderous steel I should be clasping Bible to preach the Word, and this should ever be—Love!"

"No!" she cried, bitterly. "In such cruel, wicked world gentle love is out o' place. I have more cause for hate— as you should know."

"Yet love shall someday win this poor world to kindliness, Anthony, but as for hate—'tis wasteful passion, begetting naught better than its evil self. . . . And now, if you'll have the goodness to bring my clothes——"

"However," said she, sullenly, "I hate your fine Captain Troy that is forever plaguing me with his sly mockeries!"

"No, no, child! If he banter thee, now and then, this should be no reason for such anger or——"

"Then why must he jeer me? Why must he look on me with such . . . such eyes?"

"Nay, Anthony, a cat may look at a king, 'tis said,— so here certes should be no just cause for hate. And, moreover——"

"Why, why must he flout me . . . with every look, every word and gesture, making these so hateful manly clothes the more odious? He knows I must needs wear them . . . yet why will he shame me so?"

"Anthony, I think you magnify his thoughtless raillery into more than it truly is, making it an offence where none is."

"'Magnify'?" she repeated, angrily. "'Magnify,' say you?"

"Indeed, I think you do. For truly——"

"Oh,—do I?" she cried, wildly. "Then tell me this,— why must he forever be trying to—kiss me?"

Adam's bright eyes widened suddenly, closed slowly to shining slits, and, taking his chin 'twixt finger and thumb, he sat up in bed as if lifting himself bodily thus.

"When?" he enquired, and though his voice was almost a whisper, she threw up forbidding hands and shrank away.

"Don't!" she gasped. "Don't look such . . . such death on me! So cruel—fierce, don't!"

"When," he repeated, averting his head; "when was this?" And now she saw he was gazing where hung his father's sword.

"No!" she cried. "No . . . I will not tell thee! I . . . I meant not to speak of it, but you drove me to it with your 'magnify'!"

Now at this, Adam sank back on his pillow and smiled up at her very tenderly.

"Antonia," he murmured, "when was this? I pray you tell me or I must needs seek answer of him."

"Two nights since . . . you were asleep . . . I went out on deck for breath of air . . . and the stars very wonderful bright. . . . He stole upon me ere I knew, but I broke from him and came to my cabin and locked myself in and . . . and that is all, Adam."

"And—since then?"

"I have kept out of his sight."

"Ah well, well," sighed Adam sleepily and nestling deeper into his pillow, "here was none so great a matter," and having said this, he yawned.

"Are you then so—suddenly sleepy . . . at last?" she murmured, though looking down on him with such eyes that he closed his own against their level, shrewdly questioning gaze.

"Indeed!" he answered, and yawned again.

"Why then, sleep well, and—pleasant dreams." And so, with scarcely a sound, she was gone.

For perhaps five minutes Adam lay perfectly still, his ears on the stretch; then, and suddenly, he was out of bed, had bolted the door and was hunting feverishly for his vanished garments. He found them at last neatly folded away in one of the many drawers and got himself into them with the same feverish haste. Then he combed back his white hair, covered it with his close-fitting bonnet and taking his sheathed rapier beneath his arm, began very cautiously to unbolt the door.

CHAPTER XI

HOW ADAM DARED THE CAT-O'-NINE-TAILS, AND WHY

SLIGHT as was the sound he made yet quick ears heard, it seemed, for in this moment came a gentle tapping and therewith the soft murmur of Antonia's hushed voice:

"Oh, Adam, pray let me in . . . but a moment."

Sighing, he made haste to set back the sword, and it was towards this she looked as the door opened.

"Whither go you, Adam?"

"To take the air."

Now at this she clenched her fists as any furious, young man might have done, then stamped her foot as only an angry girl might,—a troubled girl also, for instead of the furious outburst he expected, she began to plead in almost weeping tones:

"Oh, Adam, Adam, how could you try to so deceive me? And why think me such dolt or so foolish blind to be put off by your silly make-believe? To yawn and feign sleep and the glare of battle in your eyes? I know whither you would go . . . and why."

"Then," said he, making to pass her, "pray suffer me——"

"No,—no! You must not, you shall not. Oh, I was mad to tell you . . . for there was no harm done . . . indeed he was very gentle . . . he scarce touched me."

"Anthony, let me pass."

"No, Adam! Oh, for mercy's sake do not go."

"I must."

"But I vow to God there was no evil done and none meant. . . . Oh, Adam, you that spoke of love for your fellows, you must not shed blood . . . you cannot!"

"I vowed to protect you!" murmured Adam. "I took oath upon my father his memory! And such oath must be kept."

"Ay, but not now, Adam, so late from bed o' fever, not now. Wait . . . do but wait until you be stronger and more able,—wait, I do beseech you!"

"Indeed," he nodded, "there's reason in this,—to wait until I am more able. And to gain strength I must have air and movement. Come then, Anthony, let us out and walk."

Scarcely had they reached the deck, to find a cloudless sky above and placid ocean around, than was patter of small, bare feet and Smidge came running.

"Oh . . . sir," he panted, "I be that glad as youm well again, as I'me come to tell ee as they'm a-goin' for to flog Martin Frant 'crost his own gun, as be my gun too— number four, forrard, sir. So will ee go 'long o' me, if ye please, and stop 'em, 'cause you ain't afeard o' nuffink nor nobody, will ee, please?"

"But what's the man done to deserve flogging?"

"Nuffink, sir—leastways only cracking the Smiler wiv a belaying pin for going for to burn Johnny and me wiv a hot iron. So will ee come and save Martin as saved Johnny and me—please?"

Adam nodded, and following Smidge to the gun deck beheld a half-naked sailor in the act of being tied face down across one of the ordnance and beside him a bearded man in breast-plate and morion who seemed in authority.

"Who is yon gentleman, Smidge?"

"Master Danvers, sir, officer o' the deck."

"Bo'sun!" cried this officer, so soon as the victim had been secured. "Bo'sun!"

"Sir?" answered a squat, powerful fellow, stepping forward.

"The order is—twenty-five with the cat."

"Ax pardon, sir, but might I suggest the cane or rope's-end?"

"You may not."

"Ax pardon again, sir, but offence committed was doo to greatest provocation and therefore I humbly——"

"Silence and be damned t'ye! Where's the rascal Perez?"

"Yere I is, sah!" cried a jubilant voice, and from the silent ranks stepped that same mulatto fondling this time, instead of axe, the whip of many-thonged torment.

"Well, twenty-five is the order,—lay on!"

But as Perez stepped forward, eager to obey, forward also stepped Adam.

"Mr. Danvers," said he, bowing, "I crave a word."

"Oh, sir? And who may you be?"

"Adam Penfeather, at your service."

"Aha, Captain Troy's friend. I am James Danvers, sir, Master's mate. You come to see punishment properly done, sir?"

"No, Mr. Danvers, mere justice."

"Justice, sir? What talk is this? The rule o' the sea is —for strife aboardship, flogging, and aboard this ship, twenty-five lashes, and by Captain Troy's order."

"However, sir, I desire you shall hear a word on this man's behalf."

"Eh—what's this?" exclaimed Danvers, with look of indignant amazement. "You desire—you?"

"No, I demand this in the name of Justice."

"Well now rot me if I ever heard the like o' this! Who the devil are you dare so demand, sir—eh, sir?"

"A mere Englishman and therefore a lover o' justice for every man. Bo'sun, pray what is in evidence 'gainst your prisoner?"

"Sir," quoth the Bo'sun hasting to answer before his superior might frame adequate retort, "Smiling Sam were for branding a brace o' the boys with hot iron, joking like, Martin here interposes and gets hisself burned instead wherefore Sam gets hisself beat and choked somewhat by Martin, wherefore Martin is doo for twenty-five, as your honour sees."

D

"So," said Adam, turning to Mr. Danvers, "there's your evidence, sir. How say you now?"

"I say twenty-five lashes for the offence and five more for your cursed interference and——"

"Bo'sun," said Adam, "pray carry my respects to Captain Troy and say that here is urgent need of his presence."

"Bo'sun," roared Danvers, "bide where you are. Now, forrard, you, Perez, and——"

"Bo'sun," murmured Adam, coming swiftly beside this harassed officer, "suffer me!" And speaking, he whipped the astonished Bo'sun's sword from its scabbard. "Now," cried he, with threatening sweep of broad blade, "strike one blow, Perez, and I'll cut ye down. Master Danvers, I suggest you send for Captain Troy, forthwith, sir."

For a moment the Master's mate glared speechless, then, in voice thick with fury, gave the order.

And thus they stood waiting silent all, the men staring and gaping in their ranks, the Bo'sun goggling and fumbling at his empty scabbard, Mr. Danvers pulling at his beard, while Antonia leaned slender back against the ship's side,—every eye gazing at Adam, this small yet resolute person, who stood sword in hand looking on vacancy.

At last, and at his leisure, came Absalom smiling and debonair in new splendour of garments from belaced falling-band to rosetted shoes, a very gracious gentleman though masterful, supremely assured and slightly grim.

"How now?" he demanded in his pleasant voice. "Adam, why that sword?" But before he might answer, Mr. Danvers became eloquent, wherefore Adam stood mute, his sombre gaze now on the wide prospect of sun-flecked ocean.

"So then," quoth Absalom, when Danvers had ended, "you will take sword to raise mutiny on my ship, eh, Adam?"

"No! I arm myself 'gainst injustice and to protect the helpless. Hear the evidence and judge."

"I have already pronounced judgment! No man shall brawl and make trouble whiles I command. Stand aside now and suffer justice be done."

"No!" said Adam again, looking now on the weapon in his hand. "I protest here is no justice and your sea-laws brutishly cruel."

"I am the law on this ship, Adam."

"And you doom this man to the lash?"

"Ay, I do. And what then?"

"This!" answered Adam between shut teeth and, with swift, unerring stroke of keen blade, severed the rope that held the prisoner, tossed the sword clattering at Absalom's feet, looked up at last into his astonished face, and nodded.

"So,—there's your prisoner free, Captain Troy! Now, if you must lash someone, lash me. For I, too, have broke your damned sea-laws and am therefore guilty as he."

Absalom stared from the speaker's small, pale face to the sword at his feet and spoke, almost whispering:

"Now damn you, Adam, for compelling me to this! . . . Ha, Bo'sun, strip and seize him up for punishment!"

"Ay, ay, sir!" groaned the Bo'sun.

So Adam's puny form was bared and himself fast bound upon the gun and all with never a word.

"Forrard, Perez! Two shall suffice, nay I——"

"Stop!" cried Antonia, in voice that seemed to ring throughout the ship; then, drawing the hidden pistol she had been grasping all this while, she cocked and levelled it full at Absalom.

"Free him!" she commanded. "Bid them loose this valiant gentleman was once your friend, or I shall kill you this moment, Captain Troy, by God I will!"

Absalom looked at this threatening weapon, at the desperate face and wide, resolute eyes behind it and reading there his certain imminent peril, smiled.

"Lord love thee, Master Anthony, sir," quoth he, "thou art beyond my expectation and more than I bargained for, or damme! Bo'sun, cast loose the prisoner, ay—let my poor friend go free lest his so devoted young brother, or half-brother, end me so bloodily—and aboard my own ship. Now, Mr. Anthony, be pleased to uncock and put away that pistol and hereafter so often as you think on Adam's great provocation, remember Absalom's tender mercy, ay and be thou grateful to this same good, kind Absalom Troy that he hath saved thee from the vile sin o' murder." So saying, Absalom nodded, chuckled and strolled away,—while Adam, freed by many willing hands, found his own grasped between the Bo'sun's horny palms.

"Sir," said this officer, hoarsely, "here's me, Ned Bowser, vastly proud for to shake wi' such gentleman as can be such man as to stand up for Poor Jack,—ay, and here's all on us Jacks to say the same,—eh, my hearties?"

"Ay, sir, ay ay!" came a chorus of voices. "That us do and with a will!"

"Your honour," said one, "I be Martin Frant, the man as you saves, and I'm grateful. Sir, any man as dare speak up for poor Jack as dassent speak up for hisself, any gentleman as'll venter his own body to save a man, takes that man's heart out of that man and makes it his very own. Sir, I be that grateful as I can't say no more, only— ho—messmates all, a cheer now, a cheer for Master Penfeather as dare be friend to the likes o' we,—a cheer for Master Adam Penfeather!"

And with these hearty voices ringing in his ears, Adam went back aft, walking slowly like one very weary, and, under cover of this cheering, murmured:

"Antonia . . . brave soul! You saved me from that I dreaded more than death."

"But . . . Oh, Adam," she answered, speaking as softly, "he knew I should have killed him, he knew it . . . and mocked me . . . even then!"

CHAPTER XII

HOW ADAM BEGAN TO LEARN A SHIP

IT was in these days of fair winds and smooth seas that Adam set himself with his usual determination to the accomplishment of two purposes; and one of these was to instruct Antonia in sword-craft or, as he phrased it, 'that most delicate art of rapier play'. And this he did with the aid of two blunted foils shaped and fashioned, beneath his own eye, by Andrew Brent, the armourer, choosing for these lessons such hours of the long day as when the broad decks were deserted save for the customary watch.

His second purpose was to learn and know a ship, her every timber, spar, sail and rope, and found many able and humbly eager to instruct him. For now whenever he left the aftermost part of the vessel, sacred to officers and gentlemen, and went forward to waist, gun-deck, or fore-castle, he was met by smiling looks and given respectful though hearty welcome, more especially by Ned Bowser, the Bo'sun, and his two mates, Martin Frant and William Croft; and these, experienced mariners and prime seamen all, became his chief instructors.

And because Adam was not ashamed to ask questions or affronted by advice from humblest sailor or mere boy, he questioned and listened to all, and with such un-feigned and lively interest that all men became the more eager to instruct and serve him.

Thus hourly he acquired his first knowledge of sea lore, as: that starboard (or steerboard) meant the ship's right side and larboard or port, the left; the difference of stand-ing and running rigging; of blocks double and single and their uses; of braces and pennants for traversing the yards,

93

and the like. It was with Martin Frant close on his heels that he first ventured to clamber aloft to the great main-yard and, perched there with Martin beside him, learned something of gaskets, bolt-ropes, cringles and bowlines: he gazed up with eyes of awed speculation at what Martin said was the lubbers' hole and puttock shrouds, with the huge topmast soaring above with its maze of cordage, guys and stays.

Thus each day he devoted all his attention to some par-ticular part of the ship,—as, for instance, upon this morn-ing when with steady breeze the *Bold Adventuress* drove westward through a gentle sea all asparkle to an early sun.

"A fair morning t' your honour!" quoth Bo'sun Ned, knuckling bristly eyebrow and rolling forward to greet him, "I've been a watching of you and gentleman brother at your foyning play yonder, which though pretty for to watch is too furrin and niminy-piminy for the likes o' me. When I fight give me good broad blade 'stead o' them narrer tucks, and downright blows, 'tis best sooted to an English fist, your honour."

"Ay, Bo'sun, the broadsword hath ever been our weapon, yet point is speedier than edge, and therefore the more deadly."

"Well, sir, I've seen some fairish deadly sword and buckler men, in my time, at Ruffian Hall, Smithfield way. There was George Silver, for one."

"Ay, Ned, and Signior Vincentio for another, his rapier out-pointed Silver's broadsword, you'll mind."

"Ah well, sir, other days, other ways. Only when it cometh to right close work—gimme a hanger, or better still, a boarding axe!"

"For close work, Ned, so say I."

"Well, now, wot'll I show your honour this morning?"

"Why," answered Adam, looking up and around with kindling eyes, "as much as possible, Ned. First the fo'c'sle there and beak-head where the anchors hang. Ay, and the spar you told me is the bolt-sprit. Nay first, this great rope that runs up the foremast here, tell me its name and use."

"'Tis called a jeer-rope, sir, and is rove through that block aloft as be seized to the top, d'ye see, and so cometh adown the mast and is rove through this other block by the deck. And its use is for to hoise up the yards so that though the ties should break yet would they hold up the mast. And yon preventers be for the like purpose. These yere be the partners as do hold fast the bolt-sprit as you see, sir, which be further supported by the fore-stay yonder."

"'Tis great and noble spar this bolt-sprit, Ned."

"Why so it be, sir, and carries the sprit-sail, sprit top-sail and jackstaff, and its length be usually the same as the foremast."

"And what are these great timbers?"

"The cathead, sir, and yonder be the cat-hook for to trice up the anchor from the hawse to top o' the fo'c'sle."

"How many anchors hath a ship?"

"Well, there be these bow anchors, first and second bowers, for her to ride by. Then there's the kedge for calm weather or to kedge up and down a narrer river lest wind or tide drive her ashore. Then there be grapples, smallest of all anchors, wi' four flooks but no stock, for a boat to ride by or to heave aboard an enemy ship in close fight, to ketch hold o' gratings, rails and such, in order for to board her. Lastly there's the sheet anchor and greatest of all, only used of necessity, 'tis the last refuge in tempest against driving to death on a lee shore."

So they walked and talked together in eager question and instant reply until to them came John Fenn, the gunner, who, obedient to Adam's gesture of welcome, now joined them.

"Be you still learning the ship, sir?" he enquired.

"Ay, I am, Master Fenn, and was about to ask Ned if he could tell me aught concerning the azimuth, what it is?"

"Somewhat about the altitude o' the sun, ain't it, Ned?"

"Ar!" nodded the Bo'sun. "'Tis con-sarned with the sun sure-ly, also arks and merry deans, but pre-zackly how I dunno. I can lay a course true enough by dead reckoning, but these yere fancy ways goes beyond me. For this, Mr. Adam, you must ax any o' the navigation officers. I can tell ee all about a ship's tackling, sails, ropes, rigging cables, anchors, flags, pendants and the like, same as John here can larn ee all about guns and shot, sponges, rammers and ladles, but navigation ain't our consarn, d'ye see?"

"Then pray, John, show and tell me of your guns, their various names and powers,—if you will?"

"I'll be honoured, sir. And I'll best do it below on the gun-deck." So thither they went, and there John Fenn patted and explained his grim monsters on this wise:

"Sir, you must know there be guns o' many and divers sorts, and the greatest the cannon royal, as shall cast you a ball o' forty-eight pounds, then the serpent, forty-two,—the demi-cannon, thirty-two,—the cannon-petro, twenty-four,—the culverin, eighteen,—the basilisk, twelve,—demi-culverin, nine,—the saker, six,—and the minion, four. There be also swivels, called murdering-pieces, mounted above on the cubbridge heads to sweep the decks fore and aft."

"And do they all shoot ball?"

"No, sir, we've shot for all occasions, as case-shot, loaded with small bullets, nails, old iron and such in a case, for sweeping crowded decks, then there's chain and cross-bar shot to cut an enemy's rigging, there's likewise trundle and round shot."

"Why are your guns tied up in these ropes?"

"These be the breechings, sir, to hold 'em agin recoil and the pitch and roll of the deck, and tackle to work 'em."

"Where do you keep the powder?"

"In the hold till wanted, then here right handy in barrels amidship."

"Is there no danger from sparks?"

"Well—not so much, for in fight, on every tub must sit a powder boy to cover it with his latter-end, sir, and cover it, com-plete!"

"How many guns does this ship carry?"

"All too few since you ask me, sir. She's pierced for forty and mounts but twenty-five, culverins and basilisks alow here, sakers and minions aloft,—but twenty-five, and in these waters!"

"What of these waters, John?"

"Sir, on our larboard beam lays Africa,—the cursed Barbary Coast."

"You mean—pirates?"

"Ay I do. Sallee rovers, bloody barbarians and right desperate fighters all, 'tis win or die with 'em, and we under-gunned. Well, thank God, we've no women aboard."

"Women!" repeated Adam, softly. "Ha, John, now should these pirates attack us . . . we must be more desperate than they, we also must win or die,—I for one."

"And myself for another, sir, for I know what——"
He paused suddenly and stiffened to salute as towards them with leisured stride came Absalom.

Nodding to the gunner, he looked down on Adam with somewhat ironic smile, and seeing him so grim of face, bowed, saying:

"Good friend, will you be pleased to walk with me?"

So when Adam had thanked gunner John, he went with Absalom and both silent until they had reached the upper deck and this chancing to be deserted, for it was still early, Absalom spoke:

"You keep your distance these days, you and . . . your brother,—eh, Adam?"

"And each with sufficient reason!" he retorted.

"Ay, that sorry business t'other day when you forced me, for sake of discipline, to do that would have shamed us both. You'll not soon forgive me this, eh, Adam?"

"Yes, heartily, for I brought it upon myself,—also it hath served me very well."

"Ay, you are great with the men, I've seen you confabulating with 'em frequently o' late."

"Every day," nodded Adam.

"You prefer fo'c'sle to poop 'twould almost seem?"

"Ay, I do indeed."

"Well, damme, but you speak plain enough!"

"'Tis so my endeavour."

"And what a plague do you there every day. Not thinking to raise a mutiny 'gainst me, eh, Adam?"

"Captain Troy, such base suspicion shames only yourself!"

"Then what do ye there day after day?"

"Do what I may to become a seaman."

Absalom chuckled, then shook comely head.

"'Tis poor trade, Adam, mostly."

"Yet manly one always. Someday, mayhap, I shall command ship o' my own."

"Hum!" quoth Absalom, cocking an eyebrow. "And in the meantime you learn—our Tony—pretty sword tricks, ha?"

"Not tricks but an art, a craft shall prove sufficingly deadly anon."

"'Tis an apt pupil—this Tony of ours, eh, Adam?"

"Ay, truly!"

"And becoming ever more—manly, eh, Adam?"

"I am glad you observe this, and trust you to bear yourself accordingly."

"Ay ay—how should I not?"

"How indeed?"

Now at this, Absalom glanced down almost furtively at his companion's small, set visage and finding it wholly inscrutable, took him by the arm, saying:

"How say'st thou to a noggin, shipmate?"

"No, thank you," answered Adam, freeing his arm, and though he did this gently enough, Absalom scowled.

"And I'm to believe you bear no least animosity against me, am I?" he demanded.

"Yes."

"Yet you refuse to drink with me,—ay or eat with me! Why must you forsake your place in the mess and feed alone—with your beloved brother, of course, 'stead o' joining our company in the great cabin?"

"By reason that I am not at ease in company, more especially at table. I eat little and drink less, and am happier doing this alone. As for Anthony——"

"Must bide with dear brother Adam, ay ay! Ha, well, the choice is your own. Keep yourselves to yourselves and be damned to it! Ay, do as ye will, but—mind this, —when you are with your friends o' the lower deck you shall infallibly sink to their level soon or late!"

"I'll remember," nodded Adam.

"Ay, and this also, to wit: Discipline aboardship must be maintained and enforced at all times and by all means, 'tis the first law at sea,—ay, and everywhere else, for that matter."

"Well now," answered Adam, looking up into his companion's face at last and meeting his scowl with one as dark and fierce, "I quarrel with no just law, Captain Absalom, more especially such law of stern honour as can aid a man to govern and discipline himself!" With this he turned and would have gone but that Absalom stayed him with powerful hand, saying angrily:

"What mean ye by this now,—what mean ye?"

"Sir," Adam murmured, glancing from this compelling hand to the threatening face above him, "have the goodness to loose me."

"Go then!" said Absalom, in choking voice, and strode away in a fury.

Then Adam sighed, shook his head and went in quest of Antonia and breakfast.

CHAPTER XIII

HOW ADAM SOUGHT TO BECOME A SEAMAN

SAID Adam to his pupil, and both seated on a coil of rope in shady corner of the deck, for it was the drowsy afternoon hour:

"Now, Anthony, I will expound as best I may the true Philosophy of the Sword, more especially the rapier, this being the best, noblest and most deadly of all weapons."

"Nay but, Adam, how may any weapon be noble since 'tis but a tool for slaughter?"

Now at this heresy, Master eyes Pupil and shakes his head in shocked reproof, whereat Pupil nods hers, wholly unabashed and repeats with emphasis:

"An ugly tool, Adam, for cold and murderous slaughter!"

"Not so, Anthony, my faith—no! Your murdering tool is cowardly pistol or blundering musketoon whereby Brutish Ignorance may slaughter Learned Valour and from safe distance. But, as Mind is greater than mere Body so is the rapier greater than any other weapon, and it manages an exact science calling not only for the strict accordance of hand, eye and foot, but for an alertness o' the mind also. For, Anthony, he that would be a true sword-master must first be master of himself, then of his blade, so shall he be master of his adversary. You follow me, I hope?"

"No, Adam, you must be plainer. Tell me your Firstly first, as—how one must be master of himself?"

"By schooling himself to a reasoning calm, putting aside all fury of anger, heedless of taunts and all provocation. He must—— Are you attending, Anthony?" Here Pupil, whose bright glance has strayed from Master's small, serious visage, starts guiltily yet answers serenely:

"You may be sure I am."

"Then presently I shall describe and show the various lines, attacks and parries, though 'tis not quickness o' body shall make you a swordmaster so much as celerity o' mind,—to forethink your adversary and sense his intent and the line of his attack."

"Nay now, Adam, a mercy's sake! How shall any mere human forethink another except by spells and tricks o' magic witchcraft?"

At this, Master rises, the better to survey and admonish Pupil who instantly salutes him with graceful flourish of foil, saying:

"What then, have I shocked thee again, dear Adam?"

"Tricks?" he repeated, shaking reproachful head. "In this noble science there are nor tricks nor master-strokes though there be many ruffling knaves offer such at a price."

"Nay tell me, Adam, how do you forethink your adversary when you fight?"

"By anticipating his attack, luring it with a feint and, when it comes, meeting it with instant riposte which, as I've told you, is parry and counter-thrust in one,—or by volte, that is, turn o' body, letting it pass and take him with a time thrust to wound or end him as you will."

"On my soul now a most learned and bloodthirsty disquisition—or souse me for a gurnet!"

Glancing up, Adam beheld Absalom lolling on the carved poop-railing above.

"Damme, Adam, but thou'rt transforming this gentle, smock-faced brother o' thine into a perfect throat-slitting 'sdeath and blood bravo, a notable swashing, hell-fire, bully roarer, eh, Adam?"

"None o' these, sir!" he answered, narrowing his eyes on the speaker. "No, I do but make him so able in his own defence that none shall affront him with impunity."

"Oho! Affront, d'ye say?"

"Ay, I do!"

"As how? When? Where? By whom? Come, out with it."

Dumbly Adam turned from him, and thus finding Antonia had disappeared, tucked foil beneath his arm and hastened away down into the waist of the ship where stood Mr. Amos Perrin, the master, taking his daily observation of the sun. A lank person was Amos Perrin, mournful of aspect and dolorous of voice; just at present his woeful visage was twisted askew, one eye screwed up, the other glaring heavenward along an instrument such as Adam had never seen, wherefore he watched this with very lively attention.

"Sir," said he at last, unable to remain silent any longer, "Mr. Perrin, what do you?" The master turned, uttered sound like a groan and answered:

"Master Penfeather, oh dear me,—I take the sun his altitude."

"And what is that instrument?"

"Sir, 'tis called a—ah me—a backstaff, ay and a forestaff also."

"Pray, sir, how do you use it?"

"Master Penfeather, take and try for yourself. Ah, dearie me! Hold the flat o' the staff to corner o' your eye, let it rest on your eye-bone, sir, as near the corner o' your eye as may be, yet so it doth not hinder the sight. Now look at the upper end o' the cross for the sun and at the lower end for the horizon. Oh me! But if at the lower end you see all sky and no water, draw the cross nearer to you along staff,—if you see all water and no sky, slide the cross a little further from you till you see the centre o' the sun at the upper end o' the cross, then 'tis right for a true observation. Now look and see at what degree marked on the staff the cross rests and that will be the meridian altitude or its complement according to these words marked on the staff. Ah, dearie me!"

"And what, sir," enquired Adam, returning this instrument, "pray what means the word 'azimuth'?"

"'Tis an arc, Mr. Penfeather. The azimuth is an arc o' the horizon intercepted betwixt the meridian and the vertical circle, which passeth the centre of the sun, sir."

"Alas!" sighed Adam. "All this is far beyond my poor wit. How may I learn this science of navigation?"

"With pain, sir,—ah me—with pain o' laborious study. But if you be serious and intent to learn, I have books might instruct you."

"Then, do but show me how, and study I will," said Adam, "ay, and this right diligently. Will you be so good, sir?"

"Mr. Penfeather,—ah me,—I shall do my poor best for you, sir."

"Then, sir, I am so grateful I grieve to see you thus marvellous woeful and would fain comfort you."

"Impossible, Mr. Penfeather, I sorrow as I breathe, sir, 'tis so my nature since I was born a wailing babe into this Vale o' Sorrow. Go with me now and I'll lend you certain books and show ye how to use 'em."

And thus it was that Adam began his study of navigation, taking upon himself yet another labour, and one that was to tax all his resolution, and this mostly by night, for all day long he was pacing the decks and talking 'ship' with Captain Smy, or asking questions of Bo'sun Ben and other prime seamen. He sat for hours puzzling out the intricate craft of knotting and splicing; he clambered aloft to yards and crosstrees and more boldly now; he hauled on ropes and yo-hoed lustily with the men; he learned the use of compass and bittacle and therewith how to steer, thrilling with joy to the quiver of the great whip-staff that throbbed in his grasp like a live thing

And thus for Adam, at least, time sped apace.

CHAPTER XIV

"'TIS pitiful!" exclaimed Antonia who, with coat off and white arms bare, was busied at a large bowl washing certain of their too few garments.

"What is?" enquired Adam, glancing up from his books and papers.

"That in this great ship is not one single, solitary thimble. Do none of all these sailormen ever use needle, Adam?"

"Oh yes, but 'stead of thimble they use a piece of leather and call it a 'palm'. Which reminds me," said he, fumbling in pocket, "I got one for you from Bo'sun Ned this afternoon,—ay, here it is!"

"That!" cried Antonia, wrinkling her pretty nose at it. "How a mercy's name may one sew with such thing?"

"You slip it on your palm—thus, and push your needle, open-handed."

"How like a clumsy man!"

"And how like very woman you talk! Have a care, brother Anthony!"

"Nay, we're private here, Adam, thank God! And we've but four pair o' stockings betwixt us, and as few shirts, and most of these need mending. Indeed you are very hard on your clothes, Adam, you are forever up and about, these days. Twice I watched you climb the masts to-day —and so dangerous and bad for your clothes."

"Ah, but to-day also, Antonia, I steered this ship,— and for an hour by the glass! To-morrow I'm to hale on the tackle o' one of the biggest guns, number four!"

"They won't shoot off the hateful things, will they, Adam?"

"Nay, 'tis but to exercise the crews; 'twill be mere dumb show."

"I heard them shoot cannons at The Tower once, and 'twas like the crack of doom. How far away it all seems now. The Tower . . . London. 'Tis like a new world!"

"Why, so it is indeed," said Adam, turning to look at her again. "And in this new world I pray God you shall find . . . True Happiness."

"And you also!" she answered, fervently. "And yet . . . what is True Happiness?"

"Here is question, Antonia, hath puzzled all the philosophers through the ages."

"Adam, can Happiness true and abiding ever be in this sad, cruel world?"

"It is my sure hope and belief, Antonia. Though none, I think, may ever find it that seek for Self alone, since True Happiness is never selfish. I believe this blessing cometh only to such as forget self in love,—ay, and service for others."

"What mean you by such love, Adam?"

But here, and before he could reply, a voice beyond the open door did this for him, chanting these words gaily:

"Nay, Tony lad, 'tis question stupid!
  Whom should he mean but wanton Cupid,
  Little, naked, impish boy,
  Sly, tender archer, elf of joy?
  Dan Cupid that with burning darts
  Through steel and buff transfixeth hearts.
      Ha!
  Would Cupid now an arrow shoot,
  Speak, and I'll hence and leave him to 't."

"In fine," chuckled Absalom, lounging in the doorway, "do I intrude? For here's scene o' domestic bliss to touch

the heart o' poor, lorn sailorman and take him all aback,
or I'm a buttered parsnip!"

Antonia frowned and bent again to her labour, Adam
put aside his books and turned to regard the speaker
between narrowed eyelids. And when they had surveyed
each other thus for a long moment, Absalom nodded and
smiled, though a little grimly.

"Well," he demanded, "am I welcome? Ay or no."

"This depends," sighed Adam, his gaze still intent.

"Ay ay!" chuckled Absalom, though with gathering
scowl. "You bear me no malice but prefer my room to
my company. Yet here am I to . . . humble myself for
Friendship's sake. And how then, Adam?"

"Could you ever be truly humble, Absalom?"

"Don't I say so?"

"Very easily. Howbeit, come your ways."

"Am I welcome then, shipmate? We've been something
strange to each other o' late and . . . I've missed thee,
Adam, thy sober airs and gravity o' speech that match
your old man's hair. Am I indeed welcome?"

"I had not asked you else, Absalom."

"Why then, what saith our Tony?" Antonia neither
looked at him nor spoke. "Nay," said he, still halting in
the doorway, "be kind to thy poor, humble Absalom.
How,—still dumb? Then prithee, sweet Master Antonia,
sir, have I permission of thee to enter—and despite thine
arms, sweet ,round nakedness, or shall their white nudity
prevent?"

Antonia flushed painfully, yet still neither turned nor
spoke, while Adam began to pinch his chin in that nervous
way of his,—seeing which, Antonia glanced apprehensively
from him to where hung his rapier, and bit her lips and
closed troubled eyes ; then she laughed suddenly and turning
on Absalom, said with her most swaggering air:

"Sink us and burn us, Captain, never heed these bare
arms o' mine! Come in, man, and sit ye, tell us o' your
masts and sails and riggings and have ye been flogging

any other o' your men lately, damn their eyes and be cursed to 'em!"

Adam stared speechlessly, as did Absalom for a moment, then in he came, sat down, stretched out his long legs and clapping hand to brawny thigh, laughed right joyously while Antonia, folding her arms to hide trembling hands, watched him with a curious intentness that seemed to check his merriment, then seeing him about to speak, she nodded at him, saying:

"Yes, I liked you better in your grime and shackles!"

"Eh! Now damme, but did ye so, Tony?"

"Curse me if I didn't!" she mocked.

"Aha!" he chuckled. "And why so, my pretty lad?"

"You showed more natural in them than this new finery of clothes that suit you no whit."

Absalom's chuckling laugh was choked suddenly, his bronzed cheek flushed, he blinked.

"Well now," quoth he, "let me perish if I——"

"Yes!" said she, with another fierce nod, "you may perish, burn, sink, or become a buttered parsnip and the sooner the better!"

Absalom sank back in his seat and was dumb, his so ready tongue seemed paralyzed, he made futile gestures with his hands, he shook his head.

"So?" he exclaimed, at last. "'Twould almost seem I am not wanted! Ay, and a saucy, malapert, young ruffler to tell me so! 'S death, Adam,—see now what your plaguey sword lectures ha' done! Hast transformed timid-bleating ewe lamb into roaring lion, meek-eyed, whispering coyness into this fire and fury young Bobadil! Alas, alack! And yet—these pretty arms so smoothly white show not the hairy beefiness o' true fighting man; these lovely limbs were shaped for kinder uses,—ay, by Nature formed to cling, to clasp in Nature's way some happy man by Nature shaped to——"

"Nature?" she repeated. "Nature hath much to answer for, that having formed and shaped such things as toads and worms, she must shape also Captain Absalom Troy that is indeed such form, such shape——" Antonia shuddered, closed her eyes as against some horror, and turned away, while Absalom stared at her shapely back with starting eyes; and she, her face thus hidden, smiled to hear his arrogant assurance so utterly quelled that now he was actually stammering:

"Eh . . . shape . . . what shape? How then, what . . . what mean you . . . what am I then?"

"No more than that I prove you."

"Well . . . what d'ye prove me?"

"Of such sort that I will begone."

"How? Wilt run away, my hero? Wilt flourish and run? And wherefore, my handsome, my sweet, bold Antonia lad?"

"Lest I yield to temptation, Captain Troy, and dowse the hateful mockery of you with this water!"

"Do!" he nodded. "Ay, do and be—kissed, Tony!"

Antonia hesitated, then drying hands and arms slowly, she took up her coat and fronting Absalom, gazed down at him with such look as checked the words on his lip.

"If ever you do," said she, scarce above a whisper, "I so detest the touch, the mere sight of you, that I shall certainly kill you for the doggish wretch I prove you!" Then, with slow nod of her bright head, she turned and walked leisurely away.

CHAPTER XV

ABSALOM sat staring towards the empty doorway and ruffling his curly head for some little while and never a word.

"Kill me, eh?" he muttered, at last. "Here's twice she's threatened me. 'Doggish wretch,' quo' she! Doggish, by Satan!" At the word he chuckled, though harshly, and made to rise and follow, but was checked by the voice of Adam, who had remained all this time staring down at the toe of his worn shoe.

"It is to be supposed you came here with some purpose?"

"Eh—purpose?" repeated Absalom still gazing towards the doorway until, feeling a touch, he turned to find Adam leaning forward to look on him at last.

"Ay," he nodded, "some better purpose than tormenting; one hath troubles enough and to spare."

"Tormenting, say you?"

"Indeed, with your jibes and fleers and threats of— kissing!"

Now reading the fierce scorn in the speaker's small, pale face, Absalom flushed hotly, essayed a laugh, scowled and became sullen.

"I but jested with . . . with a little fool should not be here."

"No, an innocent maid that trusted to your honour, Captain Troy, and vainly it seems. I cry you shame and——" Up leapt Absalom red with hot fury, and up rose Adam, pallid with cold rage.

"How then," cried Absalom, clenching powerful hands,

"will ye dare impeach my honour so lightly—and for this—
this runaway baggage, this murderous shrew? Innocent,
d'ye say? A cut-throat gallows-bird, says I . . . and
now threatens to kill me . . . and by God she would
too."

"Sir," said Adam, hissing between his teeth, "it is to
be hoped so!"

"How? What? My life . . . for mere kiss?"

"On shipboard, yes. As for . . . 'gallows-bird' . . . I
protest you lie most foully." Absalom's comely face grew
ghastly pale, his shapely lips quivered and yet were
silent; therefore Adam continued:

"You, being once a gentleman, should know better
than affront so basely one so helpless, and this I will permit
by no means."

"Permit?" cried Absalom, with tone and gesture so
wild and threatening that Adam braced himself for the
expected blow. "Now curse your prating insolence . . .
to flout and give me the lie . . . and all for this termagent,
this——"

"Be silent!" cried Adam. "Stint and curb your lewd
tongue! I've named you liar,—go fetch your sword——"

"Hey?" sneered Absalom. "You'll play off your damned
rapier tricks on me now, will ye?"

"Every one—if needed!" answered Adam, reaching
down his father's sword. "Now begone! You shall find
me on the lower deck, it should be quieter there." But
instead of going, Absalom folded his long arms, he smiled,
he nodded.

"So ho!" quoth he, in soft, jeering tone. "'Tis as I
guessed . . . this shrewish claw-cat, this blood-thirsty
she-devil . . . you love her, eh, my poor lad? Ay, you
love her, or damme!"

And now it was Adam who stood mute with a raging
fury beyond words, an anger that seemed to rob him of
his poor strength, so that he sank upon the locker behind
him and, feeling himself so weak and futile, covered his

face in clutching hands to hide the burning tears that shamed him. Crouched thus, he heard Absalom's long legs go striding away . . . and presently come striding back; heard Absalom curse bitterly and then say, in shaken tones:

"Gallows-bird . . . dammit . . . I retract, I take it back!" Then away he went again only to return as soon; and Adam, still crouched upon the locker, heard him curse again and say, as though against his will:

"Shrewish claw-cat and she-devil . . . these also . . . I retract. . . . And now, when you're ready, come to me in the coach and there I'll essay a sword trick or so on that little carcase o' thine!" Then away he strode for the second time.

And after some while, Adam rose and with sheathed sword beneath his arm, stepped forth of his cabin and came face to face with Antonia, and he was quick to see she had been weeping.

"Adam, don't go," she pleaded, "for sake of wretched me . . . don't fight him! Oh, I know, I've been listening. . . . I heard every word."

"Why then you know that fight I must, so, let me pass."

"No!" she gasped, wringing her clasped hands. "He retracted all he said . . . so don't . . . Oh, Adam, for dear God's sake don't fight, I . . . I cannot abide it."

"Antonia," he murmured, "are you so fearful for me?"

"No, ah no, for him—for him! He is so big and reckless and you are so . . . so small and deadly, so cold and terribly sure!"

"Sure?" repeated Adam, beginning to tremble now even as she. "Yes, I am sure, but—only of myself. Are you . . . is he . . . his safety so . . . so very dear to you, indeed?"

"'Tis not . . . this . . . " she answered, her clear gaze wavering, "only I would not have you shed his blood for sake of me, Adam."

"Are you so certain I can?"

"Yes,—yes I am! For Death goes beside you, Adam, to guide your hand . . . looks out from your eyes. And he . . . Oh, all his size and strength shall nowise avail him, I know . . . I know."

"Howbeit," sighed Adam, "comfort you now for . . . he shall come to no harm."

"You promise me this, Adam?"

"Yes," he answered, sighing deeper than before.

Now as he went and slowly like one in troubled muse, there met him Sir Benjamin whom he welcomed with one of his rare smiles, saying:

"Sir, it seems long since you stood my friend 'gainst Captain Sharp and on this very spot."

"Ay, time fleets, friend Adam, time fleets, and whiles you busy yourself about the ship I shut myself up with Lord Perrow, my brother, George D'Arcy and the Devil, losing my all at cards, sir, the bones—and by each am cursed, for my luck is out, sir. But now, friend Adam, I am hoping to serve you again in your affair with Troy."

"So he told you o' this?"

"In confidence, Adam, and that I might stand thy friend i' the matter."

"Is he so wishful to fight me?"

"Indeed! Though he lays the onus on you, bidding me say he waits your retraction of certain word or your person to make it good."

"He shall have my person."

"Ha, well said!" exclaimed Sir Benjamin, bouncing with jubilant motion of his legs. "Od's my life, but I love thee, Adam, let's to 't."

So came they into that large cabin with its square windows opening upon railed gallery, this the greatest room in all the ship and called round-house or coach, where they found Absalom at table scowling blackly into the untasted wine before him. At their entrance he rose, inviting them to drink with a gesture.

"Anon, sir, anon!" answered Sir Benjamin, bowing with extreme formality. "Afterwards—perhaps." Adam merely shook his head.

"Ha, gentlemen," quoth Sir Benjamin, with a flourish, "I here venture to suggest the matter may be accommodated."

Absalom scowled and was dumb; Adam shook his head again, whereupon Sir Benjamin, his legs once more jubilant, nodded, saying:

"Then, sirs,—the sooner the better!"

Absalom caught up a silver bell from the table and rang it furiously till came Joel Bym hurrying and after him Captain Smy, more leisurely, who, looking on them sternly, groaned.

"This cometh o' breaking our rule!" quoth he, gloomily. "But if ye must to bloodshed, have at it and be done."

"Need we strip?" growled Absalom.

"'Tis more customary," answered Sir Benjamin. So off came their coats and doublets.

"Your shoes!" said Absalom, kicking off his own.

"Thank you," answered Adam. "I'll keep mine, I am a little taller so."

"Bym, my Toledo!" The weapon was brought, a fine silver-hilted rapier which Absalom slowly unsheathed, saying: "Bolt the doors, Bym!"

"Now, sir," said Sir Benjamin, baring Adam's rapier with a certain joyous officiousness, "I propose you play three veneys and let them suffice, blood or no. Is 't agreed?"

"Ay, ay!" nodded Absalom carelessly.

"As you will!" answered Adam.

"Then," said Sir Benjamin, drawing his own weapon, "after the third encounter I shall interpose. Are ye ready? On guard!"

The long, narrow blades flickered and rang together; and thus with steel grinding they fronted each other, Absalom frowning and grim, Adam's face pale and set.

For a long moment they stood staring eye to eye, motionless and dumb.

"Fight!" snarled Absalom, at last.

"When you will," answered Adam, never moving. So, with stamp of shoeless foot and hissing between shut teeth, Absalom fell to sudden, swift action,—he feinted cunningly, shifted dexterously, making his glittering point a circling, darting menace until, spying an opening in Adam's guard, he flashed in a thrust and was met by a parry so unexpectedly strong that it jarred him from wrist to shoulder and, as he stepped back to recover, Adam's blade darted, ripping his shirt from elbow to throat; whereat Sir Benjamin bounced and whispered amazed oath, Smy opened grim lips that spoke not, and the hairy Joel Bym seized himself by the beard and murmured: "By cock!"

"Veney Number One!" cried Sir Benjamin, "and 'Snoggers' a pretty play, very sweet and rare to fancy." But even while he spoke the murderous steel was grinding together again in rapid exchanges,—stroke and counterstroke, threat of flickering points at face, at throat, at body and limbs, with ceaseless clash and flurry of swift-twirling blades. At last, Adam's weapon sweeping in wide parry, seemed to leave an opening and there, as expected, Absalom instantly made his attack, which Adam as instantly avoided by supple volt, or turn of his agile body and, stepping back as Absalom drove past, lowered his point and stood thus motionless, though panting a little, until Absalom might recover his poise and guard.

"Veney Number Two!" cried Sir Benjamin. "And 's death, gentlemen all, I'm bold to aver that I——"

"Ha, damnation!" Absalom gasped. "Stint this foolery, Adam,—strike, man, strike and blood me . . . if ye can . . . What mockery d'ye make?"

"None," Adam answered, despondently, "except that I promised not to harm you."

"Eh—not——? You . . . you promised not to harm——" Words seemed to fail Absalom, and he stared dumb with indignation and amazement, therefore Adam continued:

"Ay, I did. And indeed, Mr. Troy, your play is even more reckless than I expected, so loose and wild I might have killed you all too easily. So let's be done."

"The which," quoth Captain Smy, "is gospel true."

"Ay, body o' me," cried Sir Benjamin, "that's the verity on 't, sirs!"

Absalom stared down at the rapier in his fist, shook his head at it, strode to the table and laying it there, stood, chin on breast, as if pondering some abstruse problem; suddenly he chuckled and, seating himself on corner of the table, began to laugh, and so continued until came a thunderous knocking on the door and therewith a voice, crying hoarsely.

"Sail ho! Two sail . . . bearing down on us to larboard! Pirates o' Barbary . . . two galleys bearing down on us."

CHAPTER XVI

THE SALLEE ROVERS

ADAM saw them first as two black specks far to windward yet showing plain against a luminous horizon, while all about him,—fore and aft, below and aloft, was stir and hum of instant preparation, with a confused murmur of voices that had in it something grimly joyous, this never-ending hum pierced, now and then, by shout of command and silvery twitter of the boatswain's pipe.

Now as Adam leaned to watch this oncoming menace, he was aware of Captain Smy beside him who peered very earnestly through a spy-glass.

"Are these indeed pirates, Smy?" he questioned, anxiously.

"Ay, beyond all peradventure, Adam! Pirates o' Barbary, sons of iniquity and children o' the Devil. Try a peep at 'em through my perspective glass."

So Adam took the glass and after some trouble got sight of these vessels, long and black with sweep of lofty pointed sails.

"And—oars!" said he.

"Verily, Adam, this is why they are galleys,—they can go with no wind, d'ye see?"

"Also I can see . . . steel aflicker."

"Ay, this proves 'em galleys o' war and crammed wi' rogues athirst for Christian gore, Adam. So an the wind fail us or they shoot away our spars thou shalt ha' thy bellyful o' fighting for once! And none o' your delicate rapier work or pretty foyning play,—'twill be chop of axe, push o' pike and downright stroke o' sword, for they'll lay us aboard. So I'll away to prepare me, therefore, and do thou

set by that rapier and take stout broad-sword instead, for
'twill be close and bloody work should the wind drop,
the which God forbid!"

And away strode Smy leaving Adam to watch these
distant foes with growing apprehension. For now all his
thought was of Antonia, remembering how John Fenn,
the gunner, had thanked God there were no women
aboard.

But as he watched these black specks, that seemed
to grow upon his sight, and greatly troubled thereby, he
heard a low yet very cheerful whistling nearby, and greatly
wondering what man could whistle so merrily at such
time, turned, and was astonished to see this was none other
than Amos Perrin, the Master, this usually doleful person,
who, meeting Adam's surprised glance, smiled and nodded,
he also winked.

"Sir," said he, "in this sad world be yet times for joy,
and this is one! For yonder come two devil craft intent
on our slaughter and destruction! Death, sir, and damnation! So is my soul uplift whiles heart singeth within
me."

"Nay, but why so, I pray you?"

"For that being an Englishman and therefore Christian,
'tis my assured hope this death and damnation shall be
theirs and we the instruments o' Grace by means o' steel
and round-shot to plunge 'em forthwith to the very deeps
of hell. Friend Adam, I was captured and slave to 'em
once, I with my boy, Will, and he scarce fifteen turned . . .
they whipped him to death, my young and only son,
whiles I in my fetters watched him die. So now rejoice
I that Providence shall rid the world o' yon scum and pray
John Fenn's guns shall do their business right bloodily."

"But how if the wind fail and they board us?"

"Why then 'stead o' round-shot, shall be our steel,
hand to hand,—ay, and so much the better. In two hours,
or thereabout, we shall be hard at it and . . . should I
be called to join my little son, the happy despatch, sir,

my books and instruments are for you. I've left a writing to this effect."

Then, before Adam might find words to thank him, Amos Perrin smiled and strode away, whistling happily as he went.

Forward in the waist of the ship Bo'sun Ned and his mates were busied aiding and directing divers of the men to clear for action, so thither went Adam.

"How think you of the wind, Bo'sun?" he enquired.

"Too light, sir!" answered brawny Ned, glancing up at the great spread of sail that flapped ever and anon. "Us needs a stiffish breeze and a smart helm for to weather they galleys, and be cursed to em! Hows'ever, us can give 'em a broadside or so afore they run us aboard—eh, John?" he enquired, turning where stood Fenn, the gunner.

"I reckon so, Ned. I've my lower tier loaded with ball, cross-bar and case as should discourage 'em somewhat. If they close and board—'twill be in guns, shut ports and us, every man and boy, aloft here with pike and cut-lash."

"Ar!" nodded the Bo'sun. "And me wi' old Alf here," and from somewhere nearby he caught up a ponderous axe, its haft corded and fashioned with a loop, its great blade backed by a down-curving spike.

"But," enquired Adam, "why do you name it Alf, and wherefore is that spike?"

"Why, sir, I names him Alf arter me old dad, him being the biggest man in Alceston or any o' they Down-land villages, and this being the biggest axe aboard. This here spike is for to smite into the timbers of a enemy ship whereby to climb aboard same, wherefore 'tis called a boarding axe. And when I fight I has this here lanyard rove about me wrist agin loss. And," quoth he, twirling this terrible weapon in powerful hand, "for close work there's nought may compare with a axe, 'tis very pretty, very sarten-sure. Though there's some prefers sword and others a pike, but for me ever and always—an axe. And what'll be your ch'ice, Mr. Adam, if so be youm minded for to try a stroke at they varmin?"

"A hanger, Ned, this in your belt—will you lend it to me again?"

"With j'y, sir," answered the Bo'sun, unbuckling his broad belt to gird it about Adam's slim person. "You know as it be purty sharp, ay, and so does Frant,—eh, Martin lad?"

"Ay, that do I!" answered the man Martin, saluting Adam with the stout pike he bore.

"Ha, stand by!" quoth Bo'sun Ned as a trumpet blared from the poop. "Yonder sounds the rally, and this means me," and taking the silver pipe that dangled from a lanyard upon his broad chest, he sounded thereon a long-drawn, quavering note,—whereat, up from dim gun deck where battle-lanterns now glimmered, and down from forecastle came gunners stripped to the waist and bare-armed men to be mustered aft by the Master and his mates. Then the trumpets sounded again, drums beat, and forth upon the lofty poop, a warlike figure in glittering morion and half armour, stood Absalom Troy. And his eyes were bright, his handsome face smiling and assured, his pleasant voice glad and hearty as, glancing down on the assembled company, he saluted them with flourish of sword, and spoke:

"Shipmates and Bold Adventurers all, yonder come pirate rogues to destroy us—if they can. And I would not have it other, for here's chance to prove me your mettle, to show these cursed sea-wolves that English sea-dogs can out-bite 'em. How say ye, my lads?" He was answered by a roar of cheering and the glitter of brandished steel. "Well and good, my hearties," he laughed, "yet mark this,—should they win the ship 'twill be death for all wounded and vile slavery for the rest, a slavery worse than death, or damme! So now, should they board us, let no man quail or hope for mercy, but fight as I shall fight,—to my last breath. So fight it is, my lads,—fight

hard like men, fight unflinching like heroes, fight with a
will and cheerily—like Englishmen." Here once again
voices roared and steel flashed until Absalom's upraised
hand silenced them. "Lastly, my hearties, since I would
have no one of ye die fool-like, let every man lie down
and take cover each in his place, and no man fire shot
until I give the word. Now may the Lord o' Battles love
and bless us,—and so to your stations, shipmates all, to
bide the issue and quit ye every one like men of Old
England."

Here for a third time the men cheered lustily, and Adam
with them, in which moment he saw Absalom looking down
and beckoning to him. So up to the poop went he, and
so came where abaft the mizzen stood Absalom.

"Adam," said he, his face unwontedly grave, "if the
wind fail, as I think it may, here shall be very desperate
business, for these rogues o' Barbary fight like devils, as
too well I know, for I've met 'em ere now. So it is I shall
be a very busy man and no chance for further speech wi'
thee until this action be decided—one way or t'other.
Wherefore now I would show thee my heart that may'st
know 'tis my grief to ha' given thee such just cause for
quarrel, and . . . my bitter shame to have so miscalled
. . . her, this sweet, brave soul. Indeed you see me
very . . . humbly contrite. Well now, how says't thou,
Adam?"

"That such humility honours you, Absalom, and makes
me to love you better than I thought to ever."

"I suppose," said Absalom, his keen glance now on the
lazy-flapping sails and now on the approaching galleys,
"indeed I'm very sure that there never were two men
more dissimilar than Adam Penfeather and Absalom
Troy, yet are we alike in this . . . that we do both love
Antonia. For, Adam, in this that may be my last hour,
I do protest I love her most truly and with all that is
best in me . . . and because I know she hath no kindness
for me I have been most bitterly jealous. But now instead

I . . . would fain make this love an added bond betwixt
us . . . so, Adam . . . brother . . . shall we?"

"Yea and with all my heart!" Adam answered; and
thus for a moment they stood looking into each other's
eyes while their hands met and clasped hard.

"What . . . tears, my old Adam?"

"Of joy, Absalom. And thou'rt no better. Blink, man,
blink 'em away as I do."

"Faith, Adam, I could blubber like a boy, or damme!"
So they blinked, they shook their heads at one another, they
laughed, and paced silently to and fro for a minute or two.

"Burn me," exclaimed Absalom, suddenly, "burn and
sink me but Friendship is right good thing, Adam, and
calls lustily for a noggin, yet this must wait. Meanwhile
I ha' to lay a burden on thee, brother, but first, look
yonder!" And he pointed towards the galleys which
though still distant were now so plain that Adam's anxious
eyes could glimpse the flash and flicker of their long, wet,
sun-smitten oars, their huge painted sails, the surge and
sparkle of steel upon their crowded decks. Now as he
gazed upon these dreadful ships that seemed to be con-
verging upon them, the air about him seemed full of a
flutey piping, a sound so blythe, so shrill and unexpected
that he glanced about, wondering.

"Absalom, why do our men whistle so merrily?"

"For a breeze, Adam, for a fighting breeze. The wind's
failing just when most needed. And so, 'stead o' meeting
yon rogues, as I would, with craft o' seamanship, out-
matching their cursed oars with trick o' sail and helm,
we must lie helpless, rolling like any log and they attack
us at their will and pleasure, with a curse! So is like to
be a very bloody chance medley, or I'm a mere forked
radish! In about half-an-hour, as I judge, they will be
letting fly with their fore-chase guns, heavy pieces all,
Adam, cannons-petro and baselisks most like, as by experience I know. And before then, Adam, She must be
secure out of harm's way—Antonia."

E

"Very true!" nodded Adam.

"And the only safe place is below the water-line, in the hold."

"Indeed, a very proper place!" nodded Adam again.

"So thither, my Old Adam, thither you must take her, ay, and there you must keep her prisoned. This is the labour I lay on you, and labour 'twill be, considering she's of spirit fiery and resolute,—so how you shall do this the Lord alone He knoweth."

"It shall achieve!" nodded Adam, for the third time.

"Good! Then whatsoever you hear of gun-fire and fighting tumult you shall nowise suffer her to venture forth until the business be ended."

Now at this, Adam glanced up in no little surprise.

"You mean," he questioned, "I am to remain below until the battle is over?"

"Ay, I do, Adam, I do. She is your charge to keep prisoned lest she adventure herself, as she would, God love her! She is naturally courageous and you have learned her to fight and love it,—so to cage and keep her safe becometh your bounden duty."

"And I must bide below whiles you fight, I must be idle and safe?"

"Ay, for her sake, my Old Adam. And I shall count it more heroic in thee, ay, damme, but I shall!"

"But, Absalom, I am nowise heroical, alas!"

"Ha, now what d'ye mean, Adam?"

"That I shall fight and she bide safe, ay—though I must needs tie her hand and foot."

CHAPTER XVII

TELLS HOW ADAM LEARNED A GRIEVOUS TRUTH

THE *Bold Adventuress* rolled, lazily helpless, to the languid swell of a windless sea, sails flapping idly, blocks rattling while voices muttered where the men made their last preparations for what was to be.

Now as Adam stood looking on the orderly bustle around, to him came Antonia striding very manlike, sword on hip, her bright hair covered in gleaming steel, and with her, Joel Bym bearing divers pieces of armour.

"'Tis steel o' proof, sir," quoth he, "as shall turn ye a bullet right handsome, by cock!"

"Howbeit, I want it not, Joel."

"Cap'n's orders, sir!"

"And mine, too!" cried Antonia. "Buckle them on him, Joel, my hearty." And so, willy-nilly, Adam was strapped into back and breast plates, upon his head was placed a cumbrous helmet which he instantly removed and, turning to Antonia, was about to speak when his words were checked by the boom of a cannon and something hummed through the rigging high above them.

And now all eyes gazed where, with thrashing oars and sharp prows cleaving the sullen waters to foam, the two long galleys drove down against their helpless prey.

But though the *Bold Adventuress* rolled thus helplessly becalmed, upon her lofty poop paced Absalom Troy, sword in fist, leisured of step, serene though watchful of eye: behind her stout bulwarks crouched desperate men who gripped ready steel, eager for battle; amidships stood their grim-faced officers glancing now at the oncoming foe and now up at that slow-pacing, glittering figure on the poop, awaiting his expected signal.

From the galleys, now rapidly approaching, came a sudden, wild clamour of voices, a ferocious howling,—upon the *Bold Adventuress* was no sound except the rattle of blocks and flapping of useless canvas; then the enemy's fierce hubbub was lost in the roar of their artillery followed by instant crash of splintering timbers . . . a man screamed, leapt afoot, staggered blindly across the deck spattering blood and so fell, and lay dreadfully motionless and silent.

"Oh God . . . of mercy!" gasped Antonia. "Is that . . . death?"

"Ay, I fear so," answered Adam. "Come, let us begone."

"Oh . . . but whither?"

Adam, glancing up, saw Absalom lift his sword, heard Smy's harsh voice cry "Fire!"—heard Bo'sun Ned's answering bellow. . . . Then from the ship's high, embattled side gushed smoke and flame with thunderous roar, shaking the stout vessel from stem to stern, and the foremost galley, smitten by this point-blank broadside, checked and broached to,—her lofty sail was swept away in flappy ruin, and as the powder-smoke blotted her out, rose a joyous, full-throated English cheer drowned in the crashing salvo of the second galley that smote the *Adventuress* forward and with deadly effect, for from the forecastle came screams and savage cries drowned by another rousing cheer and rattle of musketry fire.

"Come!" shouted Adam, above the increasing din. "Come, Antonia!" Seizing her hand, he urged her across quivering deck, down the wide companion and through the choking reek of dim gun-deck where by light of the battle lanthorns misted in swirling smoke, half-naked men were reloading the great pieces while little powder boys pattered to and fro. Amid all this seeming confusion Adam led the way, pausing only to snatch down one of the lanthorns, and, lighted by this flickering beam, went on—down to the orlop and thence down yet again into the

comparative quiet of the great hold piled high with cargo
of all sorts, lashed and battened trimly against the ship's
rolling. Here, reaching a kind of small embayment amid
this stowage, Adam paused to set the lanthorn very carefully in place of safety and so, to look at Antonia and
she at him, while above them the battle clamoured ever
louder, a tumultuous, never-ceasing uproar pierced now
and then by the splintering shock of shot-riven timbers,
hoarse cries, thin wailings or the deafening thunder of
John Fenn's crashing broadsides. At last, leaning near,
she spoke:

"Adam, shall you fight?"

"Can you doubt it, Antonia?"

"No. But why are we here?"

"I bring you to safety."

"And lose your labour, my foolish Adam, for I am no
more in love with safety than are you, or . . . Absalom
Troy, and so will share all perils with you."

"Nay now," sighed Adam, looking on her lovely, resolute
face but listening to that dreadful clamour above them,
"no woman should front such dangers."

"Howbeit, my Adam, since I must needs seem a man
I'll act like a man and fight."

"Not so, Antonia, you will, as I trust, remain here,—
'tis Absalom's command."

"Oh! Well, now, his commands shall never bind me, for
I despise the man. And besides——"

"Ay and besides, Anthony, I ask this of thee also."

"Then no to you, Adam, because you are my very
dear and only friend and I had liefer die beside you to-day,
since die I surely must someday, than bide here and you
be killed and I left desolate. Indeed, I fear death no more
than you,—for what have I to live for? I am but a poor
waif of the wind to be blown hither and yon! What hath
life for wretched me that I should fear to lose it?"

"Love!" he answered. "Wife and motherhood! 'Twas
for this God made thee, Antonia, and 'tis for this you

should cherish life. And 'tis for this I now beseech you from my heart to bide safe here and suffer that I now go to my duty doing my poor best, the best I may, against our enemies, leaving the hereafter to God. So now will you promise me to stay here in safety, will you on your honour pledge me this?"

"Yes," she answered in weeping tones, "yes, I promise thee, Adam. Go to thy duty and 'stead of me, I pray God shall go beside thee, dear Adam. Give me thy hand."

"My dear . . . ah no . . ." he gasped for, seizing his hand, she was kissing it. "Nay. . . . Oh, Antonia——" For now she was kissing his brow, his mouth—lips that kissed her again . . . arms that, for a moment, clasped and held her close. Then he drew away, but in his bright eyes a new and very joyous brightness.

"Antonia," said he, raising her hand to his lips, "in this hour . . . with death all about us, it is but honourable I should tell how that . . . Absalom loves thee also."

"He?" she repeated, in strange, breathless manner, "Absalom? Oh!" And shrinking back, she covered her face between quick hands. But in this face, this murmurous cry, Adam read the very truth and stood awhile rigid and dumb.

"Now God keep you," he muttered, at last. "God bless you . . . both of you!"

Then Adam turned from her and stumbled away into the darkness.

CHAPTER XVIII

TELLS HOW THEY FOUGHT

UP to the battle, to baleful roar and tumult went Adam, going slowly, heavy burdened by this sudden knowledge of irreparable loss and a grief far beyond words, and one indeed that never must be spoken; and, mingled with this pain, a fierce envy of Absalom for his bodily strength and comely, all-conquering manhood.

So came Adam to the gundeck thick with smoke, to slip in blood that fouled the littered planks, to stumble over prone shapes that writhed groaning, or lay dreadfully still and mute. But presently amid the eddying smoke he glimpsed a face he knew despite blood and grime of battle, and cried aloud:

"Ho, John . . . John Fenn! Canst use me, John?"

"Ay, I can, sir, I can," answered the Master Gunner, wiping sweat from his eyes. "Number Four is shorthanded . . . Frant's gun, forrard yonder. Martin'll show ye what to do—if he's yet alive. 'Tis pretty hot, sir, pretty hot."

Forward to Number Four went Adam, crying above the furious clamour:

"Frant. . . . Oh, Martin Frant, show me what I must do to help you." And a grim shape black with powder, answered cheerily:

"What, is 't you, Mast'r Adam! Lord love ee now here's a ploy. Lay on to this yere tackle, sir, and heave. My lads be all down but two, and she's a heavy piece is Number Four. Heave now . . . heave all and cheerily—yo—ho—ho!"

Thus Adam hove and wrought and laboured with Martin

and his two remaining men at Number Four until he gasped and sweated in his heavy corselet and yearned to be rid of it, but found no time to loose and unbuckle.

"Martin, where's . . . little Smidge?"

"Dunno, sir. He was hereabout, but now,—I dunno."

Smoke and thunderous roar of guns . . . shivering crash and shock of shot-riven timbers . . . shouts and cries . . . groans and a dreadful screaming. A vision of Martin calmly altering his gun's elevation . . . blowing on his match . . . giving fire . . . smoke and flame and thunder. A glimpse of Martin peering out and down through reeking gun-port . . . turning hand at mouth to hail:

"Ahoy, Master Fenn, they'm below us, sir . . . out o' range. They'm alongside. Ho, Master Fenn, they'm boarding of us!" And then John Fenn's answering hail:

"Gunners, stand by! In guns all! Close and bar all ports! Is 't done, lads?"

"Ay, ay, sir! All 's fast and snug, sir."

"Then pikes and cutlasses! Aloft to repel boarders. Follow me!"

A coughing scramble amid the smoke; a trampling of hasty feet; a surge of eager, half-naked bodies up the wide companion, up from smoke and gloom, out into blinding sunglare, to pause a moment with dazzled eyes and then to behold a dreadful sight of prone bodies trampled on blood-spattered deck by men who fought desperately, thrusting and hewing at wild figures that swarmed the bulwarks, a howling fury of attack. And into this merciless battle leapt John Fenn followed by his smoke-grimed gun crews, and with them Adam. . . . Cut and parry and darting thrust, blow on blow until arm wearied and breath failed.

Somewhere in the reeling press Adam heard Bo'sun Ned's hoarse bellow, and fighting thitherward, glimpsed him at last, a ghastly figure of slaughter plying great axe with terrible effect. Cut and parry and darting thrust until, loud above the raving din, rose Absalom's breathless but right jubilant cry:

"By God . . . we have 'em! To it, lads . . . at 'em, old seadogs, point and edge . . . sa-ha!"

A breathless cheer . . . clash of random steel . . . a vision of Sir Benjamin's plump visage pale now and agonized . . . a tall figure that choked horridly and went down. . . . Then Adam was hurled backwards . . . was kicked, trampled, felt pain, felt sickness . . . felt—nothing.

CHAPTER XIX

AFTERMATH

HE roused to a right pleasant coolness, a sweet refreshment and opening his eyes stared down into a bowl of bloody water whence a great hand lifted dripping clout to splash his drooping head until he gasped, and turning with an effort, looked up into the blood-spattered visage of Bo'sun Ned who instantly nodded at him, crying:

"Ahoy, Martin, he've come to."

"Yes," sighed Adam, blinking the water from his eyes "So we . . . won the fight, Ned?"

"Ay, we did, sir."

"At a price, Mast'r Adam!" added Martin Frant. "There be five o' my watch gone."

"Ay!" growled the Bo'sun, wringing the water from his clout, "yet to good purpose, Martin lad, there's them and ten more all gone aloft on the wings o' Victory, as English sailormen should ought for to go."

"Fifteen—killed?" gasped Adam.

"Ay, sir, this be the total, and two or three o' the wounded doo for to follow 'em, I reckon. This be the tally of us foremast men. As for the after guard, the officers and gen'lemen,—there's the Master, Mr. Perrin, very dead of a cannon shot. There's Mr. Danvers gone and Lord Perrow likewise, with Sir Benjamin and divers others hurted somewhat. Yet—here's you and me and Martin and Cap'n Troy right as so many trivets and nary a scrat!"

"Yet you bleed, Ned."

"Mostly furrin, sir. I've took a small cut here and theer I won't deny, but naught to matter."

"I grieve poor Amos Perrin is gone."

"But, sir, he were killed afore he knowed it. A round-shot is usually mighty quick and therefore marciful; this 'un did Mr. Perrin's business very handsome,—like a flash o' light. He's lying forrard there, along wi' the rest o' them, waiting for Job Day, the sailmaker, to perform his dooty on 'em."

"How so, Ned?"

"Roll 'em snug and sew 'em up neat in canvas, sir, all trim and shipshape. And presently wi' a round shot rove to their feet and the Cap'n and us to pay 'em our last respex, over they'll go to Davy Jones—their poor bodies to the deep, but their souls aloft—we hope."

"Why truly, Ned, into the hands of God,—and as you said, on the wings of Victory, whereto I now say—Amen! So many dead alas,—and here sit I unharmed by very miracle."

"And your steel-jack, sir!" said Martin. "Here be tidy dent in the front, lookee! A pistol ball, I guess, 'twas this dropped ee and should have ended of ee else."

"And what of the enemy?"

"Two wrecks, sir, miles a-starn of us. For, d'ye see, so soon as their business is done, comes the plaguey wind as might ha' saved us in our need and didn't. Howsomever them cursed galleys shall never make land, which is summat to be thankful for."

And now came Joel Bym, limping somewhat, who hailed Adam with cry of welcome.

"By cock, sir, I've been a-seeking of ee alow and aloft along o' your young brother as be a-looking yet—below there on the gundeck."

"Then go say I'm very well, Joel."

"Ay, ay, sir!" And away hobbled Joel, while Adam got to his legs with an effort, saying:

"Now I must find thy hanger, Ned, for I lost it when I fell."

"Nay, 'tis here, Must' Adam, and very prettily blooded . . . and yonder cometh your brother something green about the gills and no wonder, for he's young and we'm all pretty gory. Us'll swab down so soon as the lads have had a spell.

Me being Bo'sun and therefore ship's nurse, I'll away and tend her. Come, Martin lad!" And away rolled these hardy mariners while Adam turned to meet Antonia and seeing her so pale, spoke cheerily as he might.

"Blood!" she gasped, "Blood everywhere . . . my shoes are wet with it. Oh, Adam, what cruel wickedness a battle is! Thank God you are alive! I looked for you down there among those blood-splashed guns. I sought you in the dreadful cockpit where the wounded lie in their blood, crying and groaning . . . and Mr. Perks and his mates all blood to their elbows. . . ."

"Nay, such sights are not for you. Come now and lie down a while, take your ease until——"

"My ease?" she repeated, shivering. "And men groaning in agony!"

"Ay, I know," he sighed, "I know."

"Well now, Adam, if I must not fight will you have me shrink at sight of wounds, 'stead of doing all I may to ease such poor sufferers? Can you think me so heartless to take my ease and be such craven indeed?"

"No!" he answered, gently. "Yet what can you do?"

"All that I may," she retorted, and throwing off coat and doublet, rolled up her sleeves.

"Whither go you?" he questioned, anxiously.

"Downstairs, Adam! Down and yet down into the horror of that fearful cockpit—where no clean air may come and no light is save flickering lanthorns. And such work to do! Life and death! Oh, why must they have such dreadful place so dreadfully far from God's daylight? How like silly, great, blundering men!"

"Shall I go with thee, dear Anthony?"

"No, no, you would be sick, as I was at first,—very nearly. Instead go you to little Smidge, he lies in your cabin."

"Is he hurt?"

"I was looking for you, Adam, and found him lying by a cannon, between two dead men and thought him dead also, yet found he lived. So brought him up to your cabin and made him easy as I might. A great bump on his little curly head, poor lamb! Ah, 'tis sinful shame such children should be brought to sea. Take my coat, Adam, I'm going to the galley for rum and plenty of it to dose these poor sufferers!" And away she sped.

So Adam went to his cabin and beheld there outstretched a very pale little Smidge who, looking up at him with large, wistful eyes, raised hand to brow in fumbling salute.

"Ax your kind pardon, sir," said he, a little faintly, "'twas your bruvver brings and lays me yere, but if you wants to lay down I'll sheer off, sir."

Adam shook his head and blinked but answered cheerily:

"No, no. How's thy old nob, shipmate?"

"Aches me a bit, sir, it do, but I'm a fighting English seadog now, Mr. Adam, so I don't mind nor yet notice it nohow. 'Cos when Tom Benson was killed I took his cutlash and used it agin them pirits right hearty I did till I gets this yere clout o' my figurehead and couldn't do no more. So then I went asleep and dreamed as my mother was a-kissing of me and wakes up and finds as 'twas your bruvver, Mist' Anthony . . . and I was that ashamed I closes my peepers again and so he carries me up yere, though I dessay as I could ha' walked, then he lays me yere and . . . kisses me again—ay, and calls me 'poor child', 'e did, though I tells him I ain't! So please, Mist' Adam, don't let him kiss me no more, and if he calls me 'child' you tell him as I'm a seadog as poked them pirits proper,— will ye, sir, if you please?"

"Ay, ay, shipmate, I will so,—but only on condition you close your peepers now and try to get some sleep like the bold seadog you are."

"Then you don't mind me a-laying yere, sir?"

"No, Smidge, not if you sleep and obey orders as a seaman should."

"Why then I will, sir, and thankee kindly . . . for I be . . . main weary." And to prove his words, the little fellow was presently fast asleep.

Then, soft-treading, forth went Adam to see what harm the *Bold Adventuress* had suffered in the fight, and was surprised to find this so much less than he had feared.

Bo'sun Ned, this so capable man and dutiful ship's nurse, himself taut and trim as ever, was already on duty to oversee the swabbing of decks and repair of damaged rigging, while the carpenter and his mates were hard at work to mend riven timbers and plug shot-holes, and all greatly to Adam's expressed admiration, so that the men grinned and the work went the more merrily. But after some while Joel Bym came limping to say, knuckling an eyebrow:

"Cap'n's sarvice, Must' Adam, and will ee step into the roundhouse, sir?"

"Ay, but art hurt, Joel,—thy leg?"

"My starboard spar, sir, a bit of a cut though irksome, by cock."

Absalom, his armour laid by, was sitting alone with papers on the table before him and a wide belt of soft leather wherein showed many small pockets. He beckoned Adam to the chair beside him and so soon as Joel had departed closing the door, he turned with the question:

"What of . . . her?"

"Safe, Absalom, and now below in the cockpit to aid Perks and his mates."

"She should not be there, Adam, 'tis ghastly place!"

"This is why she went."

"Lord!" murmured Absalom. "Now God love her! Adam, 'tis very angel o' mercy."

"Yet a woman, Absalom, to cherish and honour."

"And . . . love, Adam!"

"Ay verily."

"Adam, hast spoke aught of . . . of thy love?"

"No."

"Hast ever loved afore, Adam?"

"Never."

"I have, alas! And so often, the memory shames me

now, for I am wiser. She hath learned me how love is no idle toy, no mere pastime but a very . . . holy thing, ay, so purely sacred that I know myself all unworthy."

"Since when, Absalom?"

"That moment she looked on me with her clean maid's eyes and vowed to kill me. Which is marvellous strange yet true as death, Adam. So, I know I have never loved afore in all my days, and, loving now, shall never love any other . . . for in all this world can be no other for me. And though she despise me I honour her therefor, since I do so truly merit her disdain."

"And art so very sure that she despiseth thee?"

"Ay, I am . . . she hath made it very sufficiently evident. And no wonder, for blind fool that I was, I have shown her ever the worst of me,—almost! But, Adam, I never believed such love could be and . . . when it came . . . I was ashamed and hid it 'neath a galliard lightness, fool talk and smirking gallantries . . . yet all the while True Love crying shame on me—even as you did, Adam. And when we fought, though meaning not to kill thee, I did my best to shed thy blood because I knew she loved thee."

"And now, Absalom?"

"Why now. . . . Love hath so changed me thou'rt dearer to me for her sake . . . so her choice o' thee is mine also. And this bringeth us to the matter in hand, to wit,—this treasure belt and these papers which were the property of Lord Perrow who was killed fighting beside me. Now hidden in this belt, Adam, is treasure of jewels, all that is left of the great Perrow heritage, being family heirlooms, the half of which I shall give to thee for——"

"To me?" exclaimed Adam, in stammering amazement. "But how . . . how can you . . . ?"

"Ay, to be sure," sighed Absalom. "I should ha' told thee . . . Lord Perrow was my only brother."

"Your . . . brother?" Adam repeated.

"Here are these papers to prove it."

"Then you . . . you are now . . . Lord Perrow!"

"Ay, verily, Adam,—lord of an acre or so and old, ruined house in Sussex, all the rest was confiscate in my father's time. We were family of power and great wealth . . . all gone like vanished dream, save for these jewels that, according to my brother's papers, are valued in London at fifty odd thousand pounds, and this now mine. For by law I am Jocelyn, Lord Perrow, but by choice I shall remain to the end o' my days Absalom Troy, mariner."

"I pray you why?"

"A title, Adam, must be lived up to, so I'll none of it. And I've even less love for my family name than I had for my poor brother, God forgive me. But you must know that my brother Eustace lived up to his title, ay and beyond it, and being some years my elder, lorded it over me all my days until at last, our mother being dead, I went to sea as gentleman adventurer and left him to lord it over others,—the which he did to such effect that he drew on him King Jamie's disfavour, though for this I nothing blame him,—was attained with other gentlemen and doomed to banishment, as you know. But girt about him was this our treasure o' family jewels, the half of which, as I say, I shall bestow on you, my Old Adam."

"But why should you give me so great a fortune?"

"Adam, thour't my friend . . . and she loves thee. This money shall make thee bold to woo and wed, so shall it be my wedding gift. Well now are you answered?"

"So well, Absalom, that I must as truly answer thee. For indeed, though most truly grateful, I can nowise accept this gift . . . having no least need of it by reason that I shall never . . . be so blest . . . to have a . . . wedding."

With the word he arose, and when Absalom would have questioned him further, he but smiled and shook his head.

So presently back went Adam to his cabin and there, seated before his books and charts, saw instead of these, the haunting beauty of Antonia's face and this gradually misted by slow-gathering, painful tears.

136 ADAM PENFEATHER, BUCCANEER

take little heed; "I d-do," gasped she, starting up from the rest of the beds. "Bu—t it all—so hot." "I care not, no, so I breathe with you this—"

CHAPTER XX

OF NO PARTICULAR IMPORT

BLAZING sun, tempered by a gentle following wind that urged the *Bold Adventuress* through calm seas of colour so deep and wonderfully blue that yet seemed daily to become more beautiful, a very joy to the eyes and one that Adam never wearied of beholding, as he was doing in this warm and slumberous afternoon from shady corner, the decks all deserted save for the customary watch; thus solitary stood Adam, and so lost in meditation that at sound of Antonia's voice and light footstep he started, almost guiltily, for it was of her he was thinking, —tormenting himself with such dream as went beyond all hope of realization, and therefore ineffably dear. Thus, as he watched her coming towards him, what wonder if his heart leapt painfully because of her warm and vivid beauty. For these weeks of sea air, of brine and glowing sunshine have deepened the colour in cheek and lip, her step is quick and firm, her every movement instinct with vigorous, new life and the pure joy of it.

"Goodness me, Adam!" she exclaimed, leaning beside him, "Each day seems hotter than the last."

"And will be," he answered, "for soon we shall be crossing the Line."

"Oh! What line?"

"The equinoctial."

"Why, whatever is that?"

"An imaginary circle in the heavens running with and above the earth's equator, and called the equinox because when the sun crosses it, days and nights are equal."

"And both equally hot!" she sighed.

"Indeed!" he nodded. "I wonder you are not sleeping like the rest o' the folk."

"I tried, yet could not, so instead went a-visiting my school."

"Eh, school?"

"The gunroom, Adam, where now my schoolboys lie, the wounded men. 'Tis well for them you got the man Troy to suffer they should be brought there, I think they'd have died else. I call them my scholars because I read to them every day then question 'em to know how much they remember. And they are all my children because all men are always children, and very babies when they're sick. And a marvellous strict parent I am . . . though in their weakness I love them all. And they are so patient, Adam, so very grateful for what little I can do . . . smiling on me through their pain, so that sometimes I could weep, but then it is that I grow stern, very bluff and gruff and swear my best at 'em . . . yet with tears o' pity in my heart. And, for their comfort, a flask of rum in my pocket to temper Mr. Perk's bitter nostrums, the biggest nip for my brightest scholar! Oh, and here's a wonder,—the man Troy can trouble his proud magnificence to visit them, and frequently o' late! He came again to-day while I was reading to them, and sat there meek as a mouse, the odious wretch!"

"Are you so angry yet against——"

"More so, Adam. For now when I chance to meet him, which is seldom as possible, he affects the most nauseous humility. But no more of him,—talk we instead of ourselves, and first of myself for, Adam, I am becoming my own trouble."

"How so, Anthony?"

"By—growing! Look at me! Since leaving England I've grown—inches! And, as I say, this troubles me. Look now, don't you mark any change? Look at me, Adam!"

Obediently he glanced at her then, looking down at the sea again, answered:

"Yes, you are—browner."

"Brown as a berry, Adam. I've no more need for Mother Martha's walnut juice. But besides this I'm growing, so that it makes me anxious lest I begin to show . . . to seem too much . . . unlike a man. Adam, look at me . . . look hard!"

Again he glanced at her, murmured a negative, and then gazed down at the sea once more, lest his eyes should betray him. At this she frowned, sighed and slipping hand within his arm, murmured:

"Have I anyways angered thee, dear Adam?"

"No," he answered, cheerfully as he might. "Lord love thee, no!"

"Yet I prove you a little . . . strange of late."

"Ay, truly, I believe I am, and no wonder—for my poor head is all a-buzz with meridians and parallels, degrees and latitudes. As, for instance, how to find the longitude of any place by the satellites of Jupiter. And 'tis to be done on this wise——"

"Nay, a-mercy's sake, Adam."

"Yet, hearken." And drawing small book from pocket, he read forth: "'By a clock or watch observe the time of the immersion or emersion of any of the said satellites which being compared with the time of immersion or emersion of the same satellites at the first meridian, the difference of time reduced into degrees gives the longitude sought.' And what say you to this, now?"

"My poor Adam, why trouble your head with such?"

"To make myself a true and worthy seaman."

"Well now, look down with me into the wonder of this ocean that groweth ever bluer and almost too beautiful for belief . . . like those islands we stayed at days agone, where was the mountain that flamed by night——"

"The Cape de Verd and that island with the volcano is called Fuoco."

"Yes, Adam,—but whither are these beautiful waters bearing us?"

"To happiness, I pray God, and a useful life."

"I pray so too, Adam. And yet sometimes I grow very fearful. . . . Have you no fear of the future?"

"No!" he answered, gently. "Since death I nowise fear and life can bring me no grief more bitter than I have known, I am resolute to meet whatso of tribulation may wait me . . . and with no repining."

"Oh, Adam, I would I were brave as thou!"

"Alas, I am not brave!" he sighed. "'Tis only that I have faith in this better part of me the which is of God, this immortal soul that is so strong to endure all things and so mighty to achieve, that all things may be possible, despite frailty o' body, since our souls, I do believe, are very part of God, living forever. See you what I mean, Antonia, see you?"

"Yes, Adam, yes, and it makes me less fearful."

"Well now, since this great, glorious ocean is also of God, His own marvellous handiwork, and is now bearing us to His purposes, let us take heart and be joyful, therefore, nor anyway dread whatso the future may hold. Is it agreed, brother Anthony?"

"Yes, Adam, with all my heart, so long as I can see this dear, white head somewhere near me I shall be bold as any lion—or very nearly."

"And now, pray you, let us talk of . . . of Absalom."

"But wherefore of this base creature?"

"He is my dear and honoured friend."

"Honoured, say you, Adam?"

"Ay I do! For indeed I know him a clean-souled, great-hearted gentleman and——"

"Yet I prove him a cruel wretch, with vile, bitter tongue."

"No, no."

"Yes, yes! And someday you shall hear me curse him to his hateful, mocking face and damn him the best I may."

"You swear very trippingly these days," sighed Adam, "and more frequently."

"Ay, I do indeed! I swagger and curse most hatefully—all to the one purpose, as you should know very well."

"Yet tell me, Antonia."

"Well," she answered, leaning closer to sigh in his ear so that her fragrant breath seemed all about him, "of late my womanhood grows upon me and . . . the more womanly I feel the harder I swear. Oh, I curse and swear amain to shame and shock my womanhood, and seem the manlier and more brutally male. Yet I abominate swearing—except when I think on him—your Absalom, this Troy,—this brute-man that could name me 'gallows-bird' and 'claw-cat'? Oh, I could swear and curse at him with purest joy, as I shall yet,—damn him and burn his eyes!"

"Can you not forgive?"

"Never! No—except he kneel and plead my pardon, woo and sue and supplicate forgiveness on his odious knees."

"Forgiveness is a blessedness——"

"But one that should be earned, Adam, and sought with diligent humility." Here she paused and turned, as, with quick patter of small bare feet, came little Smidge to make a leg and pull forelock at them smartly as any hardy seadog aboard.

"Ax your pardins, sirs," he piped, "but Mr. Anthony, sir, if you please, sir, Joe Brent says as I'm to tell ye as he be took main bad again, so will ee come please for to shift his bandage?"

"Ha—rum!" quoth Antonia, at her manliest. "Shiver and sink Joe for sly rogue, 'tis more rum he's after! Tell him no, Smidge, no is the word, not another drop or burn my neck! Nay, I'll go tell him this myself."

Now scarce was she gone, striding very man-like, and Smidge's little legs trotting to keep pace, than hasty feet descended the poop nearby, a long arm clasped Adam's drooping shoulders.

"Now Lord love thee," exclaimed Absalom. "Lord love thee for trusty friend, my Old Adam. . . . I heard thee plead my cause,—ay, I've been listening, eavesdropping right shamelessly! I heard her curse me, bless her! 'Damn me and burn my eyes,' quo' she, and ears never heard swearing so sweetly pretty! Oh, Adam, what bride for a sailorman, what wife for a buccaneer! . . . And on my knees! Ay, faith, at the first chance—down on my knees I'll go to plead her pardon even as she said; I'll woo and sue and supplicate . . . even though she flout and deny me forgiveness, eh, brother, how say'st thou, Adam?''

"Yes," he answered, with sombre gaze on the distance, "speak from your heart and . . . I don't think . . . she'll deny you."

"By heaven, I will! At the least she shall see me humble and know me contrite. . . . And now, my Old Adam, go with me for a noggin,—ay and shalt help me plot our position on the chart."

CHAPTER XXI

HOW THEY TALKED AMID GLORY OF STARS

IT was night very hot, very still, and Adam, the lanthorn drawn near, sat crouched above his books deeply intent and fiercely resolved to master the abstruse problem in navigation that engaged him. . . . But after some while, the ship being so silent, he became aware of a vague sound nearby, and raised his head to listen, then rose in sudden perturbation for Antonia was weeping very bitterly.

He stood a moment or so debating what he should do, then going to the door of her cabin, knocked gently.

"Who . . . who's there?" she questioned, breathlessly.

"Adam!" he murmured.

"What . . . do you . . . want?"

"Why do you weep?"

"Because I . . . I'm so minded."

"Oh!"

"Yes!"

"Then I grieve to have troubled you."

"Oh . . . go away!"

"Good night!" he answered softly, and went.

Yet scarcely had he settled to his studies again than came a tapping on his door; rising he opened it to see Antonia looking at him through her tears and, to his great relief, completely dressed.

"Adam. . . . Oh, Adam," she sobbed, "I am so very miserable. I do so hate myself, and this great, vile ship and everyone on it and . . . 'specially . . . one! I would I were dead, or back in England . . . our dear England . . . even though they . . . swung me on a . . . gallows!"

"Ah no!" he murmured. "No!"

"I do!" she retorted. "Yes I do, and all your fault. Oh, you meant me well I know, but see now what you have led me into . . . and I have made myself such . . . failure! I've tried so hard to seem a man . . . you've learned me to fight . . . I've made myself seem bold, a braggart and swearer, but . . . God made me a woman and . . . Oh, I do yearn . . . for my petticoats!"

"Now God love and bless thee!" murmured Adam, then laughed a little shakily, whereupon she began to laugh also, even while she wept, and to his dismay.

"Hush!" he whispered, taking her two hands in his quick clasp that could be so unexpectedly strong. "Come out with me and find comfort in the glory and wonder of God's stars."

So, hand in hand, soft-treading, forth they went to such starry splendour as may only be seen in those latitudes.

"See now, Antonia,—yonder, up from dark ocean riseth Venus in radiant majesty."

"And like a little moon, to make a glory on the sea, Adam."

"Ay, and, yonder again, hangeth the Southern Cross! And there above our mast-heads, sprawled across the firmament, is the Scorpion. So here stand we, two children o' God, amid the glory of His creation. Above us the everlasting wonder of His heaven, below us the abiding mystery of His ocean,—and this great ship no more than merest atom afloat between these His immensities."

"Yes," she murmured, "all this speaks forth the awful majesty of God . . . and He is so mighty and so remote from poor me!"

"And yet so near us, Antonia, that the griefs we suffer, the harms we do, all these are known to Him that heedeth the fall of a sparrow. For this eternal so mighty God is also our all merciful Father."

Thus Adam talked for her comfort, and his own, until

up from dark ocean rose the great, tropic moon to pale the myriad stars and show him all things touched with a new beauty,—towering sails, broad, white decks and— the loveliness of she who leaned beside him so near and yet so remote, her dreamful gaze upon the glittering, ever restless sea. Thus for a while they were silent and the night about them full of sounds grown familiar,—the sighing hiss of placid waters, murmur of wind in rigging, hoarse mutter of voices from the lookout forward and slow-pacing step where the officer of the watch kept his lonely vigil on lofty poop above them.

At last, deep-sighing, Antonia leaned nearer and spoke.

"Adam, you have called me your brother and oh, my dear, as a brother I love you, and as a man I honour you most truly. And now because you are so wise I must tell you that which troubles and greatly surprises me. This evening while you were sitting with Sir Benjamin I went into your cabin to order it and set out your books as is my custom, and found . . . him there."

"Absalom?"

"Yes. But no sooner did he see me than . . . oh, Adam . . . he knelt to me! Yes, on his knees . . . at my feet . . . and in his look no least sign of mockery. And while I stood there amazed beyond words, he . . . pleaded my forgiveness . . . stammering . . . his voice broke . . . then he leapt afoot and was gone, yet oh . . . not before I had seen . . . tears in his eyes,—yes, tears, Adam, tears! And he a man so proud and hard! What shall this mean now?"

"Truly, that he is neither."

"Then what is the miracle hath so changed him?"

"Ah, child, doth not . . . thine own heart tell thee this?"

"Nay," she whispered, "my poor heart tells me only what I would so fain believe . . . yet dare not."

"So then," said Adam, keeping his face averted, "I am to know . . . you love him . . . very greatly."

"Yes, Adam, yes . . . from the first moment he looked on me in that English lane! Yes, I love him despite myself . . . and very grievously because I know it is all . . . so hopeless!"

"Hopeless?" repeated Adam, angrily amazed. "Now in the Lord's name, why?"

"Because I am a nameless waif . . . a poor foundling and . . . oh . . . a fugitive from the Law. Ah, how could he . . . a man so great and splendid . . . ever love . . . only me?"

"Because you are indeed merely yourself . . . the Only Antonia in all this world. Never disparage thyself, for thou art one with this great glory of stars and ocean since thou, too, art God's handiwork. He made thee woman, and hath endowed thee with noble valiance of soul and sweet loveliness of body. Well, respect thyself therefore, and know thyself worthy all honour and . . . and worship and a glory to the man shall win thee. And remember this,—Beauty is a power—one of the mightiest in life, for thereby a woman may ennoble or debase a man. Beauty is either shame or a crowning glory. Oh, indeed, to be a woman and beautiful is vast responsibility!"

"Am I then . . . so beautiful, Adam?"

"Yes."

"And doth . . . he . . . think so, think you?"

"This he shall tell you himself anon."

"Oh!" said she, breathlessly. "Will he? Are you sure, dear Adam?"

"Very sure!" he answered, between shut teeth.

Now after this they were silent some while, and when at last she spoke again, it was in voice very soft with tenderness:

"Oh, Adam . . . dear, loved brother, now I pray God bless the clean, brave soul of thee ever and always . . . and so, good night!" Then, swiftly, lightly, she kissed his silvery hair and was gone, flitting silent as a ghost.

For some while Adam stood motionless, staring down

into that dark mystery of ever-moving waters and when at last he looked up it was to see the stars all dimmed through a blur of scalding tears. For as she had left him now, so she would leave him very soon to solitude and great desolation; and from the loneliness of his stricken heart he cried speechlessly to that God his so loved father had taught him was, and ever would be, his stay, his consolation and ultimate salvation so long as he kept faith.

So Adam watched the night through until the stars paled their fires and, to end his lonely vigil, came the dawn making a radiance of sky and ocean. And standing in the light of this new day, he found strength to implore a blessing on these two whose love was to make him a loveless, solitary man all his days.

CHAPTER XXII

WHICH INTRODUCES DIVERS PAGES
OF ADAM'S JOURNAL

AMONG the personal effects Amos Perrin had bequeathed to Adam was a journal, a small, stout, handy volume of many pages as yet untouched by quill, and in this book it now became Adam's custom to note down in his small, neat script the minor happenings of each day, together with such thoughts and self-communings as his lips might never utter. And since this may show him forth better than any bald statement of fact, it is deemed well to include divers pages thereof from time to time in this narrative and record of his early adventures, grievous sufferings, few joys and many triumphs, beginning on this wise :

June 2

I begin this my Journal in the dawn and with marvellous heaviness of spirit, for now I am assured beyond doubt how my hopes are all vain, and in my bitter loss can but say her will be done. And in this black hour thankful to assure myself that by no look or word have I betrayed to her that her choice and Absalom's coming happiness are my despair and abiding grief. For I, that never had woman to love, no not even my own mother that died too soon, do now love this woman so greatly that in all my life can be no other. May Absalom, that hath, as confessed, loved so many, now love this one with fervour as deep and abiding, to the assured and lasting happiness of them both, I pray God. Amen. I pray also for strength to bear myself towards them both with a cheerful amity, and that my jealousy of Ab. and envy for his happiness may nowise lead me to any word or act unbecoming the son of my Father whose sign, this grief-stricken white head, I bear upon me like his Blessing and Memorial to remind me how I must live in honour and die unfearing—even as did he.

And now since I must needs be lonely man henceforth, I am resolved to live and die (I hope) at sea, this infinite mystery where (as I do think) in day and night, calm and tempest, God is so manifest. I shall therefore devote myself more than ever to fitting myself for sea life by study of books, of ships and the men who sail therein, and thus become one of the great Sea Brotherhood. These sailor-men, for the most part, I prove to be woefully ignorant and therefore rough and suspicious, and yet therewith kindly and simple-hearted, and naught wanting to win their faith and love but justice, sympathy and belief in their manhood.

June 4

To-day for the first time Anthony and I took our places at table in the great cabin called 'coach', with Absalom, his chiefest officers and the five rescued prisoners, namely: Sir Oliver Kent, Mr. Ames, Sir George D'Arcy, Mr. Falcon and Mr. Temple, which last is kinsman to Sir Benjamin, a young, sad gentleman and silent. With these during the meal we became more familiar, and found them kindly gentlemen all, and more especially Sir George. And myself very happy to see Antonia bear herself as any young gentle-man should. The meal ended, we, Anthony and I, out upon deck leaving the others to their cards and wine, and she very full of talk anent these same gentlemen who, so long familiar to us by sight and word, were now so much better known and esteemed, especially Sir George D'Arcy. After this, to my cabin, and there much talk of ourselves or rather, of her. For since telling me of her love for Ab. she will now speak much of him and of her own hopes and fears, making of him now a hero as much too perfect and beyond her hopes, as before she had vowed him a wretch beneath contempt. And in thus confiding in me she but makes herself the more inexpressibly dear, so that the thought of our soon parting becomes a pain hard to bear.

This night I worked late at my Navigation studies, and yet, when I got me to bed, was haunted by this one dismal thought that followed me even into my dreams.

June 6

This morning, Sir Benj. hobbling on my arm, he begins to peeve and fret and on my asking the reason falls to great fury of vain oaths and fetching breath thereafter:

"Look, Adam," says he, "here's me with nigh all my poor fortune in this ship and cargo and no least idea whither we are bound, for when I question Absalom, as is my right, he puts me off with side answers, laughing mockery and evasions, so that I begin to lose all faith in him and conceive myself mortally affronted to boot."

I told him that I hoped not.

"Ay, but I do," says he with more ferocity of oaths; "he shall account to me or debate the matter wi' steel as gentleman should, so soon as I'm healed o' this plaguey wound, a three ounce ball through my nether man,— though precisely how any rogue-pirate could have aimed to hit me there, is my astonishment. Howbeit, so soon as I am able, Troy shall answer me one way or t'other." At this I counselled him patience, very earnestly, also reminding him how we had sailed for the rescue of his kinsman and other gentlemen.

"True enough, Adam," says he, "but this done, we were to open trade with my goods along the Guinea Coast and Gambia River which, as you should know, lie now far astern of us. And thus am I choused! And by Troy, this man I trusted, for, mark me,—'tis my certain belief he is minded to sail on his own account, ay and to turn rogue-pirate, Adam, and make us like rogues!" At this I protested with vehemence, and indeed no little heat, vowing he did Absalom great wrong and injustice. In the midst of which Sir Benj. stayed me with furtive gripe on my arm, and, glancing up, I saw Absalom regarding us from the poop nearby.

"What," laughs he, "at thy old plaints, Ben? Ay, faith, thy so fiery visage proclaims it. Then at the next bell come ye both to me in the coach and shalt hear that shall make thee pipe like carolling lark."

So at the turning of the next glass and stroke of bell that marks change of watch, to the great cabin we went, and found Absalom there seated with Smy and every of his officers including gunner, boatswain and carpenter and with chairs beside him for us. Scarce are we seated than he speaks, and so far as I remember, these his words.

Sirs, by the recent death of my brother, Lord Perrow, I am transmuted from poor adventurer into person of some wealth. Yet seaman I am and adventurer I shall ever remain, being so by nature. Thus Captain Absalom Troy keeping faith with himself and with you, shall more than fulfil his pledges by leading ye to such riches as goeth beyond our present hopes. And this the manner on't, to wit: We sail for Port Royal, Jamaica, there to refit and better arm our ship what time we market our cargo. This done, we bear away for an island, known only to Captain Smy and myself, called Black Bartlemy's Key, there to make sure end of this black rogue,—which good work happily accompt, we repay ourselves by plunder of his secret hoard, this great treasure of jewels and gold that is become a bye-word along the Main, for there is no man hath sailed those seas but shall hear tell of Black Bartlemy's Treasure.

"I have, for one!" cries John Weir, the first Officer. "And I also!" says Roger Challen that is now master in the room of poor Amos Perrin. And now I spoke, saying that if this treasure be so great it will certainly be well hid and hard to come by.

"Ay, to be sure," nods Absalom, "very true, Adam, for,

besides Black Bartlemy there were but four men knew of
this secret, and two of these are dead, therefore, whiles
other two escaped so hardly with their lives that to-day
Bartlemy believes them dead also,—yet are they very much
alive as ye may see, for one of these men is Captain Smy
and t'other—myself.

"This then is our true venture, and one to make us,
each one, rich all our lives. The treasure to be shared
proportionate to rank by articles to be drawn up anon
and duly signed. And now I think a noggin to drink success
upon us every man jack." So presently we all drink right
heartily, and every man now mightily uplift and eager,
indeed, as any band of school urchins. And yet, thinks I,
this treasure is yet to find.

June 7

This morning on deck with her, and though so early,
the sun extreme fierce, and the sea alive with great shoals
of flying fish that do go with a small, dry, whispering sound.
And some of these at last falling on board, we saw their
wings no more indeed than large fins. And these fish will
only leap into flight when pursued by an enemy below and,
thus flying, are often attacked by birds in the air, so that
these poor, hunted creatures have but short and anxious
life. Towards noon Absalom comes to me and I wonder
to see him girt with his sword and crowned with brave,
feathered hat, very stately.

"Ay," says he, on my remarking this, "I'm to oversee
punishment,—a blasphemous, murderous fellow and proven
thief named Jenks, wilt go with me, Adam? There sound
the drums! Wilt along?" But, instead, I went and shut
myself into my cabin, maugre the heat, not to hear or see
aught of this miserable wretch, for I cannot abide this
methodical beating of a man whose writhing body is bound
helpless to the cruel lash. I was hard at work with my
books when to me cometh Antonia, breathless and very
pale.

"Oh, Adam," says she, gasping, "they are beating a poor man so cruelly I could hear his raving outcries loud above the awful drum-beats! And . . . he is there . . . watching it done . . . and no least sign of pity! So cold . . . so merciless! Oh, he must be a very hatefully, blood-thirsty beast, at heart. I wonder how any woman creature may ever . . . love such a man."

"Yet love him you do!" says I. "Very dearly . . . with all your heart."

"Yes," she sighed. "Yes, I . . . it seems, I cannot help myself. Yet there be times I fain would hate him . . . if I but could, as I so tried and all in vain. For he is hard and proud and cruel, not like you, Adam, that are so kindly gentle." Here I must needs remind her how she had vowed me cold and terrible ere now.

"Ay," says she, "you can be so, and yet merciful too. But this Absalom wretch hath no mercy in him." Now when I chid her for so misjudging him and showed how the captain of a great ship, being one to rule the many, must therefore be a solitary man, and stern, yea even to a pitiless harshness if need be, she flares out on me naming me 'turncoat', for: "Lord, Adam," cries she, "you that withstood him so boldly once in like cruelty do now excuse him. Here's strange and mighty change in you!" To the which I agreed, saying 'all things were changed'—whereat she left me in a pet. But presently back she comes and lays hand on my shoulder, like a caress. "Adam," says she, "how are all things changed, what mean you . . . my dear?" Now to this I had no answer, and not daring to look on her, bowed head over the open book afore me yet saw it not,—for in this moment her arms crept about me and with her soft cheek to mine, she whispered: "Oh, my dear, break not your heart or mine will break with it. Such grief in your face yet never one word. Oh, I am not blind . . . I know your sorrow, I have seen love in your every look, heard it in your voice, such noble, such unselfish love as makes me very humble and . . . Oh I would die to spare you pain . . . and yet——" She said no more, but presently left me and my face wet with the sweet tears of her compassion. And all this, with her very words, I now set down here that I may read in days to come, and so reading, feel again her caressing touch and hear her broken words of pity and be blessed again by the mercy of her tears, when she is far removed. But in my mind shall ever be the sacred memory of this hour.

June 9

This morning early comes Antonia to me on deck with the foils and will have me to fence with her. So off come our coats and to it we go. And truly I find her more proficient than methought, being instant in attack, quick in recovery and feinting with such craft that twice she all-but touched me in the first rally, to my expressed admiration.

"Do I improve then, Adam?" cries she, "Do I?"

"Beyond expectation!" says I. "Your sword becomes a menace few may cope with, and your defence well nigh impregnable." Our fencing done, we walked a while, and she marvelling at this sweet gentle wind, how steadily it blows all day and every day, I told her it is named the 'Trade Wind', and great blessing to all shipmen. After this we stood to watch the wondrous blue of the sea, with the flying fish that darted above its gentle surge, and both of us leaning across this stout bulwark had so lately been red with blood and yet bore scars of steel and musket-ball.

Now presently as we stood thus, shoulder to shoulder silent, though as it were in communion, I felt her begin to tremble, and wondered therefore until, glancing round, I beheld Absalom coming towards us, who gave us Good-morrow, yet with no cheeriness of voice or look.

"In but few days, Adam," says he to me, the while he gazed on Antonia, and very doleful since she seemed to heed him no whit, "in some few days," says he, fetching a deep sigh, "we should be off the Abrollos Shoal that lieth ninety odd leagues east of Brazil, if the wind hold fair, for these are the latitudes of plaguey calms and roaring tornadoes. Treacherous seas, Adam, and veering winds very unstable and feminine, ay mighty like a woman!" So saying, he goes wandering away mighty gloomy, and Antonia staring down at the sea quick-breathing and her cheeks aglow. And presently she, too, heaves a deep sigh and with no word for me or look for Ab. away she goes in opposite direction. Whereby I judge their love is very sharp upon them both and they yet at painful logger-heads, so that the sooner 'tis spoke and they agreed, the better for both, thinks I, and straightway begin to scheme how I may contrive this to their content and happiness. The which came about with no aid of mine and in the following unexpected and tragical manner, viz.: It was in the late forenoon and few on deck, the sun being extreme hot, when out upon the quarterdeck stepped Absalom, but scarce had he appeared than from some lurking-place a man sprang upon him with flash of vicious-stabbing knife. I saw Ab. reel from the stroke, steady himself and grapple his assailant. Then even as I ran thither, I beheld Absalom, all bleeding as he was, whirl his would-be murderer aloft and heave him overboard. Now at this I checked and stood aghast, but seeing Ab. so pale and how fast he bled, I set my arm about him and so to my cabin. But in the door-way there met us Antonia who seeing him thus hurt and bloody, gives such tender cry as only loving woman's lips might utter, and runs to clasp him in the fond comfort of her arms, this Earthly Heaven. Then Absalom sweeps her up in his embrace and with her thus upon his heart and no eyes save for her, yet cried out to me, saying: "Oh, Adam, see now what wonder of joy is come upon me!"

Now as he stooped to meet her kiss, I saw her lovely face all dabbled with his blood. And so presently I turned and left them to each other, alone with their happiness.

On this same day towards evening Absalom comes to

me on deck, his wounded arm trimly bandaged and slung, and leans him beside me and for some while both of us mute.

"Well, brother Adam," says he, at last, "of what think you?" and forthright I answered:

"Of the man you drowned to-day." At this he frowns, saying: "The rogue deserved it, and 'twas better death than hanging. So enough of him. Talk we o' better thing."

"Why then," says I, "how is your wound?"

"Throbs and itches very damnably!" says he. "But this shall abate anon for I heal quickly. But I . . . I would ask favour o' thee, Adam." I asked him precisely what, being of a cautious nature, whereat he hums and ha's some while. Then, clasping sound arm about me, "Adam," says he, almost whispering, "I desire you to speak . . . to persuade Antonia that she wed me, and before we reach Jamaica." Now, greatly wondering, I demanded how this could possibly be, and where.

"Why here!" says he, stamping on the deck, "Aboardship. To-night! Smy shall marry us if only she will." Here, seeing my astonishment, he nods, saying, "Indeed, Adam, Smy, being a captain and we in mid ocean, he hath the power in law thereto, such marriages are therefore legal and binding, the world over. But she, God love her,— though my promised wife, will have us wait for Jamaica and parson. Yet I think, nay I know, a word from you shall win her to agreement. So, brother Adam, how say you?"

"No!" I answered, and instantly. "I will never try to persuade her against herself and woman's judgment, no, not I."

"Ha!" says he, eyeing me askance. "And wherefore not?" I hesitated, being much concerned and troubled, and before I might answer, Absalom starts, turns, and goes hasting to meet Antonia where she comes, though I had heard no sound of her. "Absalom," says she, leading

him back to me, "have you thanked him? Have you prayed
blessings on our Adam, as I do now? Can we ever thank
him enough? But for Adam I should have been left behind
in England with death's shadow on me! But for Adam
I should not be here,—this radiance of happiness would not
be around us, but for our dear Adam."

"Ha, true enough!" says Absalom, looking down on me
and his eyes very bright. "But for my wise brother Adam
I should ha' left thee . . . never to have known the joy
and wonder of thee. So, 'tis Adam gives thee to my love
. . . and so do I now thank God for thee, Adam."

"And oh," sighs she, "have you told him of your promise
to me? If not speak it now that I may hear it again."

"Why then, Adam," says he, slipping hand within my
arm, "when we're wed I'll go no more adventuring. I'll
be done with the sea. Instead I'll buy me a plantation and
slaves, raise tobacco and sugar cane, and bide with my
sweet wife. And by Heavens,—should we be blessed with
a son, his name shall be Adam." Now after this we were
silent all, my poor heart being too full for speech and they
regarding one another in a communion that went beyond
need of words.

"A home!" says Ab. "What blessing to find home at
last!"

"Home!" she whispered. "Oh, it will be so very nigh
to heaven it frights me lest aught of earth prevent."

"And this," says he, "is why I would have our marriage
soon . . . to-night . . . this very hour. I have spoke to
Smy and——"

"No!" says she, with a catch in her dear voice. "This
would seem no marriage."

"Yet," says he, very plaintive—humble, "true and lawful
indeed, by the ancient law o' the sea and——"

"No!" says she again, and mighty resolute, "I love not
your sea-laws."

"But, oh, my Antonia," says he, very heedful to whisper
this beloved name, yet mighty ardent.

"Nay, Absalom," she answered, whispering also, and with note of such sweet pleading that I stole away and they all unaware, so lost were they to all in this world save each other.

June 13

Coming on deck very early I find Smy gazing heavenwards like one in an ecstasy, whereupon I looked up also but seeing no more than cloudless blue, asked what he so gazed at.

"Well," says he, shaking grim head at the universe, "I watch for that which is not yet and yet shall be, or curse me for papistical Spaniard! 'Tis well you've your sea legs, Adam, for my nose warns me of a change. I smell weather in the offing." I asked if he meant a storm.

"Worse!" says he. "Somewhen, soon or late, over to wind'ard yonder you shall see 'the ox's eye'." I asked what this might be. "Tempest," he answered, "that shows first much like the eye of an ox and not much bigger, yet cometh down swiftly and with such fury o' wind as shall blow a ship's canvas to rags all in a moment, dismast or drive her bows under—down to Davy Jones. I've seen many a stout ship served so ere now." I now asked him whereabouts we were by his estimation. "Why," says he, "yonder to looard bearing sou'-westerly lieth the Island Grande wi' Santa Catalina and coast o' Brazil beyond, and these be stormy regions at this season. Howbeit, Adam, I smell tempest, and for that matter so doth Lom. You shall see us scudding under bare poles afore long." The which dismal prophecy was fulfilled and sooner than I expected. For as I sat at my studies after day of stifling heat, I was conscious of a strange, chill air and a growing darkness, riven suddenly by vivid lightning flash followed immediately by such tremendous, stunning thunderclap as I had never heard, and this merged in odd, whistling roar that appalled me. I felt the ship quake, then plunge so sheer and dizzily it seemed she must be diving headlong to the veriest deeps of ocean. And lying where this so violent movement had flung me, I waited the stifling inrush that was to drown me. But somehow this brave ship righted herself and for a moment was a lull, a strange hush wherein I heard the voice of Absalom in loud command answered by other voices and the shrill summons of Bo'sun Ned's pipe. So up I stumbled and out to a swaying deck where wet, wind-blown figures moved amid the hissing spray of monstrous waves that raved all about us and a dreadful blur of cloudy blackness above our reeling mastheads. Even as I looked, the wind smote us again, lifting the seas to engulf us,—a great, foaming wave broke inboard, filling the waist and sweeping the quarterdeck with white water so that I thought we must surely founder. But once again this noble ship freed herself and rose defiant to this raging tempest. All night long Absalom kept the deck and I with him, since no chance had any man for sleep in this fierce turbulence. And in these terrible hours I loved Absalom for his bold heart and cheery spirit where he stood by the four steersmen, conning the ship to keep her before this howling fury of wind. Came dawn at last and the tempest increasing upon us so that looking from sheltered corner upon the terror of this raging sea all lashed to foam and flattened by this great ferocity of wind, I could not think how any ship might live therein, and yet by God His mercy we do. May He have us yet in His care and in especial Antonia.

June 16

For three days we have driven before this storm and no glimpse of sun or star, so that whither we are being carried none knoweth. The poor ship's labour so violent that no man may go save by life lines rigged fore and aft, or sit or lie but must hold on against her violent rolling. And I no chance to write these days.

June 17

This day in early forenoon with Ab. on the poop, and both nigh spent for lack of sleep, when comes such blast of wind as hurled me to the lee rail there to cling for my life. In which moment, and above even this raving tumult, I heard a rending crash and beheld our foremast beat overboard, followed a moment later by the main. So lay our poor brave ship rolling helpless, buffeted by merciless seas and now battered cruelly by the shackled wreckage of her masts that smote her amain, threatening to stove her with every rushing billow. And in this dreadful calamity I prepared myself for that sharp, brief struggle in these choking waters where life must change to death and this again (as I do believe) to more glorious life. Thus I gave up all hope for the ship, but not so Ab. In this dire peril he became to me and all men the inspiration to battle still 'gainst destruction. For clapping speaking trumpet to lip, he roared above the gale: "Forrard there! Stand by, my lads, I'm with ye!" And down swaying poop-ladder went he to haul himself forward by the life-lines along foam-swept decks, and after him went I. And now he cries for knives and axes to cut the wreckage adrift ere the thunderous blows of our drifting masts breach and sink us. So to work we went, blinded by spray, staggered by rolling deck, choked and half-drowned by the waves that broke over us, we yet wrought amain to hack and hew asunder the tangle of ropes and twisted cordage. Once a great sea nigh beat me overboard but a powerful arm stayed me and Bo'sun Ned's gasping voice cheered me. And so at last we cut ourselves free of these tossing masts that were pounding our poor ship so cruelly. Thus was this peril at least averted.

June 18

To-day, thank God, the wind abating, but seas still high and ship violent as ever. This morning as Antonia, Ab., divers others and myself were in the great cabin, making shift to eat and hold on the while against the ship's violent lurches, and she making this and our consequent awkwardness reason for merriment (like the valiant soul she is) to us cometh Smy with Bo'sun Ned and the carpenter to say the ship in rolling had opened all her upper-works and seams and started the butt-ends of her planking below the waterline, and was so leaking they doubted the pumps might ever free her. At this ill news away goes Ab. to set all pumps agoing and do all that skill and determination might for the saving of our brave, sore-wounded ship.

June 19

Sea and wind falling, but alas—too late for our benefit, it seems, for despite all efforts the leak gains upon us. All this day, off and on, I have taken my turn at the pumps, though we all know this wearisome labour vain and but a means to delay the inevitable. For the *Bold Adventuress* is doomed. I write this with grief and therewith pain of body, my hands being sore blistered from the pumps. And our ill-fated ship quite steady now save for long, sleepy roll ever and anon that proves her waterlogged and soon or late must sink.

Moved by this sad thought I went forth to look on her, and great my sorrow to behold this once proud and stately vessel no more than woeful hulk and storm-beaten ruin. Now as I stood thus grieving, to me comes Antonia to slip her hand within my arm (with never a word) and lead me to my own cabin where sat Smy with open book afore him, this New Testament of King James, and with Absalom standing beside him. Now seeing what was to do, a faintness came on me and for a moment all things dimmed, perchance because of my much late exertions. So, there in my cabin, while the doomed ship was slowly sinking beneath us, these two were wed. Scarce was this done and I wished them every happiness, speaking from my very heart, than I went forth on deck and there met Sir Benjamin with Sir G. D'Arcy, they watching where men were busied casting loose the boats, pinnace, long-boat, yawl, etc.

"Thank God," says Sir George, "the boats took no damage; these shall now be our deliverance except we have another storm."

"Ay," groans Sir Benj, "or we perish by famine or thirst, or be taken to slave for damned Portugals or cursed Spaniards, or are whipped to death aboard their foul gallies, or tortured in the vile Inquisition, or slain by Indians, or——"

"Hold there, Ben, God ha' mercy, hold!" cries Sir George. "Pluck up heart now, let our late salvation be assurance of our future safety. How say you, Mr. Adam?"

"Ay, truly," I answered him, "if death come what matter the how of it so it be sure?"

Then down went I to help with the boats, and here found Smy with the Bo'sun, and both scowling to windward, and on my asking the reason for their gloom, Smy growled:

"The sooner we're away the better, Adam, for I like not the look o' things, eh, Bo'sun?"

"No, sir," answers Ned, "nor me neether. There be more foul weather acoming, or I'm a lubberly Dutchman, which I ain't!" So presently back went I to collect my papers with the books and instruments given me by poor Amos Perrin and (most especially) for my father's sword. Being here and alone I opened my Journal to set down these that are, I think, the last words I shall ever write herein. The Future is very dark and with perils abounding and whether I am to live or die is now all one to me since life hath so little to offer and death indeed may give back to me my long-lost mother and noble father. So if I go now to my death, my last prayer on this ship shall be— Lord God let Antonia be happy in this life and hereafter. Amen. And now is great ado and commotion on deck, so will

Here endeth the Journal of Adam Penfeather writ aboard the *Bold Adventuress* lost at sea, June 19, 1638.

And here also ends the First Book of this Narration.

BOOK TWO

CHAPTER XXIII

TELLS HOW THEY RODE THE STORM

"BAIL! Bail for your lives!"
    "Shake out a reef or we'm pooped!"
"Madman, you'll drown us!"
"Lubber, belay your chaffer! Shake out a reef there!"
Adam gasped to shivering wakefulness and sat up
dizzily, to be half choked by wind and flying spray; he
blinked and rubbed the water from his eyes to see a stumpy
mast with shred of sail, the awful nearness of monstrous,
hissing seas rushing to engulf him and, between his cowering body and this pursuing menace, the dripping, wind-
smitten form of Bo'sun Ned at the tiller of a boat now
soaring against angry sky, now plunging down beneath
the curving, green chasm of following wave.

"Bail! Oh . . . bail for your lives!" And now Adam
saw the man who thus cried was Sir Benjamin bailing
feverishly with sodden hat, with Sir George D'Arcy, and
beyond them many other men who wrought as desperately
with buckets, with pots, caps, shoes, hands,—anything to
free them of this invading, murderous water; but nowhere
did his eager, questing eyes see any sign of Antonia or
Absalom. And so at last he turned back to the Bo'sun and
shouted above howling wind:

"Oh, Ned . . . Ned . . . is my brother here?" And,
crouched against blinding spindrift the Bo'sun answered:

"No, sir. Bleeve he was took aboard the Cap'n's boat
. . . the longboat, sir."

"What o' the ship?"

"Lost, sir . . . Davy Jones."

"Where are . . . the other boats?"

"Only the Lord o' Marcy knoweth, sir."

"Can any boat live . . . in such sea?"

"Ay . . . mayhap,—if handled sailorly. But should she broach-to 'tis the end o' we. Ay—sure-ly!"

"How came I here, Ned?"

"You was washed adown . . . quarterdeck ladder when . . . t'other squall struck us and . . . laying onconscious would ha' been left, only . . . Smidge found ee."

"Where is the boy . . . Smidge . . . where?"

"Forrard somewheers."

"Can I anyways help you, Ned?"

"Ay, off wi' your shoe and bail, sir, the lighter she be the easier she rides."

So Adam bailed, as he did most things, with all his might, till a plump, wet hand met his and he looked up into the pale, wet face of Sir Benjamin.

"Thought ye dead, Adam," he bellowed. "There's blood i' your hair!"

"The sea shall cure that."

"The sea, ay," wailed Sir Benjamin pettishly, "this cursed sea shall cure us o' living, like as not! And death by drowning is no fit end for a gentleman,—steel or a bullet, but—water! Ha, 'sblood, I quake!"

All day they drove, lashed by hissing spray, buffeted by hooting wind, tossed on foaming seas that threatened to swamp them, yet thanks to their stout craft and the Bo'sun's deft hand upon the tiller, they rode these fierce billows until as night drew on and the sun aflame in broken cloud, seas and wind gentled and, for the time being, their danger was past. Yet now it was that Sir Benjamin, being wet and miserable, began to make loud lament to all and sundry:

"'S death, now here's damnable coil and cursed pickle! Bo'sun, where a plague are we according to your reckoning, —where?"

"Somewheers off the Abrollos Shoal, I'd say, your

honour. Wi' Brazil to looard and the Main right afore us.''

"Then are we poor English in mighty parlous case, by God! Enemies' seas all about us! For the cursed Dutch don't love us, the damned Portugals fear us and the bloody-minded Spaniards hate us! Prison, slavery or the vile torments o' the Inquisition!''

"Why now then," said Adam, seeing all men greatly downcast by these words, "since God hath protected us in the past, let us pray He so do in the future, to be our ultimate salvation. Come now, let us call on our merciful Providence. Will you, Sir Benjamin, lead us in prayer?''

"Nay, I've no gift that way, Adam, and small belief.''

"Then, will you, Sir George?''

"No, Mr. Adam, for though I've belief, I have no eloquence thereto.''

"What o' thee, Bo'sun Ned?''

"Ay, I would, sir, right hearty, but begs excuse being a bit rusty like.''

"Will any of you men forrard there,—John Fenn, Martin Frant?'' He was answered by shaken heads, hoarse muttering or sullen silence. So now, therefore, crouched in this storm-tossed boat, Adam lifted hands and voice, praying thus:

"Almighty God, Lord of Battle and Storm, Thou giver of life and death—that is yet the loving and merciful Father of all men, look down on us thy lost children in this Thy desolation of waters and be now our comfort. As we are brothers now in adversity let us live brothers henceforth to each other's help. Make us strong to endure Thy will, to suffer all things valiantly since only by suffering may a man prove his worth and manhood. Guide us, O Heavenly Father, bring us safe out of all perils from fury of tempest and rage of foes, and so at last to thine everlasting glory . . . Amen!''

Now after this, all men turned to Adam with looks more hopeful, yet none spoke until Bo'sun Ned, glancing

up at cloudy night sky and round about upon darkening
ocean, nodded and bade them let out another reef in their
sail.

So, all night long, this small, lonely boat drove through
a windy darkness and turbulent ocean that was bearing
them none knew whither, till came the dawn to show them
a wide foam-smitten sea where no ship sailed and nothing
moved save their own, solitary craft. But presently up
came the sun in glory to warm their poor, shivering bodies
and hearten them with promise of new life.

CHAPTER XXIV

TELLS HOW AND WHY ADAM MADE HIMSELF CAPTAIN

IN this boat, as in all craft that ever swam, were of necessity two orders of society, namely—the few to command (aft at the steerage since Authority sits at the helm) and, forward of this, the many who must obey. But in this crowded space these many, with some few exceptions, began to show themselves sullen and unruly, and the chief of these the man Perez who, being a powerful man and moreover feeling himself now freed of all authority and fear of the lash, became ever more fiercely defiant and quarrelsome and was abetted by others of his like, especially at meal-times. This mutinous conduct reached its climax on the morning of this second day when Perez dashed his pannikin of water over his neighbour, cursing him fiercely.

"Bo'sun," said Adam, softly, "pray lend me your knife."

Perez was yet flourishing his pannikin and making uproar when, all in a moment, came a hand to twist sinewy fingers in his hair, with another hand to lay the keen edge of a knife to his throat, then, as he crouched paralysed by the cold threat of this steel, his head was wrenched violently back till his fearful eyes stared up into the small, fierce visage down-bent above him.

"Beastly rogue!" snarled Adam. "Accursed fool, will ye waste and spill the water is the life of us all? Will ye raise mutinies in the very face o' Providence? Sit still or I'll slit your vile throat! Hearkee now,—raise your hand in strife again and 'twill be my knife in your ribs and your foul carcass overboard to poison the fishes! Now go forrard into the bow, rogue Perez, and bide there. And for your waste o' the precious water you drink none this day.

Go! Make way, forrard there!" Hand at throat and eyes wide in dumbly fearful amaze, Perez stumbled forward and all men staring on Adam in a like amazement,—this small, fierce man who grasped glittering knife so purposefully and scanned every face with eyes so keen beneath black brows and wind-tossed silvery hair.

"Now hear ye, shipmates all!" cried he, "though poor, lost castaways yet are we English sailormen, to quit ourselves as such, dreading naught, so my lads, Dreadnoughts let us be. And now, hear this! Henceforth I take charge of ye all to rule ye and command. Henceforth I am your captain to be obeyed and followed. Now if any man o' ye deny, let him step forth and match his knife with this o' mine. How say ye, shipmates, is it mutiny and murder or sailorly duty, are ye against me or to follow me, Dreadnoughts all? How say ye?"

For a moment all were silent, then, from midway in this crowded boat, up went a great, powerful hand:

"Ay!" cried Martin Frant. "Ay, ay, Master Adam, Captain you be!" Scarce had he spoken than from somewhere beside him up went another hand very small and slim and therewith the high, shrill voice of little Smidge.

"Ay, ay, Cap'n Adam, and so says I, Cap'n you be!"

And now spoke John Fenn, the Master Gunner:

"So be it, lads. For Mr. Adam can fight as well as pray, so—a cheer for Captain Adam Penfeather!"

And thus, in this wide desolation of waters, cheer they did, and heartily as only English sailors may.

"Why then," said Adam, looking round upon them all, "God make me able! And now John Fenn and Bo'sun Ned I take you for mates first and second. Sir Benjamin, I pray you take charge of such arms as we possess and see them stowed abaft. Sir George, will you oversee our store of provisions, food and drink, the which shall now be strictly rationed. Martin Frant, you are bo'sun. Now is this known and agreed?"

"Ay, ay, sir!" cried they one and all, and cheerily.

"And what o' me, Cap'n?" piped little Smidge.

"You," answered Adam, beckoning, "you shall be my own seadog to go ever beside me. Well now, Martin Frant, how many do we number?"

"Twenty and seven, sir, all told."

"Then choose your watches, and let all things go sailorly and as aboardship. First let us all turn to and clean ourselves and the boat and set all things trim and orderly. This done, Martin, take a spare sail, if we have one, and rig it for awning against the sun to our comfort. But, shipmates, above all let us each and every keep bold hearts, be of cheery fellowship, trusting in our own manhood, and the God that made us."

And so began this journey that was to test them all, body and soul.

CHAPTER XXV

HERE FOLLOW DIVERS PAGES OF ADAM'S LOG CONCERNING HIS COMPANIONS AND THEIR GRIEVOUS SUFFERINGS IN THE BOAT

TO his grief Adam found that his father's sword, this treasured relic and splendid weapon, had been left to go down in the ship and, with this, all his books, charts, instruments and papers. Thus despite all his past laborious studies he must needs trust to the Bo'sun's dead reckoning for guidance to bring them ashore ere all provisions failed and they perish miserably; and the nearest land, according to the Bo'sun and John Fenn, who had sailed this ocean before, was the coast of Brazil, to larboard, south-westerly. So thitherward, by stars and the boat's compass, they set their course.

Now it chanced that among the few possessions that Sir George had brought away was a small pocket memorandum with pencil attached, the which Adam no sooner glimpsed than his eyes glistened.

"Sir," said he, impulsively, "if you could allow me the favour of a page or so in your book I should be extreme grateful, for I would note down the names of these men the Lord hath set in my charge, together with the goods and comforts He hath blessed us withal." Gladly Sir George bestowed this book wherein Adam duly wrote down the names of these castaways, his first crew, with his estimation concerning their chances of life and death; which book, by some miracle, was preserved and divers of its pages, written small and neatly to begin but scrawled large and wavering towards the end, are here interpolated.

June 20

Those with me in the *Adventuress*.

Her Yawl.

Name	Condition	Remarks added later
Sir Benj. Trigg .	Knight .	A mighty swearer and grumbler
Sir Geo. D'Arcy .	do. .	A gentleman patient and resolute
John Fenn .	First Officer	A valiant and trusty man
Ned Bowser .	Second do. .	A right seaman and mighty help
Martin Frant .	Boatswain .	do.
Charles called Smidge .	Ship's boy .	A right seadog
Joel Bym .	Seaman .	do.
Hosea Sawyer .	do. .	
Thos. Rendal .	do. .	Died of knife thrust, July 29
Robt. Small .	do. .	Died of knife, July 28
Silas Guppy .	do. .	
Giles Tregenza .	do. .	
Job May .	do. .	
Sim Hopkins .	do. .	
James Clark .	do. .	Lost overboard in the night, Aug. 8
Charles Eady .	do. .	Died in the boat, Aug. 9
Nicholas Cobb .	do. .	
John Diggle .	do. .	Died in the boat, Aug. 6
Ian McLean .	do. .	do., Aug. 3
James Hudson .	do. .	Went mad and leapt overboard, Aug. 6
Timothy Sprake	do. .	
Wm. Tenby .	do. .	Died mad of drinking sea water, Aug. 5
James Hawk .	do. .	Died in the boat
Matt. Appleby .	do. .	

Name	Condition	Remarks added later
Jimbo . .	Steward	. A blackamoor great of body and heart
Juan Perez .	A rogue	. Shot and killed by me in the boat, July 31
Adam Penfeather	Captain	. Who, God aiding, shall

do all that is possible for the preservation of these men.
To the which end I have had collected and carefully
examined everything that may be of use, and here set
the good against the evil, thus:

Perils to be expected	Blessings to our gratitude
Storm and tempest	. A stout boat and able mariners
Dangers of Mutiny	. The arms all stowed abaft and six resolute men.
Rage of foes . .	. 15 firelocks, 12 pistols with powder, and ball, 14 swords, 7 axes, 25 sheath knives.
Hunger . . .	. 2 casks salt beef, 1 of pork with 3 bags ship's biscuits.
Thirst . . .	. 4 small kegs of water. (To be strictly rationed forthwith.)
Sickness . .	. 1 medicine chest small and very inadequate.

Now though Adam is careful to set down much concerning winds and currents, squalls, strange fish, baffling airs
and maddening calms, with mention of their 'torment of
sunshine' despite their awning, there is about it a certain
monotony might weary the reader. So, passing this record
of sufferings becoming ever more acute, we come to this
—in a writing that begins to show much less neat and
regular.

July 28

Still no breath of wind and the sun now a plague, his
beams, reflecting from glassy ocean, a blinding torment.
Most of the men deject and some mutinous again by reason
of the thirst that affects us all, cry out upon me very

bitterly, demanding or begging a sup of water to appease them. And of those crying loudest are Juan Perez, Tom Rendal and Robt. Small. These so violent against me, I show them the pistol I must keep ever by me to protect this precious water that is now our very life, yet such pitiful little of it remaining that, in my heart, I know we must all perish except we sight land or are blessed with rain. At mess time great pity is it to see how all eyes glare at the water Sir G. D'Arcy doles out from our last small keg, a quarter pannikin each man and this no more than mere swallow can scarce moisten our parched tongues. Some there are who gulp this little at once and groan for more, and others who sip and sip till it be gone, —whereby came tragedy on this wise, viz.: Tom Rendal having swallowed his ration, sees Robt. Small sipping thus, snatches the pannikin and spills all is left to Robt. of this most precious water, whereon Robt. draws knife and stabs Tom desperately who, none the less, cuts Robt. into the throat whereof he instantly died and very bloodily. I did what might be for Tom Rendal, and thereafter said a prayer and hove Robt. Small overboard. And all of us mighty downcast.

July 29

This forenoon died Thomas Rendal of his wound so, after prayer for his soul, committed his body to the sea. Our water nearly gone, so that I told the crew our portion must now be reduced by a half that we may perchance live longer to hope for land or sight of some ship. The sea a flat calm and still no wind, and the soft lapping of water against the boat but an aggravation to our torment that increases on us with every hour, and suffering dreadfully manifest in every face. And, in this long agony of dying, strange it is to see how differently men do show from that expected of them. Sir G. D'Arcy uncomplaining, oft now sinks in stupor. Sir Benj. now prays with fervour, cursing only by habit and then feebly. Ned sings or trieth

and, finding this vain, weeps in his hand. John Fenn sits
long hours quite mumchance, yet when he speaks his
words are cheery. Martin Frant is forever looking for the
ship that never comes, and twice in the night had cried
'twixt sleep and wake: Sail ho! and to our bitter dis-
appointment. Little Smidge lies at my feet and as oft
as I touch or speak him, smiles so that I could weep for
the young, brave soul of him. The other poor men snarl
and sigh and moan, sleeping and awake, and many now
cry out on me for their murderer that I will not let them
drink, and I sit meekly dumb, since strength and life are
failing me, only I keep faithful watch on the water, all
that is left, that none steal it that yet may prove our
salvation.

Aug. 5

About noon Wm. Tenby, against all advice, drank greatly
of sea-water and towards evening was seized of a madness
and jumped to death or any might prevent.

Aug. 6

This morning at dawn came a breeze to cheer and refresh
us, yet later died away and we the more woeful. Towards
evening John Diggle cried with great voice dreadful to
hear, and within that hour was dead. Also on this grievous
day, because of cruel sun James Hudson took a fit and leapt
overboard.

Aug. 8

Calling the roll this morning Martin reports a man
missing, which proved to be James Clark, who we suppose
stole himself overboard to die soon rather than by this
slow agony of thirst.

Aug. 9

To-morrow, except it be God His will to send us a ship,
I suppose we must die all. Our water now so minished
there is scarce a gill for each man. No wind and this sun

a fiery torment. This noon Charles Eady is dead. . . .
A day of agony wherein Death creepeth very near. . . .
This night, waking from troublous dozing, I hear customary
sounds of anguish with delirious ravings. And, thinks I,
better to have drowned with the brave ship than this
slow agony of dying. Strove to pray, yet could not, my
mind being in strange daze and dazzle of wild thoughts.
I now beheld a moving shape in the darkness, dull gleam
of steel, a hand outreached fumbling where lay our few
remaining sips of water. So reaching my pistol whence
it lay, I leaned forward and saw this rogue thief was Perez
and shot him into the face that he sank and lay asprawl
at my feet and none heeding. Then fell I again to my
daze and dazzle, nor roused till Ned shook me and Smidge
cried. Then I saw Perez slain and his blasted head beside
the water keg.

Aug. 11

Morning.

I think many lie dead and all nigh thereto, for none
able to stir save only myself. And this do mind me how
Perks said that men little and small are most vital. Night
cometh and death   here is the end of all suffering
          think Sir G.   dead at my feet   brave
little Smidge all dead now   they lie still   is
blessed relief   long pain soon I too   done my
uttermost best. So   this last hour   Antonia,
my beloved, and only   Pray God   spared her
like suffering   bring her to joy happiness and me
through death to His abiding Glory. Amen.

Here ends Adam's last entry aboard the boat, written
in failing hand very hard to decipher and with words
omitted.

CHAPTER XXVI

HOW ADAM LED THEM UP OUT OF SLAVERY

THE *Santa Barbara* galleasse, urged by her many groaning slaves, was making for the rich and populous city of St. Juan de Leon; upon her gilded poop, beneath silken awning and surrounded by his officers and gentlemen, sat Don Esteban Peralta, Captain General of the Coast and Governor of Panama. Tugging at one of the great starboard oars, shackled hand and foot, his lean body scarred by the whip, blackened by fierce suns, agleam with sweat, ridged and knotted with the thews of constant labour, Adam Penfeather swayed and swung in time with the stroke; back and forth, to and fro, with no respite, eyes shut against the sun, mouth agape for air, he rose and fell to the never ceasing swing of the long, heavy oar.

From aft came sounds of laughter, with the music of flute, harp and viol on an air made sweet with burning spices; around Adam was the sobbing moan of driven men, crack of whips answered by squeal of pain or snarl of hate, with the foul reek and stench of these crowded rowing-benches, and in his desolate heart the voiceless cry:

"How long, O Lord, how long?"

They rowed four to the oar, with twenty oars a side, for a great and powerful vessel was this *Santa Barbara* galleasse. Immediately before Adam was the brawny back of Bo'sun Ned, beyond him laboured a groaning fellow with back as wide, as sunburned and muscular but more whip-scarred,—and this moaning, sweating much-beaten wretch none other than Sir Benjamin, transformed by hardship from plump pomposity to a lean, great-muscled ferocity. Scattered among the other beaten slaves were Sir George

D'Arcy, John Fenn, Martin Frant, Silas Guppy, Simon Hopkins, Timothy Sprake, Nicholas Cobb, Matthew Appleby, Giles Tregenza, and Jimbo, the great negro, all that survived of the twenty-seven, Adam's first crew.

Sway and creak of the oars, pant and groan of labouring humanity, these men that, used and beaten like savage animals, now snarled and hissed or cowered to the whip like the savage animals they were indeed, or would be. So the great oars swung and swayed to the beat of heavy timing mallets as they urged the *Santa Barbara* upon her course.

The sun was declining westward when the stroke of these mallets ceased and the oars were stilled at last, for they were in the harbour entrance guarded by its two grim castles wherefrom drooped the golden standards of mighty Spain. Trumpets shrilled from the galleasse answered by thunderous salute from ashore, and the *Santa Barbara* paddled her stately way towards this goodly town, her home port, that rose in terraces from seashore to the green foothills that sheltered it, with lofty mountains beyond.

And now at word of command, the ponderous oars were swung inboard and the galleasse glided gently to her berth alongside the quay while the slaves, drooping in weariness, clashed their fetters and muttered harshly or cursed fiercely under their breaths and in half-a-dozen different tongues, and none more fiercely bitter than Sir Benjamin as he rubbed sweat from his scowling eyes with great, gnarled fists.

And now as they waited thus, growling like chained and hungry beasts, while the lordly Governor, his gentlemen, officers and soldiers went ashore, Sir Benjamin turned to glare across brawny shoulder at one who sat dumb in his misery, gazing away across the harbour with haggard, patient eyes.

"What, Adam, ho, Adam, are ye praying again? Are ye supplicating your so just and merciful God, are ye praying? But to what avail? What o' mercy hath your

Lord o' mercy ever shown us, ay—or justice? What ha'
we ever done to merit this hell o' shame and misery?
Where's the justice o' this and where the mercy? And
where is He, this God o' yours, if there be a God? Back in
England, mayhap, along o' law and order,—not in this
abomination!" And with his woeful gaze in the one direction, Adam answered, gently:

"All I know is that He liveth . . . to be our salvation
soon or late. . . . Without this belief, this sure hope, I
. . . should run mad and perish like the brutes."

"Brutes, d'ye say? Well, what are we but beastly
brutes, foul o' body, sick o' soul, to labour thus in our
sweat and filth until, like as beasts, we sink to brutish
death? Call now on your God and see an He will deliver
us! Beseech Him to a miracle on our behalf."

"Ay, I will, Ben, as I have done . . . very oft."

"Yet bide we in hell, Adam! Two years of anguish since
that accursed Spanish ship plucked us from clean death
in our boat to die thus foully! Two long years o' shame
and agony."

"One year, eleven months and four days, Ben."

"And each day, Adam, each hour a link in our chain o'
misery. Look,—ha, look around us on these human brutes,
these foul two-legged beasts that once were men,—look
and know, as I do, that there is no mercy, no justice and
no God!"

"And yet," sighed Adam, "and yet He liveth! He was
the God of my—father."

"Ay," snarled Sir Benjamin, "and left the poor gentleman to hang! I say there is no God, no——"

"Lord, sir," exclaimed Bo'sun Ned, hoarsely, "avast
now and likewise belay! God or no, we'm Englishmen to
take rough along o' smooth and make the best o' both,
so what I says is,—let's do 't. And now, Cap'n Adam,
what might you be a-staring at so on-common hard, sir?"

"Yonder, Ned, the galleon," and he nodded wearily
where, with cables hove short, rode a great and splendid

ship brave in gilding and new paint, from lofty forecastle to towering poop with its railed galleries, glittering windows and tall crucifix between great poop lanterns and the name *Santissima Trinidad* in richly carved and gilded characters.

"Ah, they tell she'm a treasure ship, sir, and doo to bear away for Spain on to-morrow's flood. They builds 'em big and vast, do these Spanishers. Ay, she's a eyeful, lots o' paint and gold carvins, but she'll be heavy on her helm, I'll warrant me, and lubberly on a bowline."

"And her people," sighed Adam, "nigh all her company will be ashore to-night for the fiesta."

"Ay, sir, you can hear the townsfolk a-twangin' and a-tooning up their music a'ready. A banket wi' the Governor and all they dons and senoras and——"

A trumpet nearby drowned his voice; hoarse commands were shouted; the slaves were loosed from oar and bench to be marshalled in double rank. Then, jangling in the chains they must always wear, they stumbled ashore between their armed guards, through a narrow street and so to a long barracoon that was their prison when ashore, into which they were herded like so many cattle and where, like cattle, they were fed with coarse though bounteous fare to keep them in full strength, and so were locked and bolted in for the night.

Here in this foetid gloom, Adam made his way to that corner beside the massive door which he had made his own by past strife, and where he was used to sleep surrounded by these twelve survivors of the twenty-seven he was wont to call his Dreadnoughts. Here now he sank down, weary back against rough, stone wall and all about him the usual sights and sounds,—fierce, hairy faces, naked bodies, snarls and oaths, English and French, Spanish and Dutch, with other tongues besides; a harsh, discordant babel accompanied by the never-ending clash and jangle of fetters.

Adam closed his eyes, made himself deaf and let his mind soar free—and thus, by the blessed magic of Imagination, he was out and away from this sordid misery; he was a man of great achievements seated in the cabin of his own ship, plotting a course should bring him to the Golden Haven of Desire where, instead of wealth or fame, Love was to meet him with yearning arms outstretched in glad welcome, arms that were to clasp and lift him high as Heaven.

A sudden hand clutched his arm, shattering the dream very painfully, and Sir George D'Arcy spoke in his ear; now this hand was quivering and this voice uncertain, breathless with some deep emotion:

"Adam . . . ! Oh, Adam. . . . !"

"Yes, George."

"A voice . . . by God, I heard a voice, Adam . . . a voice from without . . . beyond the door . . . and a scratching . . . a scratching, d'ye hear? Either I'm mad at last or dreaming . . . which I'm neither . . . someone called your name beyond the door . . . out yonder in the free air . . . the cool, clean night. Listen!"

"I hear nothing, George."

"No . . . no—nor I, now. Mayhap I was indeed but dreaming. Ay, dreaming as I ever do, Adam, that this misery is but fearsome nightmare and that soon I shall wake to find it so. And unless I do . . . and soon, Adam, I shall kill myself and be done, for I can bear little more of this."

"Hush!" whispered Adam, sitting up suddenly. "Listen, George, ha—listen!" A soft, faint tapping on the massive door, a vague, muffled whispering beneath it.

"Cap'n Adam. . . . Oh, Cap'n Penfeather—ahoy!"

Adam was down upon his face, whispering through the gap 'twixt door and worn flagstone:

"Yes . . . yes! I am here. Who wants me. . . . ? I am Adam." And close to his ear came the whispered answer:

"'Tis only me, sir, your old seadog Smidge. I 've stole the key . . . guards and all be drunk to-night, so I took the key and be agoing for to open door."

"Easy, Smidge! Softly, old seadog,—unlock but open slowly, and but an inch or so . . . careful now, old shipmate!" And presently came faint sound of oiled lock, squeak of heavy bolts, unheeded by any save Adam and D'Arcy. Then as the ponderous door moved, Adam arose, whispering.

"Warn our Dreadnoughts, George, them only, bid 'em stand by and wait for me." Then, unheard and unseen, Adam edged himself through the narrow opening—out into the sweet, cool freshness of the night, and closing the door, beheld, in the starry dusk, a small shape dight in the splendid livery of a page.

"Smidge!" he whispered. "Oh, God bless thee, Smidge, I—— Ha, what's yonder?"

"Only drunk soldiers, sir, a-singing i' the guard-house."

"How many?"

"Two—three, I dunno exackly, Cap'n."

"Bide here—no, get you to Ned and John Fenn, bid them go round and warn every man to be ready yet silent to wait my coming . . . silent or all's amiss."

Then Adam turned and, speeding on naked, soundless feet, came to the guard-house, so long familiar, where lights gleamed and a drunken voice sang unmelodiously, and peering in through open doorway he saw four men, three who sprawled fast asleep and snoring and one whose misfortune it was to be awake and sober enough to glimpse the brown, sinewy arm outstretched towards the naked sword that chanced in reach. The man started afoot, groped for the pistol on littered table and, in that moment, choked and died. . . .

Then, sword in hand, back sped Adam to hear a murmurous hum from the roused slaves and stifled clink of fetters. Then Adam swung wide the door and standing before them outlined against starry background, lifted sword and spoke in hushed tone and well as he might in English, French and Spanish:

"Silence for your lives! In the harbour lies ship to our

deliverance, her officers and crew ashore, she is our only hope of life; except we take her we be all lost men to die by fire, noose or torment, so take her we must and silent as maybe . . . keep your chains from least rattle. Now line up, two by two, and follow me."

And so these men, made desperate by cruel usage and cunning by fear of death as cruel, followed Adam's white head—out and away from bestial suffering to chance of freedom and hope for new life. A grimly silent company, they flitted through the dark, by narrow alleys and crooked ways, with ears on the strain and eyes that glared watchful on the night, hands griping silenced fetters ready to smite and slay for dear freedom, they followed the gleam of Adam's silvery hair.

From the town above them came sounds of life and revelry, with fitful strains of music; from the harbour below them rose the sighing, languorous murmur of the flowing tide. They reached the haven at last, this grim and silent company of ghosts; they launched the nearest boats lying there, manned and paddled them cautiously, with oars, stretchers, or eager hands, towards where, riding at her moorings, lay the great galleon *Santissima Trinidad* with none aboard save drowsy anchor watch. Nearer they crept until she loomed mightily above them, a vast shape in the velvety darkness. Boat after boat they reached her, and man after man they boarded her, climbing her lofty sides with gripping fingers and clutching toes; by port-cills, broad rubbing-strakes and carved mouldings they clambered up—and up; then some man's fetters clashed loudly, a voice challenged from above to end with a dreadful suddenness.

Panting and breathless Adam surmounted the broad bulwark, and with him, after him, his desperate company, mostly experienced sailors, who instantly set to work, some swarming aloft to loose sails, others to cast off moorings, while John Fenn and his fellows looked to the ordnance.

Suddenly, from somewhere below, a voice crying out in

Spanish was answered by an English curse, this followed by the thunderous discharge of a caliver.

"Rouse away!" shouted Adam, running towards the steerage.

"Ho, sheets and tacks!" roared Ned, amidships.

"Gunners, stand by!" shouted John. "Here be matches a-plenty, thank the Lord! Bring me yon lanthorn, Sim! Ha, the dons are yare to us at last, they've marked summat amiss! Be ready now!" Even as he spoke, lights twinkled in the castles to right and left of them, drums beat and trumpets blared a wild alarm. Then came the shattering roar of cannon to fill the night with thunderous tumult and echo as awfully in the distant mountains.

And at this most fateful moment that was to be their death or salvation, Adam standing upon this lofty poop, in his filthy rags and scarred nakedness, raised sinewy arms to starry heaven and cried aloud:

"A wind, oh God! Now of Thy kind mercy, send us a wind!" And, like an answer, it came—to fan his haggard brow, to stir his long, white hair, while down below him on the quarterdeck, Sir Benjamin, looking back on the town where bells now clamoured and many lights hovered, exclaimed very piously:

"Ha, thank God for this good wind!"

"Ay, she feels it!" chuckled Ned, with his gaze on the huge bellying sails, and then came he clambering up the poop ladder where Adam conned the ship, with Silas Guppy and Nicholas Cobb at the steerage.

"Hard a-larboard! Easy . . . as she goes! Starboard,— so! Amidships. Steady as she is!"

Slowly the huge vessel gathered way, while guns boomed from the castles and their shot began to whizz ever nearer, what time from town and harbour came growing din and confused uproar.

"'Tis pity," said Adam, looking thitherward, "ay, 'tis great pity we might not have fired their shipping. See, Ned, there's one making after us already!"

"Ay, but we've the wind of her, Cap'n."

"How many are we, think you, Ned?"

"There's a hundred and sixty-eight o' the galley, sir, but with others we be somewheers about a hundred and seventy-four, sir, I reckon, for——"

"No! A hundred and seventy-five, sirs!" piped a shrill voice. "For here's me, sir, and wiv a cutlash, Cap'n Adam, sir!" And from somewhere appeared little Smidge and on his shoulder a sword long as himself.

"Ah, Smidge!" cried Adam, clasping an arm about him. "Now God forgive me, I'd forgotten thee! How came ye aboard, shipmate?"

"Froo one o' the gun ports, sir, that's how I got me this yere sword so fine, and nobody stayed me 'cause o' my Spanish rig. Ye see, Cap'n, I were page to the Governor's lady, I were, and can speak the lingo—somewhat."

"And but for thee, Smidge, we were all of us back yonder . . . caged like so many animals. Ay, 'tis thyself hast made us men again. Now for this, Smidge, I make thee my own seadog and special officer to be ever near me." Thus said Adam, to the boy's tremulous joy, while his keen eyes watched now the harbour astern and now the headlands before them.

"Below there!" he cried suddenly. "Ho, John, 'tis no matter for the castle batteries, they'll soon be out o' range, man our stern-chase guns, for we're pursued."

"Ay, ay, sir!" cried John, cheerily. "Lord, 'tis sweet to tread deck again and handle such guns, cannons royal and culverin! With such we might battle a whole fleet—of dons or Portugals."

Presently up came the moon in glory to show them the city, growing ever smaller, its white houses agleam against a vast background of dark forest and soaring mountains, —and before the broad, white decks of this great ship where many dark figures were so eagerly at work with hoarse laughter, rolling sea-oaths and snatches of song, rejoicing in their new found freedom and the wide ocean all aglitter with moonlight and stirred by freshening wind.

But Adam looked oftenest where astern of them came a ship of war under great press of sail; suddenly from her bow came puff of white smoke and a round shot hummed through the sail above his head, but as the report woke the echoes, it was answered by the harsher roar of the *Santissima Trinidad's* heavy stern-chasers aimed by John Fenn, and, when the smoke cleared, the pursuer's fore-topmast was seen to hang in flapping ruin.

Then from Adam's company rose such cheer as these shores had seldom or never heard, a deep-lunged bellow of savage exultation, the jubilant cry of slaves becoming men once more.

And so, with a fair wind and none left to bar her course, the great *Santissima Trinidad* bore out and away for the open sea.

CHAPTER XXVII

HOW ADAM TOOK COMMAND OF THE
GREAT GALLEON

HO, for the piping song of wind in cordage and rigging, with creak of straining blocks and mighty yards! Ho, for the surge and hiss of tumbling seas at foaming fore-foot, for the joyous lift and roll of this great ship that is bearing them out from the black hell of misery and servitude, from stripes and shame—away across windswept ocean to a new life and the Golden Indies.

And now, feeling something of this rapture, these men that had so lately been slavish wretches cowering to the whip, made haste to rid them of their fetters, shameful badges of their degradation, and then to sing and dance, to cut capers and play leap-frog like so many happy boys, but thereafter to show themselves for the savagely revengeful brutes hardship and bestial usage had made of them (Adam included) and in the following manner.

With Jimbo, his gigantic negro steward, in attendance, Adam was blessing himself with a hot bath and sensing all the luxurious comfort of it, when to him ran little Smidge, tumbling over his ponderous sword with haste.

"Oh, Cap'n Adam," he panted, "they've found they Spanish dons as was hiding below and be a-dragging of 'em up for to kill and murder 'em! Oh, sir, come and stay 'em . . . come quick!"

Up leapt Adam, snatched on his breeches, or what remained of them, caught Smidge's sword from him and ran out on deck where the great, tropic moon made all things plain to see and showed a howling scurry of naked savages who, with merciless fists and clawing fingers were at their dire work on one whose pale, blood-spattered face and torn clothing were evidence of horrors yet to be. . . .

But in upon them burst Adam, a small, silent, hard-smiting fury using the flat of heavy blade to such dire effect that the raving mob scattered and showed two— the half-swooning Spaniard and the hairy, inhuman ferocity whose powerful clutching hands had begun their dreadful work.

"Loose him!" cried Adam; the hairy savage roared and spat, so Adam smote him down. Snarling, the fellow made to rise, took Adam's bare foot in his face and was dashed to the deck half stunned; yet even then he would have risen, but squealed instead to the goring steel that nailed him to the planking. Then with foot on the man's hairy throat, Adam laughed, wrenched free the sword and fronted the many-handed menace that now threatened him.

"Off . . . ye dogs!" he panted, twirling the long blade in sinewy hand. "Back, ye vile scum or I'll bring bloody death on ye. I'm Captain here . . . ay, Captain o' this ship to be obeyed, d'ye hear? Now forrard two o' ye and take me up this two-legged beast. Heave him overboard if dead, if not—tie him up till I can tend him—away with him. The rest o' ye fall in,—line up or——" Here again he made fierce play with his sword, driving his snarling would-be assailants before him, this way and that, striking them with flat of blade, checking them with point until he had them lined in some degree of order.

"Now," said he, padding up and down their sullen ranks, "I am Captain Adam Penfeather, your captain, and one ye shall obey or, by the God above us, I'll be death for some o' ye afore I die. Ho, Dreadnoughts!" he shouted.

"Ay, ay, Adam! Here, sir! With ee, Captain!" cried the Twelve, mustering about him.

"Martin Frant and you, Ned, look to these murderous slaves I mean to make into men again. Choose your watches,—nay first, since they're so foul outsides and in,

let 'em heave buckets o' water over each other till they
be something sweeter. Smidge, your Spanish is better than
mine, desire this don to follow me."

And so, long sword aglitter and white hair gleaming in
the moonlight, back stalked Adam to his interrupted
bathing and, lying in this joy of warm water, bade Jimbo
go and do all he might to the comfort of this ill-used
Spaniard.

Now after some while when Adam came to dress he
found that instead of his own poor rags, Jimbo had laid
out for his selection so many strange, rich garments, such
splendour of satins, velvets and gold embroidery, such
luxury of lace and fine linen, with stocking of silk, shoes,
buckled and rosetted, boots short and long, of fragrant
leather themselves soft and pliant as velvet, indeed such
magnificence of attire as should be worthy to grace only
the high and noble person of a Spanish Grandee of loftiest
lineage and bluest of blood.

Adam surveyed these many wonders, as he had the
magnificence of this spacious cabin, with eyes of awe,
then, having no other, proceeded to choose such as he
thought fittest and get himself into them, turning as he
donned each garment to watch its effect in the long, silver-
framed mirror nearby. Thus at last he beheld himself no
more the naked, scarred wretch but a very dominating
personage, a stately gentleman of such gracious bearing
and dignity that he marvelled at the potency of tailor's
needle and the magic of clothes.

Thus arrayed, he entered the great cabin whose luxury
of carving, silken hangings and rich carpets seemed less
awesome now by reason of his own splendour. Here Jimbo,
with Smidge to aid, was comforting the hurts of the
Spaniard, who instantly rose and bowed with such ceremony that Adam found himself bowing as graciously.

"Sir," said this young Spaniard impulsively and speaking in very good English, "I beg you to accept my very
humble, grateful expression of thanks."

"Pray be seated," said Adam, "and indeed you speak excellent good English."

"Sir, I was with our Ambassador in England, first two, then three years. I was well acquaint with your Prince that is now King Charles, and have many friends there, though our nations, alas, are nothing friendly. I am Luiz Alphonso y Valdez, and your very grateful servant. But for you, sir, I had died . . . extreme ungently."

"Don Luiz, I am happy to have served you. Were you an officer aboard this ship?"

"No, sir, a passenger, I was going home—to Spain. But now——?" Don Luiz spread eloquent hands and bowed again. "I am your prisoner and glad to find myself in so noble hands . . . those of a gentleman of England. And, sir, I beg to say that my father will pay generous ransom if——"

"No, sir," answered Adam, "you will pray consider yourself passenger still until we fall in with the first Spanish ship able and willing to your transport."

"Oh, sir . . . sir," stammered the young hidalgo, "I crave to learn the name of my so generous captor and . . . host, if you please."

"Sir, I am Captain Adam Penfeather——"

It was now that with knock on door, Sir George D'Arcy entered and all he wore, besides grime and matted hair, was a pair of ragged, canvas drawers; dumbly he stared from Adam to Don Luiz who recoiled with a very evident disgust.

"Adam?" he exclaimed, at last, "Lord love me, I . . . I'd never ha' known thee!"

"Don Luiz," said Adam, rising, "I have the honour to make known my good and dear friend, Sir George D'Arcy . . . George, I present Don Luiz Alphonso y Valdez." Sir George, arm a-flourish, bowed with an extreme of ceremony: Don Luiz, opening his fine, dark eyes very wide, leapt afoot to do likewise, gasping:

"Honoured, sir!"

"Don Luiz, the same, I vow!" answered Sir George,

smiling. "You behold me, sir, but lately from a rowing-bench aboard the *Santa Barbara* galleasse——"

"George—ho, George!" bellowed a familiar voice, and in upon them strode Sir Benjamin who, besides dirt with shag of hair and whisker, wore nothing save a breech-clout yet who (having boomed astonished curses at Adam's changed appearance), being now presented to the young Spaniard, instantly bowed, flourished, bounced and made great play with his legs which, no longer chubby, showed lean and corded with hairy brawn.

"'S blood, sir, a joy!" he exclaimed. "Let me rot and perish, sir, if 'tisn't purest joy . . . to play hosts to grandee o' Spain in Spanish seas aboard Spanish ship, with Spanish wine, and ourselves but late all foul and filthy, bleeding and bloody slaves aboard a Spanish ac-cursed galley. I say, sir, you are and shall be our right honoured guest or may I burn, choke and perish! And now, Adam, where is the wine, prithee? Can't we find ever a bottle, or say two wherein to pledge this our worthy gentleman don?"

Adam rang the silver bell beside him, whereat the quick, soft-footed Jimbo appeared bearing three bottles on tray of massy silver.

So they bowed all three and drank to Don Luiz whose pale cheek flushed as he bowed and drank to them. And thus they continued to drink, more especially Sir Benja-min, who called toast after toast, until Adam left them and came to his own cabin, or rather this spacious apart-ment of luxurious comfort chosen for him it seemed by his zealous servant Jimbo, and which must have been designed for a lord high Admiral at the very least. Now among its many furnishings was a richly inlaid writing standish with silver fittings, sheaf of quill pens and shelf of books above. Choosing from these a book of many pages and heavily bound, that he thought must be the ship's log book, Adam selected one of the pens and began writing, as follows:

"On board the *Santissima Trinidad*
this third day of May and year of Grace
1640

"In this night of May begins for me a new life. For here sit I, Adam Penfeather, aboard this rich and glorious ship, within a splendid cabin, clad in Spanish magnificence of dress that by good hap and because I am grown somewhat and fuller of body, do fit me very well. And now all my thought is this, viz.: How best to rule this wild company, these poor, fierce, brutalized creatures, to lift them up and back again to manhood and this best of all manhood as I do think, namely English sailormen. Whether to attempt this by suasion of prayer and exhortation or by method less kindly. Memo. To-morrow early, must order all firearms to be shifted abaft, and stored beneath the coach where they shall be ever to hand and under my own eye. As regards these poor men, am now resolved on prayer and exhortation with show of instant and extremest ferocity whensoever needful. And now before sleep will forth on deck to know all well and the watch alert."

This night, instead of straw and stone floor, Adam lay between fragrant sheets on bedstead richly carved and gilded; but what with all this unwonted comfort, splendour, and events of this most fateful day, sleep he could not, and therefore summoned Jimbo, who came instantly, though stifling vast yawn behind huge, black hand.

"Jimbo," said he, motioning the black giant to be seated nearby and who goggled but obeyed, "where is my boy, Smidge, my small seadog?"

"He am berry bountifully asleep, sah, in de li'l cubby next door 'longside, Cap'n Adam, sah."

"Why then let him be. To-morrow you shall set him a bed in the corner yonder."

"Yessah, berry good, sah."

"To-morrow also, first thing, you will look out clothes for Sir George and Sir Benjamin as you did for me."

"Hain't no manner of need, sah, berry good clo'es in ebery cabin abaft heah, great plenty clo'es, sah, and all berry splendorious!"

"Good! Now another thing, Jimbo, these long years of trouble and suffering have shown you for a man brave in hardship and faithful to me, therefore I shall double your share of all profits."

"Do-double him, sah?" stammered Jimbo, with great show of teeth. "Oh, Cap'n! Oho, Cap'n Adam, you is a berry elegant, noble, Christian gemman. Amen and de Lord bress yo' eyes an' limbs, now and ever more, Cap'n!"

"You will be chief steward aboard this ship, Jimbo, and my fighting man ashore."

"Yassah, yassah! I don' lak fighting, but when I has to fight I fights berry hearty, sir."

"What o' the man I had to stab to-night?"

"Berry sore and groansome, sah, and mighty curseful! Him called Tom Ash and rowed next to me in de galley."

"Howbeit, Jimbo, I took care to bleed him only, through th' upper arm, he shall do well enough till morning. Now hearkee, I mind you were familiar with all the slaves, Jimbo."

"Yessah, I knows 'em ebery one, and friends wid ebery one as be friends wi' me till I quarrels and then I hain't."

"Well now, Jimbo, I want you to tell them, each and every one of them, that Captain Adam Penfeather is a man very fierce, very cruel, quick to shoot or hang any rogue disobeying orders or fighting with his fellow. I want you to terrify 'em beyond my need of killing any one of 'em. Now is this well understood, Jimbo?"

"Yessah, it berry sho'ly am. I'll tell em as yo' am de bloodiest, cruellest, frociousest Cap'n that ebber commanded any ship in de Main."

"Why then, good night, Jimbo!"

"Thankee, sah, and de same to yo' and many ob dem wid de berry sweetliest ob sweet dreams, sah."

CHAPTER XXVIII

TELLS HOW ADAM SET ABOUT TRANSFORMING SLAVES INTO MEN

GOING on deck next morning Adam beheld a resplendent gentleman, enjoying the early sun, who, turning in leisured promenade, disclosed the lean features of this new Sir Benjamin and he, catching sight of Adam in his rich attire, glanced down at his own splendour and laughed, sweeping off feathered hat with courtly bow, saying:

"Lo, Adam, rigged forth like lordly don I feel but the more English, and shall never believe how that yesterday I was miserable slave—until I see my poor, scarred back,—if I ever do. And yet, Adam my hearty, let me die but I must needs confess and solemnly protest that our bitter hardships and privations ha' their uses."

"Why so I think," nodded Adam, "they should make us something wiser."

"True enough, Adam, and besides they ha' given me a new palate for wine, a boy's joyous, indiscriminate appetite for my food and made better man o' me than ever I was afore. Aha,—look now yonder where George struts in his like-stole finery!"

"Ay, faith!" laughed Sir George. "And see again down yonder on the half-deck our naked rogues o' yesterday, their wondrous transfiguration!" And he gestured where divers of the men were parading themselves or mocking each other in their new fashion of garb and wide Spanish breeches with coloured hosen.

It was this same morning, after breakfast, that by sound of trumpet and drum, all men were summoned aft where Adam, standing above them on the wide quarterdeck, thus addressed them:

"Let all men hearken now. We have been brothers in our sorrows and pain, let us be brothers still, true to each other, obedient to our duty and faithful to our God, the Almighty Father of us all that by His mercy hath delivered us from slavery. But to do this, ye must be men. Ay, and men ye shall be, clean outside and in, and this either by your own will or my contrivance. Ye that were poor slaves cringing to the lash, brute beasts lusting for vengeance, shall be men again to respect yourselves and each other. And the first means is to be clean o' body,—so, every man o' ye every day shall sluice himself down or be soused overboard from the lee yardarm. This is an order! Moreover, ye be for the most part, English sailormen, than whom there are none better men in this whole, wide world, so be ye thankful therefore to the God that made ye so and, remembering how He hath brought us out of great tribulation, pain o' body and anguish o' soul, let us praise and give Him humble thanks all our days. To the which end, shall be prayers at morn and evening daily by beat o' drum. And this is another order! Lastly, ye men of my command, remember this,—he that proves worthy shall have honour and reward, he that is proven rogue shall lie i' the bilboes or swing at yardarm. Remember, lastly, that ye are all, each and every, sons o' the Lord that made ye. And so—dismiss!"

And now it was that, with the unknown Spanish shipmaster's backstaff and instruments, maps and charts, Adam at last put the result of his studies into practice, laying a course to keep a good offing from Coast of the Main whence pursuit might come,—galleys and ships of war. This morning as he paced the quarterdeck, the sweet, clean wind about him, the sun above and sparkling ocean below, he was a man very humbly reverent and deeply grateful for this present good, while the *Santissima Trinidad*, her huge, painted sails outspread, her brasswork and gilding bright and gleaming, was bearing him to his destiny,— to that future which, hold what it might of hardship and suffering, could have no terrors for one who had endured so much and was ever ready to die.

Presently, espying the Bo'sun below, clad in his new finery of raiment, he hailed him cheerily:

"Ho, Ned, come you hither!" So up the broad, richly-carved ladders came sturdy Ned, his bronzed face new shaven, his blue eyes glad and bright as the sun-flecked ocean. "Well, Ned man, how think ye of our ship? Look at her, Ned, look at her,—so vast and powerful, and Lord only knoweth what o' treasure below. How say you of her, Ned?"

"Why, sir, I answers you, and says as how this yere *Saintissimus Trinidaddio* be like these same Spanish breeches as covers me,—wi' their tiers o' buttons, their braid and galloons,—overly broad i' the beam and too trig and fancy for plain sailorman. She's painted like any Jezebel,—a bluff-bowed, heavy starned, lubberly glory she be! Yet I'm proud of her and have had our rogues a-swabbing and a-polishing of her right zealous, Cap'n."

"What think you of 'em as a crew, Ned?"

"Foul and wild, sir! Wolves to snarl and tear the first chance they gets, ay—and us the first shall feel their teeth and claws, b' reason of our cargo, for 'tis said as this yere *Santa* be full—choke full o' gold."

"How many do they number, our wolves?"

"At the last muster, sir, they was a hundred and seventy-four not counting boy Smidge."

"And of these, how many English?"

"Some 'eres nigh a hundred, sir, the rest being only Frenchies, Dutch, Portingales and a few Spanish gallers-birds—and suchlike duffle."

"In fine, Ned, six more than rowed aboard the galleasse. And, as you say, wolves all! Yet I'll tame 'em, or die i' the endeavour."

"Which, sir, die you likely will and all honest lads with ee, for should these yere raskells make chance to rise agin you and mutiny, as well they may, there be only us to

withstand 'em, us as you calls your Dreadnoughts, twelve
men, counting you three gentlemen!"

"Ay, Ned, but then dreadnoughts we are indeed and
brothers all, that well do know and trust each other, fair
or foul, and this is far better than mere numbers. Also
I shall be instant to check the least show o' mutiny. And,
moreover, the small arms are all secured abaft, I hope?"

"Ay verily, sir, i' the dawn, and all asleep save us
Dreadnoughts, every musket, pistol, axe, pike and sword
all safe under lock and key where you give order, and
guarded beside, same as the cargo."

"Talking o' this, Ned, you've had no glimpse of our
lading, eh?"

"No, sir, nor nobody will except you so order. I've set
Nick and Silas well armed for to see as nobody shall."

"Why then, Ned, we'll below, thou and I, this moment
to take stock o' things, and softly, man, softly now!"

So down they went from deck to deck of this great
vessel until they came to the lazarette where Silas Guppy
and Nicholas Cobb sat dicing, but with pistols and muskets
in reach. Taking a spare lantern Adam led on, Bo'sun
Ned following, and down until they reached the spacious
hold where the reek of bilge was sweetened by rich, spicey
odours, cloves, ginger, cinnamon, tobacco and the like.
Here they found merchandise piled and shored to the
very cross-timbers; and so, unseen by any eye, began their
investigations. And, after some while they paused to stare
on each other like men who scarcely dare believe what
they see; thereafter, seated in odd corner with the light
between them, they shook their heads at one another and
still without a word. . . .

Gold! In bars, ingots, dust and coin. Chests of moi-
dores, sacks of pieces of eight. Bales of Orient silks and
rich brocades, spices, carved ivories, sugar and much
beside. A treasure so stupendous as went beyond words;
so for a while they sat dumb and continued to shake their
heads at one another.

"Lord!" exclaimed the Bo'sun at last, in hoarse whisper, and wiping furrowed brow, "Lord love us! A fortun' beyond count!"

"Enough," said Adam, whispering also, "and more than enough to make every wise man of us rich for life!"

"Ay, sir, except it be our death! For should noos o' this get abroad, the scuppers shall spout blood, ay—and ourn first of all!"

"So I think, Ned,—at present. So, for the present, no man, fore or abaft, must learn o' this. An armed guard shall be mounted, also the hatches must be battened down. See you to this, Ned, and choose only our Dreadnoughts to its doing."

May 4

I write in great amazement and not a little troubled to find we are laden with a treasure far beyond my expectation, a great curse of gold that, second only to woman, is cause of more sin and bloodshed than aught else in this troubled world, and may yet bring death on many of us should news of it reach these lawless rogues I must needs learn to rule and govern. In this moment great comfort is it to know all the firearms are in keeping of my Dreadnoughts. So if this is to become a ship of death we few may have some small hope of living. This new anxiety, putting me in mind of the man I hurt yesterday, I buckled on sword, and with Smidge to bear such medicaments as methought needful, to the forecastle there to be greeted by fierce looks from many but no word. I found this man, Tom Ash, extreme weak from loss of blood, and therewith all wild savagery so drained out of him that, while I did my best to his comfort, he talked of his mother in England and wept. Which do give me great hope I may win him back to manliness and self-respect, since only a man indeed may weep. Having washed and cherished his wound to his instant relief (by reason of my much experience while a slave) I bade him come abaft to me daily for treatment, and so left him a humble man and grateful. This same morning by sound of tucket and drum our wild fellows were mustered for prayers and after brief supplication I began to exhort them from the Psalms, choosing passages at random, in the midst of which one cried out very lewdly and with much blasphemous ribaldry. On this, I drew the sword I had been heedful to wear against such expected trouble and nodded to Martin who, instructed beforehand, thrust another sword into this blasphemer's fist and I stepped to him with point advanced. But, seeing me so ready, this fellow let fall his weapon, refusing combat. So when I had beaten him somewhat with flat of my sword I ordered him into the bilboes forthwith. But scarce had two of my Dreadnoughts laid hands on him than from his fellows rose prodigious clamour and ferocity of uproar, vith flash of drawn knives very threatening, and close about us. So I pointed them where above us on the poop stood John Fenn with a small murdering-piece aimed and ready to discharge upon them, whereat they all stood as it were astonished. But now, well knowing that if I am to tame and rule and presently win these men to me I must do it by my own force of hand, I chose me the tallest and fiercest showing of this fierce company and demanded his name. His answer was snarling obscenity. "Rogue," says I, "step forrard." "Not I," says he, and mocks me for my lack o' size and with much foul invective. "Who made you captain o' we," he demanded, "you that was slave like us and no more, who made you captain?" I asked him who dared deny it. "Why, I do," cries he, groping for his knife again. "Very well," says I, "take up yonder sword, follow me to the poop, where all may see, and let us now prove which is the better man and more able to command. Come!" cries I, making myself seem fierce as possible. "Follow me, rogue, or by my blood, Master Fenn's gun yonder shall blast some o' ye to per-dition—come!" Then I turned and mounted to the poop, and praying with my every step that the God of my Father would nerve my arm. And so indeed He did, and to such effect that very soon I had this desperate fellow bleeding in six or seven places and finally, after a close parry, beat the sword from his failing grasp and him, thus defenceless, backed to the rail, there to lean, he being something faint and ready to sink. So, calling for water, etc., I bathed, anointed and bound up his cuts and glad to find none of them of any moment. This done, back went we to deck below and the company now very silent and altogether seemly the while I besought them to lift their hearts in gratitude to God for His present mercies and our late deliverance and to remember how we are all the children of His love. And all men now attentive to my discourse, bowing their heads reverently to the final Amen. Thereafter I gave order they should be exercised at our ordnance now and every day at this hour, bidding John choose his mates and gun crews, telling him also that what I desired in action was not so much accuracy of fire at long range as speed of fire at close quarters. At this John became very joyous, being great lover of his guns, so that presently this great ship was all a-quiver with their thunderous discharges, and the men for the most part very brisk. While this was yet adoing, I, with Ned, Sir G. D'Arcy, and Sir Benj. to that spacious cabin 'neath the coach we had made the armoury, and glad to see this ship so very well armed both small and great, with many pistols, muskets set very orderly together with swords, pikes, axes and moreover divers suits of body armour, one very rich and precious. This night in my sumptuous cabin, and Smidge fast asleep in his cot as ordered, bethinking me of our so great and perilous treasure, I knelt praying God His aid to win this crew to their duty unto the ship, themselves, and to me, and their souls, one and all, to His Glory. And so got me to bed with assured hope my comforter.

Adam was scarcely dressed next morning when came little Smidge, still heavily armed, to salute smartly, saying:

"Begs to report, Cap'n, as they two rogues wot you fought and wounded, sir, is come aft for treatment as ordered."

"Very well, Smidge. Bid Jimbo bring bowl of warm water and the medicine chest, then admit our patients and stand by to see what I do, for I would have you able to treat a wound, set a bandage and do a little rough surgery anon, Smidge."

"Ay ay, sir. Though I'd rather fight like a seadog should ought for to do, Cap'n Adam."

"Why, so you shall—if needful. Though 'tis better to heal a man than harm him."

"And you do bofe, sir, so I'll try bofe too."

"Then first lay by your great sword and hurry."

Thus presently in came these two of Adam's wolves now looking very sheepish because little Smidge had each by an arm, leading them into this splendid cabin to front this small, very masterful captain, who surveyed them with such keen scrutiny and whose movements were so quick and light as he removed coat and rolled up snowy shirt-sleeves.

"Thomas Ash, step forrard!"

"Ay ay, sir!" says maimed Ferocity No. 1, in groaning voice, yet obeying smartly, none the less. "Pain be powerful sharp, sir. Oh very bad it be, sir."

"Ha!" says Adam, knitting black brows and smoothing white hair. "Pain is ofttimes a powerful deterrent, Thomas, and sometimes a stimulant to better things. Doff his bandage, Smidge, and easy now!"

"Ay ay, sir!" pipes the boy. "But, please, how'll I come at him and him so high up above me?"

"He shall come down to you. Kneel, Thomas!"

The man hesitates, glances sideways at scowling Ferocity No. 2, looks at Adam and obeys. So, while this burly fellow kneels that the boy may bare his wound, Adam selects divers lotions and salves from the medicine chest and Ferocity No. 2, this great, red-headed fellow, tall nearly as Jimbo, looks on 'neath lowering brows and clenches his big fists,—in which moment Adam speaks though seeming not to look up from the bandage he is preparing.

"Well?" he demanded, sharply. "Why d'ye scowl and clench fist. No matter! What's your name?"

"Tregenza."

"Tom, Dick, or Harry?"

"Neither. It's Giles,—as ye might ha' known on that cursed galley, you heard it oft enough. Ay, and you doctored the fetter-galls on my wrist."

"So I did to many others, Tregenza, my own included."

"And," snarled Tregenza, "I don't kneel to any man, no nor boy—not I!"

"Then ye may go!" said Adam. "You have no doctoring from me."

"You!" cried Tregenza. "You poor, little half-man! I could snap ye across my knee, ay—choke the life out o' your pitiful carcass with my bare hands!"

Adam, still busy, troubled to glance up at the speaker and shook his head.

"Oh no!" said he, gently.

"Ha,—what d'ye mean, little man?"

"That you'd die too soon."

"Die? Who—me?" sneered this big man. "And by such puny wretch as you? Ay, you'd call your fellows and have me shot down, murdered, for sure."

"This moment, if need be!" nodded Adam. "Look yonder!"

Tregenza looked, Adam leapt, his sinewy fist smote up hard beneath the big man's ear, his dexterous foot tripped him, and Ferocity No. 2 thudded full length on the rich carpeting, made to rise and was checked by the knife-point that menaced him.

"Kneel!" said Adam, standing above him.

Tregenza, making as if to obey, flashed out his own knife instead, took the toe of Adam's shoe beneath his chin, groaned, dropped the knife, sank down again and so lay mute and still.

"Now," said Adam, breathing short, "off with his bandages, Smidge, whiles I tend Ash." But the boy stood motionless, staring on this great fellow struck down in his strength and so terribly, until Adam laughed, saying: "You're not afeard o' the brute now, are you, old sea-dog?"

"N-no, sir!" gasped Smidge. "No, I ain't afeard o' nobody nor nothing . . . not when I'm along o' you, Cap'n, sir."

"Why, very well!" nodded Adam, turning to Ferocity No. 1. "Now let's 'tend to you, Thomas."

"Ay ay, sir, ay ay, but—not like you just tended to Giles there, Cap'n! Oh, not that way, Cap'n."

"Tush man! Sit you in this chair. Well now, here's pretty scar as does us both credit, Thomas! You're healing apace. Had you been an evil liver alongshore, here would have been pus and inflammation. Life aboard yon galleasse hath its compensations truly and despite whip and manacles! Your blood is become sweet, Thomas, and pure as a clean boy's. There now! Hold this pad—so, whiles I fetch a turn about it with the bandage."

"But, Cap'n, blast my eyes, sir, and axing your pardin, but you . . . you hain't been and gone and . . . killed pore Giles, 'ave ye, sir?"

"Not quite, Thomas. Only enough to quiet the devil in him awhile. You behold him tamed for a little, no more."

"Ay, sir, but looked like as you'd kicked his figure'ead clean adrift, Cap'n."

"How does your arm feel now, Thomas?"

"Sweetly soothsome, sir—though 'twould be better yet, if ye'd be so kind, for a tot o' rum, sir."

"At proper season, Thomas. Now, off with ye!"

"Ay ay, sir, and thankee kindly, I'm sure. My sarvice to ee, Cap'n!" So saying, Tom Ash made a leg and rolled himself away. Then Adam turned to see little Smidge kneeling beside Tregenza.

"Oh, sir," said he, looking up, anxious-eyed, "will I give him a tot o' rum or sowse him wi' water?"

"Neither, shipmate."

"But he . . . he don't seem like . . . coming to, sir."

"He will, Smidge, give him time. Now leave me and bid Jimbo see no one disturb me till I ring."

"What, must I go, sir, and leave you alone . . . along o' yon murderous, great man?"

"He isn't murderous now, Smidge."

"But . . . when he comes to—if he ever do, how then, sir, if you please?"

"I'll manage him, shipmate, somehow."

"Will I leave ye my cutlash, sir?"

"Thankee no, messmate, clap it on, and take his knife with you also." Very unwillingly Smidge obeyed while Adam, having dressed the unconscious man's wounds and ordered and closed the medicine chest, sat down and took up his quill.

Thus when at last Tregenza opened his eyes it was to see Adam seated at the table, writing busily and yet who now spoke without looking up:

"Your wounds are all dressed and doing very well, Giles. You are indeed a fine-made, powerful fellow but, which I think is better, I perceive you are one of some education. What were you in England?"

And crouched on the floor, staring on his questioner in strange, dazed manner, Tregenza answered, like one in a dream and speaking against his will:

"A law student . . . in my father's office . . . in Helston."

"You preferred the sea, then?"

"Being only a cursed, fool boy . . . yes, a seaman . . . then carpenter's mate."

"Good!"

"How? How good? It's brought me nought but evil . . . how good?"

"Because," answered Adam, laying down his pen at

last and turning to look at Tregenza, "I need a ship's carpenter, and I'll try you."

"Eh? Me? You'll try . . . me . . . after what——"

"Report to Ned Bowser, the master. Say I sent you."

Giles Tregenza got to his feet, with an effort, felt his chin with a painful solicitude, scowled at the floor, the gilded beams overhead and finally, at Adam.

"Sir," he began, and choking on the word, stood dumb again.

"Well?" demanded Adam, turning again to look on this great fellow who fumbled with his hands and shifted so awkwardly; thus reading the trouble in his blue eyes, Adam did that which was so rare with him, smiled.

"Sir," said Giles again, "this is the second time I would have killed you . . . and joyed in it! Though why, only the Lord knoweth. Belike 'twas because I saw ye on the galleasse for such little man and small and no account at the oar, and always so meek seeming, never daring to cry out 'gainst cruel injustice or rage 'gainst our oppressors. . . . Such puny man and now, on a sudden, setting yourself up for master of us all."

"Hast said it, Giles!" quoth Adam, rising. "Master of ye all am I, and will be henceforth, whiles I live! Captain of this ship until a better man shall displace and kill me, for indeed kill me he must, Giles, and make very sure I am dead."

"The which, sir," said Giles, shaking his red head, "there's no man aboard may ever do, for master indeed you are. I began to think so yesterday when we were at the steel together, to-day I know it. Captain are you henceforth and I your man and . . . proud to own it."

Adam rose and began to pace slowly to and fro across the wide cabin and presently to speak his thoughts like one in self-communion:

"To know our own mind, to be faithful to our word and what we believe our duty . . . to have faith in ourselves, our destiny and in God . . . to bear these deep

in our heart with a green memory of that small island
so far across the seas . . . to live ever worthy of our
England . . . all this, I think, is summed up in the word
'honour'. And 'tis this maketh an Englishman able to
rule and shall lift little England into the very forefront of
the nations . . . someday . . . mayhap . . . As for myself,
I was meek and uncomplaining aboard the galleasse because
I do not cry out or rage 'gainst adversity, for that I believe
pain and travail are sent to tempt and try us, and should
make us but the wiser and stronger, and therefore so much
the better men. Also I believe the Almighty is a God of
Justice and Mercy shall make of our sufferings a crown of
glory, hereafter. . . . So now, Giles Tregenza, I shall believe
you honourable, as Englishman should be; 'tis for you to
prove me wise or mere fool. Go now and report for duty."

Without a word, Tregenza crossed to the door, turned
as if to speak, saluted instead and strode away. So,
presently, Adam sat down again to his writing and had
filled two close-written pages when, with thunderous
knock, the door swung wide and in strode Sir Benjamin.

"S'death, Adam!" he exclaimed, flourishing the sheathed
rapier he held. "Bloody mutiny's afoot!"

Adam rose and from beneath a pile of loose papers,
drew the pistol they had concealed.

"Art sure, Ben?" he enquired, cocking the weapon.

"'Od's my life, that am I! So's George! George saw.
. . . George heard! Ho, George, where a plague are ye?"

"Here!" answered Sir George, entering as he spoke.

"Ha, well now you'll bear witness, George, 'tis that
cursed, red-headed, great rogue, Adam, that same arch-
villain you fought at prayers——"

"Ah!" murmured Adam, and uncocked the pistol.
'You'll mean Giles Tregenza."

"I don't know his infernal name, but 'tis that same
ill-beseen, foul-advised hell-hound——"

"A very tall, red-haired, seemly fellow!" nodded Adam,
and laid by the pistol.

"Eh? Seemly, says you? Man, I'm telling ye o' this same tall, great, ugly rascal, this scoundrelly, very lewd rogue provoked you lately to blooding him and very handsomely ye did it! Well, this ill-conditioned knave comes swaggering up to myself, George and Ned——"

"I should scarce call it swaggering," Sir George demurred, "striding would be the word, Ben."

"Smite me dumb, George! D'ye think I don't know swagger from stride? Up swaggers he, and 'pon the quarterdeck, mark ye, Adam, with some cock and bull tale of promotion, mate or coxon, and as I live, oozing damnable mutiny at every accursed pore!"

"Sweat, Ben! Should rather call it sweat," murmured Sir George, "the sun being so pestilent hot!"

"And I say 'twas mutiny, so plain and manifest that had I been armed I'd ha' been at the rogue! As 'tis, Adam, staying but to snatch sword, I'm here to demand he be instantly clapped i' the bilboes."

"Not so, my Benjamin,—yet awhile, at least," answered Adam, "he is too lately ship's carpenter."

"Eh—eh?" gasped Sir Benjamin, recoiling. "He . . . ship's carpenter . . . an officer . . . this proven rascally, murderous——"

"Even so, our ship's carpenter, Ben."

"Well now, strike me deaf, blind and bleeding if I ever heard the like o' this! A villain to be cut and chopped one day and promoted officer the next! Ha, and when he brings his like rogues down 'pon us to slit our throats, how then?"

"Yourself shall have the hanging of him, Ben."

"But, if you must have carpenter, why . . . why i' the foul fiend's name, choose this fellow?"

"Since you ask, well—I like his looks, the set of his chin, the cock of his eye."

Here Sir Benjamin, finding adequate retort quite beyond even his powers for the time,—snorted, bounced, and strode away.

CHAPTER XXIX

HOW ADAM MET MUTINY—AND QUELLED IT

DAY after day westward rolled the great *Santissima Trinidad*, manned by a crew that gradually, from savage contempt, learned to fear and then respect this small, masterful captain whose silvery, old man's hair was in such strange contrast with the flaming youth of his quick, keen eyes that, like his ears, missed so little of what chanced around him; this man in whose slim body dwelt soul of such potency and inexorable will, backed by an unexpected muscular strength and power of endurance. A captain this who showed so contemptuous of dangers and moreover so extremely ready and able for personal combat. Here, then, was a man for men to follow; and so, in the end, follow him they did, through storm and battle, defeat and triumph—many of them to—the very end.

Thus, day after day, these men were mustered and stood very reverently now, morning and evening, to be prayed over and exhorted; thereafter, and as regularly, they manned the guns, especially those great pieces of the lower tier, to load and fire, sponge, charge, ram and fire again and all at topmost speed, until the ship was veiled in smoke to her lofty topmasts. While this was doing, Sir Benjamin and Sir George, with their files of musketeers, were banging away at marks set afloat for the purpose; and standing alone upon the towering poop their little Captain watched all that was done, swift to admonish yet as quick to praise.

Now as Adam stood looking down on this great ship that was his to command and these sturdy fellows who were learning (he hoped) that discipline which should transform them from lawless rabble into a crew of hardy, self-respecting mariners and lusty fighting men, up to him came Ned Bowser, himself all that an English seaman should be from curly head to Spanish shoes.

"Cap'n Adam, sir," said he, lifting two fingers to bristly eyebrow, "seeing as how, sir, I begs to ax a favour."

"What is it, Ned?"

"Why, sir, seeing as how you've rose me above myself by making of me Master o' this yere ship *Santa*, and there-fore quarterdeck officer where I don't nowise belong seeing as how my nat'ral rank is bo'sun, and nat'ral place the lower deck, to live and mess comfortably and nat'rally forrard instead of aft most on—nat'rally, and therefore dis-comfortably, along o' you and t'other gentlemen in the great cabin, I now axes you as a great favour, seeing as how, to be therefore ex-cused therefrom."

"Meaning you would liefer remain bo'sun, Ned."

"Pre-zackly, sir! For d'ye see, though you made me Master, Natur' and myself made me a bo'sun, which ʃ being, bo'sun I'd be, according. Is it agreed, sir?"

"No, Ned. You are the primest seaman aboard; had you knowledge o' navigation you should be my lieutenant. You are also . . . my good friend, like stout John Fenn. Ay, you and John are as my right and left hands . . . men I shall ever trust. Also, Ned, as Master you will receive greater share of—our cargo. Therefore, Master you shall remain and mess whereso you will."

"Thankee, sir, and heartily."

"How think you of our crew now, Ned?"

"Better and better, sir,—though there be rank bad uns among 'em as no man couldn't tame nohow, nowise and nowhen. But for the most, sir, you be working wonders on 'em by working of 'em—constant. Good food, plenty o' work and a ready fist backed by justice—no crew could ax fairer."

"I sent Giles Tregenza to you this morning."

"Ay, sir, which as-tonished me, for you'll mind him as

one o' the worst aboard yon galley, a fur'ous, ill-conditioned raskell. Up he comes and tells as how you says as
how he is carpenter."

"True enough, so I did."

"But then he says, says he, as he can't, seeing as how
he weren't never nowise apprenticed to the trade and
therefore not able for to do justice to hisself, sir, or you,—
and off he goes."

"An honest fellow, Ned."

"Or wilful and bone-idle, sir."

"Let us say 'honest'. Howbeit, a carpenter we must
have. There should be one among so many."

"So there be, sir, ay and one o' the best and likewise
worst, him being Toby Drew, as was carpenter aboard a
King's ship once, but a precious black rogue now. Ay, one
o' the four worst villins aboard yon galley. There was him
and Tregenza and Will Vardon and Sam Morris always
in trouble, and the lash only made 'em worse. You'll
mind 'em, sir, seeing as you doctored 'em pretty frequent,
'specially that time as we fouled the wreckage and broke
three oars as nigh tore their hands off in their shackles?"

"Ay, I remember," answered Adam, glancing down at
his own scarred wrists. "We must bear these marks to
our graves, Ned."

"Well—now, sir, these same four bad uns be ripe for
mischief, ay and a-stirring up others! I've had my weather
eye on 'em, so's Martin, and I've likewise got two of our
Dreadnoughts a'watching of 'em constant."

"So?" murmured Adam, pinching his chin. "Then have
this man Drew brought hither to me with show o' force,
an armed escort, two of our lads shall suffice, and let this
be done instantly, Ned."

So presently this man shambled aft between Timothy
Sprake and Matthew Appleby, an ungainly, bow-legged
fellow, scowling first on one, then the other, and lastly on
Adam, who dismissed his two Dreadnoughts with a gesture.

"Well, Toby," said he, looking into the man's sullen eyes, "this is better than the galleasse."

"You works us pretty nigh as hard."

"Ay, I do indeed, and shall,—but with no irksome shackles or bloody lash—yet, not yet, Tobias. No man shall be flogged aboard my ship,—except he earn it, and then, 'stead o' one lash shall be nine!"

"Ha, so you'll dare threaten us wi' the cat, eh?"

"The cat, yes, Tobias, and thereafter plenty o' salt to heal bloody backs and then the bilboes. For, as I tell ye, on my ship I'll have——"

"'Tis no ship o' yourn!" quoth Tobias, fiercely. "She belongs to us—us as took her wi' naked hands and 'spite our chains! I says she's our ship, and therefore a free ship, and us to 'lect our own captain! Ay, and lookee you, Adam, as was no better than any of us aboard yon hellish galley, no nor so good, being only half a man, I'm telling ye she's our ship, and bloody end to them as shall gainsay us!"

"Howbeit, Tobias, I do gainsay ye!"

The man turned and spat, very ostentatiously, to leeward, and sneered:

"That's you!" he nodded. "Ay, you'll soon go overside! Ha!—ye don't think the likes o' you can trample the likes o' we, nor yet steal for yourself what belongs to us, do ye? We bides our time . . . this here ship is for us —us as won her by our own sweat and blood!"

"Ah, blood!" repeated Adam, in musing tone, and crossing his arms, stood with head bowed as one very pensive, awhile. "Talking of blood, Toby," said he, at last, "you were never nigher to losing yours and your life than—now!" And speaking, he advanced a leisured pace or so, uncrossed his arms and Tobias Drew recoiled suddenly, staring horrified at the muzzles of the two small pistols so near his flinching body.

"You . . . won't . . . murder me . . . ?"

"Let us say . . . execute ye for insubordination. Why, you poor fool, without me you and like brutes would ha'

been at each other's throats days ago and the half o' ye
dead. Without me, to watch and navigate, you'd blunder
into capture—death or the slave benches again. I'm life
to ye all, your only hope for safety! Use that block-
head o' yours and know I speak truth. I'm your only hope,
and ye threaten me with death—'overside' was your word!
Now for this, on a King's ship, you would be hanged—
you know this, don't you? I say you know this?"

"Ay, ay!" groaned Tobias, with fearful up-glance
towards the great mainyard. "But this . . . this ain't
a King's ship, thank God, sir."

"No," sighed Adam, "therefore I may shoot ye now or
have ye flogged to death anon, according to sea law. And
this you know also."

Tobias licked his lips, glanced at the speaker's small,
grim face and nodded miserably.

"You, Tobias, with Tregenza, Vardon and Morris were
raising a mutiny against me, I know it . . . so you may
as well confess. Speak, rogue."

Tobias nodded again instead.

"And for this, your penalty is to be swung, kicking and
choking, to the mainyard as warning to like rogues. Have
you aught to say?"

"No, sir, since you know all about it,—only this . . .
I'd ha' ye to know, likewise, 'tis myself is the ring-leader,
and so begs kinder treatment for Morris, Tregenza and pore
Vardon as lost his starboard eye in the galley and as you
tended so kind. . . . And lastly, sir, I'd rather be shot
than hung if 'tis all the same to you, sir."

Adam took a slow turn across the deck, and when
Tobias looked again, his hands were empty, the pistols
had vanished.

"What then . . . captain . . . is it . . . the rope?"
he questioned, in broken voice.

"This depends on yourself, Drew. To-day I promote
you to Master Carpenter, to-morrow I may promote you
yet higher—in a noose if you so deserve. Meanwhile, I

trust you to play the honest man with me and be worthy
my clemency."

"Carpenter . . . ? Sir, did ye . . . say . . . Oh, Captain, do you . . . am I——"

"Go forward now and report you to the Master."

"But, sir, I—— Captain, d'ye mean . . . am I to——"

"Go! And bid Vardon and Morris here to me. Come
now, despatch!"

Then Toby Drew squared his brawny shoulders, saluted
so vigorously that he quivered from heel to head, and
strode away like different man, for he bore himself erect
now and shambled no more; and little dreamed he how
the small, fierce Captain who watched was praying, with
a dumb fervour, that this change might endure. Yet
when, after some while, two other furtive-looking men
reached the poop, they were met by one whose eyes were
a savage menace and whose biting words pierced even their
cynical brutality, because they had once been honest
men and English sailors.

"So ho, my beastly rogues and right bloody-minded
villains, ye plot mutiny and murder, do ye! You that
were born of English mothers to be their joy are become
their blasting shame, to die like dogs."

"Ha, then there's been Toby Drew peaching on us,
curse him!" snarled one, an evil, pock-marked, one-
eyed fellow. "Sam, us'll slit his dirty weasand for
this!"

"Not you, Will, nor yet me, b' the looks o' Master
Adam. Well, what's it to be, master? You've got us fair
caught, I'll not deny. So, if we're doo for to swing, carry
on! We don't betray our poor messmates for to save our
necks like yon Toby Drew, blast his deadlights."

"Speak for your ownself," cried Vardon, laying hand
on the knife in his belt, "belay or I'll bowel ye! If Toby
can win free his way, I can—this!" So saying, he flashed
out his knife and leapt full at watchful Adam,—to be met
by flame and smoke, and crying once, in thin, bubbling

voice, he dropped to his knees, sank to his face and lay still,—and the decks below athrong with startled faces.

"Up with this carcass—up, I say!" quoth Adam, gesturing at Morris with smoking pistol. "Heave and hang it across the rail that all like rogues may see a rogue dead of mutiny."

So Vardon's unlovely, dead body was lifted and propped across the carven poop-railing, and all men staring in such awed silence they might hear the quick patter of his life blood on the deck below.

"Look now!" cried Adam, tapping this still form with smoking pistol-barrel. "Here is man would have murdered the Captain o' this ship, wherefore he is dead. Let any like rogues beware. Bo'sun, send two men for this body, let it be prepared for burial. This day at sunset we will commit William Vardon's carcass to the ocean, beseeching God's mercy on his everlasting soul. Dismiss!"

"And now, sir, what . . . what o' me, if y' please?"

Adam turned to look into the speaker's pallid face, noting the level glance of his grey eyes, the resolute set of mouth and chin, despite the sweat that trickled upon haggard brow. Thus stood Adam a while, pinching his chin.

"You are Samuel Morris, I think?"

"That same, your honour."

"And guilty as your mate Vardon. You and others were biding a chance to kill me, as well I know."

"Then sich being so, I says nought,—only——"

"Well?"

"Though wishful for to take the ship, I was agin killing you. Bible Oath, sir!"

"Also you refused to betray your fellow rogues to save that roguish neck o' yours."

"Yessir! I did and I do. And there's plenty of 'em."

"Well, they see I'm prepared to meet murder day or night. Now tell me, Sam, if you can be so true, so faithful, to these mutinous fellows, why can you not be as true and faithful to your duty and me?"

Now looking at his questioner, Morris saw (and to his wonder) how this lean face was no longer grim but sadly wistful and lit by eyes no longer fiercely accusing but very kindly appealing; and opening his lips to speak, Morris was dumb, and, being unable to meet this so unexpected look, hung his head.

"Have you no answer for me, Morris? Then go forward and talk the matter out with your fellows, and when you find answer, come back to me with any you will and tell me. Now, you may go."

"Go, sir? But . . . but . . . I thought——"

"Ay, go you and think, Samuel; think hard and talk with your messmates, asking yourselves,—if it be not better to live honest men all, faithful to the ship, to me, and to each other, rather than rogues I must kill, as I most certainly shall if forced thereto. Off with ye now and bring me answer for yourself and fellows when you have decided to be either honest sailormen I may trust or felons for certain chastisement." This said, Adam went below, leaving Sam Morris a free man and therefore a man greatly astonished.

May 5

This evening in the coach after supper with Sir Benjamin, Sir G. D'Arcy and John Fenn, Don Luiz having retired early, there is much talk concerning our crew and my shooting of this man William Vardon whose poor body now lies so deep and many miles astern. And though they all commend this act of mine as necessary to the well-being of the ship, yet my mind, then as now, is greatly troubled therefore. To kill, even of necessity, is dreadful business, and shakes me to the very soul, so that I begin to doubt I can ever hang any man howsoever guilty. And this do trouble me in another fashion, viz.: Lest being too unready to take life I thereby endanger the lives of all, and thus prove myself unfit to command and keep order and peace. And here (thinks I) what strange, paradoxical virtue is Peace if it may only be maintained by war or force of arms! Sir G. D'Arcy now begins to question me whither we are bound and where I am taking the ship. "Though," says he, "being a fugitive and penniless, 'tis all one to me, Adam."

"Ay, or me either," groans Sir Benjamin, "seeing I am no more than poor naked, sorry wretch in no fit condition for return to England with that comely estate as befits a gentleman. So whither you take us, Adam, is no least matter, and yet we'd—fain know, since to be anyways ignorant is to be damned. How say'st thou, John Fenn?" And John (a steadfast, quiet man) replies by saying he has few friends in England and no family, and desires to share my fortunes foul or fair, so long as he may, the which, and from such right Englishman, greatly comforted me, as I told him.

"Ay," says Ben, "but whither do your present fortunes lead us, Adam?"

So I told them I was setting our course for Port Royal, in Jamaica, since 'twas there my good friend, Captain Troy, intended, and I was very fain to know if they had been spared to come safe thither.

"'They?'" says Ben. "You'll be meaning Absalom and your young brother, Anthony, he was taken into the pinnace with Troy I mind, a pretty lad, a dainty, young gentleman."

"Though," says George, "so shy and mighty retiring I saw less of his company than I would. Now here, to change the subject, I went on to say what little I knew concerning Jamaica, how that Port Royal is a resort of ships and merchants of many nations, and therefore a good market." At this word Sir Benjamin falls to bewailing his trade goods lost in the *Adventuress* and very mournfully. Now seeing these are trusty men all, and my very good friends, I told them (in some part) of the riches we carried aboard,— whereat Sir Benjamin soars from deeps of gloom to pinnacle of joy and so to a rhapsody, saying how he will to England forthwith and buy back his family estates and

H

so to Court, as gentleman of fashion, whiles George and
John and I follow our own thoughts, mine this, to wit:
Could I but recall the past few hours, William Vardon
should now be alive with chance to become, mayhap, an
honest man or die of roguery by other hand than mine.
And this thought so troubled me that I presently bade my
cheery companions Good night, and so to my cabin. Yet
even so, this memory haunted me so that, despite my
prayers, sleep was long a-coming, and when at last it
blessed me, I started up broad awake thinking I heard
again poor William Vardon's wailing, childish death-
cry. Now to comfort myself, I bethought me of the gentle
Christ, and how He had said He came not to send peace
but a sword. I thought also how He had buffeted the
money-changers and kicked over their tables. And so
again to sleep, only to dream of Vardon dead at my feet
and myself looking down on him to see ah,—not his evil
face but the lovely, oft-dreamed features of Antonia all
marred and fouled with blood. And so, to banish these
horrors, I got me dressed and went forth to meet the dawn.

May 8

This morning on the gun-deck with John when from
above comes cry of sail-ho with great stir and ado. So
up go we forthwith to the poop and there find Ned peering
to starboard through a perspective-glass at this distant
ship that is no more than blink of white on the horizon
bearing from us, as I judged, north-westerly. So for some
while we stood all three scanning her through our glasses
and I began to deliberate with myself whether we should
go about and stand away from her lest she prove Spanish
warship in quest of us, or bear down on her and speak
her in the faint hope of news concerning Antonia whose
dear memory has been with me in my darkest hours,
coming to me in my anguish like sweet and fragrant breath
of Heaven, as it ever may, I pray God. I was yet un-
decided when Ned says that by her rig (now more distant)

he judges this a Spanish ship, whereupon I was about to
put to him this question that vexed me, when he spoke,
saying he was pretty sure there was something amiss, and
bidding me watch her closely. This I did, and now saw she
was behaving very oddly,—coming up into the wind only
to fall off again, and this repeatedly, so that it was manifest
she was under no guidance. This deciding me, our course
was altered to bring us to her soon as might be. There was
stiffish breeze, and this great ship, despite her bluffness,
being clean and new-scrubbed, made such fair going that
after what seemed great while, yet sooner than I expected,
we had good sight of this ship and made out her name to
be *San Cristobal* and later, as she yawed, saw her much
scarred by battle, and from her mainyard five dangling
shapes that swayed with her every lurch.

We held on until so near we might glimpse her decks,
beholding which, I took glass from my eye to look at Ned
and he at me. "Pirates!" says he, with great oath, and he
no swearer as a rule. "What now, sir?" he questioned.
For answer I hailed and ordered a boat hove outboard.
So with yards braced aback we drifted near this poor ship
and presently brought to within half a pistol-shot of her.

Then Ned and George, John and I, with four men all
well armed, rowed to and boarded this ship, clambering up
by means of trailing cordage, and stood appalled, for blood
seemed everywhere and amid it all, lashed to the mainmast,
a dripping, shapeless horror all ringed about by shattered
bottles that had battered him to death. Ned was muttering, though whether prayers or curses I knew not, Sir G.
D'Arcy reeled to the side and vomited. I, shivering, drew
my two pistols instinctively and looked to their primings,
and then nigh dropped them in new horror as from 'twixt
two huddled bodies that lay abaft, and scarce seen behind
the starboard poop-ladder, a dreadful shape up-reared
itself, beholding which, Ned cried on God very awfully,
for this ghastly, blood-dabbled thing was a woman, who
ran crouching, to fall at my feet calling out piteously in

Spanish to show mercy on her for Mary and sweet Jesus' sake. So I raised her gently, speaking her kindly as I might in my broken Spanish, and beckoning John, bade him take her to the galleon and give her to the care of Don Luiz.

Then with George and Ned, I went to and fro about this ravaged ship, and in the great cabin found four other women dead and in such cruel and shameful circumstance as I may not describe. And when we had salvaged such few things as might be of any use or value, I ordered this poor ship, this dreadful monument of man's vileness, to be set afire, and so presently back to the *Santissima T*. Then with yards braced to wind we stood away, leaving this ship, *San Cristobal* well aflame. And in about an hour, we with fair offing, the fire reaching her magazine, she blew up, hiding her shame forever in God's clean ocean. And now in my body such faintness and within my soul such great bitterness and horror that I could not bear company, so went and hid myself in my cabin, bolting the doors. And after some while, took pen to make faithful record, and therewith this most solemn oath before Almighty God, viz.: That henceforth, the Lord aiding, I will be the Absolute Death and Perfect Destruction of any pirate that Providence see fit to send within my reach, to rid the world of this and like Pests, and the world of such inhuman monsters could have worked such barbarous shame and ghastly suffering aboard this ship called *San Cristobal*. Amen.

Writ this same day though later.

I had but just set down this most solemn vow and the ink not dry, when Smidge, knocking, cried out that the Don begged word with me. So unlocking the door I bade him be admitted.

He entered immediately, very pale and fervently grateful for this saving of a noble lady of Spain, her name Dolores de Gomez, "who," says he, hands and eyes lifted heavenward, "thanks to the Blessed Virgin and holy saints, 'scaped the unspeakable usage of her mother and sister and their two waiting-women. But, alas, sir, her noble father they murdered, killed him by throwing glass bottles . . . the captain and officers of the ship they strung up to the yards and forced overboard such of the crew as refused to join them." I now asked if the lady had told him aught of the rogues had wrought this evil. "Yes, sir," says he, "my lady says 'tis a pirate ship called *Joyous Lark*, commanded by an Englishman, one James Sigsbee, and long cruising the Main, and much feared, and spoke of as being a consort of this most infamous pirate named Black Bartlemy." And when I had learned thus all I might concerning these villains (and this little enough) I bade the young Don go comfort this poor lady the best he might with assurance of her present safety.

So thus, as if in answer to my vow (above solemnly recorded), comes this news of James Sigsbee and his ship *Joyous Lark*, the which, thinks I, is like a sign from Providence how I am destined most certainly to be the future destruction of this wretch and his vile company, and thus begin fulfilment of my oath. And this, God aiding, shall be accompt in His own good time.

CHAPTER XXX

TELLS BY WHAT ARTIFICE ADAM BROUGHT THE "JOYOUS LARK" TO DESTRUCTION

AND now is to tell what further preparations Adam made and the artifice he used to the accomplishment of his vow, and why so few suspected his design until he brought it to pass in his own subtle though determined manner.

Daily, morning, noon and night, he swept the wide horizons with perspective glass while he kept men constantly aloft on the look-out, with promise of gold piece to the first who should glimpse a sail.

Day after day he stood to watch John's gun-crews at their drill and ordered extra rum for those most apt and zealous; he did the same with the musketeers, thereafter planning with Sir Benjamin and Sir George how best to station them for close fighting, and how they should give fire, rank by rank, one file to shoot while the other reloaded.

He chose the most splendid of the armour, and this of black steel richly damascened with gold, its close-fitting burgonet adorned with scarlet plume,—all of which he had conveyed to his cabin and placed in charged of Smidge, to the boy's tremulous delight.

Thus as he stood of a certain morning, glass at eye, sweeping the vague distances, came Sir George new-risen, for it was early.

"Good-morrow, Adam!" said he, stifling a yawn. "D'ye never sleep? Last thing at night and first in the morning and always o' late with that glass at your eye. Why are you forever on the watch,—what is it you look for?"

"Ships!" answered Adam, laying by his glass. "Ships, George, for this is the Main, and we should fall in with plenty anon, and if Spanish I would speak her on account of Don Luiz, according to promise and also . . . seek news of Absalom and . . . Ay indeed I would fain question every ship 'twixt here and the Barbados."

"Nay but, Adam, remembering we are so rich laden,—how if we sight one of these damned pirate vessels?"

"Then she'll sight us, George, and know us instantly for Spanish treasure ship by our mere rig and bravery o' paint, so must we fight or run."

"And what should you do, Adam?"

"Both, George."

"Now how in reason can that be?"

"And moreover," said Adam, his gaze on the distance, "I've an odd feeling, George, a strange premonition, or say foreboding, we are destined run foul o' the *Joyous Lark*, soon or late."

"God forbid!" exclaimed Sir George, with fervour.

"As you say, George. And yet . . . if God permit I shall do my best to her absolute destruction."

"How then, you'd risk——?"

"Everything, George, to such good purpose, and my own life first of all."

"But, Lord love you, Adam, this would be——"

"Our duty, George."

"No no, Adam, I was about to say stupendous folly! With such crew as ours all untried in fight 'twould be adventure wild and quite impossible."

"Ay verily," nodded Adam, "duty often seems so . . . yet I hold few things to be impossible. Now tell me, talking of this *Joyous Lark* have you had word with the Spanish lady o' late, the poor, gentle soul?"

"She keeps very close, Adam, and small wonder. But last night she being on deck for breath of air with the young Don, I ventured to bow and pay my respects, whereat she tried to speak, but fell a-weeping instead, and so left us, very pitiful."

"Ay truly," sighed Adam, "the *Joyous Lark* hath left its foul brand upon her soul, ay and others beside, and will again—except such evil be destroyed."

"If ye please, gentlemen," piped Smidge, appearing at this moment with his usual suddenness, "Jimbo says as breakfast be awaiting for you t' eat."

"Why then, lead on, my seadog, and eat we will, eh, George?"

"Faith yes, I'm ravenous! And by this same token, Jimbo is very excellent cook."

"Ay, and a man, George."

It was this same morning, after a busy hour or so with his musketeers, that Sir Benjamin, puffing and blowing and somewhat pettish because of the heat, clambered to the poop where Adam paced, his eyes questing as usual to windward.

"Adam," quoth he, mopping tanned visage, "I'm a dog,—I say I'm a lewdly-yapping cur if ye don't work us plaguey hard and beyond all reason!"

"Ay I do, Ben, yet with purpose very reasonable!"

"Well now, Adam, I'm here to know just what precisely is your reason that I and all men aboard must so labour and sweat, sweat and labour till, what with our so laborious sweat, we might as well be sweating again at cursed labour aboard that thrice blasted galleasse! Come now, what's your reason, in a word? Pronounce!"

"In a word, Ben, safety."

"Ha, safety is it? Now if you mean our hellish rogues, these imps o' Satan and spawn o' the devil, our rascal crew,—eh, Adam?"

"Ay, ay, my Benjamin."

"Then I protest there is no reason, for since you killed Vardon they're tame enough."

"And to keep 'em so, I work them, Ben."

"Ay, but lookee, Adam, thou'rt turning this galleon

into very ship o' war on tip-toe for bloody strife, 'stead o' peaceful trader speeding for port to be our fortune."

"I am," nodded Adam, grimly, "I am indeed! This *Santissima Trinidad* shall be death and destruction to any dare attack."

"Well and good, Adam! But—having proper regard to her so precious cargo that is to be our future good, our joy, ease, luxury and Old England, indeed the summit of our hopes, and crown of our ambitions, minding all o' this, thou'lt run no least chance of attack but run there-from rather, ay at first glimpse of strange sail, you'll bear up and stand away on opposite course, like wise man and prudent commander, eh, Adam, eh?"

"As you say, Ben. Though I'd have you remember how this ship is heavy on her helm and something slow, whiles these Spanish warships and pirate vessels are rigged and built for speed."

"Ay, and choke-full o' fighting-men, Adam, whereas we, alas, are undermanned! Now minding this and our cargo and the very desperate courage o' these vile pirates, I say far better run than fight—to risk our lives and so much beside,—eh, Adam?"

"As thou sayest, my Benjamin."

"Ay, I do, but—hell and furies, man,—what say you?"

"Well, I say we are a floating lure to every pirate and buccaneer in the Main, Ben, for with our paint and gilding we are treasure ship right manifest. We are Spanish from trucks to waterline, and Spanish we'll seem, yet fight like Englishmen if need be."

"No no, Adam,—talk not o' fight, 'tis a naughty word and likes me not—with so much treasure below. To fight with naught to gain and all to lose were merest crass folly, and very damnable fool's ploy. As a beggar with all to gain I'll fight the world, but as rich man with all to lose I'll flee so fast from danger that my nether man shall be hid in the dust o' my going. So, Adam, like most wise and sapient commander, you'll turn and run at first sight of any sail, come now! Promise me this in holy Friendship's sacred name."

"Ben, you shall see us clap on every inch o' canvas we can carry, though, as I say, she is a slow ship, built rather for strength and comfort than speed!"

"Howbeit, I take marvellous comfort in thy promise, Adam, to flee all hazard o' battle or loss thereby of our treasure. Ay, here's comfort. So now, being parched wi' very sweatful labour, I'll go quaff a cup or so o' wine to our safe and speedy anchorage at Port Royal, eh Adam?"

"Ay, Ben, go drink to thine own prosperity. Take all comfort for thy share o' the pelf . . . this loot, this damned gold and the curse of it."

"Hey? The curse, says you?"

"Ay I do. 'Tis curse and plague say I. For there is no curse in all this world like love o' gold and the fear of losing it, can so blight the soul to the begetting of avarice, fear, hate and murder."

"Eh . . . eh . . . what?" gasped Sir Benjamin, "I protest you . . . you shock me . . . very damnably! Now lay me bleeding if I ever heard the like o' this! All I can say is . . . smite me deaf, blind and dumb if——"

"No no!" said Adam, with one of his rare laughs. "A dumb Benjamin would be beyond nature and therefore impossible!"

Sir Benjamin glared, snorted and strode away to appease his consuming thirst forthwith; but scarce had he gulped the wine Jimbo had poured than from above rose that most arresting cry:

"A sail! Sail ho!"

Up bounced Sir Benjamin instantly and out upon deck, bellowing:

"Where—whereaway?"

"Astern of us to windward," answered Ned, glass at eye. "She'm too far yet to make sure, but by her length o' spars and cut o' canvas I'll say as she ain't Spanish."

"Ha, you hear that, Adam, you hear?" cried Sir Benjamin. "Now, fulfil me your promise, man."

"Ay ay!" answered Adam, focusing his own perspective glass upon this distant ship. "Let them make all sail, Ned, every stitch. Then come you to my cabin. As for thyself, Ben, go muster and arm your musketeers! For, as I've told, our *Santissima* is heavy sailer, and should we be pursued 'twere well to stand prepared."

"'Od's body, Adam,—one would think you expect battle and bloody strife anon!"

"As you say, Ben. But what I say is,—what will be must be, wherefore it behoves us to be ready."

So saying, Adam smiled rather grimly, tucked perspective glass beneath his arm, and so went to his cabin; and here presently Ned coming to report all sail now set, found him gazing thoughtfully from stern window at this distant vessel.

"Sit down," said Adam, without moving, "sit ye now and hearken to me. If, as you think, yon ship is no Spaniard then I take it she is some pirate or buccaneer and if so, 'tis my earnest hope she may prove that same *Joyous Lark* intent on more vile havoc and plunder. Indeed, Ned, I verily believe she is."

"Then, sir, she'll be on-common heavy armed and manned."

"Beyond all doubt, Ned. Howbeit I am determined on her absolute destruction."

Ned drew a deep breath, rose to his feet, staring on this small, soft-voiced speaker but, meeting his eye, sat down again and shook his head.

"Meaning, Captain, as you'll . . . fight her?"

"Indeed!" nodded Adam. "I shall bring her to close action so soon as may be."

"The Lord forbid, sir!"

"Nay, I believe the Lord so ordains, Ned, and hath sent her hither to His just vengeance and her final doom."

"But . . . Oh Lord love us, Cap'n Adam,—how can we be sure as our rogues shall fight?"

"Because the most of them are Englishmen, thank Heaven! Moreover, we Dreadnoughts will show 'em how. For fight we shall, and sooner the better. And this the way on 't. 'Tis certain she sees us,—very well,—so soon as she alters course to pursue, we, as if in panic, shall do the like, making to run from her, and this shall be proof to every man aboard how anxious I am to avoid battle and spare them all the least danger thereof . . . but—now hearkee! I have read of a contrivance called a 'sea-anchor', which is a sail outspread on spars, that, cast overboard, shall hold and stay a ship very handsomely."

"Ay, sir, for sure. I've rigged many a one."

"Why then, Ned, you shall now go rig another and all unknown to any o' the men save trusty, chosen few. Then stand by, and so soon as I give order to alter course, you shall let go our sea-anchor astern to check and hinder our speed. So thus and despite our vast spread o' sail our pursuer shall rapidly overhaul us and, thinking we fly in terror, shall be the more assured and less prepared for heat of our welcome. Now, is this understood of thee, Ned?"

"Ay, sir . . . though . . . when I think on all that gold below as is to be our fortun'——"

"Ha,—this curse of gold!" snarled Adam, in sudden fury. "This damnable evil that can so pervert and corrupt the best and bravest——"

"Nay now, sir!" quoth sturdy Ned. "Belay, Master Adam, I was but saying, seeing as how we'm rich, one and all,—why run chance o' losing all? And yet, seeing as how you be my Captain and orders being orders, all as I therefore says is, ay ay, sir, dooty being dooty, so be it!" And, touching bristly eyebrow, away rolled this hardy seaman, leaving Adam to pace up and down, scowling on this far-off ship; presently, however, he took quill and penned this:

A list of all officers aboard the *Santissima Trinidad* prior to our action with suspected Pirate.

Name	Rank
Ad. Penfeather	Commander
Ed. Bowser	Master
John Fenn	Gunner
Nick Cobb	Gunner's mate
Silas Guppy	do.
Sir Benj. Trigg	Captain of Musketeers
Sir Geo. D'Arcy	2nd do.
Martin Frant	Boatswain
Matt. Appleby	Boatswain's mate
Timothy Sprake	do.
Tobias Drew	Carpenter
Sim Hopkins	Carpenter's mate
G. Tregenza	Cockswain

And I humbly pray God we may all answer the roll-call when this fight be over and these pirates utterly destroyed.

Amen.

This written, he summoned Smidge to belt, hook and buckle him into his splendid Spanish armour, and so went clashing to and fro to get used to the irk of it, while the boy watched in an ecstasy.

"Now, shipmate," said he, surveying himself in the mirror, "go seek John Fenn, Sir George, Martin Frant and Sir Benjamin and bid them to the coach ten minutes hence for council of war." So away sped the boy while Adam clanked down below where Ned, Toby and Sim Hopkins were busied to fashion the sea-anchor.

"How goes it, Ned?"

"All ready and ship-shape, sir."

"Very well. Stand by to let it go when I hail."

Then up he went for his perspective glass, and so to the poop, and peering thence at their pursuer, saw her

now much nearer, plainly standing in chase of them
beneath great press of sail. Hereupon he hailed below
where Ned and his fellows waited in the steerage; he heard
Ned's answering cry, then the splashing plunge of the
sea-anchor, and thereafter was aware how the great ship's
career was sensibly decreased,—and so with furtive smile
curving his lips, Adam betook himself to the coach.

Thus Sir Benjamin and his companions, turning to
sound of opening door, stared at sight of this grim, warlike
figure booted to the knees and thence sheathed in burnished
steel, but grimmest of all the lean, bronzed face framed
in steel and crowned by nodding, scarlet plume.

"'Od's body!" exclaimed Sir Benjamin. "'S blood,
what's this?"

"Strategy!" answered Adam, taking his seat at head
of the long table. "You behold in me a Spanish Admiral,
a proud and noble gentleman o' Spain, with Spanish
colours at our main and, as I believe, a pirate coming
down wind on our quarter in chase of this treasure ship
o' Spain. So it behoves us now to take counsel how we
shall meet his attack."

"Eh—attack?" exclaimed Sir Benjamin, bouncing in
his chair. "Why, by not meeting it, by bearing up and
standing away and avoiding any chance o' battle. We're
all agreed on this, and most heartily unanimous, eh, sirs?
You, George, speak now and tell him how we are determined."

"Why yes," said Sir George, "for truly and indeed.
Adam, seeing we have so much at stake our best strategy
should be to elude all strange ships and shun every chance
of attack, to set every sail possible and use every means
and sailorly device and cunning artifice——"

"'Tis done, George, 'tis done!" nodded Adam. "Sail,
device and artifice, and yet despite all this our pursuer
gains on us so fast their shot will be flying about our ears
ere long. And 'tis no wonder we are pursued since this
great galleon, with her paint and gilded bravery, is a

challenge and resistless lure to all predatory craft. So
must we handle and fight her like the Englishmen we
are. And this the way of it. Yon ship I believe to be a
pirate intent on our blood and pillage——"

"God forbid!" exclaimed Sir Benjamin, piously.

"Amen!" said Adam. "And may He thereto aid our
John and his men to aim true and fire speedily. Now
hearkee, John! With your greatest pieces double-shotted
you shall bide with closed ports and never a blink of gun-
muzzle, while you, George and Ben, with your musketeers
shall lie hid in points of vantage. Then will I in this
armour show myself on the poop like proud Don in solitary
estate. So shall these rogues come on amain all unsuspect-
ing and assured until at my word ye loose off every piece,
every musket and gun smiting them point blank and so
close as, I pray the Lord, shall prove their soon and very
complete destruction. Well, how say ye?"

"Say?" moaned Sir Benjamin. "I say if fight we must,
with a wannion,—fight we will, ay, and with a will, the
closer the better! For I'd liefer die person of affluence
aboardship than perish a pauper ashore."

"And pray," enquired John Fenn, his eyes bright and
eager, "how near shall you let 'em come afore we fire,
Captain Adam?"

"About pistol-shot, John. I shall take care to keep
them bows on, then, before they can bear up to give us
their broadside, we shall rake 'em fore and aft with
ours."

"Why then," quoth John, rising as he spoke, "at such
close range our weight o' shot should do their business
very surely."

Their method of battle thus agreed, forth they went
on deck to watch the approach of this ship that Adam
was hoping might indeed prove to be the *Joyous Lark*.

"She comes apace!" said Sir George.

"Ay, and with freshening wind!" nodded John. "A
sweet fighting wind if this lubberly, old *Santa* of ours

was a bit livelier; she goes surprising heavy! I knew she was not speedy, but——"

"Speedy?" exclaimed Sir Benjamin, stamping and snorting with impatience as he rolled fiery eye up at their great spread of straining canvas. "She's speedy as a snail! Why, dog-bite me—she crawls! Ha, smite me blind and speechless but she creeps like a slug, a very louse!"

"Indeed," said Adam, his steady gaze to windward. "She is perhaps something slow, but——"

"Slow?" groaned Sir Benjamin. "She's a worm! 'Tis pestilent lousy ship shall be our destruction yet or I'm a dog! See how yon devil's craft gains on us, she grows with every minute."

"Ay, Ben, she sails three feet to our one," said Adam, glass at eye. "She'll be at us with her fore-chase very soon."

"And we to make no reply, Captain?"

"Not a gun, John, till I give word. And . . . ah yes," said Adam, steadying his glass, "it is as I expected . . . she is—— But look for yourself and tell me," and he gave the glass to John who, after some focusing, answered cheerily:

"Ay, she's the *Lark* sure enough! And a powerful ship, sir."

"Yes, she's sufficiently formidable, forty guns or thereabouts, eh, John?"

"And fairish heavy pieces, sir. Now if she has chance to luff and bring her broadside to bear——"

"She never shall, John, trust me for this."

The *Joyous Lark* was now so near they could see her plainly for a fine, stout ship heavily sparred and armed, though not so high built as the towering *Santissima Trinidad*. Now as they watched her coming against them in her prideful might, Adam drew the long rapier he wore and with its glittering point gestured where from her lofty mainmast broke and fluttered a great flag that showed a black skeleton on yellow ground, this blazon of merciless piracy that was lately become the plague and terror of these seas.

"See now yonder!" said he. "She flaunts her defiance and black shame, 'tis flag of infamy,—and this one, at least, God aiding, shall affront His seas no longer. And now, sirs, I suggest you go muster your men to their stations,—nay, first bid Martin pipe the crew aft for word from me."

So presently Adam, coming to the quarterdeck rail, looked down where the men were ranked, men who scowled, muttered, stared in wonder or grinned to see him in this splendour of Spanish armour. Suddenly he lifted sword as if in salute, and with blade thus upraised and glance that swept each watching face, waited until all muttering ceased and, in that moment, spoke them loud and clear:

"Ye that were slaves are now men, and being men are all children o' the Lord that, being our merciful Father is also the God of Battles to strengthen us for victory ever and always so long as our cause be just. Well now, yonder against us come sons o' the Devil, joying in iniquity, to be our death. So to-day we fight for our lives 'gainst wickedness and cruelty, and therefore to the glory of the Lord. And so, my Dreadnoughts all, taking God with us into the fight, we cannot fail, let come what may. Remember this and fight your hardest, doing your duty like men. And now to our posts!"

And thus it was that Adam began to fight the first of his many battles, though he gives very brief account of it in his Journal, and indeed it seems to have been a short but decisive action; and what he writes of himself is this:

About three o'clock the *Joyous Lark* began firing at us with their fore-chase and no man aboard the galleon more inly perturbed than myself, insomuch that my knees shook as I mounted the poop ladder while my poor body shivered within my splendour of steel, like the craven that I truly am, and yet conceal for very shame. For being of singular cautious nature, with a mind quick to apprehend and overly imagine dangers, I see these perils all so greatly magnified I should never dare them but for my so great and constant desire to be worthy my father that lived and died unfearing. And so thus in this first hour of battle, foreseeing what horrors might be, I felt myself all aquake with a nauseous swimming in my bowels, so great was my dread. But bethinking me how the fate of this great ship and all on board lay in my care, I nerved myself for what was to do, crying within me on the Lord (yet again) for strength and wisdom thereto.

So with this prayer in his heart, up to the poop went Adam and there, his armour flashing back the sun and scarlet plume dancing in the breeze, paraded in solitary state like a proud noble of mighty Spain. And for such indeed it seemed these pirates mistook him, for at sight of his splendid, lonely figure, they raised a shout inarticulate as yet, though fiercely derisive, and opened a brisk fire with their two fore-chase guns.

It was as Ned came up the steep poop ladder that a shot struck the bulwark hard by, filling the air with splinters and Adam was hurled to the deck, whereat rose a howl of jubilation from the *Joyous Lark*; but as Ned ran to lift him, Adam scrambled to his feet and laughed.

"Eh, you're not hurt, sir?"

"Nay . . . this armour . . . saved me!" Adam gasped. "But they're marring our paint and finery sadly."

"Ay, sir, but no more, for yon ball h'an't so much as pierced our timbers! She's stout built is our *Santy*." Even as he spoke, another shot whizzed through the bonaventure sail above them, followed a little later by yet another, and so near that Adam flinched in spite of himself while Ned ducked, saying:

"'Tis getting pretty hot yereabouts, sir!"

"It is!" nodded Adam.

"Why then, sir, seeing as how, don't ee think 'twould be as well to take cover in lee o' the mizzen, say, or lay low out o' sight?"

"Ay, I do indeed, so down with thee, Ned."

"Why then, you first, sir."

"No, no! I wear this armour to show like a Spanish grandee, Ned, and who ever heard o' proud Don so far forgetting his dignity as to crouch to mere cannon ball? So, down with thee, ha take cover, man, this is an order!" So while Ned squatted obediently in shelter of the high bulwark, Adam paced to and fro, glancing, now at the decks below, where men lay so very still and watchful, grasping cocked muskets and waiting his command, and now at their threatening foe astern whence now, with their great shot, came musket balls to whine and hiss about him.

"Who is at the steerage, Ned?"

"Si and his comrade Nick, sir, able men and trusty both."

"You warned 'em to stand by for my word?"

"Ay, I did, sir, and they'm both a tip-toe wi' years on the stretch at this moment, I warrant me."

"Our sea-anchor serves us well, Ned."

"Ay, sir," he answered, fidgeting with the ponderous boarding axe he bore, "but don't ye think 'tis about time 't was cast adrift and we bore up to give they rogues a broadside, they'm getting pretty close."

"Another ten minutes or so."

"Ten minutes?" exclaimed Ned, peering over the bulwark. "Why . . . Lord love us I can see 'em plain as may be."

"But I would see them plainer yet, Ned."

"Sir, if you wait much longer you'll be too dead to see em at all."

"That's as may be, Ned, but when we do fire it shall be point blank to do their business perfectly."

Thus Adam paced and talked, with death whizzing about him, and Ned crouched and argued, fidgeting with his axe, while the *Santissima Trinidad* rolled sluggish upon her course with no answering sound or sign to the fierce clamour that came down wind from her pursuer,—the jubilant shouts and cheers of a crew exulting in their strength and used to victory.

The musketry fire grew hotter; a bullet clipped a feather from Adam's burgonet, a second grazed the mast beside him, a third smote and whined from his armour, staggering him; then cried Ned:

"Oh, Cap'n, will ye die afore you order we set about 'em? Will ye suffer they run us aboard?"

"Not so, Ned, for—now is the moment, these your orders: Let slip the sea anchor! Down helm! Lee tacks and braces hale aft! See to it!"

So away hurried Ned, shouting . . . whereupon the great yards creaked round and as the mighty galleon bore up, thus turning her broadside to the foe, Adam stepped to the quarterdeck railing and lifted his sword; at which expected signal so long and eagerly awaited, the Bo'sun's pipe twittered and Matthew Appleby passed the word to fire. Then from the *Santissima Trinidad's* towering side John Fenn's heaviest guns roared, gushing flame and smoke and slaughter. . . . And in this awful moment came little Smidge, from some corner where he had lain hid, to slip his hand into Adam's firm clasp until, remembering, he saluted smartly instead and drew his sword.

Now presently, the smoke clearing, they saw the battle was won, for the *Joyous Lark*, smitten and raked fore and aft at this close and deadly range, lay a shattered ruin her fore and mainmasts gone, her once crowded decks a red horror direly confused. Yet to make all sure, Adam bade them bear up, and the galleon fetching about, let fly her larboard guns. . . .

And so was an end of this ship *Joyous Lark*, for presently down she plunged, stem foremost, to hide her evil in the blue deeps of ocean; only where she had been was drift of floating wreckage crowded with miserable wretches who wailed in the face of Death, imploring mercy,—and all in vain.

But as Adam commanded the galleon's yards to be braced to the wind, Sir Benjamin bellowed from the quarter-deck, and up the poop ladder came Sir George, stumbling with haste.

"Oh, Adam, wait—wait!" cried he, breathlessly. "The survivors, Adam,—what o' them?"

"There are none," answered Adam, watching where the sails were being trimmed.

"But there are, Adam, there are! Men are drowning yonder . . . can't ye see, don't ye hear?"

"Ay, I do, George. But I remember also those dead women aboard the *San Cristobal* . . . their shame and agony! I think of . . . of another woman who may have been so abused! As for their murderers yonder, these beastly rogues, I give them the clean sea and sailorly death here, rather than strangling noose ashore where they would rot and foul the air on gibbets."

Then going aft he hailed the steersmen.

"Helm a-starboard! Keep her north-westerly." And so the *Santissima Trinidad* bore away on her old course for the Barbados and Jamaica, soon to leave behind her no more than floating wreckage.

Then, with Smidge trotting at his heels, Adam went down to his cabin and there rid of his cumbrous armour, wrote down a brief account of this action for witness his vow had been fulfilled.

CHAPTER XXXI

WHICH IS OF NO PARTICULAR IMPORT

WITHIN a week they came to the Barbados, where Don Luiz and the heartbroken Spanish lady made their grateful farewell; and here, while Sir Benjamin (who showed as prime man of business) made some traffic of their cargo and Ned saw to the ship's overhaul and plenishing of her stores, especially fruits and fresh water, Adam took the pinnace and with Sir George D'Arcy and chosen crew all 'very well armed', went seeking news concerning the survivors, if any, of the *Bold Adventuress*. Which is best and shortest told in Adam's own words, thus:

Buoyed up by that desperate hope which has lived within me despite many fearful doubts, we sailed and rowed and marched to and fro and about these islands until, our laborious days running to weeks and no word to comfort or encourage us, I at last determined to go back aboardship and sail for Jamaica there to assure myself, once and for all, if Antonia lived or was dead. Much discouraged and greatly deject I, with Smidge, Jimbo and seventeen of our men, chief of whom were Giles Tregenza and Tobias Drew, that are become my staunch allies these days,—we were, I say, marching seawards to rejoin Sir G. D'Arcy and others in the pinnace, when we were arrested by that (to me) most terrible of all sounds—the agonized screaming of a woman. These piteous cries coming from beyond a high wall that bordered our going, I beckoned Jimbo, who took me standing upon his shoulders and thus hoisted

me so that looking over this wall I saw a woeful yet too
frequent sight in these plantations, viz: An Indian girl
rove to a post bleeding 'neath the whip of a negro, an
Indian youth writhing in bonds and a stoutish white
man richly habited, sprawling in cushioned chair to
watch this torment and a pistol in his fist. As I looked,
he cried (and in English) "Enough!" The negro stepped
aside whereupon his white master (and an Englishman
alas!) levelled and shot this poor, screaming creature,
ending her miseries instantly; then he gestures with
smoking pistol toward the Indian youth. The negro
raised his blood-stained whip, but I shot it out of his
hand then, tossing the discharged weapon to Smidge,
got me over the wall and coming to this white man,
enquired very civilly his name and condition.

"Why," says he, "I am Philip Dalton and master
here, so who the devil are you?" "Adam Penfeather,"
says I, and catching up a gold-knobbed cane from table
whereon stood bottles and glasses, I struck him smartly
across his plump visage therewith, naming him a foul
disgrace to our England, then, seeing he wore rapier,
drew my own and bade him defend himself. At this,
his negro raises great haloo, and comes at me and others
also, but him I disabled with my second pistol, whereat
over the wall leaps Jimbo and the rest of my men,
eager for strife. Then, while Mr. Dalton's servants,
black and white, stood cowering, we fought. But this
man, being of gross habit and marvellous inapt with
his weapon, was instantly at my mercy and I greatly
minded to end him, but instead was content to let him
blood in several places and finally transfixed his sword-
arm from elbow to shoulder and holding him thus painfully helpless, forced him to kneel. And when he had
sworne thus to show more kindness on his slaves thereafter or God smite him dead, I left him alive, a very
sore and sorry man. So back to our pinnace, and this
Indian youth now following me like my shadow and

with most fervent and lively marks of loving gratitude for his deliverance. Reaching the seaside, he makes such urgent appeal to be taken with us that I could not well refuse. Towards evening we came aboard the galleon, and myself now so intent for Jamaica (there being Absalom's rendezvous and my last hope for news of Antonia) that despite Sir Benj. his reproaches and pleas of "much present good business," we hove anchor this same night and bore away for Port Royal.

And thus did Adam save alive this poor Indian who was to become his willing slave, faithful servant, loving friend and finally his salvation, as is yet to be recorded.

CHAPTER XXXII

HOW ADAM BECAME PENFEATHER, THE BUCCANEER

NOW though Adam's navigation had guided them truly thus far, it seemed they were not yet to reach Jamaica, for scarce had they left the Barbados than the weather became so threatening that, as Adam writes, he struck his topmasts, thereby (and with God his grace) escaping certain shipwreck in great gale that drove them far northward through terrible seas for very many days, but the ship so trim and stout that, when at last this storm abated, she was little the worse for all her cruel buffeting. So (writes Adam) "after long and weary travail with many and divers perils, we came into that sea named Caribbean whose blue waters do cradle isles of such beauty as passeth description."

Yet describe them he does, their luscious fruits, noxious reptiles, coral beaches and palmetto groves, with much concerning their wild peoples, their strange customs of life. Also in Adam's Journal is a long catalogue of the many Spanish ships they met; of which (as he writes) "having plundered somewhat, especially of provision, powder, shot, etc., we suffered to depart no whit the worse." There are also many brief, though grim, descriptions of "pirates lured to their perfect destruction, they being duly burned or sunk and never a survivor."

So for a year or more the great *Santissima Trinidad*, with her crew of now experienced, hard-fighting seamen, roamed the seas, showing like treasure-ship of Spain and thus seducing all predatory craft to be destroyed by the speed and accuracy of her heavy broadsides, so that the last earthly sight many a dying rogue beheld was the

grim figure in black, Spanish armour, whose lifted sword
glittered, as it were, in salute to their dying. . . .

And yet some few survivors there must have been, for
the name of Captain Adam Penfeather rang throughout
those seas as a leader of victorious daring, though merciless as he was bold. So that the *Santissima Trinidad*
became (later on) no more a lure to be chased in certainty
of easy victory and rich plunder, but a hard-smiting
terror to be shunned at all hazards.

Thus Adam's fame grew week by week and month by
month, until whensoever his tall ship came surging into
port or haven, men flocked to serve under commander so
bold to dare and so fortunate in his daring, so that as
time passed his crew had grown to twice its number and
these Englishmen all, many of the Coast Brotherhood
and everyone chosen by himself.

So ' Penfeather, the Buccaneer,' grew famous, and waxed
from strength to strength, his silvery hair or scarlet plume
became the sure gage of victorious fortune for all to
follow.

It was at this time that ship-captains less fortunate
sought to join company and sail beneath his command
and vainly, until, learning of the horrors committed in
the prisons of the Inquisition

"and especially (writes Adam) those of Panama, Porto
Bello, Carthagena, St. John, and Santo Domingo and all
rich cities, I determined to rescue these poor victims from
torture and torment of fire, and levy tribute on their
oppressors therefor. Thus, having news that in the city
of St. John was to be one of these mass burnings of men
and women, heretics and others, in presence of great concourse assembled to watch their agonies and called an Auto
da Fé, I sailed against this city as Admiral of twelve ships
of the Coast Brotherhood or Buccaneers, all well manned
and armed. Having forced a landing in two several places,
we stormed all defences and whiles divers of the Buccaneers

burned and pillaged the town, I with my company broke
open the prisons, freed all therein and so got safe back
aboard ship with little booty yet smaller loss, and later
cometh Sir Benjamin himself wounded, his company few
but heavy with loot.''

So passed some eighteen months of fighting at sea and
battles ashore, thus briefly narrated, till came that day
when the storm-beaten, battle-scarred *Santissima Trinidad*
came in sight of Jamaica at last, to the great joy of all
aboard, more especially Sir Benjamin, and the trembling
anxiety of one.

CHAPTER XXXIII

TELLS HOW THEY CAME TO JAMAICA

ALONE stood Adam in this early forenoon, his brooding gaze upon this island that grew upon his sight with every forward surge of the vessel,—a vague, blue shape of uprising from bluer ocean; but when he would have surveyed this through his perspective glass, found it impossible because of the nervous quiver of his hands and inward quaking. So instead he leaned there on the carved poop-rail staring with great, wistful eyes. At last his agitation became so great that he went down to his cabin and sought relief therefrom with pen and ink. And since he can best describe his trouble, and its cause, in his own words, here they are:

In sight of Jamaica at last where I am to know, and certainly as may be, if Antonia be alive or dead. And my harassed mind in great turmoil therefore, since now I must needs think on all the many chances against her having weathered and come through so many grievous perils unharmed, as—famine, sickness, mutiny and shipwreck. Or been taken as captive of Spain and the terrible Inquisition to die by torture or fire, or fallen the helpless prey of accursed pirates, to suffer—oh God forbid it—such vile shame and brutish violence so foully manifest aboard the *San Cristobal*, the which nauseous fear hath driven me to such pitiless doing against all pirates soever. And indeed which fear even now so haunts and sickens me that I cannot bear to write, but must up again into the clean air.

"Oho Adam, so there she lies!" cried Sir Benjamin, bouncing and strutting on jubilant legs. "Jamaica at last, and ourselves deep laden with vasty treasure, aha! 'Od's my life 'tis noble isle, a fair anchorage and famous market for our wares, our princely loot and kingly plunder. Yonder is our means of much enrichment, our future fame and . . . Old England, God bless her! England and prosperity, Adam; eh? Why, smite me stiff in gore if y' aren't all of a quake and pallid as a shark's belly! What's amiss, man, what's to do? Yonder, I tell ye, lieth our joy—fortune, fame, and riches."

"Ay, and—the truth, Ben! Truth at last,—good or ill!"

"Truth quotha? What truth?"

"If they be living or dead. Ay . . . dead and lost these four long years and more . . . Absalom Troy, Captain Smy . . . and . . ."

"Your young brother, eh, Adam, that pretty, young gentleman, alas! Well, there with them also was kinsman o' mine, my cousin Temple,—poor Tom! And each and every vanished like so many dreams! Four years about, Adam! Four woeful, weary years of battle and tempest since we lost our fellows, their sweet companionship, 'mid cruel perils in plaguey cruel, vile and evil world where violence is king with grisly Death his consort foul. So, Adam, old shipmate, we were wiser now to esteem them dead and lost to us a while—until the Great Reunion . . . if there be such indeed—as you believe, eh, Adam?"

"Ay I do!" he answered, fervently. "I do with all my heart, this life were mockery else. So . . . if they be dead . . . well, they have thereby attained to fuller life and shall, mayhap, greet us kindly when cometh our turn to die."

"Why, here's good thought, Adam, though mighty lowering and melancholic. Thou'rt an odd, mournful soul for such vastly fortunate buccaneer, victorious captain and merciless fighter."

"Not merciless—no!" sighed Adam. "Say rather—a worker for Justice and Law in wild places,—a Scavenger o' the Seas. No man hath suffered by me save those fore-doomed by the Law. Such malefactors as sin where Justice may not reach them save by me. And whatso I have done against these wicked men I am ready to answer for at any time, here on earth, Ben, or aloft at the Last Great Tribunal.''

"Ay ay, Adam. But no more o' this, 'tis moot point and grisly subject, so talk we o' life and the joy of it for,—hearkee in thine ear,—at my last and most secret compu-tation, we are grown rich beyond even mine own expecta-tion,—never a man o' the crew but will receive a thousand guineas and more for his share, ay—even little Smidge! As for thyself, Adam, being Captain-general, thourt one o' the wealthiest commanders afloat to-day! For myself,—though 'twill grieve me sensibly to part, I am for England by the first ship thither bound. England! And affluence! I'll buy me back our family estates, become a power in the country and figure o' splendour at Court! Oh, Lord love thee, Adam, come now and let us drain a goblet, clink cannikin and toss a pot to Old England, ourselves and the golden Future,—come thee now!''

CHAPTER XXXIV

HOW ADAM HALTED 'TWIXT DOUBT AND CERTAINTY

THE sun was in its decline when they anchored before this rich and populous city of Port Royal to be presently surrounded by a great flotilla of boats of every kind thronged with people of every sort from languid ladies and fine gentlemen rowed by liveried slaves, to native piraguas filled with vociferous humanity, black, yellow and tawny. Yet each and every eager for sight of this now famous ship of ' Captain Adam Penfeather, the Buccaneer,' whose exploits had made him so notorious and whose tall vessel, though scarred by battle and stress of weather, yet showed much of her former splendour.

So the citizens of Port Royal, who throve greatly by marketing the cargoes of merchant adventurer, but far more by the rich lading of buccaneers and pirates, gave resounding welcome to the great *Santissima Trinidad* from boats, canoes and crowded quays, since report spoke her as ship crammed with treasure to the very hatches.

But Adam, having scanned these many faces with eager, questioning gaze, now fixed his wistful eyes upon this famous city that was for him the one place in all the world because of the one woman whose feet might have blessed the pavement of its busy streets and palm-shaded squares. Motionless he leaned, chin in hand, gazing on this oft-dreamed city where he knew, instinctively, was to be found the answer to that anxious question had troubled him these four long years; here he was to know at last if Antonia lived or was dead. So now, preferring doubtful hope to final and hopeless certainty, he made no least effort to know this answer, for his fear so far out-weighed hope that he shrank as yet from seeking the truth of it for himself. Thus stood he until espying Sir George on deck below he beckoned him up to the poop.

"George," said he, his gaze still on the distant mountains, "I take it you will go ashore with Ben?"

"God love you—yes, Adam! Life calls yonder, all the bustle and joy of it. But you'll with us, surely?"

"No . . . not yet, George, lest in the midst of such joyous life I learn . . . of death."

"Ah, you mean our lost shipmates of the poor *Adventuress ?*"

"Ay, I do. And most especially my good friend, Absalom Troy and . . . his lady."

"Eh? Lady? Mean you his wife, Adam?"

"Indeed, George."

"But how . . . who . . . when had he a wife?"

"Howbeit, George, as my trusty friend I ask you to . . . to make persistent enquiry ashore . . . wheresoever you go . . . for our lost friends. Ask first for Captain Troy, and if this fail, then enquire for him as Lord Perrow. Wilt do this for me?"

"Assuredly, Adam. But for Troy's wife now, pray tell me——" But at this moment Sir Benjamin appeared, bellowing joyously and in resplendent attire (looted from some ship), a magnificent personage from arrogant-curling feather to jingling, silver spurs.

"Ha, plague and confound me!" he exclaimed. "I say curse me with everlasting torments but 'twill never do, Adam! Art never going ashore in such damnable, dismal rig? That coat,—those breeches——"

"Will remain aboardship, Ben, and myself in them."

"So thou'lt not join us, Adam? Then I'll away to convene the chiefest merchants and so forth. I'll sound the markets and open negotiations. Also I've ordered Frant to have the sally port manned and ourselves piped away for mere look of it. There be many eyes upon us, Adam, and it behoves us to carry ourselves somewhat preciously."

So these two splendid gentlemen descended with dignity into their waiting boat and were rowed ashore while Adam went to his cabin and there found Smidge hard at work, with rags, oil and soft leather, on his armour (this constant labour of love) cherishing the many dints and scratches that hard service and close action had wrought upon the burnished steel.

"Lookee, Cap'n Adam, sir," cried the boy, "here's where a musket ball hit ye! And here's where you was poked very hard wi' a half-pike the time they pirates boarded us fore and aft, two ships they was—off Hispaniola. And on your helmet the mark of a sword though I think as how 'twas a naxe, and——"

"Ay, my old seadog, 'tis a good armour and has served me well."

"Yessir, 'tis always a-serving and a-saving of you because you always seem trying to get yourself killed, sir."

"Yet am I alive, Smidge."

"Because o' this armour, sir,—so this is why I keeps it bright."

"Well, leave it now and bring me your lessons, first the sentences I gave you to copy, then the four sums. You've done 'em, I hope?"

"Ay ay, Cap'n, the very best as I could . . . only . . . I wrote some blots by accident, sir, and one o' they sums wouldn't let me do him nohow . . . and, if you please, sir, I got a complaint to lay afore you."

"What is it?"

"Why then, Cap'n Adam, I don't want for myself to be a scholard,—just being your own seadog is all as I wants for to be until I grows me into one o' your Dreadnoughts like Si and Toby and Nick what can't write a stroke, sir, and says as how they don't want. So I'd liefer be your sailor than try for to be a scholard, sir."

"But I wish you to be both, Smidge, so that someday you'll be able to navigate and command your own ship. How old are you?"

1

"Why jist afore I takes to the sea, I hears as I were ten years of age, sir."

"So that now you are about fourteen,—ha, and a very backward scholar for your age. Now bring your lessons for my correction."

"Ay ay, sir,—only first, axing your pardon and by your leave, I got jest one more complaint——"

"What now?"

"This yere Indian savvige, sir, as be always looking and staring and follering o' you and never a word . . . ay and running for to serve you afore me. Well, sir, he aren't wanted—not wi' me always ready for to look arter you, Cap'n Adam. So what I says is—let's tell him for to sheer off, if you please, sir."

"No, Smidge. Instead we will make him your messmate. Remember what cruel suffering we saved him from, and what he must have endured. I think he is sad, lonely and silent only because he has no English."

"He can talk Spanish, sir—a bit, though not so good as me."

"Very well, you shall teach him English and how to read, write and cypher."

"What—me, sir?" wailed Smidge.

"Yes. And this is an order! I set him in your charge Now bring me your lessons—no, first go fetch hither our Indian."

"He's out yonder now, sir, standing off and on."

"Then bring him in here."

Smidge obeyed, though unwillingly, and presently returned followed by this tall young Indian who saluted Adam with joined hands touching first his breast and then his brow.

"Smidge, ask his name slowly and in your best Spanish."

The boy did so, whereupon this silent Indian's dark eyes lit up, and touching himself with slim, brown finger, he made answer in soft, liquid tones:

"Yarimao, Capa-cupa, Guan-uco, In-ca!" Then, pointing

to Adam, he bowed, saying, "El Capitano Ad-dam," and, gesturing towards the frowning boy, contrived to say: "Smee-eege."

"Well now," quoth Adam, "if he be Inca he is no mere savage. We will call him Mao and he shall be your friend, Smidge, I hope. However, I trust you to look after him."

"Ay but—how, sir, if you please?"

"See he is properly clad. Show him the use of a sword and how to speak English and, as I say, to read and write. By teaching him, you shall better learn yourself. Report to me both after supper. Now, off with ye."

"Ay ay, sir. Bear alongside o' me, Mao; I'll do my best with ye, 'cording to orders, to learn you A.B.C. and how to be a Englishman."

CHAPTER XXXV

HOW ADAM MET BLACK BARTLEMY

DAYS passed, but Sir George and Sir Benjamin (busied ashore with much traffic) bringing no least news of their lost companions, Adam at last determined on an expedition to explore the island himself nor cease his quest until all was known. His mind once made up, he set about it,—that is to say he reached for the silver bell beside him, then paused, arrested by sound of music slowly drawing nearer. Acting on sudden impulse, he rose, went forth upon the lofty stern-gallery and thence beheld a ship's longboat, but this a thing of splendour with silken canopy whence came this languorous music and rowed by brawny fellows in gorgeous livery.

Now perceiving this luxurious craft was making for his ship, out on deck went Adam, wondering. And thus he presently beheld a creature of supreme elegance who minced in his walk and held very daintily a gold pomander to the delicate, arched nose of him, a gentleman garbed all in black from arrogant-curling feather in bejewelled hat to the toes of his dainty shoes; diamonds glittered and pearls shimmered in the creamy laces at his throat, gleamed on one finger of his slim though muscular hand, sparkled in the gold hilt of his long rapier and flamed upon his arching insteps. This sombre magnificence was followed by a great, swaggering fellow who flourished bright steel hook in place of left hand, chewed tobacco voraciously and spat with ferocity, right and left. Beholding Adam, this gentleman ambled forward languidly, bowed graciously, sniffed at his scented pomander delicately and murmured:

"Lemme die, sir, but your ship reeks damnably o' tar!"

"Which, sir," answered Adam, bowing as graciously, "I prefer infinitely to the reek o' musk, civet, or suchlike cattish smells."

"Aha!" murmured the gentleman. "A hardy mariner, I perceive, very bluff, extreme tough, though something small as mariners go,—yet nevertheless, hardy! And now, sir, pray go inform your Captain I would ha' word with him, one Adam Penfeather, called The Buccaneer."

"You behold him, sir."

"Now do I, indeed? Sir, I am astounded!"

"And whom do I astound, pray?"

"Oh, sir, I am Captain Bartlemy, called 'The Black'. Other names I have, or had, but in these outlandish latitudes it contents me to permit such as will to name me Black Bartlemy, a title, sir, perhaps not wholly unknown to . . . even yourself."

"Indeed!" Adam nodded. "I know it for name of much detested rogue and pirate notorious."

Black Bartlemy's delicate nostrils quivered as he sniffed at his pomander, while his tall follower's hook glittered in sudden menace and he spoke in blustering tone:

"So ho now, ye hear him, Captain? This paltry skipjack,—ye hear him?"

"And you, Tressady, I would not hear, so—be dumb!"

"As you says, Captain, as you says!" quoth Tressady, spitting ferociously, while his master viewed Adam with faint-smiling arrogance.

"So you are the Captain Adam Penfeather they call The Buccaneer, and more bloody and merciless than any rascal pirate in The Main,—a choice, hypocritical smug that calls on God and blasts poor sailormen to hell! Ha truly, Captain Adam, thou'rt sober, smock-faced manslayer of deeds so splendidly atrocious I am here with some thought of enlisting your powers with mine 'gainst Santo Domingo, a place of much wealth, sacked years agone by Frankie Drake, but far richer booty to-day, and—what's more to me, famous for the warm beauty of its women. Now

Fame, sir, except she lie as usual, speaks you as crafty strategist ashore, and an artful strategy is required since the city is well-seated for defence and therefore difficult to assail. Well, now, myself and yourself, with eight or nine other captains to my command, might contrive very well. Say three or four weeks hence . . . by surprisal. How say you?"

"First," answered Adam, "I would say if your mannerless rogue fouls my deck with his beastly spittle again, or flaunts that hook of his, he shall be kicked overboard,—and secondly, Black Bartlemy, I invite you now to leave in fashion more seemly."

"Ha, Captain, he crows!" exclaimed Tressady. "He croweth like very small bantam cock on his own dunghill, —he crows and be damned."

"Silence!" said his captain, and with such look that the big fellow quailed and, lifting hook to hat-brim in sullen humility, was dumb, while his master surveyed Adam beneath languor of drooping eyelids.

"Might one ask the wherefore of your refusal, sir?"

"Because I've no will to be associate with one so black as Bartlemy."

"Well now, Sir Buccaneer, can it be possible you mean to affront me . . . you?"

"Would this so astound you . . . again, sir?"

"Beyond expression! For, Captain Adam, despite your extraordinary bloody reputation, you are in your person so very much the opposite of a Goliath or, say a Hercules. Hitherto such misguided heroes or venturesome braggarts as have dared me and died of it, have been sizable braggarts and——"

"Sir," retorted Adam, his keen eyes narrowing, "you may now remove yourself."

"Anon, sir, anon," answered Bartlemy, smiling engagingly. "I hurry myself for no man, few women, and take orders from neither. Also you tickle my fancy, being so very much other than expected. Ah yes, and in this plaguey weariness called Life, the unexpected hath a charm. I find you a creature anomalous, neither boy nor man, with hair like a hoary patriarch, eyes of a devil and the smug, sanctimonious airs of a Puritanic, psalm-smiting preacher."

"Have you done?" enquired Adam, studying the pale, arrogant features of the speaker, this once handsome face now marred by evil. "Have you finished?"

"By no means, Captain Adam. You have, sir, incredible fact,—affronted me, and this is so new in my experience that it becomes my pleasure to inflict you upon myself to our mutual exacerbation. Thus we may continue to affront one another by look, by gesture and by word, though with due punctilio, until we attain the natural climax of drawn steel—its delicate insinuation,—to the content of both and demise of one."

"Verily," said Adam, pinching his chin thoughtfully, "by all accounts 'twould be meritorious act and for the general good to rid the world o' you, Black Bartlemy."

"Many have tried, sir, yet do I live and flourish as the bay tree. But yourself, now, might succeed where so many failed, I say—you might, though I gravely doubt it. You were wiser to curb your valorous and vaulting ambition and—remain alive."

"For instance," continued Adam, as if Bartlemy had not spoken, "I might with justice hang you from the yard-arm with your ruffian, as pirates both."

"Certainly, Captain Hypocrite, since we are but two and your buccaneer cut-throats all about us," murmured Bartlemy, "but then I should as certainly . . . take you with me. . . ." As he spoke, his slender, right hand was armed suddenly with a dagger, its narrow, triangular blade glinting evilly.

"I see!" nodded Adam, and folded his arms.

"No,—but you shall!" smiled Bartlemy, and tossing the dagger aloft he caught it dexterously by the blade and thus showed the haft—of gleaming silver exquisitely wrought in the form of a naked woman who seemed to stand poised upon his fist a shape of wicked beauty. "Lo now, Sir Captain,—here she stands! My Silver Woman! This priceless wanton! Many fair women have I possessed yet none so fair as this . . . my Silver Lady whose kiss is —death! You behold her, sir?"

"Ay, I do," answered Adam and, uncrossing his arms, showed the two small pistols he held drawn and levelled; Black Bartlemy tittered, bowed graciously again and now fronted their menace empty-handed.

"So?" he murmured, smiling. "Well, shoot if you will and end Black Bartlemy with craven's pistol 'stead o' valiant steel. Yet this were so preposterous easy I am certain you will not."

"Truly," said Adam, staring into the dark eyes that, beneath their sleepy-drooping lids, watched him so shrewdly, "this is not that murderous hangman's ship called *Ladys' Delight*. Now if it were, and I in your case, you would murder or hang me—by mere force of habit, eh, Black Bartlemy?"

"Captain Adam, to answer you faithfully, I believe I should. Though, as you suggest, merely because I am Black Bartlemy the—um—'detested rogue and notorious pirate' and must live up to my so heinous reputation. So you, sir, as Penfeather, The Buccaneer, and puritanical smug who drowns men wholesale and prays over 'em piously whiles they perish, should abide as truly by yours. Thus, sir, as you detest pirates and I have as lively a contempt for sanctimonious Judases, let us here make an end of wordy speechifying by earnest endeavour to end one another."

"With pleasure!" answered Adam, returning each pistol to its hiding-place.

"Now, sir," said Bartlemy, "when you have snuffled prayer or sung psalm, I am wholly at your service," and he laid one finger to the jewelled pommel of his rapier, "and best—ashore, I think?"

Adam, fingering chin, surveyed his soft-voiced challenger; then suddenly instead of prayer or psalm, he intoned solemnly:

> "'There be two at the fore,
>   At the main be three more
>   Dead men that hang all of a row . . .'"

Black Bartlemy's sleepy eyes widened, then he smiled and nodded with affable condescension.

"Ah!" said he. "So you've heard poor Troy's poorer jingle? Yet this is fame, sir! For these sorry verses, becoming a chantey, do trumpet me abroad, so that though I am happy to be rid of him, I shall regret he will make no more songs o' me henceforth."

"Meaning," enquired Adam, finger and thumb at chin again, "that he is dead?"

"Worse, sir! Troy lieth fast in clutch of the Holy Inquisition whose saintly, though zealous, familiars and sons o' the Church shall teach him a death vastly unpleasant . . . yet scarce more so than I might ha' done had mine been the good fortune to take him."

"How know you of this?"

"How should I not? Sir, I have my agents all along the Main. But, to be frank, this good news, Troy being one o' my few abominations, these glad tidings were given me by one of his crew, a petty rascal he marooned,—and called Abnegation Mings."

"And where lieth this Troy prisoned?"

"In dungeon of the Holy Office at——" Black Bartlemy paused to sniff at his pomander again, viewing his questioner slyly askance, then, finding him dumb, enquired: "Pray why would you know, Sir Buccaneer?"

"No matter!" answered Adam, stifling a yawn, "I was curious to learn if his wife was prisoned with him, but——"

"Wife?" exclaimed Bartlemy, almost forgetting to be languid. "Absalom Troy—with a wife? Can the poor, fond wretch have sunk to wedlock when any woman may

be had for the taking—by such as we? Troy wed,—not
he! Knowing the man, I'll not believe it of him. Have
you, perchance, seen his—um—reputed wife?"

"I have."

"A lovely creature, ha?"

"Yes."

"Then you may take it she, if a wife, is wife of another
man, wife filched from doting spouse,—or she is some
loose, pretty doxy, or shameless baggage, some warm,
luscious——"

"Enough!" snarled Adam, then checked the fierce
retort upon his lips; but Bartlemy's eyes, keen as Adam's
own, had seen the grim tightening of jaw, the tensing of
small, powerful body,—and he bowed, tittering, while
Adam, aware that he had betrayed his consuming anxiety,
raged within himself therefor, yet watched the pale,
mocking face before him serenely, none the less.

"Captain Adam, unhappy lover,—pray forgive me that,
all unwitting, I have traduced a wife so dear to yourself!
For I must now believe this—um—twice beloved wife is
indeed poor Troy's beloved wife and sweetly naughty
spouse. But—oh alas,—she will be,—ah woe,—the unhappy lady captured with him, and now prisoned, poor
soul, to burn anon and not, alas, with ardent love for husband or lover, but mid cruel flame to expiate her pretty
peccadilloes. Think on't, sir,—her tender-sweet body to
fry . . . to shrink and shrivel in the scorching fire——"

"Hold,—a mercy's sake—hold!" cried Adam, like one
distraught and goaded past endurance. "Tell me . . .
where is she to die? Tell me!"

"Alas, sir!" Black Bartlemy paused to sigh, to shake
languid head. "Alas that lady so fair, so warmly kind
should so . . . very warmly die! And where, sir? Oh,
strange and woeful fact, where but at . . . San Domingo!"

Now at this, Adam smiled grimly and, turning, beckoned
where Smidge and the Indian Moa paced watchfully together
hard-by. "Smidge," said he, "go fetch my rapier." Then,

looking on Bartlemy. "Now," quoth he, "I know you for base liar would draw me to your design by contemptible trick. Let us go ashore lest I foul my deck with your rogue's blood!"

Black Bartlemy bowed, saying:

"Sweet gentleman, my boat awaits you."

"Sir, I prefer my own."

Thus presently, with John Fenn as his second and sheathed rapier beneath arm, Adam was rowed ashore. Here the principals, having bowed to each other, went side by side, their two seconds behind them (and a small, furtive shape behind these again), until they reached a place sufficiently remote from observation.

"This shall do, I think?" enquired Bartlemy, halting.

"Very well!" answered Adam, his glance upon the ground.

"Then," said Bartlemy, easing himself out of his upper garments, "the sooner the better, sir."

"Yes," answered Adam, doing the same.

And so, having saluted, they advanced against each other; scarcely had their blades crossed than, through their contact, Adam sensed all the latent power and cold ferocity of his smiling antagonist and prepared himself accordingly. For a long moment they stood motionless and watchful,—then Adam, making a tentative thrust, gave an opening, met the instant attack with violent parry and a counter-thrust so near that Bartlemy leapt out of distance and lowered his point; now, though he laughed, his eyes, sleepy no longer, showed wide and fierce, instead of languor was vigour and speed of movement backed by arrogant assurance and an indomitable will. All of which Adam was quick to note as they faced each other, each alert and strung to deadly purpose. Slowly they approached again, then with sudden, harsh cry, Black Bartlemy leapt, plying point and edge; back went Adam one pace and two, parried an upcut at his face, answering it with a thrust that checked his enemy, who put it by so narrowly his shirt was ripped open beneath his arm. Bartlemy laughed again, though breathlessly, but in that moment with false disengagement, his lightning point was through Adam's arm and, leaping back from instant counter-thrust, he bowed.

"First blood . . . to me, sir!" he panted. "Shall this suffice?"

"By no means," answered Adam, shaking head at Smidge, who had leapt forward at sight of the blood; "indeed, Black Bartlemy, your play, being uncanonic, interests me. So, when you have fetched your breath and feel able, let us begin to fight."

"Eh, fight, sir? Must I kill you then?"

"Why, sir," answered Adam, his wistful glance now upon an inequality in the ground beyond his enemy, "this is as the Lord wills."

"Ha?" sneered Bartlemy. "Shall I wait whiles you say a prayer first?"

"'Tis done, sir, and I'm ready."

"So be it!" said Bartlemy, and advancing with airy flourish, took his ground.

Clash and ring of vicious steel that flickered in close and deadly action; stamp of feet and hiss of quick-drawn breath; skill and scorn of death against murderous craft and imperious will. To and fro, up and down, back and forth, they fought with no stay or respite now, changing their ground with nimble volts and dexterous passes, while slowly yet surely, Adam compelled his enemy in the one direction. Bartlemy's fleeting smile had vanished, his breath came short, the sleeve of his sword-arm was a fluttering rag; Adam was spattered with his own blood, his face showed pale, his eyes half-closed; then his point faltered wide and, with gasping, triumphant cry, Bartlemy drove in powerful, finishing thrust—was jarred by violent parry, strove to recover, tripped and, as he fell, felt his sword beaten from relaxed grasp—and thus lay defenceless, staring up from the point that pricked his throat, to the merciless eyes staring down on him. So, for a moment, both were still and dumb, while the blood from Adam's wound splashed down upon Black Bartlemy's face.

"Well . . ." said Adam, at last, " it is . . . high time you were . . . killed!"

"And 'twould seem . . . that time is . . . now!" gasped Bartlemy, and, settling himself more comfortably, looked up at scowling Adam and smiled. "Sir," said he, "you now behold me . . . ready."

Very slowly and as if against his better judgment, Adam backed away.

"John," said he, "my handkerchief."

"Here, sir,—shall I lap it about your wound?"

"No, pray give it to me."

So with the handkerchief, Adam went back to his still prostrate enemy who gazed serenely up at the cloudless sky and hummed a merry air to himself.

"Sir," said Adam, "you need this, I think."

Smiling graciously, Bartlemy accepted the handkerchief and therewith wiped Adam's blood from him, then rising with his usual languid ease, beheld Adam being helped into his garments by a small, eager boy and a placid Indian youth, while John Fenn was sheathing his rapier.

"Captain Penfeather, my thanks and—your handkerchief!"

"Black Bartlemy," answered Adam, a little mournfully, "you may keep it in memory of one who might—nay who ought to have killed you . . . and yet did not . . . and to my present wonderment. But should there ever be a . . . next time . . . then and most certainly kill you I shall."

And presently, with John's handkerchief about his hurt, his rapier beneath John's arm and his two devoted and awed young seadogs following, Adam went back to his waiting boat.

CHAPTER XXXVI

TELLS OF JOY AND A GLAD REUNION

"PRO-DIGIOUS!" exclaimed Sir Benjamin, mopping brow and glancing at his companions' intent faces, from Adam leaning motionless in his chair, to Ned Bowser who stared with round eyes and mouth agape.

"It is a sum," continued Sir Benjamin, "of such amplitudinous magnitude as doth far transcend the loftiest expectations of—even myself! We sit here vastly wealthy men all and therefore persons o' power to command o' this base, slavish world whatso we desire."

"Ay but," questioned Adam, sitting up suddenly, "heark to yonder tumult! This curse o' gold begins to work upon the crew."

"They do but rejoice, Adam, and not without due reason, or I'm a cur-dog! For there's never a man o' them but hath two thousand, five hundred odd broad pieces to his share, worked out in proportion,—so stupendous is our fortune!"

"Faith," laughed Sir George, "there's seldom been richer booty to divide. I'm all amazed to find myself so preposterous wealthy!"

"And I!" said John Fenn, shaking his head, "I can scarce believe it yet."

"Nor me likewise!" quoth Ned. "Which, seeing as I'm so rich, I dunno what I shall do wi' myself, or how spend so much good money."

"For mine own part," said Sir Benjamin, "I sail for England with the first ship I may. For England now summons me home with golden clarions."

"And I'll with thee, Ben!" cried Sir George, "England is—the only place, and home—ah 'tis a blessedness!"

"Well now," demanded Sir Benjamin, "what o' thyself, Adam? What holdeth the golden future for thee?"

"Work!" answered Adam, somewhat grimly.

"Nay, I protest!" exclaimed Sir Benjamin, bouncing in his chair. "Work, in a rich man, is folly and worse, as I shall now prove. For, mark me—a rich man, having no need o' work, yet working for mere love o' work, pandereth to his own lust and passion for work, and thus doeth his poorer neighbour out o' work, and so becometh a menace and stumbling block to all that needs must work to live. Ergo, the rich worker is a curse,—so curse him heartily,—say I!"

"Also," continued Adam, "the sea is my home, and there is work for me hereabout that I am called unto and best fitted for. So my destiny is here."

"Why then, 'twill grieve me to part with thee, Adam, after all these years of trial and close fellowship,—ay, 'twill touch me very sensibly, or call me dogsbody!"

"Indeed," sighed Sir George, "it hath been a good and great companionship, Adam, a true friendship."

"So truly great," said John Fenn, "that I bide with you, Captain Adam, so long as I may."

"Ay, ay," growled Ned, "when I mind how 'twas me as larned ee to know a ship,—what I now says is, such being so and seeing as how, I'll bear along of ee, poor or rich, and no thought o' parting company till Natur' passes the word thereto——"

It was now that a knock on the door interrupted them, and Martin Frant stood on the threshold, an angry man who jerked thumb over broad shoulder, saying:

"Ship's company is away, sirs,—took shore leave and sheered off for good, by look o' things."

"Desertion?" bellowed Sir Benjamin. "Ha—malediction! What's the meaning o' this?"

"Gold!" answered Adam. "'Tis the curse of gold beginning to work in them, Ben. Most of the poor rogues will be drunk to-night, sick in a week, ruined in a month and destitute. . . . How many remain aboard, Martin?"

"Scarce fifty, sir."

"Why, very well, say to these I will sign them on for a new venture, at double rates, and bid 'em pass the word to their fellows when they go ashore."

"Ay, sir,—and at double rates?"

"Yes, Martin. The crews I command shall be ever the stoutest seamen and best paid of any afloat. Let this be known to all. Say also that every man is free to go ashore, but all such as remain faithful to the ship and me—these I shall never forget."

"Howbeit," quoth Sir Benjamin, so soon as Martin had departed, "you are like to be deserted by all here pretty soon, Adam, except you go ashore likewise. For who will bide cramped aboardship when he may live in luxury ashore?"

"I shall, for the present," Adam answered. "So now, Ben, you are leaving, I take it?"

"Ay, 'od's my life—that am I! And George likewise. I've taken goodly house nobly furnished, Adam—and with servants, slaves and so forth, in best part o' the town. George bides with me until such time as we take ship for England. There we shall live as gentlemen o' circumstance should, surrounded by all those comforts, refinements, precious amenities and delicate whatnots denied a man aboardship. I was hoping you might be induced to join us—eh, how sayest thou, Adam?"

"My thanks, Ben, but I've too much to employ me, as —first and foremost to seek news of our lost friends. Then to re-victual and choose me another crew, and after that —the Spanish Main."

"Why then," quoth Sir Benjamin, rising, "you will visit us often, I hope, and I shall come aboard frequently as may be."

So they took leave of each other, Sir Benjamin somewhat boisterously, Sir George regretfully,—and were presently gone.

Thus alone, Adam summoned the boy Smidge, saying and cheerily enough:

"Now, my old seadog, go bid Master Frant muster and arm a shore-going party, six men shall suffice. Then warn Jimbo to make preparation for a week's hard march inland."

"But, oh, Cap'n, sir, will you march to-day and your arm scarce healed?"

"'Tis well enough."

"Well then, Cap'n, won't you let me size it up in a sling for you, cosy like?"

"Nay, I'm no cripple! Come, help me on with my coat —easy now! So!"

"If you please, Cap'n Adam, sir, you'll suffer I march wi' you, I hope?"

"Ay, shipmate, according to promise."

"And may I bring this here Moa along of us, sir,—to keep him out o' mischeefs while I'm away?"

"To be sure, Smidge. Now off with ye, I'm busy."

So away they sped and down sat Adam to write up his Journal and despite the throbbing of his wound.

He had written busily for some time, and this a brief description of his meeting with Black Bartlemy, when he heard the door open behind him and thinking this was Smidge, spoke without looking round:

"Are the men armed and ready?"

A deep sigh answered him, and glancing over his shoulder, he sat rigid and speechless. Slowly he turned, then was afoot but, striving for utterance, could do no more than gaze wide-eyed because of the heart-swelling joy that thralled him and half blinded him with sudden, burning tears.

"Oh, Adam! Have you no welcome . . . no single word for me . . . after all . . . the years?"

The same dear voice so softly sweet yet touched with a deeper note of sadness, like the wistful eyes tear-bright with such look of yearning tenderness that he bowed his head, and when at last he spoke all he said was:

"Antonia! My . . . dear!" Then he was before her, kneeling to clasp and kiss the hands that clung to his and seemed to tremble beneath his lips.

"Now, I thank God!" he murmured. "For here is the hour I've lived for . . . dreamed of through all these weary years!" So saying, he rose and drew her to a chair and stood looking at her and she at him until, flushing beneath his gaze, she turned to survey this great cabin.

"You are . . . very splendid here," she faltered. "They say you are a famous captain . . . wonderfully fortunate. . . . And you are grown . . . taller, broader . . . also you are great, as I foretold . . . so long ago . . ."

"Four years, Antonia, and all this time I have . . . carried your dear memory . . . in my heart. And to-day you are . . . in my care again and . . . even more beautiful."

"Yet I feel old . . . very old!" she whispered tear-fully. "Grief hath aged me . . . my sweet baby died . . . of the cruel heat . . . and my husband is lost. Oh Adam . . . !"

"Lost?" he repeated. "You mean——"

"Dead or living . . . only God knoweth. A great tempest destroyed our crops. . . . Then Absalom gambled desperately and lost. . . . So, with the last of his money he and Smy fitted out a ship and sailed for Bartlemy's Island. But they were wrecked, and captured by the Spaniards, they and all that were left of their crew, only Master Perks and Joel Bym escaped and brought the news. So am I twice bereaved, and in my loneliness and trouble, come to . . . you. . . ."

"And I very humbly thank God that He hath sent you . . . to my care again!" exclaimed Adam, fervently and, not daring to say more or even look at her just then, began to pace up and down the spacious cabin while she, because of his breathless sincerity and deep tenderness,

watched him through slow-gathering tears. Then, to check
her weakness, she spoke in lighter vein:

"I have heard much of you this last year and more,
Adam, for of late scarce a ship has come in but with some
news of your doings, tales of your fierce battles that I
could well believe, and of your pitiless cruelties which I
would not and do not believe! For I know you could never
be merciless, Adam,—ah no, never you!"

"Merciless?" he repeated, suddenly arrested; and now
taking himself by the chin he pondered this as he had
never done. "Merciless!" said he a second time.

"Yes, Adam," she answered, watching him with a glory
in her eyes because his gaze was averted. "They say you
fight savagely and drown men without pity, which I know
for wicked lies and——"

"No, 'tis truth, Antonia."

"But . . . Oh, Adam," she gasped. "You couldn't
kill and drown men . . . helpless men!"

"Ay, but I could, Antonia, indeed I have. God forgive
me! When I thought you dead, this seemed but act of
justice on your possible murderers. Yes, I have sunk
every pirate ship we met. I have destroyed, giving no
quarter to any . . . and because of you."

"Oh, but how," she cried, rising to her feet, "how of
me and why . . . why?"

"Believing you dead, Antonia, I deemed myself the
Lord's instrument of vengeance, to bring death on your
murderers and the slayers of other such hapless innocents.
. . . I have imagined you dead so often . . . and in
so many dreadful ways, in especial . . . one! So, for
your sake, or my sick dread for you, I killed of these
pirates, these blasters of innocence, all that I might, lest
some of these had perchance wrought like shame on you.
. . . Well, what is done is done, and I stand by it now
and hereafter. But no more o' this,—pray sit down and
tell me more of yourself. I'm hungry for news,—nay, first
of Absalom, where was he captured, where lies he now?"

"At Santo Domingo, in prison of the Inquisition."

"So," murmured Adam, "a rogue spoke truth!"

"'Tis a great, rich city they say, Adam, and very strong."

"Ay, I know it. How long since was Absalom taken?"

"Scarce a month, though 'tis over a year since he sailed."

"Over—a year!" repeated Adam, pinching his chin again, "Though he promised you, nay vowed to give up the sea and devote himself——"

"He is of—of roving nature, Adam, and would have been content to bide with me but that our crops, first the cane then tobacco, failed . . . our slaves deserted and so . . . came ruin."

"Do you mean—absolute ruin?"

"Yes."

"Then how, being alone, how do you live?"

"By my needle . . . sewing, and I do well enough . . . people are very kind." Up again started Adam and went pacing to and fro until Antonia began to laugh at him, though rather tearfully. "Oh, Adam, how well I remember that way you have of . . . pinching at your poor chin . . . when anyways vexed or troubled! Nay, my dear, come you now, sit down and leave your poor chin alone. Sit here beside me and listen while I tell you." Mutely he obeyed and now, for the first time, noticed how very plain and simple was her attire and how worn and frayed her shoes that, even as he viewed them, she hid beneath her gown.

"Well, first you must know our plantation lay on the other side of Jamaica, this is why the news of your coming took so long to reach me, for there I live in a . . . dear little house somewhat like an English cottage though not so pretty, of course,—but all that remains of our property. So there I live alone with my Caruna, who is all that remains of our many slaves, and is devoted to me, and with our needlework we contrive very well, and fruit in

Jamaica costs so very little. So don't frown, Adam, or pinch your chin at me or worry and vex you for me."

"Ay, but I must!" he answered, almost fiercely. "I must and shall—until you are safe aboard my ship and 'neath my own eye."

"Oh but, Adam, I . . . I couldn't."

"Woman!" he exclaimed. "Girl, lass, child,—dear brother Anthony, I'll not permit you shall bide alone in any cottage,—ha, and with all manner of blackamoors, mulattos, Indians and the like two-legged dangers roving about."

"But I'm not alone. And besides——"

"Howbeit, I'll not endure it, no—not after four long years of such dread for you and direful anxieties. I'll send some of the crew to fetch away such gear as you desire, though I can rig and furnish you very handsomely here aboard the *Santissima Trinidad*. Also you shall be lodged like a queen, and may bring three or four waiting-women if you will."

"I should need but Caruna. But——"

"So here then shall you live and sail with us for Santo Domingo."

"Ah, you . . . you mean?"

"To rescue your Absalom or perish with him."

"Oh, Adam!" she murmured, and covered her face, yet spoke in passionate, breathless manner: "You were always kind . . . generous and very gentle! But now you . . . overwhelm me. Indeed you are the same dear Adam,— the years have made you only greater."

"Antonia," he sighed, venturing to touch her bowed head very gently, "you are so infinitely . . . dear to me! And now God, in His mercy for me, has given you to my care again as He did aforetime. So are you my sacred charge until I . . . bring you safe to . . . your chosen man."

"My . . . chosen . . . man?" she repeated, whispering the words as if to herself, and Adam felt her tremble

. . . then she looked up at him and he fell back a step and began to tremble also. . . .

But now came a rapping on the door and Smidge appeared, saying:

"Oh, Cap'n, if you please, the men be ready and—coo!" The boy snatched off his seaman's bonnet and came rigidly to attention.

"Smidge!" said a soft, sweet voice, and this stately lady rose, she actually reached out her arms as if to embrace him, whereat Smidge gaped, recoiled, and fled.

"To be sure," said Antonia, smiling a little ruefully, "he never saw me in petticoats. He is grown to fine boy, Adam."

"And shall grow to fine man, I hope. But now, Antonia, aft here to larboard is cabin most luxurious, with bath, ewers and basins of silver, a bed of silver and ebony, silk hangings, rugs and carpets—all meant for some noble Spanish lady, but fit for any queen, and so most apt for you. I have sometimes . . . dreamed you there . . . never thinking it could ever be realised . . . yet this is why I have kept it private always. Come you now and take possession."

So thither he brought her, and she in an ecstasy because of the luxurious splendour and yet delicate beauty everywhere manifest.

"Oh!" sighed she. "Indeed 'twas some grand lady,—ah no, only a very woman could have made such dream come true . . . these rich broideries . . . this dainty china-ware . . . this most lovely bed."

"And 'tis a very woman will sleep in it this very night."

"To-night? Oh—but, Adam!"

"Ay, to-night, Antonia! You shall nevermore be out o' call of me until . . . Howbeit, this night you sleep here. I'll send for your Caruna at once, she should be with you ere sunset. Well now, at the next bell, in about half-an-hour is dinner, till then I'll leave you to grow used to your new home—for home it is and shall be."

"Stay, Adam—stay!" cried she, turning on him radiant-eyed. "Go, wait me in your cabin, I have something for you that I've kept . . . treasured all these years—wait!" Away she sped, but was soon back again bringing him that at mere sight of which he uttered joyous exclamation and leapt afoot.

"Yes, your beloved father's sword, Adam! 'Twas the last thing I brought away from the poor *Adventuress*."

So Adam took the sword and with it her two hands also and, kissing them, felt their slender fingers all roughened with toil, so he kissed them again very reverently until was another rapping on the door, and at Adam's bidding, in came John Fenn to know when the expedition must start.

"At once, John. But first . . . Antonia, here stands my good and valiant John Fenn, of whom I can tell much, —John, you behold my lady Perrow, Captain Troy's lady." John flushed, made his bow, said he was honoured, and turned to be gone, but Adam stayed him, saying:

"I want you to land a shore party to fetch aboard my lady's woman and . . . pray give him the particulars, Antonia."

This she did with such gentle grace that sturdy John alternate bowed and flushed, then strode away in haste to do her bidding.

"And now," said Adam, sitting down with his father's sword across his knees, "tell me how we came to miss each other when the *Adventuress* was abandoned."

"Well," she answered, leaning back in her chair to view his lean, bronzed face and masterful bearing with quick and deepening interest, "I had seen you on deck just before that last terrible wave struck us, then you were gone . . . they said you were swept overboard and lost. But this I wouldn't believe, so ran to your cabin, calling for you and 'stead of you, found only your beloved sword. And this made me know something frightful must have happened to you, because you would never have left that

to go down with the ship. So I caught it up and ran to
and fro calling for you until Absalom came and snatched
me up and bore me to the boat, and I still crying for you.
Then, what with grief, the wild confusion and terror of it
all, I swooned away, and when I awoke—nothing to see
but our tossing boat and foaming waves all about us. Then
followed three terrible nights and days . . . with my
heart breaking for you, so that I could not bear to look
on the hateful sea because I thought it had killed you . . .
and when it grew calmer I hated it the more,—though I
remembered how you had said you wished to die in God's
great waters. On the fourth day we were taken up by an
English ship, the *Lion*, of Bristol, that carried us safe here
to Jamaica, and here I have been ever since, thinking you
surely dead, until just eleven months and . . . four . . .
five days ago. At first I dared not believe it, but when I
was sure——"

"Well?" he enquired, for she had faltered to a sudden
stop.

"I . . . oh I was . . . glad . . . !" she murmured, bowing her head above the hands that were clasping each other so nervously. "Now tell me of yourself,
Adam. How, 'stead of lying deep in ocean, you are greater
man than I dreamed, and the famous captain I prophesied
. . . and how ever you came by this great, splendid
ship . . . and if you thought of me . . . very often,
and if so . . . why,—oh why were you so long a-coming
to Jamaica . . . and me? Tell me . . . everything!"

"Why, 'tis a long story," he answered, his gaze down-
bent to the sword on his knees, "ay, and something painful
to recall. You see I . . . thought my heart was dead.
I have written something of it down in my Journal,
but——"

"May I read it . . . sometime, Adam? Oh pray,
pray suffer that I read it someday . . . soon."

"Well . . . yes," he answered, very dubiously,
"though I have set down much that I could nowise

utter . . . so that perhaps it were better you should not——"

"Oh, but I must . . . every precious word! Adam, I pray you, don't gainsay me . . . oh, don't change your mind and deny me such small comfort—nay, indeed I shall not suffer it. . . . But now tell me as much as you may. What happened to you in the boat?"

"Agony!" he answered. "And death for many of us . . . and all on Death's very threshold when we were picked up by a Spanish ship, carried to St. John's and there made slaves,—these be the enduring marks of my bitter servitude!" And he showed her his wrists.

"These scars?" she murmured.

"Shackle-marks!" he nodded.

"Oh, Adam . . . ! Oh, my dear!" she gasped. "My poor, tormented Adam. . . ." She was beside him on her knees, kissing those scars until the sword fell and lay unnoticed,—until, feeling him wince, she looked up in quick alarm.

"Ah, did I hurt thee, Adam? This bandage on your arm?"

"No no," he answered, stooping for the sword, "it is no more than small hurt I took this morning."

"Pray how?"

"In some . . . petty disputation."

"More battles, Adam?"

"Lord no, child."

"Ah, then 'twas a duel. Who with? Tell me of it, my dear. Nay," she sighed, seeing him hesitate, "am I become so strange you will no more confide in me? Am I so altered and less to be trusted?"

"Nay indeed," he answered, "you can never seem strange to me, Antonia, or I to you—I hope. But truly there is so little to tell, save that my opponent was this same Black Bartlemy of whom one hears such wild tales."

"This terrible creature! This monster of iniquity! Why, Adam, indeed his wickedness is a byword, his very name carries terror. The mothers of Jamaica fright their naughty children by saying Black Bartlemy shall have them unless they're good."

"Yet is he no more than veriest human, Antonia, though a something exceptional rogue, yes . . . an original, a quaint, new-fangled villain."

"And you fought this . . . this dire wretch and are yet alive!"

"Ay, but . . . I suffered him to live also and wondered why at the time. But now I . . . yes, now I know."

"What is it you know?"

"That I spared him by the Lord's will that he might aid us to rescue Absalom."

"Ah, not—not this man, dear Adam! Seek no aid of this evil wretch,—trust rather to your own strength and skill."

"So I would, Antonia, as with God's aid I have ever done—though 'twas mostly to mine own interest. But to-day I think of Absalom, his peril . . . and Santo Domingo is city strongly embattled as well I do know, and my *Santissima Trinidad*, though ably manned and heavily armed, shall achieve little 'gainst so strong a place. Castles and shore batteries. We must have other ships,— a fleet!"

So saying, he rang the silver bell and Jimbo instantly appearing:

"Look now," said he, "here is the lady Perrow, Captain Absalom's lady. She will occupy the larboard cabin. See to it, Jimbo, ay, and open the chests and lay out that lady's gear, gowns and dresses, caps and so forth."

"Yessah, dis berry instant-moment, Cap'n!" And flashing his teeth, he bowed and vanished.

"Gowns? Dresses? Oh—Adam!"

"Why yes, I forgot to tell you, there are chests and presses full o' them—gowns, caps, shawls, with other garments of all sorts,—silks, laces, 'broideries,—enough to last your life-time."

"Oh, my gracious heavens above! And you forgot any mention! Adam, how like you!"

"Well, they await your ladyship. Jimbo will be shaking 'em out for your inspection——"

"Jimbo shall—not!" she cried, and sped away like a carefree girl.

Then, buckling on his father's sword, Adam went out on deck and summoned Ned Bowser and John Fenn.

"Yonder!" said he, pointing them where, at no great distance, rode a stately black ship.

"Ay, she'm a likely craft!" quoth Ned.

"And powerful gunned!" said John.

"Come in last night she did," added Ned, "about the middle watch, 'twould be."

"Well," said Adam, viewing this great ship with narrowed eyes, "she is the *Lady's Delight*."

"Eh, Bartlemy's cursed ship?" exclaimed Ned. "Lord love my eyes! Now what's she, ay, and him, adoing here along? What do they rogues want, I wonder?"

"I think word with me, Ned."

"Ha!" cried John. "By reason we've sunk so many of his rogue friends and consorts."

"Howbeit, I'm going aboard him—now."

"Nay now—God forbid!" cried Ned. "Why, Lord love you, this were like lamb to butcher, your throat to his bloody knife! So, Cap'n Adam, seeing as how, I begs as how you'll hearken to me and be advised."

"Nay, 'tis for you to hear me, Ned. I want to shift our anchorage somewhat . . . warp her head round to starboard. . . . And you, John . . . listen to me now, hearkee both. . . ."

CHAPTER XXXVII

HOW ADAM MET BLACK BARTLEMY
FOR THE SECOND TIME

THUS, after some while, with Smidge (armed to the teeth) beside him in the stern sheets, Adam was rowed to this great, black ship whose towering masts taut rig, and graceful lines he admired as only true seaman might. Being come alongside he nodded, whereat his coxswain Tregenza hailed cheerily:

"Ship ahoy! Rig the gangway—Captain Adam Penfeather coming aboard!"

Steel flashed on deck above and the entry-port was manned; then, bidding Smidge remain in the boat, up went Adam to a broad, white deck where, to right and left of him, stood files of armed men commanded it seemed by this same tall rogue Tressady who, striding at Adam, halted suddenly within a yard of him to leer and flourish:

"Why sink and drownd me!" he exclaimed. "I say drownd and sink me if it a'n't the little, crowing captain, the game-cock whiffler as——"

"Tressady," said a voice above them, "close that vile mouth and remove your viler carcase! Captain Penfeather be welcome aboard my *Lady's Delight*. Will you hither to the poop or shall we to my cabin?"

"The poop, sir," answered Adam. And thither he mounted to a deck scoured snowy-white but spread with rich Orient carpets and rugs beneath a silken awning, a place of delicate luxury more like a dainty lady's boudoir (thought Adam) than deck of a fighting-ship.

"Pray be seated, sir. Here is wine very rarely precious, or strong waters—excellent cordials if you prefer."

"Thankee—nothing!" answered Adam, taking the nearest chair.

"Ah, to be sure," murmured Bartlemy, "the very abstemious Puritan, the primly ascetical Buccaneer! Why then, sir, if 'stead of debasing your soul with drink you would uplift it with short psalm or briefer prayer, I can be patient." Adam, leaning back in cushioned chair, merely smiled on the smiling speaker who filled himself a glass of exquisitely cut crystal with amber wine, bowed to him and sipped daintily, saying:

"Your health, Captain Adam,—for the present."

"Black Bartlemy," said Adam, surveying him leisurely, feature by feature, "I am wondering if you are ever yourself?"

Bartlemy set down his glass and opened his sleepy eyes so wide that he may be said to have actually stared, then he shrugged languidly and answered:

"Sir, I am that I am and all I seem."

"On the contrary," said Adam, shaking his head, "you are verily so much other than you show, that I am, as I say, wondering if you ever permit yourself to lay by these affectations, when alone of course, and become the creature you truly are?"

Once again Bartlemy's eyes widened and then, having sipped his wine and pondered this question, he shook languid head, murmuring:

"Sir, I detest riddles. Pray be more explicit to let me know what the devil you may chance to be talking about. If, as I dimly suspect, 'tis of myself, then I take leave to declare you very damnably impertinent."

"Howbeit," continued Adam, smoothing the bright pommel of his father's sword, "I have glimpsed 'neath your mask and know you, for all your villainous repute, no more than poor, weary soul at odds with yourself, your fellows and your God, and therefore lost 'mid a great darkness and, in your secret heart, very fearful. You will deny this, even to yourself, yet I know—and so do you."

Now for a long moment they stared upon each other eye
to eye,—then Black Bartlemy did that which, for him, was
very strange,—he forgot to be himself, and gave way to a
wild paroxysm of fury. Gone was his sneering, icy calm,
his gracious languor, his fine, courtly grace,—instead was
stark savagery. He cursed and swore with all the coarse
invective and foul heartiness of a tarry mariner; he smote
the table with passionate fists and glaring on Adam,
vilified him 'twixt gnashing teeth, until, words and breath
failing him at last, he sank back in his chair and wiped
sweat from his brow with the back of clenched fist. And
this, oddly enough, seemed to recall his self-control, for
catching himself in the act, he whipped out dainty, be-laced
handkerchief and having used this delicately, instead of
smearing fist, he sipped his wine, smiled on Adam and
bowed.

"Sir," he sighed, "as one swordsman and *maître d'armes
académique* to another, I do here acknowledge a palpable
hit and cry: '*Touché!*' Indeed, you have tongue nimble
and unexpected as your sword. Sir, I can appreciate wit,
I can admire swordcraft, but though you possess both, I
regret to say you prove yourself so extreme detestable
that I propose to rid myself of you once and for all."

"Steel again?" enquired Adam.

"Ah no, sir, rope! As I warned you no later since than
yesterday. Ay, I warned you. Yet this morning you
thrust yourself upon me, adventuring here to put me to
proof. Well, you shall find me man of my word, though
indeed you should have known I should certainly keep such
promise."

"Sir," answered Adam, "I am so aware o' this that,
being an extreme cautious, not to say timid, man, I have
taken due precaution."

"Ah?" murmured Bartlemy rising. "May I enquire
precisely what?"

"My ship!" answered Adam, rising also. "You will
observe, if you'll trouble yourself to look, she now lies

to command yours with her whole broadside. I have but to give the awaited signal and your *Lady's Delight* will cease to be. My guns are heavy and may rake you fore and aft."

Black Bartlemy looked and, seeing this was so, nodded.

"Ah but," he enquired, "would your men sink me with their captain aboard?"

"They would certainly heed my command, sir. I am obeyed on my ship."

"Then why a plague are ye here?"

"To say I will sail with you against San' Domingo."

"So! You've changed your tune then. May I ask why?"

"Captain Troy is my friend."

"Ha,—you would storm the prison whiles we sack the town?"

"Precisely. And shall claim my share o' plunder thereafter."

"And suppose I also have changed my mind, and given over all thought o' such expedition?"

"Then I shall sail alone."

"You know the place, its defences?"

"Ay, I do."

"Then you will agree that any man who would attempt such place alone, is a fool."

"Or a friend!" said Adam, turning away.

"What, Sir Buccaneer, will you depart?"

"Ay, I've told you my mind."

"But I've not told mine."

"No matter," answered Adam, coming to the poop ladder, "when you have decided, ay or no, you may send me word."

"Ha, the devil I may!"

"Howbeit, Black Bartlemy, 'tis still no matter. I were wiser to have no truck with Iniquity. So, I take my leave of you, Sir Roguery!"

"By God!" exclaimed Bartlemy, between white teeth,

"I'll watch you dance the Tyburn hornpipe yet, the yard-arm jig!"

"Or I shall see you bleed——"

"Ah—ah!" smiled Bartlemy. "This minds me to humbly enquire—pray how is your wounded arm? Not too painful, I hope?"

"And sufficiently able, I thank you," Adam retorted, dropping left hand suggestively on rapier hilt. "Though I came on serious business."

"Oho, and be damned! Do I infer that to cross steel with me is but merest pastime, a bagatelle, as the French say?"

"No," answered Adam, gravely, "a pleasure. I find unholy joy in single combat, more especially with this noblest of weapons the rapier, and more truly so if my opponent prove skilled or with method other than mine. Alas, 'tis pleasure I deny myself often, lest it grow on me and become a ruling vice."

"Well now, let me burn if I ever heard or met the like of you, Captain Adam."

"'Tis well to be individual, sir. And so, good-bye t' ye."

"Nay, where's your hurry?"

"Nowhere. Only I prefer the more spaciousness of my own ship."

"That bedizened, lubberly galleon o' yours!"

"Indeed she is both, but, as I say, spacious."

"If you would sail with me on this expedition, you were wiser to sell such hugeous, clumsy hulk and get you a ship of speed and power more suitable."

"But the *Santissima Trinidad* suits me very well. There is no more powerful ship afloat, and as to speed, I've found her fast enough ere now."

"Meaning you'll keep her."

"Indeed. And, now returning to her, I take my leave of you."

"Then hearkee, sir! Should I determine on this venture

against Santo Domingo, and there is most delicious reason that I should,—I cannot assemble my consorts under at the least . . . nine or say eight weeks . . . nay, it must be ten."

"Too long!" said Adam. "For the reason that takes me thither, is a friend's life."

"You mean Absalom Troy?"

"Ay, I do. He lieth in prison of the Inquisition in peril of torture now, and death by fire in the next murderous Auto-da-Fé. This I know."

"True!" nodded Bartlemy. "But I also know Absalom Troy, and to my cost,—and can now assure you on my word, or oath—if you'll credit these, which you won't,—that Troy is in no least danger of torment or death, now or hereafter. You will demand how I know this so certainly, and I answer,—from my secret agents. I have spies everywhere, ay, even in the Holy Office itself,—one Grand Inquisitor and a host of lesser fry,—as saintly fathers and ghostly familiars. For in this world, as doubtless you have proved, money can buy what you will. And I, sir, have vast deal of money—as perchance you may have heard?"

"Ay, I have. But here take issue with you anent its power. Money cannot buy honour, truth, justice, the sun, the stars o' heaven, or any of the great, simple realities."

"Yet, sir, it can buy their similitudes, their likeness and seeming,—and this suffices me."

"Ay but," retorted Adam, "you are so merely Bartlemy the Black!"

Bartlemy simpered and bowed.

"Oh, sir," he murmured, "your very deeply obliged!"

"Well now," Adam demanded, "why is Troy, though a prisoner, exempt from harms and safe from immediate danger?"

"Purely because he is—Absalom Troy! 'Tis very wily gentleman of flexible morals and no beliefs to plague him; a fighting man bold as lion in battle yet no fool martyr to peril body for any snivelling creed or canting religiosity."

K

"You are suggesting he is renegade and turncoat?"

"Captain Adam, I inform you how Troy, careless of any religion hitherto, is now professed Catholic to save his skin, —being no fool martyr, as I say. Believe me or not, sir, this is precisely the news of him as I had it lately from one of my most holy, yet trustworthy, secret agents."

Adam stood musing with his troubled gaze on the distance so long that Bartlemy smiled, saying:

"'Twould almost seem you credit my word and actually believe me. If so, indeed, then you will perceive there is no need for your so passionate haste or burning anxiety on Troy's behalf. Therefore, since despite my better judgment I permit your oddity to exercise odd attraction upon me, I now give you rendezvous ten weeks hence at Dead Man's Key, which lies in latitude——"

"I know it, sir, having careened there."

"Well, there will we convene in ten weeks' time. Is it agreed, Captain Penfeather?"

"It is!" nodded Adam. "Ten weeks hence I shall be there. Till then, Black Bartlemy, ay, and thereafter, I pray God preserve you from—Black Bartlemy." Having said which, he turned and went down to his boat, leaving Black Bartlemy staring on the distance, in his turn, and with very sombre, brooding gaze.

"CAP'N ADAM, sah, de lady Perrow she in her lady-ship's cabin berry extremious busy, sah, and singing so sweetsome as any bootiful bird in de tree and—wid de door locked, sah!"

"And how should you know this, Jimbo?"

"Why first I hears it lock, sah, den berry tendersome I tries it and finds it am locked, and so den it am as I hears her singing like——" He paused and gaped, he flashed his teeth, bobbed his woolly head and vanished; then Adam, glancing round, very nearly gaped also at the radiant vision smiling on him so wistfully; a splendid woman shyly conscious of her beauty and yet troubled also. Pearls shim--mered on her round, white throat that rose from deep collar of lace, a broidered gown, girt by jewelled girdle, clung about her shapeliness,—she was one with the splendours around her.

"Oh. Adam!" she sighed. "Now indeed I am decked like a queen . . . this glory of jewels! These silks and laces! This cannot be just . . . only me! I feel like a . . . a walking dream."

"Yet truly," he murmured, "you are such glorious reality that I know at last the true reason and wherefore of jewels."

"I found them in a coffer . . . a little, beautiful casket and at first scarce dared touch them."

"Yet have they been waiting for you, Antonia. And now, thank God, here are you to claim them at last."

"But these are worth a fortune and I . . . I could never accept such gift from you, Adam."

"Ay, but you will. You shall take them from .   . your faithful, loving . . . brother!"

"Half-brother!" she reminded him smiling, though with tears in her eyes. "But, Adam, I . . . oh . . . my dear."

"Avast, Anthony! Belay, messmate! What are a few such trinkets 'twixt the likes o' you and me? Say no more about 'em, or——" Here, with loud double knock, Jimbo presented himself to bow profoundly to Antonia and say to Adam:

"If yo' please, Cap'n sah, beggin' yo' pardon and excuse, but yere's dat ol' Joel Bym come aboard and begging de favah ob speech wi' you."

"This is well. Say I'll with him anon."

"Pray," said Antonia, "suffer he come here to us."

"Right gladly, if you will. Bid him hither, Jimbo."

Thus presently came Joel, as bronzed and hairy, as trig and sailorly as ever, for, though his worn garments betrayed poverty they were neatly patched and darned as only true sailorman might.

"Sir," quoth he, taking off battered old hat and crushing it nervously in his powerful hands, "by cock, but I'm glad for to clap eyes on ee again, ay, that I am, sir—and my lady too!"

"Then give me your hand, Joel. Now sit down, man, sit down. Jimbo—rum! Come, wet your whistle, Joel, then pipe up and tell what's chanced you all this time."

"Plenty, sir, by cock, and most on it hardship, and lastly shipwreck and a Spanish prison till us won out, Surgeon Perks and me. And since that, sir, what wi' plaguey wound I took and one ill luck atop of another here in Port Royal, I've come down to working in the cane-brakes along o' poor black slaves, sir, ay, by cock, I have!"

"You might have done worse, Joel. Howbeit, here are you aboard with me again, and here you shall bide if ye will."

"What, sir, will ye 'list me?"

"Ay, right gladly, Joel."

"Lord love ee now . . . and on this ship as be called the *Golden Fortun'*! And to sarve under you as be so famous and lucky! Oh, Cap'n Adam, I dunno what to say, only— by cock, I'm that amazing glad as I can't find no word for it."

"Then take a sip o' rum, Joel, then sit back and tell us of your last voyage with Captain Absalom and what befell."

"Why then, first, sir, here's poor Cap'n Absalom's noble plantation ruinated by weather, by cock! So he tries for to right hisself by cards and horses, and ruinates his money affairs. So then he begins ruinating hisself wi' rum, by cock! Ay, goes from bad to worse, down—and down, till Cap'n Smy and me and Surgeon Perks takes him in hand and brings him up short, ay, with a round turn. So the end of it is, we scrapes together what money we have and fit out a ship for to try our luck agin' Black Bartlemy his treasure. But luck proves con-trairy, our ship springs a leak as forces us to make for one o' the Keys. But then comes a wind as blows so fierce and foul it drives and wrecks us, by cock—right beneath the very guns o' Santo Domingo. And so, after a stiffish fight, we're taken—all as is left of us, and clapped fast into prison o' the Inquisition where poor Cap'n Smy, being an officer and refusing very fierce to turn Papist, is put to the torment—frequent! And him only the fiercer therefor and more defiant . . . though he groaned right piteous whenso they tortured of him,—and small wonder! By cock, I can hear him yet! Sometimes I hears him in my sleep and wakes all of a sweat I do. As for me, I kills me one o' the guards and won free, along o' Surgeon Perks. And so, Cap'n Adam, here am I back now along o' you and mighty glad therefore, by cock!"

"But," demanded Antonia with a dreadful, trembling eagerness, "tell me, Joel, what of my . . . what of Captain Absalom Troy?"

"Why, my lady, I . . . I dunno. Ye see he was took away to . . . another part o' the prison."

"But you . . . must have seen him now and then, oh surely?"

"Why . . . no, mam!"

"Then . . . you must have heard tell of him."

"No, my lady . . . leastways . . . only off and on like."

"Well . . . what did you . . . hear?"

"Why naught, mam, naught to matter . . . except as him and Cap'n Smy had . . . fell out like."

"You mean quarrelled?"

"Ay, summat o' that kind, mam."

"What about—tell me, Joel, tell me!"

"So I would, my lady, if . . . if I might. All as I know is that Cap'n Smy was . . . well . . . a bit set again him, fierce like."

"How know you this?"

"For that poor Cap'n Smy was often dragged through my cell afore and after torture . . . and cry out, he would, and mighty sharp and bitter . . . by reason o' cruel pain, I guess."

"Oh, but why . . . why would he cry out against his friend, Captain Troy, so bitterly?"

"Why, mam . . . my lady, this I can't tell . . . not knowing, d'ye see?"

"Joel, do you mind any . . . any one of the words he cried against Captain Troy, any of the many things he said—do you?"

"No, mam."

"Think, Joel, think! Tell me, and speak the very truth, —what do you remember?"

"Nothing, mam, not nohow, my lady—nary a thing!" answered Joel, cowering beneath her level gaze and smearing knotted fist across his moist and furrowed brow.

"Then why do you shrink, Joel, and look so strange?"

"My lady, I . . . I can't abide for to . . . to think on they torturings . . . the groanings and cries . . . so cruel frequent! Ay, and there was others besides poor

Cap'n Smy . . . women too! And there'd ha' been me belike if I hadn't broke prison."

"But . . . Captain Absalom was never tortured . . . not once, say you, Joel?"

"Nay, my lady, I . . . never said as much . . . he may ha' been, for all I know. Ay, belike he was."

"Though you never heard of it."

"No, mam, I never did. And this should be your comfort, sure-ly, my lady."

"I . . . wonder!" she whispered. "I wonder! For there be worse things than torture, Joel! At the least I think so. One may save body by losing honour, ay, by losing one's . . . very soul."

"Rum!" quoth Adam, suddenly. "Joel, you forget your rum. Toss it off, man, then go forrard to Ned Bowser, the Master, and say I've enlisted you one of our Dreadnoughts."

"Ay, ay, sir! And thankee kindly in all gratitood, by cock!" And gulping his liquor, away strode Joel with such suspicious haste that Antonia leapt up as if to follow, then turned on Adam instead.

"Ah!" she exclaimed. "Why did you send him away so suddenly? And why did he evade all my questions? Oh, what think you of it, Adam?"

"That you plague yourself to no purpose. And so I——"

"Don' go fo' to lay yo' great, black paws on me, yo' hugeous, blackymoor-niggerman, else I claw out bofe yo' great, frightsome eyes,—so I warns yo'!" cried a deep, rich contralto voice beyond the door, at which sudden, fierce outcry, Antonia smiled wanly, saying:

"Yonder is my sweet little Caruna!"

As she spoke, the door swung wide and in strode a gigantic young negress, tall, very nearly, as Jimbo himself; a ponderous, leathern trunk was balanced lightly upon her head, a huge bundle beneath one shapely, muscular arm, a large basket beneath the other, and girt about her waist hung a long, broad-bladed knife.

"Oh," cried she, ridding herself of these heavy burdens
with a supple, graceful ease, to clasp her mistress in vastly
protective embrace. "Oh, now de kind Lord be praised
as I see yo' safe, my Bootiful Lady Precious! Dese bru-
talious sailormen fo'ce me to go wid dem, dey brings me,
all a-trimble, onto dis great ship, and now dis hugeous
black fellow roll him big gogglesome eyes at me like as
I was any man's trash. . . . I think p'raps J better
stick him wid my knife."

"No, Caruna, not so, child! You mustn't harm him
because he is Jimbo, a good, kind friend, like everyone
else on this fine ship. So now make your reverence to
Captain Adam, stop frowning at our good Jimbo and
follow me."

The stately young giantess, finger beneath chin, made
Adam a gracious curtsey, flashed dazzling smile at the
startled Jimbo, caught up her ponderous burdens with
astonishing ease and followed her 'Beautiful Lady Precious'
from the cabin.

"Well, Cap'n Adam, sah," quoth Jimbo, rolling his
eyes heavenwards, "all I says is—Lord pre-sarve me from
dat brimstonious, black, she-debble, murdersome, female-
wench,—Ah-men! And, sah, if yo' please de supper be
sarve in haff-hour, berry specialious and wi' me and my
two stewards in our bestest rig,—so shall I set out de gold
plates and dishes in honour ob yo' Bootiful Lady, sah?"

"Very well!" said Adam, and went forth on deck quite
unaware of the eyes that watched and the light feet stealing after him; so came he to the spacious gunroom where
sat Ned with John Fenn and Martin Frant exchanging
news with Joel. At Adam's sudden entrance they rose all
four, but taking the nearest chair he motioned them to
be seated, and sat looking on them and they upon each
other and all now mute.

"Well," demanded Adam, "why are ye all suddenly
dumb? And such gloomy, hangdog looks! Speak, somebody."

"Why, sir," answered Ned, fingering the empty pannikin on table before him, "these yere tidings o' Cap'n Troy has took us all aback."

"Ay, sir," said Martin, "'tis bit of a shock like and hard o' belief—not as I mightn't ha' done the very same in like case."

"And I!" quoth John Fenn, frowning down at his clenched hands. "Torture is mighty powerful persuader! And . . . yet——"

"Ah!" sighed Adam, leaning back in his chair. "Now speak me your tidings, Joel."

"So I will, sir, though very unwilling, by cock! Not as I hold it agin any man for to turn his coat—wi' they devils a-waiting to torment and hurt his poor body. Hows'ever, sir, the truth on 't is, Cap'n Troy has turned Papisher—ah, and cursed Spaniard into the bargain!"

"Are you sure o' this?"

"As death, sir! I was there along o' Cap'n Smy and four or five others. Ay, there was us, and they black-hooded familiars all about us,—brought afore the judges, seven o' them they was, and all stark-faced shave-polls, and they ask a rare mort o' questions in Spanish and good English too, and at last puts it to him, ay or no, if he will turn Papist and save his soul of his own accord by embracing the true faith or have it saved for him by torment of fire." Here Joel paused to look round upon his audience and shake his head.

"Continue!" said Adam.

"Well, sir, Cap'n Absalom smiles on 'em all very gay and answers summat as I didn't nowise onderstand then, and no more I don't now."

"What was his answer, as near as you remember his exact words?"

"Why, sir, he turns and looks up at a great picture as hung on the wall, a likeness o' the Virgin Mary 'twas, and says he, and these his very words, sir, says he: 'I, like a certain great gentleman o' France, am ever ready to bow and kneel to a lady,' says he, then takes off his hat and goes down on his knees afore this picture. Then these seven judges nods and some smiles and beckons him and presently away wi' them he goes,—and so it ended."

"But you saw him after?"

"Ay, I did, sir, often—through the narrer port-hole o' my cell, a-walking with the Governor and his lady and a rare lovely, handsome creeter she be—and all on 'em merry as grigs, by cock! For, d'ye see, the Governor's palace gardens be alongside this yere place as they calls Holy Office. So I see Cap'n Troy pretty often, him being such great friends wi' this same Governor, Don Esteban de Majo—and his fine lady."

"What of Captain Smy?"

"Ah, sir, it do irk a man's soul and turn his very innards for to see him now, him as was so hale and hearty, now a ruination, his poor body all seamed and twisted by the cruel torment,—so thin and feeble he can scarce go alone! Ah, but his spirit so fiery as ever, and tongue so fierce agin all Papishers, and most 'specially agin Cap'n Absalom! By cock, such names and such curses on him."

"What names?"

"'Traitor' was one, sir, 'craven-coward' and 'damned renegado', with others as I now disremember,—but, Lord,—'twas enough to shake a man's heart and smite his very soul for to hear him. This was why I dassent and couldn't tell aught of it to his sweet lady,—now could I, sir?"

"No, Joel, no! And let none ever hear of it save us four. This is an order!" So saying Adam rose and mounting to the poop remained thus aloof, pacing in solitary thought until came Jimbo, sumptuously arrayed, bidding him to supper.

"And, sah, I have made everything berry splendorious for yo' bootiful Ladyship,—de gold plate, sah, and fresh flowers on de table."

"Good!" said Adam and went down to the great cabin.

And yet, despite this splendour of gold and crystal, savoury viands and rich wines, this, their first meal together, proved a sorry business, for Antonia seemed lost in a troublous abstraction, eating little and seldom speaking, until Adam, with a gesture, had dismissed Jimbo and his two negro assistants; then she pushed her plate aside and leaning chin on hand propounded this question:

"Adam, what is true bravery?"

"Conquest of fear!" he answered, thoughtfully. "And bravery is different and quite apart from courage which, being naturally fearless, is a gift of God."

"How is it different, Adam?"

"Because the merely brave man, being greatly fearful, puts on a mask of bravery to the world and, by force of will, shames himself to such a desperate and fearful valour as may equal that of the truly courageous."

"And which of these, think you, is—Absalom?"

"He is naturally fearless."

"You—believe this, Adam?"

"I know it, Antonia."

"Oh but—how can you?" she demanded, in broken, gasping whisper. "I say . . . how can you . . . when you know . . . that to save his body from pain he . . . has lost his soul? Yes . . . renounced his Faith . . . his God! A renegade and coward . . . a traitor to Heaven."

"Hush, Antonia, in mercy's name!" exclaimed Adam, whispering also. "How can you judge him so harshly? How dare you be so sure of this?"

"Because when you went down to the others, I stole after you . . I listened! I heard Joel speak the hateful truth and . . . thought I should die of shame and grief! Now all that I feel is—shame! Oh, if Smy could be so brave, so resolute and faithful to endure so much, why could not . . . Absalom? 'Tis because one is a true man—but the other—no more than garish sham and make-believe. So

now, because Absalom, fearing torture, has forsworn his
Faith and God, I will as surely renounce my——"

"Oh, pray hush, Antonia, and hear reason! For if a
man have no particular faith how can he possibly be untrue
to it? I tell you he cannot, and therefore must needs think
it merest folly to suffer pain for one creed when all such do
seem to him of small account. Also a man may believe in
and worship God no matter what his creed."

"Ah, but," she gasped, "but if he abjure and forswear
in fear of bodily pain . . . he is craven coward and basely
unworthy! And think, Adam, think of the noble army of
martyrs, men, and women too,—were these indeed holy
martyrs or only—misguided fools? And Smy was man bold
to endure, well, why could not . . . this that was—my
man?"

"Because, as I say, he is of no fixed belief or deep con-
victions, Antonia. Yet he is no craven, as well we know,
and of nature warm-hearted and lovable."

"Oh!" cried she, wildly. "Why must you plead for him
—you of all men?"

"Because," answered Adam, bowing his head, "in his
dire situation I . . . might have done . . . even as he."

"Now shame on you, Adam!" she exclaimed. "To so
defame yourself, and with lie so manifest and foolish!
Friendship should have its limits. And you have never
feared chance of pain or death . . . and life for me is none
so precious that I cherish it overmuch. So when death comes
I, like you, shall be ready. As for . . . Absalom now?
Well, he has saved himself but lost—all else!" So saying,
she turned and, with no Goodnight, left Adam to pace the
deck, a man very pensive and grievously troubled.

CHAPTER XXXIX

CONCERNING ANTONIA, THE WIFE

HE was on deck betimes next morning and instantly aware that Bartlemy's great, black ship had gone, had stolen from her anchorage in the night and vanished like an evil dream; now this, reminding him how much there was to do, he instantly set about it early though the hour, by summoning his officers to counsel.

And presently, seated with them in the coach, he looked round upon the stalwart forms and honest faces of these tried friends whose loyalty and faith in him had never wavered through the years, these his devoted Dreadnoughts who had fronted death with him so often; and his heart swelled so that for the moment he could not speak, yet when he did, his words were short and to the point, as usual:

"Six weeks hence we sail against Santo Domingo to deliver our friends and other poor captives there prisoned. So, Ned, pray overhaul the ship, her every rope, spar and timber. You, John, will see to it we have good store o' powder and shot for all arms. You, Martin, will take a shore-party and beat up for recruits, enlist as many of our old crew that you may find and are willing for another venture."

"Lord love you, sir," quoth Martin, "we'll ha' no lack o' men, I'll warrant me, for the old *Santy* is known ashore as the *Golden Fortune*. So there's a mort o' prime seamen ready and eager, ay—'twill be case o' selection as usual, sir."

"The *Golden Fortune?* 'Tis a good name, Martin."

"Ay, so 'tis, sir. But she'll always be the old *Santy* to us Dreadnoughts, Cap'n Adam."

"And we sail in six weeks, sir?" enquired Ned. "And for San' Domingo! Shall we attempt such city of ourselves,—just us?"

"No, we join a fleet at Dead Man's Key."

"Nay, but surely this is one of Black Bartlemy's known haunts?"

"Verily, John. For 'tis with Bartlemy, and his like, that we sail."

"Eh? Bartlemy?" exclaimed Ned. "And us as do be ever sworn foes to all rogue pirates? Which seeing as how, I now demands,—Cap'n Adam, do you tell us as you'll sail and consort wi' this black and bloody villin?"

"Ay, I do!" answered Adam, grimly. "Damme, but I'd sail with the devil to deliver a friend from such hell o' suffering, such agonies as Captain Smy hath endured, and maybe is enduring even now,—ere they burn his poor, maimed body at the next accursed Auto-da-Fé."

"Ay, but supposing as Bartlemy, being the black rogue he is, shall play you false, deceive you and all on us to our ruin, death and destruction? Think on this now, sir!"

"I have done, Ned, and am determined. For what poor, mean wretch is he that will set selfish prudence afore friendship and will not risk all for his messmate! Howbeit, because Bartlemy is indeed the Black, and this venture hazardous beside, I will constrain no man to it. Whoso doubts his fortune, let him bide here in Port Royal, but, as for me, I sail with Black Bartlemy 'gainst Santo Domingo."

"No!" cried a voice, and the door swung wide to show Antonia, radiant as the morning and vital as the breeze that came with her, sweet and fresh from clean ocean. "No!" she repeated, while all gazed on her, and none spoke or moved until Adam rose.

"Good friends and shipmates all," quoth he, "here you see our latest shipmate to sail with us on this venture. 'Tis my honour to present ye to the lady Perrow, wife to lord Perrow whom ye know as Captain Absalom Troy."

Up rose they one and all, to make her their reverence,

yet none to recognize 'young Master Anthony' in this sweet-eyed, stately lady who, having acknowledged their greeting with such gentle graciousness, took the chair Adam proffered saying:

"I pray you all be seated—and forgive my so sudden intrusion—but oh, sirs, who sails with Black Bartlemy, sails with—death!"

"Yet must I," said Adam, at this grimmest, "lest death take our good valiant friend Captain Smy that, as we know, having suffered cruel torments, must burn anon. So, to save him from the fire, sail I shall, let come what may."

"And I'll with thee!" cried John Fenn.

"Me too, Cap'n!" quoth Ned.

"And I. And I!" cried they, one and all.

"Now God love ye, old Dreadnoughts!" said Adam, fervently, "This I hoped for, ay, and expected of ye. Come now, let us drink to—our lady Perrow and success on our venture." So drink they did, though first, up rose sturdy Ned, glass a-brim, to say:

"My lady, speaking for myself and messmates all, mam, what I says is as this here old *Santy Trinidaddio*, though apt to be a bit lubberly on a bowline, lady, is yet lovely ship for to look at, more especially since Cap'n Adam lengthened her topmasts,—but to-day she be lovelier by reason o' you, mam, and us be proud to have ee aboard and therefore our shipmate. Which, seeing as how, my lady, I now takes off my glass to two o' the loveliest things as a sailorman's eye can wish for to ob-sarve, a lovely ship and a beautiful woman,—you, my lady!"

"Oh . . . Master Ned!" she murmured, brokenly. "Such kind welcome makes me want to weep for gratitude . . . and joy. For your words have made you all my friends, and this great ship a . . . home to one who was . . . very solitary. So I thank you from my heart,—each one of you."

Now when they had honoured this toast and gone about their various duties,

"Oh, Adam," she exclaimed, looking on him through sparkle of tears, "what kind, good men you gather to you! But why will you risk their lives in Black Bartlemy's power,—why sail with such wicked man?"

"Because I needs must," he answered, frowning at his wine-glass.

"Are you angered against me, Adam?"

"No," he answered, still without looking at her, "only I am very troubled for you . . . your great bitterness 'gainst Absalom. This shall never make for your future happiness . . . man and wife . . . "

"Happiness?" she repeated, softly. "This fled me long since and left . . . desolation."

"God forbid!"

"Ah, would He might! I prayed He would, indeed, very often I prayed, and all to none avail. Yet I do not complain."

"Ay, but you do, Antonia, you do."

"Only to yourself, Adam, and never until—now."

"And wherefore now?"

"Because now, besides being unfaithful to me, he is faithless to God."

"Unfaithful . . . and to you?" demanded Adam, grim-lipped.

"And I forgave him," she sighed. "Truly I did . . . because he was my choice, my . . . husband. Only I chose a dream within a dream and, waking, found reality nowise like the splendid vision in my poor, foolish dream. . . . Nay, my poor Adam, look not so stricken. I shall not speak of this again, nor ever trouble you with——"

The door burst open and in leapt Jimbo, gasping:

"Oho, Cap'n! Oh, ma lady, fo' de Lord's sake per teck me from yo' murdersome wench! She say she stick me wid her knife. . . . And she will, too, and I shall pass to heaven in ma blood."

"Ah no," hissed Caruna, creeping towards the cowering

giant, knife in hand, "not to heaven. I s-s-send yo' to de brims-s-stone, fiery pit, yo' hugesome, black tief."

"Caruna," cried her mistress, interposing, "what means this naughtiness?"

"Oh, ma Lady Precious, dis great, blacksome nigger-man he come crawling into yo' ladyship's own cabin fo' to steal——"

"No, no," wailed Jimbo, "to make de bed."

"Well, how dares yo' touch de bed o' my Precious wid yo' great, black paws——"

"Caruna, give me that knife!"

"Oh but, ma sweet Precious——"

"You have no need of it on this dear ship where every-one is so good and kind—especially poor Jimbo. Smile on him, Caruna, smile I say—this moment!"

The stalwart young negress glared on shrinking Jimbo, and then obediently flashed her splendid teeth at him in smile that was ferocious grimace.

"Now, my Caruna, the knife—give it to me!"

"Oh ma lady Precious Sweetness, dis knife save yo' once . . . de time dat drunk sailorman would ha' savage yo' and——"

"I remember you nearly killed him, yes! But there is no such wickedness to kill here, Caruna, so give me the knife now, and go with me!" And mutely Caruna obeyed.

"Oh, Cap'n Adam! Oh Lord!" gasped Jimbo. "Yon black she-debble wench,—ma innards be shook and all of a quake!"

"Why then take heed not to go near my lady's cabin again."

"No, sah, no, sah—nebber, nebber no more!"

"Then bid young Smidge and Moa to me with their lessons."

CHAPTER XL

CHIEFLY CONCERNING ANTONIA, THE WOMAN

AND now to Antonia this stately, battle-scarred ship became a home in best and truest sense; a small, compact kingdom ruled by Adam and, with him, order and an all-pervading cleanliness above deck and below, and where her own gentle graciousness won respect and eager welcome from all. Only Adam, because of her too-appealing beauty and helpless dependence upon his care, held more aloof, for her mere presence and constant nearness was a joy for him akin to pain. Her grief became his sorrow, the wistful sadness in her eyes made him yearn to fold her in the comfort of his arms: and because this desire must be fought and mastered, he would often seem morose and gloomy. At which times he would busy himself about the ship with John and Ned, or shut himself in his cabin or, as upon this present occasion, have himself rowed ashore. But now, standing on busy quay, he must pause to look back where the *Santissima Trinidad* rode at her anchors, because this tall ship was blessed by the presence of the One Woman and therefore had become for him a holy shrine.

So Adam looked, sighed and turned away to the task he had set himself. And this to visit the many crowded inns and riotous taverns of this lawless city in quest of the late members of his fighting crew, these hardy sons of the sea, who, squandering their wealth fast as possible, must soon be destitute and seeking new employ. But such of these as he chanced upon were either too happily drunk, too much in love with life ashore, or not yet sufficiently impoverished to heed his offers. And some of them he rebuked kindly, some he rated fiercely, and others he belaboured soundly with sheathed sword until they fled him, howling.

It was as he passed down a certain ill-famed street, with Jimbo and two chosen Dreadnoughts on his heels, that he heard sudden uproar with fierce laughter and a woman's scream, and though such clamours were usual hereabouts, yet to Adam that scream was a challenge not to be ignored. So he quickened his step and, turning a corner, beheld a red-faced man in tarnished finery seated beside an open wine butt,—in one hand he flourished a slopping quart-pot, in the other he grasped a struggling woman, who seemed of the better sort, while divers onlookers laughed, cheered, or cried shame.

"Basta!" cried the man. "Listen, for now I speak! I am Brazillo! You drink, madama bella, you drinka wi' the brave Brazillo—no? Ever'body what comes must drink health to Brazillo or take wine in face or steel in liver—yes! So now you drink, ma bella—no? Yes?"

"No!" said Adam. The man turned and loosing his trembling captive, stared on Adam in drunken astonishment.

"Is eet you, my so little man, dare say Brazillo the no? Then now I make you drink or slit your t'roat. I am Brazillo! I laugh, I keel, I kiss all womans, I——"

"Jimbo!"

"Yessah?"

Adam made a gesture, whereat Brazillo was seized in mighty hands, whirled aloft, plunged headforemost into his own wine butt and left kicking helplessly while the awed beholders scattered. Now as Adam turned to be gone, he was arrested by a remembered voice:

"Hold, sir! Hold, I beseech, for the swinish sot oweth me good money and must drown, asphyxiate, and perish in his own weakness, to wit—sack, or is it wine of Oporto? No matter, drown he will, and my money lost, except someone clap him by the nether man and hale him forth.

. . . Why, as I live, and by the blessed Aesculapius—surely I behold again good Master Adam, pardon—Captain Penfeather, the Buccaneer, the famous 'Golden Captain'! Surely, sir, you'll mind me—I hope?"

"Truly!" answered Adam, reaching his hand to this very shabby and somewhat woebegone speaker. "You are Master Perks."

"Indeed, sir, I am that same and yet not the same, —*eheu fugaces*! For time, sir, hath dealt me divers and many unkindly buffets. I joy you yet remember me, for I—— Oh, by Galen and Hippocrates,—yon bullying Brazillo is still a-drowning."

"Somewhat!" nodded Adam. "Ay, pretty well. Howbeit you may heave him forth, Jimbo."

"Yassah! Him not quite dead yet, sah, him still work him legs a little." So saying, Jimbo grasped these now feebly-stirring shanks and jerked their owner from the barrel, dripping wine and more dead than alive.

"Ha! Hum!" exclaimed the little surgeon, kneeling to examine this spluttering, sodden bulk with professional eye. "He shall survive,—i'faith 'twould be hard to kill such arrant rogue, more especially with wine! But now, sir, pray what brings your nobility in such doghole as this vile street,—if I dare enquire?"

"I seek men o' my late command, Master Perks."

"Oh, sir, they are famous, and keep to the better parts o' the town. For, being of wealth abounding, they are very lords of creation, to be run after, fawned upon, and cheated until—their money gone, they shall become mere poor jacks again to be shunned, and to starve or creep back to sea. There be well nigh a score of 'em in the town clink, prisoned for drunkenness, fighting and—other male offences."

"Why then, I'd fain have 'em out. Could you aid me in this?"

"With all my heart, sir. There needs but to see the right persons—with small honorarium, palm-oil, sir, delicately

administered. Go with me and I'll show you the method
and way on't."

And so, when Adam had interviewed and feed certain
officials, twenty-three members of his late crew paraded
before him, their new finery of garments somewhat bedraggled, themselves, for the most part, woebegone and
pallid with excess.

"Well, my poor hangdogs," quoth he, running his eye
over these dejected 'lords of creation', "see now what
evils prosperity ashore brings on ye! Queasy stomachs,
prison and the devil! Ye that are Englishmen all,—ye
that were o' late right hardy mariners, prime seamen bold
for all hardship, now show no better than so many whey-
faced, spiritless, slouching wastrels! So now—who'll 'list
with me for a new venture and be clean men again? Who's
for the wind and the sea and the stout *Santissima*? Who'll
follow me for another bout with perilous fortune? Whoso
will—let him step forrard."

And, as one man, they stepped.

"Very well!" nodded Adam. "Report yourselves on
board where Master Bowser shall warn ye when we sail.
Dismiss!"

"Sir," said the little surgeon, as they went on again,
"I was on my way to you with proffer of myself and service, when we met. For, sir, among other evils, I fell sick,
lost my practice, and am to-day well nigh destitute. 'Twas
good friend o' mine who advised me to your service, for
verily a surgeon you'll need if you would attempt San'
Domingo as I'm told."

"Told?" repeated Adam, halting suddenly. "Who
told o' this—this that should be secret?"

"An old and trusty friend, sir."

"Ay, but who, man, who?"

"Joel Bym, for——"

"So,—the fool tattles!"

"Not he, Captain, never Joel! He and I have lain
prisoned together waiting the torture, striving to comfort

and hearten each other to endure. Ay, we are friends united by prayerful adversity, and what such friend telleth me, under pledge o' secrecy, is inviolate—if only for his sake. Joel Bym is no loose-tongued chatterer,—nor I. But now, sir, I make bold to warn you—should you attack this strong city for mere rescue of your friends, you adventure much o' jeopardy to little good."

"How so?"

"For that poor Captain Smy is no more than shattered wreck of a man sighing for the easement o' death, whiles Captain Troy sighs as deeply—for a lady! Ay, and she the Governor's wife, Donna Juana, though Captain Troy calls her Joanna,—and an extreme beautiful creature she is."

Thus Mr. Perks chatted brightly and Adam listened gloomily until they came to the busy quays and harbour where, greater than any other ship, rode the stately *Santissima Trinidad*, brave in her new paint and gilding.

"A noble vessel, Captain Adam!" quoth the little surgeon. "A splendid craft! I am honoured to serve in such and under you. When shall I come aboard?"

"At your convenience within the next month. Meanwhile pray take this money for your present expenses and on account, nay—take it, sir, all of it. And so farewell."

Then Adam went down to his waiting boat and was rowed towards the galleon, scanning her from waterline to lofty topmasts with sailorly eye,—yet with all his thoughts on Antonia.

And she it was who came to greet him with such look in her eyes and smile on her ruddy lips that, yearning amain to clasp and kiss her, he greeted her the more formally, scarce looking on her lest he betray the passion that shook him; and she, chilled by this, presently left him. So came he into his cabin, and having nothing better to occupy him just then, opened his Journal and began to read it (which he had never troubled to do ere now) and found in it such mention of Antonia, with full though unconscious betrayal of his hopeless love—words penned in haste of the moment, that he decided she must never see it.

Now by some odd chance it was of this she spoke that same evening after supper.

They were pacing the deck, side by side, beneath a sky ablaze with stars, with a cool breath from the sea tempering the heat of this tropic night.

"Adam, when am I to read your Journal?"

"Never!" he answered, impulsively.

"But," said she, with a catch in her breath, "but you . . . promised."

"Did I, Antonia? But 'tis very ill-writ . . . badly expressed . . . jotted at random. . . . Howbeit, I have changed my mind."

"You have indeed!" she sighed. "'Tis greatly changed, and is changing towards me more and more of late."

"Nay, surely——"

"Yea, surely!" she retorted, "you grow so cold and strange to me I begin to wonder why you were so insistent I must live on your ship, for now that I am here, you do all possible to avoid me."

"I have much business."

"And make more—to keep yourself remote from me."

"Antonia, this is but your imagining."

"Adam, this is veriest truth. You do all you may to avoid me, and I . . . grieve for it."

"Then you grieve very easily."

"Ay, belike I do!" she murmured, with unwonted humility. "For it nigh breaks my poor heart to prove such change in thee that I accounted so very faithful and changeless. Have I anyway offended or angered thee?"

"Lord, no! No, indeed."

"Then I must needs think fame and prosperity have turned thee into singular cold, hard man."

"Ay, perchance they have, Antonia."

"Even—with me, Adam."

"Ay, especially . . . with you."

"And prithee why 'especially'? Tell me this! Ah, will you not? Have you any answer?"

"No!"

"Then let us sit yonder and I will tell you." She led him where Jimbo had set chairs for them and a table with refreshments, and here seated, she leaned to peer at him in the starry dusk.

"Oh, Adam," she murmured, "dear fool! You make yourself seem cold and strange to me because . . . here in this strange world so far from our England . . . you love me now as you did then."

"More!" said he. "God help me,—far more! In England I was little more than boy, here to-night I am a man and one who . . . needs . . . God's help." Now, at this, she leaned nearer as if she would have kissed his bowed head, yet did not, only she asked, and very tenderly:

"And so . . . because you are Adam, you are . . . afraid of Adam?"

"Yes," he answered. "I fear myself greatly . . . for that I am . . . only a man and so . . . passionately human and alive! But, Antonia, I do so love you . . . I had rather die than bring any least shame on you or . . . the sacred memory of my father."

Here she leaned nearer yet and touched her lips to his silvery hair.

"Dear Adam," she whispered. "Brave, clean-souled man, 'tis so that I, too, love thee, and knew it all too late . . . and this is my abiding grief."

"Oh, Antonia!" he gasped. "Oh, my dear. . . ."

"Fear no more, beloved man," she sighed, "for though I yearn and long for you, yet my love, like thine, is of such sort, so true and deep, that I also would far liefer die than lead thee to dishonour. So trust me, Adam, and thine own dear, strong self, as I do, and shall be no more need of fear betwixt us or idle make-believe. We go on perilous venture where death may wait us, so, whiles we live, let us be dear friends and companions as of old. Think not of me as your friend's wife, or woman to love, but only as your own faithful Anthony to love in all innocence." Then she rose, and he doing the like, she leaned and kissed him upon the brow and so left him,—and in his heart a deep joy that yet was now pain indeed.

But in the days ensuing, Adam found such carefree happiness as he had never known, and such indeed as was to bless him never again.

For in these days, whose memory was to be his abiding comfort and consolation, he learned how to laugh and find strange, new joy in everything around him; and though he was busy as ever, Antonia was often beside him, helping him with his business letters, checking items of incoming stores, or casting up accounts. Daily also she would sit with Smidge and Moa at their lessons, setting them sums that were never too difficult, helping them with their spelling, and praising their reading,—so that they were soon utterly devoted to her.

Thus passed these days of joyous peace while the *Santissima Trinidad* made ready for sea and prepared for battle.

CHAPTER XLI

CHIEFLY CONCERNING ADAM AND ANTONIA

A ROUND head peeped in at softly-opened door, two brown eyes stared and vanished, yet Adam had seen, and spoke instantly:

"Smidge!"

"Sir?" The boy reappeared, saluted smartly and stood at attention.

"This is the second time you've peeped at me this morning."

"Yessir."

"Why, pray?"

"First time—whistling, sir. Second time—singing."

"Boy, explain yourself."

"First time, sir, I'm a-passing of your cabin when I hears somebody a-whistling so loud and merry as makes me for to wonder who, so I peeps in, Cap'n, and I scarce believes my eyes, sir."

"Why not?"

"'Cause it was—you, sir!"

"Eh? Me? What d'ye mean?"

"A-whistling, sir, so glad and merry—you!"

"Oh? Well—yes, perhaps I was."

"And the second time—singing, sir. I peeps again and, Cap'n Adam—'tis you again, only a-singing this time!"

"Was I, Smidge?"

"Ay, sir, that you was,—leastways you was a-trying very hard. Which I never heard you sing afore, sir, no, nor yet whistle neither. And then—last night, sir!"

"What o' last night?"

"Laughing, sir—you! Ay, laughed and laughed you did."

"Astonishing!" murmured Adam.

"Yessir. That's what I say."

"Nay but, my old seadog, why shouldn't I sing or whistle, and laugh—like other men?"

"Because you ain't like any other men, Cap'n."

"Lord, boy! And why not?"

"Because, sir, there's only one Cap'n Adam in the world, and you're him."

"Oh . . . well," quoth Adam, pinching his chin. "You can run off—no—bring me your lessons, you and Moa, I've neglected 'em of late."

"Sir, I begs leave to inform you as there ain't need for you to trouble about us, 'cause we've said and writ our lessons very regular along o' your lady."

"Eh—my lady?"

"Ay, sir, yourn and Caruna's Lady Precious, and she do say as we be very good scholars,—'specially me! Very kind she is to both on us, Moa and me—never scolds us, like you, she don't, sir, and if she do 'tis so gentle-like as makes us work and try our best, 'specially me,—her being so kind!"

"Too kind perhaps, eh, old shipmate?"

"No, sir! She's always kind to everybody—'specially me! This is why I can't abide for to see her shed tears, sir, and weep so pitiful."

"Weep, d'ye say? Where? When? Why?"

"Yesterday 'twas, sir, wept very bitter, she did—ay, Cap'n, and 'twas all along o' you!"

"Lord love me! But how—how have I—what d'ye mean, boy?"

"Well, leastways, sir, 'twas your book."

"What book?"

"The one as you used to be always a-writing into. 'Twas last evening, sir, and I was just a-going to knock on her cabin door—with warm water like I always do, and I hears her give a kind o' moan-like, and then sobs. So I opens the door very soft and there she is a-kneeling by her bed and a-weeping all over your book. So then, afore I can stop myself, sir, I says, 'Oh, my lady', I says, 'please don't weep, mam.' So she looks up and smiles at me with her tears a-falling, and reaches out her hands to me. So I goes and comforts her 'cause of her tears, and wipes 'em for her on a corner o' the bed-sheet. And then, sir, she says what I shan't ever go to forget. 'Oh, Smidge', says she, 'when you grow up into a Dreadnought, promise me you'll always be good and brave, faithful and true like he is, and take care of him for me when I'm gone.' So I asks her, 'Who, mam?' And she says, 'Cap'n Adam,' says she. Then I ask her why she's going away and where to? But she only smiles and shakes her head so sad-like that I felt like I should weep too like I do now, sir, only, being a seadog I couldn't, and so——"

"Ad-am!" cried a happy, ringing voice nearby.

"Coo!" exclaimed Smidge. "That's my lady, and me nigh weeping! Don't tell her, if you please, sir, as I told you."

"Adam, may I come in?"

"Surely!" he answered, rising; thus as Antonia entered by one door, Smidge vanished by the other.

"Are you busy?" she enquired diffidently. "Am I . . . shall I be in your way?"

"Never!" he answered, with fervour. "But now, pray has your ladyship brought back my Journal?"

For a moment she was mute and very still, then she smiled and sank before him in a slow and gracious curtsey, saying:

"Oh, sir, the naughty baggage stole it back into your desk last night whiles you were busy on deck, slyly, as she stole it away. Alack, this fine ladyship is not a very scrupulous lady, I fear, perchance because she is such mere female and therefore curious as Mother Eve. I trust you are nowise angry with her, good Master Adam, because she is here to beg you will take the air with her before supper."

CHAPTER XLII

A MAN, A WOMAN, AND A SWORD

TIME has sped, and the *Santissima Trinidad*, well stored, armed, and manned by chosen crew, lies waiting to go out on the ebb, for the wind is light and baffling. Upon the poop, with Smidge (heavily armed) beside him and Moa hard by, stands Adam, glancing now up at towering masts with their vast spread of sail, and now away to windward, whence comes no wind worthy the name; on quarterdeck below paces sturdy Ned in hoarse confab with John Fenn; forward in the waist Martin Frant is busy with his two mates as a boatswain must be at such time; in the great, gilded stern-gallery is Antonia gazing upon the city with wistful, sombre eyes, until, as if warned by some vague premonition, she shivers violently and goes within.

Thus no one aboard sees the horseman who comes galloping so furiously along the quay and who, leaping from saddle, hails the nearest boat.

And presently up the galleon's steep, curving side comes Sir George D'Arcy, his finery somewhat dishevelled and himself flushed and breathless with haste.

"Adam!" he cries, glad-voiced. "God love thee, old friend,—I could not suffer thee sail without me, after all. England must wait. Say thou'rt glad to see me on board again."

"Right heartily!" answered Adam, as their hands met. "Thou'rt mighty welcome, George. But what o' Sir Benjamin? Comes he also?"

"Not he, Adam, no no. He is away up country. So I stole we hither unbeknown to him. Nay, Ben is for

England in the *Falcon*, sailing next week, and vows nought shall prevent him. But as for me,—though I have paid half my passage-money in the *Falcon*—she sails without me."

"Ha, and there's the wind at last!" cried Adam. "Hast brought the breeze with thee, George?"

And now on the broad decks below was cheery stir and orderly bustle; hoarse commands, trample of feet about the windlass, wail of fiddle and deep voices raised in plaintive chorus.

"Anchor's a-trip, sir!"

"Ay ay. Lee braces—haul! Sharp your bowlines!" Creak of blocks and tackle as the great yards were squared to this freshening breeze; but as the tall, stately galleon began to move from her anchorage, down wind came a faint yet familiar bellow:

"*Trinidado*—ahoy! Belay . . . belay! Bear up! Bring to! Stand by and let me come aboard."

All this was roared in stentorian tones from a boat whose oars beat and thrashed foam in desperate pursuit; a boat wherein a person of splendour bounced and flourished and waved long arms aloft, alternately hailing the ship and cursing his hard-driven oarsmen: "*Santissima*—ahoy! Pull, ye lousy dogs, pull. What, am I to be baulked by such bone-idle, misbegotten spawn? Pull, dog's leavings,— arms and legs and backs to it—pull, ye lubbers! Ship ahoy! *Trinidado*, heave to or be damned!"

Then Adam laughed, and others with him, the yards were backed and thus, after some while, Sir Benjamin clambered aboard spluttering oaths and puffing maledictions.

"I'm a . . . dog——" he gasped. "I say, hang me . . . for lewd cur if . . . this isn't right cursed . . . manner to treat . . . thine old and valued . . . friend and . . . trusty messmate, Adam . . . or may I sink and . . . perish in blood! I say Hell's furies, man."

"Nay," laughed Adam, "hush thee, my Benjamin,

catch thy wind, pay thy poor, blown boatman, and then explain thyself and most sudden appearing."

All this being done, Sir Benjamin glanced up at straining sails and humming cordage, looked round about upon trim decks and wide ocean, stretched his brawny legs with that bouncing motion peculiar to himself and exclaimed full-throated:

"Aha! What wouldn't fool George give to be back here with us!"

"He is, my addlepated ass, as you might ha' known, so bray not!" said Sir George, stepping from behind the mast which had screened him.

"Ho!" exclaimed Sir Benjamin with another bounce. "Ha! Why then, what I say is—let us forthwith toss a pot, twirl a can, and drain a beaker to and for old Friendship's noble sake. How of it, Adam?"

"Ay, with all my heart."

"Lord!" exclaimed Sir Benjamin when they were seated to their wine, "who'd be a landsman to live in noisy, dusty town when he may ride the foaming wave, breast the crested billow and expand his soul in the immensity of sea and ocean? To live a man among men with no peevish shrew or guileful woman, strong in Beauty's insidious lure, to enslave and win him to folly o' love and so to fret and fume and plague himself with ten thousand jealousies, heart-blasting cares and soul-shattering disillusions! I'm done with all women, thank heaven, and now drink confusion on their wilish arts and——"

Sir Benjamin gasped and was dumb, gazing in rapt astonishment at the vision of gracious loveliness that had dawned so unexpectedly upon his startled vision, this tall and splendid woman (thought he) this truly magnificent creature,—this proud and stately gentlewoman whose serene glance seemed to rebuke his wide and oafish stare. Sir Benjamin felt at a loss as they rose to greet her.

"My lady," said Adam, "pray permit that I make known to you my old friends, Sir George D'Arcy and Sir Benjamin

Trigg. Gentlemen—my lady Perrow who sails with us for rescue of her . . . husband, lord Perrow, better known to us as Captain Absalom Troy."

Never had Sir George's bow been more courtly, never Sir Benjamin's broad back more supple or eloquent legs more expressive of the powerful emotions that stirred him.

"Your ladyship's very humble servant!" murmured Sir George.

"Madam," quoth Sir Benjamin, "the same, though ten thousand times more so! My lady Perrow, your advent, so unexpected, smites me dumb! Your gracious presence aboard this ship glorifies its every timber with a . . . as I say a glory far beyond my poor telling, a delight past my powers of expressing,—madam, I am speechless!"

"And yet—so extreme eloquent!" she retorted and laughed, whereupon they all laughed, and none more heartily than Adam.

"But," said she, "I'll out on deck to feel this sweet wind and watch Jamaica fade in distance, for . . . who knows if I shall ever see it again?"

"Ay, do," said Adam, crossing to his desk, "I must work awhile."

So, away she went with Sir George to bow and hand her forth into the air and Sir Benjamin to flourish and proffer his arm, though the ship was steady enough, and neither of them to recognise the one-time swaggering young Anthony in this beautiful and gracious lady. But presently to Adam, busy with map and charts, back came Sir Benjamin to stamp and puff and fume until Adam turning, enquired:

"Eh, Ben, what now?"

"George! Damme, he chatters! Let me perish, I say sink me in blood if I can get a word in edgewise! He chits and he chats,—first of our sufferings in the accursed boat, then of our bitter, shameful slavery aboard the damned galleasse—and she, magnificent creature, wasting her bewitchments, and heedless of her own beauty and my so manifest homage, hangs on his fool words and—myself perfectly unheeded! So, leaving George to weary her until she sigh for better company, I come to thee, old shipmate, and being here, would fain know whither we sail and what's our venture?"

And briefly Adam explained.

The legs of Sir Benjamin conveyed him to the nearest seat and there deposited him, whereon their owner sat to stare and, for the moment dumbly; then drawing deep breath, he exclaimed:

"San' Domingo? The chiefest and most potent city, castles and batteries! Black Bartlemy? The rankest rogue and pirate of 'em all,—pillage and plunder!"

"As you say, Ben."

"To rescue our friends,—this were good purpose and notably virtuous, but the means, I protest to be infernal, hellish and damnable! Must I consort with roguish dastards, hobnob with knaves, make fellowship wi' villainy and common cause with debauched rascaldom? Oh, horrific and most detestable thought!"

"And," murmured Adam, "'tis besides a very rich city!"

"Ha! Forsooth, here's some slight, I say some very pitiful small—amelioration. . . . Nay but—the lady Perrow? Will you carry so much o' beauty, wit and tender loveliness into these bloody perils, Adam?"

"She comes of her own desire and imperious will."

"Ha, a something wilful lady, eh, Adam? Yet she ventures her lovely self for rescue of her spouse! A right heroical lady! Ah me, a vastly fortunate man is Absalom Troy. . . . And here, praise Bacchus—cometh Jimbo with a bottle!"

"No, sah," answered Jimbo, bowing, "bottles on table, sah. Me come to say de suppah am sarve."

This night, the first of their voyage, supper was a glad and joyous meal, like many that were to follow; but when, with laughing curtesy and merry Good night, Antonia left

L

them to their wine, she bade Caruna to bed and went to
that lofty deck whence Adam was wont to command the
ship, and sitting there, became a woman forlorn and very
woeful, who looked up at the glory of stars through a film
of scalding, bitter tears. And yet when at last Adam came
on deck, as was his custom, to see that all was right with
the ship, he started to the whisper of his name, and looking
up, saw her laughing down on him from the poop railing.

"My dear," he murmured, "you should be asleep."

"Nay, I will not waste life, this precious time, in such
idle fashion and on such night!"

"But surely this is much like other nights, Antonia."

"Is it, Adam?"

"No!" he answered, fervently. "Nights and days have
never been so wonderful or time so precious as . . .
since you came . . . back to me."

"Then now . . . come you up to me, Adam—no, I'll
come to you . . . we will sit a while and look, as you
once taught me to look, and marvel at God's handiwork.'

"Nay but, Antonia——"

"Ah," she sighed, "have you no wish to bide with me
. . . this little while?"

"Ay, God knoweth I have."

"Then sit here beside me and with God above and all
about us I will now tell thee something."

So down they sat, close together in the glimmering star-
shine; but she remained silent so long that Adam began
to pinch his chin, glancing at her askance the while.

"Adam," said she, at last, "because I was thief and
stole your book I am proud and happier than I thought
to be. For in those close-writ pages I read a tale of such
noble love . . . so pure and selfless that it humbles
me . . . and yet crowns me with glory. Yes, I stole
your Journal days ago,—thank God! I crept like guilty
thief and searched your books and papers until I found
it. And though I felt so guilty there was something delicious
in such thievery as I went speeding slyly away with it,

and my heart so beating I scarce might breathe. And
when I was safe locked in my cabin, I sat looking at this
dear, stolen thing and scarce dared open it. But—when
I did, Oh then I forgot all else, the long years vanished
as I read, and I was back where I belonged—with you,
my Adam,—dying with you in the boat, suffering with
you in your chains and slavery. . . . Ah, but what nigh
broke my heart was the tender way you wrote of me . . .
my madly foolish choice,—and never, ah never one word
of blame or bitterness or selfish repining! As I read I saw
you suffer again, and because of mere, foolish me,—
dreaming of what might have been, the deep happiness
that would have been but for my folly,—such joy instead
of cruel solitude and yearning emptiness. In the first hour
we met I wondered at you, Adam; your tenderness and
fierce boldness, your ever gentle care of me, your fearless-
ness of all men and all things,—and always this wonder
grew in me and only when it was . . . too late . . .
did I know this for the wonder of love. I thought I knew
you in those days, Adam, but now—Oh, now that I have
grieved and suffered and triumphed with you in those
pages of your book, now indeed I know you for such man
that I humbly pray God will suffer me . . . someday
. . . in this life or the next . . . to come home at last
to the heaven of your dear arms."

With this she rose, suddenly, and before he might speak
or stay her, she hurried away, leaving him more solitary
now than he had ever been.

Up from placid ocean rose the great moon, rising in a
serene radiance that paled the myriad stars and made a
glory on the sea. Above him and around was brooding
peace and a deep tranquillity, but in Adam's mind was
storm and surging tempest. For Captain Penfeather, the
Buccaneer, and man of fierce life and action, was at bitter
strife with gentle Adam, this unselfish idealist and reverent
son of Puritan sire.

He thought of easy-going Absalom carefree and gay;

he thought of Antonia, her past sorrows and present loneliness . . . her warm beauty, the wonder of love he had seen in her eyes, heard in her voice. He recalled his own loveless, solitary life. . . . And now, if he would, he might know the joyous fulfilment of his dreams . . . for she was his own, the one woman predestined to him from the first . . . she was his for the taking. And he was captain and master of this ship and his own destiny. . . . The seas were wide . . . and there were islands . . . a paradise on earth! Yes, he was captain and master, but . . . she was Antonia whom he had loved with a reverence far above and more enduring than passion . . . she was Antonia and in his care. Yet was she mere woman as he was merest man, and life was very uncertain. Ay but . . . in her bewitching body, that must someday fade and pass, was a deathless soul pure and unsullied that looked from her calm, gentle eyes, all glorious with truth and unashamed—as yet.

So thus, while Adam paced the deck and the moon soared high above him, his two selves battled for mastery.

At last, warned by the ship's bell and changing watch that it was past midnight, he went slow-footed to his cabin and chancing to espy his father's sword where it hung beside his bed, took it down, scarce knowing what he did, unsheathed it and saw the long blade very bright, thanks to Smidge's unremitting, loving care. So for a while he stood gazing on the gleaming steel, but thinking only of this most beloved woman. At last, sighing deeply, he sheathed the sword, placed it upon nearest chair and, being in no mood for sleep, turned to go back on deck and saw Antonia, cloaked and very pale, leaning in the doorway as if faint.

"Oh, Adam!" she gasped, shuddering violently. "Oh —I dreamed I was dead and . . . lost . . . lost in a great darkness . . . very terrible! Does this mean I am indeed to die . . . soon . . . I that am so full of life?"

"Ah no—no!" said he, hastening to comfort her. "Dreams, they say, do ever go by contrary."

"And yet . . . I know!" she whispered, breathlessly. "I feel . . . I am going to . . . my death. And I have not lived . . . so very long!" He had taken her shaking hands and, finding them deathly cold, was striving to warm them with his burning lips, his cheek.

"Speak not of death," he pleaded. "Oh, my Antonia, dear woman I so love . . . never think of death!"

"Nay but I must," she gasped. "I must, for . . . indeed I . . . cannot help. So, whiles I have life I would fain live . . . fully as I may. . . . Oh, Adam!"

"Beloved," he murmured, drawing her to his lips, "you . . . mean——?"

"I love thee!" Even as she spoke, he clasped her in his arms and then, to her joyous wonderment, swept her up to his heart and was bearing her whither he would. But as he carried her thus, heedless now of all else in earth or heaven save that she was for him—the one and only woman predestined to this hour, he blundered into a chair—something fell clattering, and he saw this was his father's sword. Instinctively he freed her and looking down on this treasured relic, this emblem of honour and high rectitude, he groaned and sank to his knees, looking up at her like one in agony.

So, for a long, breathless space, they gazed into each other's eyes above this sword that glittered between them; then, leaning down to him, she kissed his furrowed brow, his tear-bright eyes, his quivering lips.

"More than life and beyond death . . . I shall love thee!" she whispered. Then she turned away and left him with his honour and yet a man very despondent and full of grief.

CHAPTER XLIII

HOW THEY CAME TO DEAD MAN'S KEY

"EXCELLENT!" exclaimed Mr. Perks, beaming down on the map Adam had copied and added to with such deft precision.

"I perceive you are no mean cartographer, sir. And your scheme of onfall and attack promises well, I dare to affirm."

"Ay, Cap'n!" quoth Joel Bym, "I don't see as us can anyways fail, by cock!"

"We must not!" said Adam grimly, as he pointed to a small, neat cross he had just made upon the map, "Here, you tell me, the wall is something ruinous and apt for climbing—and no need o' ladders?"

"Ay, about there, sir,—and never a ladder! 'Tis bit of a breach-like i' the stonework as a man may go up very handily—leastways sailormen like we."

"And you will be able to find this place again—in the dark?"

"Sure-ly, sir! 'Twas there as Master Perks and me took cover the night as us 'scaped."

"Verily!" nodded the little surgeon. "And with the dons clattering their pikes unpleasantly near."

"Well now," said Adam, intent upon his map, "beyond this wall is a garden, and beyond this again, a narrow street leading past the Monastery of San Francisco and market square and so, betwixt the Governor's Palace and prisons of the Holy Office. From here a broader street runs direct to this—the West Gate, that I mark with another cross. I have these bearings right so far, Joel?"

"Ay, by cock!"

"Perfectly, sir!"

"Then," continued Adam, "from this West Gate, going due south, we reach the main and seaward parapet, and following thus eastwards, come to the castle and defences flanking the Ozama river."

"And vastly strong they are!" said the little surgeon, shaking his head, "and armed wi' many batteries of great cannon, sir!"

"So then," nodded Adam, "we must depend on the element of surprise which, thanks to your information, I think shall succeed and——" he glanced up as came Ned to say:

"We'm closing wi' the island, sir, Dead Man's Key— bearing nor'-easterly, and 'leven ships wi' their cables hove short. Shall we run down to 'em?"

"No. Close within half a mile and anchor. For, d'ye see, Ned, though we must needs sail with these pirates we'll have little truck with 'em as may be."

"Ay, ay, Cap'n Adam! Which, seeing as how, so says I."

"Is the lady Perrow on deck, Ned?"

"Ay, along o' Sir Ben and George, looking on these yere ships through perspective glass."

"Then say I beg she'll speak with me here."

Thus presently, seated alone and busy with his map and charts, Adam started to her quick, light step, and as she entered, rose to place a chair for her close beside his own.

"Antonia," said he, with such look and tone as brought the rich colour to her cheek, "on . . . that night . . . you had proof how I love you far better than myself."

"That night!" she repeated, leaning nearer. "It is a sweet and fragrant memory . . . it is our deathless glory . . . that, loving as we do, we can look on each other all unashamed . . . because you were Adam!"

"And you," he answered, "you the woman made sacred to me by such love as shall never die, but with our immortal souls, live on forever. And this certainty is my comfort and makes me bold to meet the future, and patient to endure whatsoever must be. And when Death come, soon or late, he shall be God's angel to unite us at last beyond all parting. . . . Yet now, beloved, because you are so dear and infinite precious to me, I would have of you a promise, a most solemn pledge, Antonia."

"Which I shall give you with all my heart, Adam,—when I have heard,—perhaps."

"And there," said he, smiling, "there spake my cautious Antonia! Well now, I plan to attack San' Domingo by night and, so doing, this ship must lie close against the castle and surely take some scathe. Therefore I want your promise, your word of honour, that you will remain in the shelter I have had prepared for you below the waterline where no chance shot may reach you."

"Where shall you be, Adam?"

"Rowing hard up the Ozama river with muffled oars."

"And with me close beside thee, my Adam."

"No!" he exclaimed, "you shall not—I am determined!"

"Ay but—so am I!" she answered, very tenderly, though with the utmost resolution. "Dear love, how foolish to think I would cherish my life while you peril yours! For if . . . you are to die, then I could not live, I will not! So don't pinch your chin at me and shake that dear, white head. I am determined beyond all argument! Therefore the matter is settled—thus!" And leaning to him suddenly, she kissed the lips that would have denied her will.

"But . . . oh, Antonia, this expedition may be hazardous!"

"Dearest," she murmured, "I am bold for any peril by reason of your own brave words—'if Death come he shall be God's angel to unite us for ever'—so how should I fear to die?" Now at this he would have kissed her—then started with sense of guilt as steps approached, a hand knocked, and in came Sir Benjamin like blusterous sea breeze.

"Ha, your gracious pardons! But, Adam, there's a ship calling us, a great, black ship making wafts and signals repeated."

"Then this should be Bartlemy's ship."

"Well, as I say, she is flaunting divers flags and wafting signals very persistently."

"She'll doubtless weary anon."

"How? Will ye make no answer then?"

"Not I, Ben."

"But Lord smite——" He strangled the oath, coughed and bowed to Antonia, "but Adam, if it be indeed Bartlemy signals, he will be wanting you in conference and council o' war . . . to shape plans and so forth."

"Well, he shall find me here with plan ready for him if——" A stumbling clatter heralded the entrance of Smidge somewhat encumbered by the great sword he wore, though he contrived to salute the company smartly enough.

"If you please, sir," he began.

"Wait," said Adam, "why so heavily armed, shipmate?"

"Acting service, sir, ships in the offing . . . your specialest bodyguards, sir, me and Moa. And now Mr. Bowser begs leave to report as how a boat, a eight-oared galley, bearing down on us."

"Ay," nodded Adam, "and in it doubtless the person I am expecting."

"Then," said Antonia, rising, "you will wish to be alone," and giving Sir Benjamin her hand, away she went with him.

Adam sat conning his map and adding certain other details until the cabin door swung wide to admit Black Bartlemy, a sombrely splendid, though peevish, magnificence, whose bow was stiff and tone arrogant as he demanded:

"Captain Penfeather, how is this, sir, how the devil is this? I have been signalling you aboard me this hour and more—and no least notice taken!"

"And I," retorted Adam, "have been expecting you ever since I anchored and no sign of you until now."

"Expecting me? Ha, the devil you have!"

"As I say, sir. And now, since you are here at last, pray trouble to seat yourself and let us to business,—nay, first I have wines and cordials which, I dare to think, you may pronounce worthy and precious as your own."

"I am here for other than drinking."

"So I suppose."

"And why a plague are you not anchored yonder with the rest o' my ships?"

"You may call it a whim, sir. Also I am expecting to bear away for Santo Domingo to-night."

"To-night, d'ye say? Then I am to inform you such expectation is wide o' the mark. We shall not sail until to-morrow noon at earliest."

"You have doubtless some good reason for such delay?" demanded Adam, pinching his chin.

"Most virtuous buccaneer," drawled Bartlemy, "you, to use your own words, may call it—a whim."

"Why then," said Adam, smiling, "be pleased to sit and explain this whimsicality, also your plan against San Domingo—if you chance to have one."

So they bowed and sat down together; then, lolling back in his chair, Bartlemy stretched his shapely legs, sighed and answered:

"We should be off the town about noon two days hence. Then in line ahead we shall affront their coastwise batteries and the castle. Under cover of our broadsides I shall land three companies to assail the town from land, sea and river. Three thousand men and over . . . very sufficing to the business. So, good Captain Adam, there's my plan, simple and forthright."

"Indeed!" nodded Adam. "And a very haphazard, piratical, bloody botch you'll make on't!" He said this with such biting contempt that Bartlemy, forgetting to lounge, sat up to scowl.

"Captain Penfeather," he demanded, with show of strong, white teeth, "you become offensive."

"Ay, faith, Black Bartlemy, I do my best that way—

because your lubberly, bungling methods offend my better judgment and make your superb incompetence all too manifest."

Bartlemy made as if to leap from his chair, but leaned back instead, and, becoming more languid than ever, fanned himself gently with laced and perfumed handkerchief.

"Pray speak on, sir," he murmured, "proceed, I beg. Your portrait of our famous Bartlemy interests me profoundly. A 'lubberly bungler and superb incompetent', say you. And yet he is truly a man so famous, say I, and therefore humbly beg the reason for your censure and lofty reprobation."

"Fame?" said Adam. "A bag o' wind! Howbeit, should you attempt storming the seaward parapet, much less the castle and river defences, you will certainly lose the greater part of your men to no——"

"Ha!" exclaimed Bartlemy. "What matter so I win the city? Shall a little necessary bloodshed so shock thee, most tender buccaneer?"

"Ay, truly, sir, if wasted and shed so wantonly to no purpose. 'Twould seem you abide by the pirate maxim, to wit—'the fewer to share, the greater the sharing'. Well now, I'll waste none o' my company by such contemptible ineptitude and brutish foolery. Black Bartlemy, I'm done with you."

"Sir . . . now by Satan this is defiance."

"Nay, call it the commonsense of one who will not share the certain disasters of mere incapacity."

"Now curse you, Penfeather, I've sacked many a town ere this!"

"I know, ay and know," sighed Adam, wearily, "little peddling towns, never a one so strong as Santo Domingo. Truly I find your method so inadequate, indeed so fatuous that I prefer to dispense with your company. So soon as you are off my ship, I bear away to do this business without your aid and therefore with more certain hope of success. I now take pleasure to bid you Good-day!" So saying, Adam rose and bowed.

Now Black Bartlemy, being endowed with that intuitive judgment of men that had gone far to make him the formidable power he was, checked the furious retort upon his lip, mastered his fierce anger and, lolling back in his chair again, surveyed the speaker very heedfully,—his lean, resolute face framed in its strangely white hair,—his look of indomitable power, of serene and absolute confidence.

"You think to succeed alone?"

"Ay, I do indeed!"

"Sir," said Bartlemy, in greatly altered tone, "there are but two sorts of men would make such vaunt,—braggart fool or man sufficiently assured. So, believing you no fool, I would beg to learn what gives you such confident assurance."

"Here," said Adam, pointing to a great volume on the table, "in this book, taken in the ship, are many maps with plans of divers towns and cities o' the Main, and among these, one of Santo Domingo, very fairly drawn, its every street, wall and gate aptly set forth. Also in my company are two men were prisoned there yet escaped by a certain breach i' the defences. Now, where two came forth, two hundred may steal in, and more especially at dead o' night, and the city suddenly alarmed by gunfire against the castle and all men thither running in panic disorder, what time I and my company enter unseen and fire the city behind them. Thereafter I force the prison, free and arm the prisoners and set wide the gates to the main body of my landing-party. Such is my design,— belief in my men, and myself, is my assurance."

"*Quod erat demonstrandum!*" exclaimed Bartlemy, leaning forward with the alert look and gesture that proved him man of action. "Pray show me this map, Captain Adam, and let me hear more of your scheme."

So, while Bartlemy conned the map and listened, Adam explained by word and pointing finger. This done, Black

Bartlemy looked up and—smiled; but now, seeing the sharp, white teeth behind these curling lips, Adam felt a sudden qualm, and folding the map, scowled down at it, while his visitor laughed softly:

"Captain Adam, San Domingo is good as ours! We sail —to-night! And now I shall be happy to make trial of your wine—if you, being buccaneer of such exalted virtue, will stoop and dare to drink with pirate so completely damned as Black Bartlemy?" Adam merely rang his silver bell whereat appeared Jimbo bearing a large tray on which stood bottles of many shapes and sizes; setting these in orderly array he goggled at their notorious visitor, bowed and vanished.

"Do we drink—together, sir, ay or no?" enquired Bartlemy.

"Ay!" answered Adam, taking a bottle at random. "Pray make your choice." This Bartlemy did and with some care; then, having filled his glass, enquired again:

"Come now, shall black Villainy pledge peerless Virtue, or spotless Virtue pledge Villainy? Do you drink to Bartlemy, sir?"

"No!" answered Adam, lifting his glass, "I drink—not to Bartlemy the Black, but to that younger Bartlemy his mother loved to kiss."

Then Adam raised glass to lip, but, instead of doing likewise, Bartlemy sat motionless, staring down into his wine as if he saw a vision there.

"Captain Adam," said he at last and very softly, "I grieve infinitely that I did not kill you!"

"So then," retorted Adam, as softly, "doth remorseful memory bite so deep? Thus might the angels yet have hopes of thee."

Slowly Bartlemy lifted his head, laughed savagely, made as if to hurl his wine at Adam's face, drank it instead and rose.

"'Tis then agreed," said he, reaching for his jewelled hat, "we sail this night. I'll away to give the needful orders."

CHAPTER XLIV

TELLS HOW THEY FOUND ABSALOM TROY

NIGHT riven by the red flashes of gunfire. Thunderous broadsides of dim ships answered by the heavier artillery of the town from lofty parapet and looming castle;—and Adam seeking high and low for Antonia a last word, when he is checked by a hand plucking his sleeve, for he wears no armour, and turning, beholds a strange man who flashes a sword at him,—instinctively he reaches for his own, hears a bubbling laugh and stands aghast to see this threatening stranger is Antonia.

"So, I shall pass!" said she. "And in your clothes again, my dear, but these much more splendid and a little tighter, alack—than those of four years ago."

"But . . . Antonia, this is madness! And the boats manned and waiting me."

"And so you behold me ready . . . to fight beside you," said she, making a graceful, dexterous pass in the air with her sword. "I've never forgot your lessons, Adam, to bear my point—so! And parry close—so!"

"Now God help me!" he exclaimed desperately. "Here's a wild extravagance, mad folly and needless risk."

"Then, dear man, fool I'll be, but I'll make thy perils mine, and if Death challenge me I'll greet him with a kiss and thine arms about me, I pray God. Yes, to-night 'stead of cowering in lonely safety, I'll live with thee—or die! So come . . . my beloved!"

Down into the foremost boat they went, with none to heed or recognize her in the darkness; then seated in the stern-sheets of the leading boat, with Antonia close beside him, Adam gave word and they moved off into the sombre waters of this Ozama river.

"Are you forrard there, Joel Bym?"

"Ay, sir, along o' Tregenza——"

"Here's me too, sir, if you please!" piped another, and most unexpected voice. "And I've brought Moa along, seeing as how us be your bodyguards, sir."

"I gave orders you were not to come, Smidge!"

"Ay, but not to me personal, sir, seeing as me and Moa was hid in the boat awaiting—we couldn't nowise let you go to battle wivout your special own seadogs, Cap'n Adam, sir."

"Oh, bless his heart!" murmured Antonia.

Soft ripple of vague water stretching before them into gloom and a gathering darkness as the flash of roaring artillery gradually faded behind them. Shadows to left and right, the one topped by mighty walls and battlements, the other crowned by mazy thickets and dense woodlands, and the dark river winding between. Bubble and hiss of muffled oars strongly plied, rippling murmur of cleaving bow,—on and on until gun-flashes were hidden and their roar grown faint with distance,—until at last spake Joel Bym in harsh whisper:

"Easy all—so! Larboard, hard a-larboard!"

The boats turned in towards the bank, and grounded softly; with scarce a sound their crews landed and ranged themselves beneath a massive wall up-soaring into darkness. Then with Joel leading and Adam and Antonia close behind, the silent company followed this wall until Joel halted to fumble in the darkness and whisper harshly:

"Yere we be, by cock! Follow me, Cap'n."

Up they clambered, by jagged and broken masonry, up to a narrow cleft, there to take breath, and so—over and a blind scrambling down—into a wide vagueness where trees loomed and leaves rustled faintly in the gentle night wind. Here they mustered in rank and followed whither Joel led . . . by a narrow street . . . past silent buildings . . . until before them rose a dark mass that was the embattled West Gate. Forward they crept into its deeper shadow where Adam, whispering, halted them and with Joel to left and Jimbo to right of him, stole where a light beamed from the half-open door of a guardroom in which two sentinels (made lax and faithless to their watch by long security) snored in unison, despite the distant tumult, an empty wine-flask on the table between their unconscious heads.

"Pistol-butts!" whispered Adam; the three crept forward and so dealt with these unwary sleepers that their slumber became more profound and they were left securely gagged and deftly pinioned.

Then the great gates were swung wide to their shipmates waiting outside, an eager company led by Sir Benjamin, Sir George and Ned Bowser grasping his ponderous boarding axe.

"Yo-ho!" bellowed Sir Benjamin. "Whereaway, Adam?"

"The prison of the Holy Office. Lead on, Joel."

So on they went at speed, careless now of what sound they made, for the battle roared louder as they advanced. They reached the prison which no man guarded, all being gone to defend the city or fled into hiding. They broke the gates, they burst open the doors, they forced bolt and bar and chain of gloomy cell and noisome dungeon. So they freed the prisoners and by Adam's order, mustered them in the spacious Hall of Judgment. Here lamps and tapers had been left burning whose light showed the black-draped seats of the Inquisitors ranked below a noble painting of the Holy Virgin who seemed to look down upon these misused, woeful prisoners with a sweet compassion; or so thought Adam as, with Antonia beside him, he glanced at these many faces pallid with long prisonment and haggard with suffering. But amongst these miserable ones he saw nothing of Absalom or Captain Smy until came Joel bearing in his arms a—something . . . a half naked shape so twisted, scarred and shrunken that Adam recoiled a step, while Sir Benjamin gasped a whispered oath and Sir George turned away, covering his face.

"Shipmates—ahoy!" shrilled Smy, in thin, quavering voice, "what, dost not know me, Adam? Dost not recognize what Papish devils ha' left of me? Well, now ye be come I cry 'Glory—Alleluia'. For I know the Lord hath spared me to see His vengeance on this wicked city. Let it flame to Heaven! Let it go up in the smoke of its abomination! Let it be blasted from the earth——"

"Old friend," said Adam, clasping these bony hands, "thank God we find thee alive to our cherishing."

"Nay, Adam lad, I want no cherishing save the Lord's hand to stay and still my heart and His good earth to hide this poor ruin the torment hath made o' me."

"Prithee, old friend, where may I find—Absalom?"

"Troy say ye—Absalom Troy? This for him!" And Smy spat venomously. "He is anathema! He is abomination accursed! Apostate . . . coward . . . false to his woman and his God . . . 'scaping the torture now but to flame in Hell and know its torments hereafter! Where is he? Set me down, I can hobble so far, set me down and I'll bring ye to the forsworn craven, set me down!"

So Joel set him down, a figure of misery limping so painfully that, at sign from Adam, he was taken up, and very tenderly, in Jimbo's mighty arms.

"Ay ay!" shrilled Smy, with dreadful, piping laugh. "I'm scarce the man I was! Forrard, Jimbo, and take thy bearings from me."

They crossed dim, wide gardens to a shadowy courtyard where a fountain played and beyond this, beheld a great house whence a path of radiance cut athwart the night from a wide doorway. Halting his company Adam peered up at this noble house where no one moved and from which came no sound.

"Forrard!" piped Smy. "'Tis the Governor's house, 'tis the noble Don's palace,—forrard!"

"Nay—hearken!" said Adam, for his quick ear had caught a sound at last,—the wailing accents of a woman, a man's soothing murmur.

"Stand by, all!" said Adam to his silent company; then, drawing sword and with Antonia beside him, he stepped into this flood of warm radiance and through wide doorway into a richly furnished very spacious ante-chamber,—to see a swooning man upon a couch whereby knelt a darkly-beautiful woman, and, before these, Absalom Troy, a naked rapier glittering in ready hand as he turned. . . .

"Adam!" cried he, in sudden, joyous amaze. "Oh, my Old Adam! Is it thyself indeed? Now God love thee, shipmate, I thought thee bloody pirate and this the end, or souse me for a gurnet! But since thou art here thou'lt have men hard by,—so here's very miracle o' salvation! For lookee, yonder lieth Don Esteban the Governor of Hispaniola and the islands, a very proper, right noble gentleman, Adam, wounded to death. I've but now borne him out o' the fight,—and there—his lady Donna Joanna. . . . To-night the city was attacked by pirates, led, they say, by that black rogue—Bartlemy, intent on plunder, murder, Adam, and ravishment. So hail thy men, and let us do what we may to save the city and these, my dear friends. How? Why d'ye look on me so?"

Instead of answering, Adam glanced at Antonia who, unrecognized as yet, was gazing—not at her husband, but upon the lady Joanna, her dark, rich beauty.

"Adam, old messmate, why d'ye hesitate? While we stand here, Bartlemy wins the city, women and children being slaughtered! Oh, man, why d'ye hang i' the wind? You that is my blood-brother!"

"Yes," said Adam, at last, "because of this, I am here to rescue Smy from fiery death and bring you safe back to your . . . home, Absalom."

"Then by God," cried he, wildly, "you lose your labour, for I'll never desert these that befriended me! Here stay I to their defence . . . ay till the city go up in flame and we perish with it! I'll die fighting or ever they shall drag Joanna to shame and brutality."

"Do you love her so much, Absalom?"

The words were softly uttered, but, at sound of this soft voice, Absalom started so violently that his sword clattered to the floor.

"Antonia!" he gasped.

"The lady is indeed very beautiful!" murmured Antonia. "Do you love her with all your heart—truly and indeed, Absalom?"

Now, looking haggardly into his wife's gentle face, Absalom answered, whispering:

"Yes . . . yes, before God, I do . . . nor can I help it . . . now or ever!"

"Then stay you to her defence . . . and I pray God keep you . . . both." And so Antonia turned and went out into the darkness, leaving Absalom staring after her like a man in agony.

"Adam," he groaned. "Oh, my Old Adam, what . . . what must I do?"

"Return to . . . your duty."

"Duty?" cried Absalom. "What o' my duty here? How may I leave . . . these to perish? Ravishment and murder? How may I in God's name?"

Now looking on this dying man, this beautiful, fear-shaken woman, Adam bowed his head, saying:

"Truly, Absalom, only God knoweth. I can but pray, as did Antonia, God keep you—both!"

CHAPTER XLV

HOW ABSALOM BROUGHT THEM TO CAVE OF REFUGE

"HOW now, Adam, what's kept ye?" cried Sir Benjamin in hot impatience. "Here we be, two hundred and fifty choice lads, ardent souls and very eager, and—a marvellous rich city."

"An evil city!" piped Smy in his dreadful voice. "'Tis city of abomination! A wicked and merciless people that torments and burns the godly . . . Smite them, smite them in the name o' the Lord, for this is the hour of His vengeance,—smite and spare not!"

"'Sblood!" bellowed Sir Benjamin, flourishing sword. "That will we, Smy, never doubt it! So whither now, Adam? Do we march for the castle first, or——"

"The ship!" said Adam.

"Eh? The ship? Adam, d'ye mean——"

"The ship!" he repeated. "We have done all I came to do."

"But think, Adam, ha—damme think! The city lieth open to us, a vast booty, loot and a pretty pillage for the taking."

"Ay, though not by us, Sir Benjamin. Our booty is Smy and yon hapless prisoners, so am I content. We are for the ship! Dreadnoughts to your ranks and march!"

"March?" shrieked Smy. "March, d'ye say? Will ye sail off and leave the Lord's work undone? Will ye dare turn aside from working out the vengeance of God?"

"Nay, if such vengeance belong to God, Smy, to God I leave it. . . . Forrard to the ship,—march!"

Sir Benjamin stamped and swore, the men growled but obeyed, while Smy, struggling feebly in Jimbo's great arms, cried shame, and called down curses upon Adam, who nowise heeded, but knew a great content, for into his clasp came the joy and comfort of Antonia's vital hand.

Slowly they marched, a hoarse-muttering company unwilling to leave thus empty-handed when so much treasure might have been theirs. Yet, because of their small, grim commander, march they did until he checked them suddenly with uplifted sword as, faint though plain to hear above the distant battle-roar came that (to him) most terrible of all sounds—a woman's agonized screaming.

"Come!" cried he, and turning, began to run, followed eagerly by his now joyous men. Back came they to the palace where red flame curled and flickered, and into that spacious ante-chamber, to see—the Governor Don Esteban terribly dead, Absalom, backed into a corner, defending himself against many assailants, Donna Joanna struggling half-naked in Tressady's merciless arms, and Black Bartlemy, sword in hand, watching her writhing loveliness with avid eyes.

"Bartlemy! Dastard and murderer!"

"Penfeather,—cursed buccaneer!"

Then while the palace flamed about them and all men paused to watch, they leapt at each other and fought— with no grace of posture, no airy delicacies of play, but like fierce haters intent on each other's destruction. Thrust, parry and counter-thrust, agile shifts of body and quick foot-work until suddenly Adam seemed to trip,—Bartlemy's long blade drove at him . . . wavered, fell . . . and looking down at the steel that had transfixed him, Black Bartlemy choked . . . laughed and, as Adam wrenched free his blade, stumbled blindly to his knees, sank to his face and lay motionless.

But now was sudden outcry, with rattle of musketry from the darkness without, a wild clamour of shouting. . . . Spanish soldiery and armed citizens seemed all about them in fierce onslaught, men who fought with

merciless desperation, heedless of wounds and death, as
men will fight in defence of home.

So was din and uproar of close and furious combat, a
wild confusion of struggling bodies and random blows.
. . . Fire and smoke and ceaseless effort.

"Antonia! Oh, Antonia!"

"Here, my Adam!"

They were out beneath the stars at last, breathing deep
of the night air, lit by a ruddy glow that showed Antonia
beside him and all about them men of his shattered company. But at his word they fell into rank, fifteen only he
counted, but among these Ned, Joel, with Tregenza,
Appleby, Ash and Cobb.

The palace was now doomed, its great ante-chamber a
glowing furnace where no living thing might be; and
looking on this, haggard-eyed, Adam breathed a prayer and
turned away. . . . Away from sparks and devouring
flame, through a cool darkness where leaves rustled fitfully,
through silent streets with none to stay them, for the
battle had roared into the distance, out unchallenged
through the West Gate and into a glimmering dusk that
brightened upon them, little by little, as up rose the late
moon to show them a flat, grassy expanse or savannah,
shut in by dark forest and distant mountains. Here Adam
halted to look about him.

"What course now, sir?" enquired Ned, cleaning his
axe-blade with handful of grass. "Are we for sea-coast
or river?"

"The coast, Ned, there to join Sir Benjamin and the
rest—if we may. But first, did you, did any man here see
aught o' my boy, Smidge?"

"I did, sir," answered Tregenza; "he was i' the thick
of it and laying about him very stoutly."

"Ay, sir, and wi' Moa, your young Indian, along of him
likewise, Cap'n. Mebbe they won away along o' Sir Benjamin when the dons turned tail and Sir Ben's company
hard a-starn of 'em."

"Well, now," said Adam, peering at his fifteen survivors, "I'll see which o' your hurts most needs my care."

"Why none o' we, sir!" they answered in cheery chorus. "No no, Cap'n. We be well enough and handsome. . . . A bit o' blood here or there but naught to harm, sir."

"Show me! You, Will Farren,—your fingers drip! Bare me your arm—so! Here's rill should soon drain your life. Out with your shirt-tail!"

William Farren obeyed, and from this garment, by Adam's direction, tore a strip wherewith his bleeding was presently stopped. So now in this desolation, with the moon to light him and Antonia to aid, Adam performed such rough surgery as he might; in the middle of which business hearing a cautious hail, he glanced up to behold Moa with his arm about a bedraggled Smidge who limped. And never were youth and boy greeted more heartily than by their messmates, though Adam shook reproving head at them.

"Sir," said the boy, saluting, "begs to report as I have convoyed this here Moa safe and sound 'cept for bit of a cut in 's arm. And I got me trod on and trampled somewhat, which don't matter, but . . . oh, sir . . ." the boyish voice quavered tearfully, "oh Cap'n Adam, I . . . lost my sword, sir!"

"Shalt have another, old seadog. But——"

Adam paused and turned to the now familiar sound of a thin, querulous voice upraised in fierce expostulation, and beheld Captain Smy writhing feebly in the powerful arms of Absalom Troy.

"Loose me, accursed renegade, loose me, I say!"

"Easy, Smy, easy now! Bide still lest thou do thy poor body more harm. So ho, Adam,—here come I, a poor, lost soul that hath indeed lost everything save life, good sword, and stout arm. Wilt take me along, Old Adam?"

"Indeed, Absalom. 'Tis for sake of you and Smy we are here. So now are we sixteen swords. Come!"

On they went again and now all silent because of Smy's bitter taunts and Absalom's ready answers, they conversing on this wise:

Smy: "Loose me, Troy! The touch o' you is abomination, cursed false—Papist and traitor that ye are!"

Absalom: "Yet am I no traitor to thee, Smy, nor to thy God that made us all. I do but—adapt myself to circumstance."

Smy: "To save your coward's hide!"

Absalom: "True enough! What, dost groan? Do I bear thee comfortably thus, old messmate? God knows I'd spare thee any least——"

Smy: "Talk not o' God to me, Master Mock Papist!"

Absalom: "Then let's say—devil burn me but I'd fain spare thee any further pain, Smy. When I look on thy poor body I could weep! And what—what hast gained by such grievous suffering?"

Smy: "A clean soul! The fire of agony hath purged away all dross. Soon I shall stand before the Lord, strong again, perfected and made worthy by woes endured for His sake. But as for thee,—ha, thou Absalom that for dread of a little passing agony could forswear thy Faith—thou——"

Absalom: "Ay ay, old lad, I'm bound for Hell and the torment hereafter, the brimstone pit, dread Avernus and—— Ha—didst flinch again! Do I jar thee, Smy?"

Smy: "Nay! But wherefore drag my useless carcass along? To what avail? I'm done wi' life, and yearning for death and the Abiding Glory. So, put me down, leave me, I say."

Absalom: "Nay, I'll never leave thee, old shipmate, or I'm a shotten herring! While there's life there's hope,—if not, I'll see the last o' thee for old friendship's sake."

Smy: "I'm no friend o' thine!"

Absalom: "No matter, thou'rt friend o' mine, and therefore——"

"Hush!" said Adam, halting suddenly. "Listen!"

A vague sound growing louder to the thud of flying feet; a great, black shape outlined against the rising moon; the gasping voice of Jimbo:

"Oho . . . Cap'n Adam . . . Spaniards! Hundreds . . . t'ousands! Dey come for . . . burn de boats and dey kill us too! Black Bartlemy what . . . you kill so splendorious . . . him not dead, sah . . . de pirats carry him . . . back to de ships. Sir George him wounded, sah, de dons fight berry good, and Sir Benjamin lose plenty men . . . but fight him way to de boats. . . . And now more Spaniards chase me, only I . . . run berry fast for you, Cap'n and . . . warn you dey's coming!"

"Whereaway, Jimbo?"

"Astarn o' me, sah . . . pikes and muskets . . . hundreds and t'ousands, sah."

"Bear up for the woods!" cried Adam. "Starboard all!" But, as he spoke, heard a distant clamour, and glancing thither, saw the moon flash back from corslet and morion, with the brandished steel of their pursuers.

"Aha!" exclaimed Absalom. "They've sighted us! Let's run for 't, Adam! Once in the woods I know a refuge shall serve us handsomely,—caves above the sea, can we but make 'em."

"Ay!" said Adam, drawing sword. "Jimbo, take Captain Smy——"

"No!" said Absalom, "I can bear him, the poor soul's scarce heavier than puling babe."

They reached the forest, and in this welcome shelter paused to take breath and glance back at their pursuers,— fierce soldiery and vengeful citizens who cried death on them, and flourished musket or pike.

"How many d'ye make 'em?" questioned Absalom. "Nigh a hundred, eh, Adam?"

"More!" he replied, glancing askance on the one so close beside him that her hand might touch his unseen.

"Ay," quoth Ned, twirling his axe, "more they be, I

rackon, sir, but we'll make 'em fewer anon, if they cross
our hawse or run foul o' we."

On they went again, plunging deep into leafy glooms,
amid underbrush and thorny tangles so dense they must
hew a path with axe and sword,—on through a windless,
reeking darkness shot athwart by level moonbeams; stumbling over unseen obstacles, sliding in mud and quaking
ooze, splashing through dim streams and sullen pools until,
halting at last, Absalom gasped:

"Ho, Jimbo . . . your trick . . . with the Captain. . . ."

"Fools—fools!" screeched Smy, as the gigantic negro
cradled him in mighty arms. "To drag such useless burden!
Set me down . . . toss me in a pool . . . leave me
with the Lord!"

"Him berry extremious light, sah! I've carry him so
easy as de newborn piccaninny child."

"Then damn your black skin, Jimbo!" cried Smy,
humanized by indignation.

Out from that dense vegetation they struggled, up from
the dark and humid shadow into vivid moonlight that
showed a wide, grassy plateau rising steeply to a jagged,
rocky summit that overhung the sea, the sight of which
gladdened Adam's heart, so apt was this for defence.

"There," said Absalom, pointing, "is our cave of refuge
to command the steep,—and there again, scarce a hundred
yards where the cliff edge breaks, is path down to the sea
and a headland, with your ships just beyond, yet no way
of reaching 'em save by swimming."

And now, speedily as might be, they built a rampart
across the mouth of this deep cave with such rocks and
boulders as lay to hand. This done, Adam took count of
their arms:

"Eighteen swords," quoth he.

"Nineteen!" said Antonia.

"Twenty!" shrieked Smy. "Though light as puling
babe and mewling piccaninny, I'm yet man enough to smite

for the Lord, I that was baptized 'Smite-the-Devil'! So give me sword, one o' ye, or, better yet, firelock or pistol, for I can, with vasty effort, pull a trigger."

"And," said Adam, cheerily, "so thou shalt, Smy!"

"We've but eleven muskets, sir," said Tregenza.

"Yet twenty-three pistols and good store of powder and shot."

"And—a boarding axe!" quoth Ned.

"And I still ha' my knife, sir!" cried Smidge.

"No, lad, you and Moa, with Tom and Matt, will be re-charging our pieces,—ha, see yonder!"

Flash and flicker of steel in the dark forest below, with growing stir and rustle,—then an ominous hush. . . .

Adam glanced to left and right at the grim faces of his companions showing pale yet resolute in the now radiant moonlight, and spoke them cheerily:

"Dreadnoughts all, here shall be notable good fight and our method this, to wit—and mark me well! We shall let them charge within close pistol-shot ere we give fire, aiming low, then—down muskets and meet 'em with steel whiles our second rank shall reload and fire as chance offers. Is this understood?"

"Ay ay, sir!" they answered, in hearty chorus. And thus they waited, the few against the many, for what must be.

CHAPTER XLVI

WHICH IS CHAPTER OF PARTING AND FAREWELL

NINE were they, some faint with wounds and all weary, who crouched behind bullet-starred, blood-smeared barricade, with a sinking moon to show the trampled plateau strewn with stark shapes that lay still and silent or writhed, groaning.

"Smidge, are you there, boy,—and Moa?"

"Ay, sir."

"How are we for powder and shot?"

"Nigh all spent, sir."

"Ay," quoth Ned, "enough for another volley or thereabouts,—and then——"

"Steel!" said Adam. "Who died last, Ned?"

"Farren, sir,—here, poor lad, of a pike-thrust. And yonder lies Nick Cobb, and here abaft o' me, Tom Ash. And poor Cap'n Smy's a-slipping his cable, a musket ball just as we beat off the last attack, Cap'n Absalom have carried him aft into the cave. But now I rackon the dons has their bellyful, see how thick they lie afore our rampire! We've discouraged 'em at last—I hope!"

"Have we . . . beat 'em off . . . for good, sir?" gasped Giles Tregenza, wiping blood from his face.

"Ay, they'm done, Giles, by cock!"

"Or muster for another attempt, so be wary!" sighed Adam. "Howbeit we must get word to the ships . . . the cliff path yonder. I want a volunteer."

"Well, here am I!" said Absalom. "I know the path and 'tis easy swim to the ships. Smy's pains are over, he died cursing me, but just at the end . . . kissed me! Well now, I'm ready—yet first . . . Tony, Anthony, I beg word with thee."

340

Slowly Antonia rose and went where her husband waited in dimness of the cave and there for a brief while they spoke together. Then coming where Adam watched, musket in hand, Absalom loosed off belt and sword, saying as he did so:

"I, old messmate, that would have won so much, have lost all. And the lady Joanna is dead, or worse, and her child, her little, pretty daughter Joanna that was my play-fellow . . . God knoweth——? A sorry business! And now, Adam, if this should be our final good-bye—wilt give thy hand to the man hath wrought such misfortune on himself—and others?"

"Ay, truly, Absalom! God keep thee now and bring thee to happiness at last."

"Spoke like my Old Adam! And if there be true happiness in this world—God grant it to thee."

Then, watched anxiously by all, Absalom climbed the barricade and began to walk and then to run as, from the shadowy woods, death flamed and roared at him. They saw him reel, steady himself and run on and on until suddenly, as if cut down by Death's unseen, remorseless scythe, he swayed and plunged headlong. . . . Yet, even then, he crawled painfully a yard or so, lifted hand feebly as if in farewell and moved no more.

"So now—I go!" cried Jimbo, leaping afoot. "Me berry good runner extremious fast and swim like de fish—only better—look now!" So saying he cleared the rampart with mighty leap and was away at speed wonderful to see, but not in direct line, for, as the woods blazed death at him, he leapt, he ducked, bounding from side to side and, reaching the cliff-end, uttered triumphant howl and was gone.

And now for the weary seven was season of alternate hope and despair, of fierce onfall and desperate defence, with long periods of tense waiting and anxious watching for the next assault, till the moon, sinking lower, began to pale her splendour.

So they fought and watched, while the shadows deepened upon them and the moon's rim touched ocean, making a

glory soon to fade, and in the air a chill that was the dawn.
. . . And then, vague at first but waxing louder, a sound
from seaward, the steady oncoming tramp of feet, a hoarse,
familiar bellow, a rousing cheer. . . . At which glad,
right welcome sound, Adam rose to hail in answer, was
clasped in two arms, covered by a soft body, as, from the
stealthy shadows, muskets flamed and roared again . . .
and he was looking down into Antonia's stricken face.

"My dear one," she whispered, brokenly, "they would
have . . . killed thee."

Heedless of all else, he bore her into the cave and laying
her there, fumbled with shaking hands to come at her wound.

"See, Adam . . . beloved . . . the dawn!"

But looking on the red horror that marred the white
beauty of her bosom, Adam knew he looked on death, and
his heart failing at last, seemed to die within him.

"Antonia!" he groaned.

"My Adam!" she murmured. "Day breaks . . . and
I am . . . on thy heart . . . my home and resting
place . . . at last . . . God's angel hath . . . united
us . . . forever! Now . . . husband . . . kiss thy
. . . bride. . . ."

So Adam kissed her and, nestling to him, she murmured
faintly, "I . . . shall be . . . waiting——" The rest
was a sigh.

She was dead and his heart with her . . . the world an
emptiness, a desolation wherein he must walk, a solitary
man all his days . . . Antonia was dead!

He was aware of stir and movement about him, of voices
that called, of hands that touched him gently, but he
heeded only the lovely, placid face upon his breast, the
eyes uplift to his, the lips faint-smiling.

So must he remember her all his life,—placid and beautiful and smiling upon him through death. . . .

Rising at last, he walked stiffly to the barricade and
saw the sky all flushed with the splendour of sunrise, and
stood trying to imagine the pure soul of her shining some-

where in that infinity of glory . . . waiting for him . . . waiting! And he was alive and she must wait, and he yearn, through how many more weary years . . .?

A hand touched him, an arm clasped and led him, the hand and arm of Sir Benjamin, his ruddy face haggard and streaked with tears.

"Dear Adam," said he, hoarsely, "she loved . . . and died for thee . . . as I hear. And now . . . a last look——?"

Then Adam was gazing into an open grave wherein mid green leaves to make a bed, she lay, the faint, sweet smile yet upon her lips. Kneeling, he kissed her for the last time and strove to pray, but finding this vain, rose at a touch and went between Sir Benjamin and Sir George D'Arcy, stumbling like a blind man. . . .

"Wer't wounded, George?" said he suddenly.

"My shoulder, Adam, a sword-cut. But thou . . . Oh, Adam, come away . . . go down to the boats."

"Ay, ay, George,—yet first——" He turned and went hasting back but, coming where she had lain so placid and beautiful, saw no more than a mound of earth whereby stood Ned and Giles Tregenza with bowed heads.

"So then," quoth Adam, looking up and round about him wide-eyed, "here is—the end! Dreadnoughts to your ranks,—down with ye to the sea."

They obeyed him instantly, and presently were marching down the cliff path with Adam last of all.

Now when they were all embarked, with oars shipped ready to push off, Adam remained looking down on them with that same wide, vacant stare.

"Come, Adam, prithee come now!" said Sir Benjamin, reaching forth his hands.

"No!" answered Adam. "No, I am done with ships and the sea . . . my heart is dead and buried—up yonder. So now hearkee Ben and George and Ned,— hearken every man of ye to my last will and testament. I, Adam Penfeather, believing that God is all merciful, do

therefore believe in a life hereafter, a life of glory everlasting. And this is my testament! I do now bequeath
all I am possessed of to be divided equally among my crew
and those I named 'Dreadnoughts'. The *Santissima
Trinidad* shall be sold and the money to found a hospital
for seamen, in Port Royal, and called 'Antonia'. And
this is my will. Is't understood?"

"Ay, to be sure, Adam, but now I pray you——"

"Smidge, come you here!" Eagerly the boy obeyed,
sobbing and half blind with tears.

"Oh, sir. . . . Oh, Cap'n Adam . . . I loved her
too! So now let me bide with you, sir, wherever you go
. . . take me along o' you. . . . Oh please!"

"No!"

"Ah, Cap'n Adam!" The boy was on his knees, arms
upraised in passionate supplication. "Don't go . . .
without me . . . take me . . . for her sake."

"For her sake be a man, Smidge, brave and bold, faithful and true."

As he spoke, Adam did off his sword and girt it about
the boy, saying as he did so: "This was my father's sword
that I loved and treasured for his sake. Thus now, in this
day of parting and farewell, I give it to thee, boy, hoping
and believing thou shalt grow into a man even as she said
—'valiant and brave, faithful and true'. Remember this
and keep thine honour bright and life clean as this good
steel. And so—Farewell!"

Then Adam turned from them all, heeding no one any
more, and went slowly up the path where Moa, the Indian,
stood motionless awaiting him.

And thus, weaponless, moneyless, with only this Indian
youth to companion him, Adam Penfeather went to face
his destiny, which, because of his resolute soul, was to
bring him at last through peril and hardship to honour,
glory and a noble dying.

The which is yet to tell.